Tomorrow, Inc.

Also co-edited by Martin Harry Greenberg and Joseph D. Olander

Run to Starlight: Sports Through Science Fiction
(with Patricia Warrick)

The City 2000 A.D.: Urban Problems Through Science Fiction
(with Ralph Clem)

The New Awareness: Religion Through Science Fiction
(with Patricia Warrick)

Tomorrow, Inc.

SF Stories About Big Business

Edited by MARTIN HARRY GREENBERG
and JOSEPH D. OLANDER

TAPLINGER PUBLISHING COMPANY | NEW YORK

First Edition

Published simultaneously in Canada by Burns & MacEachern, Limited, Ontario

Library of Congress Cataloging in Publication Data

Tomorrow, inc.

CONTENTS: Spinrad, N. The age of invention.—McComas, J. F. Brave new word.—Pohl, F. The tunnel under the world.—Griffith, A. W. Captive audience.—Jakes, J. [etc.]

1. Science fiction, American. 2. Science fiction, English. 3. Big business—Fiction. I. Greenberg, Martin Harry. II. Olander, Joseph D.

PZ1.T62 [PS648.S3] 813′.0876 76-11057

ISBN 0-8008-7746-2

Acknowledgments

Grateful acknowledgment is made for permission to include the following copyright material:

"The Age of Invention" by Norman Spinrad. Copyright © 1966 by Mercury Press, Inc. Reprinted by permission of the author.

"Brave New Word" by J. Francis McComas. Copyright 1953 by Fantasy House, Inc. Reprinted by permission of the author.

"The Tunnel Under the World" by Frederik Pohl. Copyright © 1954 by the Galaxy Publishing Corporation. Reprinted by permission of the author.

"Captive Audience" by Ann Warren Griffith. Copyright © 1958 by Ann Warren Griffith. Published 1953 in *The Magazine of Fantasy and Science Fiction*. Reprinted by permission of the author and Lester Lewis Associates.

"The Sellers of the Dream" by John Jakes. Copyright © 1963 by the Galaxy Publishing Corporation. Reprinted by permission of the author and his agent Richard Curtis.

"The Subliminal Man" by J. G. Ballard. Copyright © 1963 by Nova Publications, Ltd. Reprinted by permission of the author and his agents, Scott Meredith Literary Agency, Inc., 845 Third Avenue, New York, N.Y. 10022.

"Dreaming Is a Private Thing" by Isaac Asimov. Copyright © 1955 by Fantasy House, Inc. Reprinted by permission of the author.

"Company Store" by Robert Silverberg. Copyright © 1959 by Ballantine Books. Reprinted by permission of the author and his agents, Scott Meredith Literary Agency, Inc., 845 Third Avenue, New York, N.Y. 10022.

"Business as Usual, During Alterations" by Ralph Williams. Copyright © 1953, 1956, 1957, 1958, 1959, 1960, 1962 by Street and Smith Publications, Inc. Reprinted by permission of the agents for the author's estate, the Scott Meredith Literary Agency, Inc., 845 Third Avenue, New York, N.Y. 10022.

"Criminal in Utopia" by Mack Reynolds. Copyright © 1968 by the Galaxy Publishing Corporation. Reprinted by permission of the author and his agents, Scott Meredith Literary Agency, Inc., 845 Third Avenue, New York, N.Y. 10022.

"Owe Me" by John T. Phillifent. Copyright © 1974 by Conde Nast Publications, Inc. Reprinted by permission of the author and his agent, Virginia Kidd.

"Patent Pending" by Arthur C. Clarke. Copyright © 1954 by Popular Publications. Reprinted by permission of the author and his agents, Scott Meredith Literary Agency, Inc., 845 Third Avenue, New York, N.Y. 10022.

"Captive Market" by Philip K. Dick. Copyright © 1955 by Quinn Publishing Company. Reprinted by permission of the author and his agents, Scott Meredith Literary Agency, Inc., 845 Third Avenue, New York, N.Y. 10022.

"Something for Nothing" by Robert Sheckley. Copyright © 1954 by Robert Sheckley. Reprinted by permission of the Sterling Lord Agency, Inc.

To Fred Pohl, who tried to warn us

Contents

Introduction

Modern science fiction highlights the impact of science and technology on human beings and on the social, economic, and political institutions in which they live. Although large business enterprises have been featured in many science fiction stories and novels over many years, the treatment of corporate and business relationships did not become pronounced until the early 1950s. But when science fiction writers turned their attention to these subjects, it was usually in indirect ways. To be sure, topics such as advances in transportation, the development of transistors and computers, the political and cultural implications of television, and military weaponry were thoroughly treated; but the *private sector* which produced this technology and sold it for profit remained in the background.

Indeed, within an important group of academically oriented writers and critics, the question of whether these issues were effectively dealt with at all has become an issue in a debate which is recorded in the journal *Science Fiction Studies*.* Answering the charge that American science fiction has ignored Marxism, Ursula LeGuin points out that science fiction is "unAmerican," for it postulates "open universes" which challenge not only the prerogatives and claims, but also the permanence of advanced capitalism. Defenders of American science fiction could go further and point out the long and distinguished list of stories and novels that criticize the present economic system. This literature includes *Player Piano* by Kurt Vonnegut, most of the work by Frederik Pohl and his collaborators, the impressive body of work contributed by Mack Reynolds (especially his *Mercenary from Tomorrow* and *Time Gladiators*), and many of the stories in this book.

It is also true that most modern science fiction implies a major assumption that runs counter to deterministic theories of the state and

* This debate can be found in *Science Fiction Studies* (Fall 1973), pp. 84–94; (Spring 1974), pp. 213–14; and (Fall 1974), pp. 269–76.

economy. Individuals are responsible for the evil in most science fiction, not the systems in which they find themselves, and it therefore falls to individuals to take corrective action. Most science fiction writers would probably agree with supporters of big business when the latter argue that corporations are neither ethical nor unethical but are whatever individual decision-makers mold them to be. Individual and personal responsibility, not collective accountability, is a major theme running through most modern science fiction. If there is evil in the human condition, the literature of Marxism looks for its source in the nature of the social structure; the literature of science fiction seeks it in the nature of human beings.

In the debate about the relative importance of structure versus individuals, this is not to say that science fiction ignores the capacity of structure to magnify the impact of individual evil. Science fiction writers become involved with the treatment of structure and systems in many ways, since they constantly pit individuals against them. Indeed much science fiction is profoundly antisystem (if not subversive) in its insistence upon the inevitability of change. Even writers who have been labeled "conservative" or "reactionary" like Poul Anderson and Robert Heinlein exhibit strong reservations about the power of large bureaucratic structures in both the public and private sectors.

Rather than characterize and evaluate science fiction solely in terms of these issues, an analysis of it should stress the opportunities it gives the reader to reflect on our own nature as individuals and on the nature of our collective concerns. When modern forms of social organization are tied to a market-oriented economic system and a democratic political system, a logic of competition is developed which becomes the cultural fabric of society. Such is the condition of Western civilization. The Hobbesian picture of constant conflict between individuals in a "natural" state is not far removed from the contemporary American scene. Science fiction is an important part of this scene and allows us to consider how power is developed and institutionalized through this logic of competition inherent in our economic and political institutions. It can envision what roles economic institutions may play in our future or what the future of business civilization may be like.

Certain major themes have been developed by science fiction writers in their treatment of business. One is *imperialism*. The exploration and settlement of our own and other galaxies is a standard plot in science fiction. In many cases, stories are modeled after the history of European settlement and exploitation in Asia, Africa, and Latin America. Although early science fiction treated the "natives" harshly and found little difficulty in justifying their liquidation and the exploitation of their planets, some writers since the late 1930s have treated these subjects with much more sensitivity, even occasionally allowing the "natives" to turn the tables on their presumably superior conquerors.

The struggle between human and machine has been a major concern in science fiction since Mary Shelley's *Frankenstein.* In this contest science fiction has vindicated the human being, although writers like Isaac Asimov have pictured a future in which the technological creations of human civilization may prove superior in the long run. A commonly employed plot involves the emergence of an elite who operate the machines for their own profit. In addition, the issue of what to do with the newly unemployed masses has received attention by many writers, a frequently used technique being "bread and circus" societies—e.g., in *Gladiator-at-Law* by Pohl and Kornbluth—to distract the former laboring classes from considering their obsolete roles.

Still another theme is *advertising* and the drive to consume. Science fiction has, especially from the 1950s, numerous stories portraying gullible men and women (housewives being singled out as a class) constantly victimized by advanced advertising techniques. Consumers were pictured as helpless against these forces which could only be defeated from within by a revolt of some of the very individuals who made the system operate. The entire production-consumption process received great attention in American science fiction between 1952 and 1964 when the subject was getting increased coverage in popular nonfiction exemplified by authors like Vance Packard and David Riesman.

An additional theme is the replacement of entrepreneurs by persons with technical expertise. This theme finds expression far beyond the boundaries of stories concerned with the future of business, for it pictures societies dominated by a "new class" of technicians, planners, and scientists who, often successfully, challenge the old economic and political elites for power. Also frequent is the story that deals with *the consequences of productivity*—notably pollution and the general destruction of the environment. Science fiction anticipated the tremendous environmental costs of the modern industrial system long before these were generally recognized and discussed. Partly as a reaction to these concerns—although the form has a long and honored history in science fiction—many stories and novels have been written on the development of small, rural, and Utopian communities that represent replacements for their large, dehumanizing, and ecologically dangerous urban predecessors. This succession is rarely by design, for the setting is usually a postholocaust civilization endeavoring to survive and rebuild. There is often a strong moral tone in these works, which suggests that human beings justly deserve such retribution when they cannot control their own technologies and the economic systems which support them.

Another frequently appearing theme is *business-related crime*. Industrial espionage and fraud are common topics in science fiction and are represented in this book by Mack Reynolds's "Criminal in Utopia" and John Jakes's "The Sellers of the Dream." In these the fundamental values and principles of business are examined, discussed and challenged.

Finally, some science fiction stories portray the *business of the future*. This type of story features new business forms made possible by technological developments, usually but not always without an ideological message. Examples from this volume include "Dreaming Is a Private Thing," "Patent Pending," and "Business as Usual, During Alterations."

What do these themes tell us of the future, of the role of business, and of the way capitalism is dealt with in science fiction? The controversy surrounding the proposals of the Club of Rome for a no-growth economy * is appropriate if we are to answer this question. Capitalism rose to dominance in the Western world through the Industrial Revolution, although the cause-and-effect relationships are not clear. But its continued dominance has certainly been helped by two major factors—a relatively cheap labor supply and inexpensive sources of energy. Both of these resources appear to be fast disappearing. Struggles over the control and distribution of the remaining resources of our planet are just beginning, and this conflict may intensify and become more dangerous, especially considering the continued spread of nuclear weapons. In response to this problem, many argue for greater centralization of the planning process. It is doubtful this can be accomplished without a consequent loss of personal liberties. Science fiction has been portraying this vision of the future for decades.

* *The Limits to Growth*, D. H. Meadows et al. (New York: Universe Books, 1972).

It has also anticipated the present tendency to distrust "bigness" in all forms, whether in big business, big government, or "the bureaucracy." Science fiction writers have infrequently treated the subject of unionism, but when they do a tone of distrust is used. This is congruent with science fiction's general distrust of mass social movements. The present feeling that the centralization of power in society must end if we are to solve our problems and to ensure human freedom will probably continue to find expression in the literature of alternatives. Post–World War II science fiction confronted and exposed the pretensions of American corporate power. If it has not supplied us with workable alternatives, it has at least shown what the consequences of uncontrolled economic power may be like. Sometimes through parody and satire, sometimes through straightforward adventure stories, it has shown us the nightmares and dreams which a business civilization can generate. For that alone, we should be grateful.

NORMAN SPINRAD

The Age of Invention

Norman Spinrad is a West Coast writer with a pyrotechnic style. He has produced a number of memorable novels and stories, including *Bug Jack Barron, The Men in the Jungle,* and the controversial *The Iron Dream.* But Spinrad is even better when working with the short story form, witness his "The Big Flash," "No Direction Home," and the unforgettable "The Last Hurrah of the Golden Horde." This collection begins with one of his best and most ambitious tales, a macrocosmic and hilarious overview of the dawn of business civilization.

One morning, having nothing better to do, I went to visit my cousin Roach. Roach lived in one of those lizard-infested caves on the East Side of the mountain. Roach did not hunt bears. Roach did not grow grain. Roach spent his daylight hours throwing globs of bearfat, bison chips and old rotten plants against the walls of his cave.

Roach said that he was an Artist. He said it with a capital "A." (Even though writing has not yet been invented.)

Unlikely as it may seem, Roach had a woman. She was, however, the ugliest female on the mountain. She spent her daylight hours lying on the dirty floor of Roach's cave and staring at the smears of old bearfat, moldy bison chips and rotten plants on the wall.

She used to say that this was Roach's Soul. She would also say that Roach had a very big soul.

Very big and *very* smelly.

As I approached the mouth of Roach's cave, I smelled pungent smoke. In fact, the cave was filled with this smoke. In the middle of the cave sat Roach and his woman. They were burning a big pile of weeds and inhaling the smoke.

"What are you doing?" I asked.

"Turning on, baby," said Roach. "I've just invented it."

"What does 'turning on' mean?"

"Well, you get this weed, dig? You burn it, and then you honk the smoke."

I scratched my head, inadvertently killing several of my favorite fleas.

"Why do that?" I asked.

"It like gets you high."

"You don't seem any farther off the ground than I am," I observed. "And you're still kinda runty."

Roach snorted in disgust. "Forget it, man," he said. "It's only for Artists, Philosophers and Metaphysicians, anyway. (Even though Philosophy and Metaphysics have not yet been invented.) Dig my latest!"

On the nearest wall of the cave, there was this big blob of bearfat. In the middle of it was this small piece of bison chip. Red and green and brown plant stains surrounded this. It smelled as good as it looked.

"Uh . . . interesting, . . ." I said.

"Like a masterpiece, baby," Roach said proudly. "I call it *The Soul of Man.*"

"Uh . . . *The Sole of Man?* Er . . . it *does* sort of look like a foot."

"No, no, man! *Soul,* not *sole!*"

"But, Roach, spelling hasn't been invented yet."

"Sorry. I forgot."

"Anyway," I said, trying to make him feel a little better, "it's very Artistic." (Whatever that meant.)

"Thanks, baby," Roach said sulkily.

"What's the matter, Roach?" I asked. He really looked awful.

"We haven't eaten in a week."

"Why don't you go out and kill a bear or something?" I suggested.

"I don't have the time to waste on hunting," Roach said indignantly. "I must live for Art!"

"It appears that you are dying for Art," I replied. "You can't do very much painting when you are dead."

"Well, anyway," said Roach, in a very tiny voice, "I'm a pretty lousy hunter in the first place. I would probably starve even if I spent the whole day hunting. Or maybe a bear would kill *me.* This way, I'm at least like starving for a Reason."

I must admit it made a kind of sense. Roach is terribly nearsighted. Also amazingly scrawny. The original ninety-pound weakling.

"Mmmmmmm . . ." I observed.

"Mmmmmmm . . . *what?*" asked Roach.

"Well, you know old Aardvark? He can't hunt either. So what he does is he makes spearheads and trades them for bears. Maybe you could . . . ?"

"Go into *business?*" Roach cried. "Become bourgeois? *Please! I* am an Artist. Besides," he added lamely, "I don't know how to make spearheads."

"Mmmmm . . ."

"Mmmmm . . ."

"I know!" I cried. "You could trade your paintings!"

"Cool, baby!" exclaimed Roach. "Er . . . only why would anyone want to trade food for a painting?"

"Why because . . . er . . . ah . . ."

"I guess I'll just have to starve."

"Wait a minute," I said. "Er . . . if I can get someone to trade food for your paintings, will you give me some of the food, say . . . oh, one bear out of every ten?"

"Sure," said Roach. "What've I got to lose?"

"It's a deal then?"

"Deal, baby!"

I had just invented the Ten-Percenter.

So I went to see Peacock. Peacock lived in the weirdest cave on the mountain—all filled up with stuff like mooseskins dyed pink, stuffed armadillos and walls covered with withered morning glories. For some reason which I have not yet been able to fathom, the women of the more henpecked men on the mountain give Peacock bears to make the same kind of messes in their caves.

Peacock is pretty weird himself. He was dressed in a skintight sabertooth skin dyed bright violet.

"Hello, sweets," Peacock said, as I entered his perfumed cave.

"Hello, Peacock," I said uneasily. "Heard about Roach?"

"Roach?" shrilled Peacock. "That dirty, dirty man? That beatnik with the positively *unspeakable* cave?"

"That's him," I said. "Roach the Artist. Very good Artist, you know. After all, he invented it."

"Well, what about that dreadful, dreadful creature?"

"Well, you know your friend Cockatoo—?"

"Please, sweets!" shrieked Peacock. "Do not mention that *thing* Cockatoo in my presence again! Cockatoo and I are on the outs. I don't know what I ever saw in him. He's gotten so unspeakably *butch.*"

Cockatoo was this . . . uh . . . *friend* of Peacock's . . . or *was.* They . . . uh . . . invented something together. Nobody is quite sure what it was, but we've organized a Vice Squad, just in case.

"Yeah," I muttered. "Well anyway, Cockatoo is paying Roach twenty bears to do a painting in his cave. He says that having an Original Roach in his cave will make your cave look like . . . er . . . 'A *positive* sloth's den, bubby,' I think his words were."

"Oooooh!" shrieked Peacock. "Oooooh!" He began to jump around the cave, pounding his little fists against the walls. "That monster! That veritable *beast!* Oooh, it's *horrid,* that's what it is! What am I going to do, sweets, whatever am I going to do?"

"Well," I suggested, "Roach is my cousin, you know, and I do have some pull with him. I suppose I could convince him to do a painting in *your* cave instead of Cockatoo's. Especially if you paid *thirty* bears instead of twenty. . . ."

"Oh, *would you,* sweets? Would you really?"

"Well, I don't know. I do kind of like you, Peacock, but on the other hand . . ."

"Pretty, pretty, *pretty* please?"

I sighed heavily. "Okay, Peacock," I said. "You've talked me into it."

So Peacock got his Original Roach for thirty bears. Next week, I went to see Cockatoo, and I told him the story.

I got *him* to pay *forty* bears. Forty and thirty is seventy. Which gave me seven. Not bad for a couple hours' work. I better watch out, or someone'll invent income tax.

I saw Roach last week, the ingrate. He has moved to a bigger cave on the *West Side* of the mountain. He has a fine new leopard skin and *three* new women. He has even invented the Havana cigar, so he can have something expensive to smoke.

Unfortunately, he has discovered that he no longer needs me to make deals for him. His going price is eighty bears a painting. I, like a dope, neglected to invent the renewable exclusive agency contract. Can't invent 'em all, I suppose.

Roach has become truly insufferable, though. He now talks of "art" with a small "a" and "Bears" with a capital "B." He is the first Philistine.

He is going to get his.

How do you like my fine new leopard skin? Would you like one of my Havana cigars? Have you met this new woman yet? Have you seen my new cave?

I can buy and sell Roach now. I am the first tycoon. How did I do it? Well . . .

Hog was the mountain bum. He never trimmed his beard. He didn't have a woman, not even an *ugly* one. He laid around his filthy cave all day, doing nothing but belching occasionally. A real slob.

But even a jerk like Hog can throw bearfat and bison chips against a cave wall.

I made an Artist out of Hog. I did this by telling him he could make fifty bears a day just by throwing bearfat and bison chips against the walls of other people's caves.

This appealed to Hog.

This time I did *not* neglect to invent the renewable exclusive agency contract. It was another ten percent deal.

Hog gets ten percent.

Then I went to Peacock's cave. I stared in dismay at Roach's painting. "What is *that?*" I sneered.

"That, sweets, is an Original Roach," Peacock crooned complacently. "Isn't it divine? Such sensitivity, such style, such grace, such—"

"Roach?" I snorted. "You *can't* be serious. Why that Neo-pseudoclassicalmodern stuff went out with the Brontosaurs. You're *miles* behind the times, Peacock," I said, thereby inventing the Art Critic. *"The* Artist today is of course the Great Hog."

"Hog?" whined Peacock. "Hog is beastly, beastly. A rude, stupid, smelly thing, a *positive* slob. Why his whole cave is a wretched mass of slop!"

"Exactly," I answered. "That's the source of his greatness. Hog is the mountain's foremost Slop Artist."

"Oooooh. . . . How much do the Great Hog's paintings cost?"

"One hundred bears apiece," I said smugly. "Cockatoo is already contracting to—"

"I told you never to mention that *creature* to me again!" Peacock shrieked. "He must not steal an Original Hog from me, do you hear? I simply couldn't *bear* it! But all this is getting so *expensive* . . ."

I gave Peacock my best understanding smile. "Peacock, old man," I said, "I have a little business proposition for you. . . ."

Well, that's all there was to it. You guessed it, now when Peacock makes one of his messes in some henpecked caveman's cave, it always includes at least one Original Hog, or maybe a couple Original Treesloths—Treesloth being another jerk Artist I have under contract. I sell the painting to Peacock for a hundred bears, and he charges his suck—er, *client, two* hundred bears for the same mess of bearfat and bison chips. Peacock calls this Interior Decorating.

I call it "Civilization." Maybe it'll last for a couple of months, if I'm lucky.

J. FRANCIS McCOMAS

Brave New Word

J. Francis McComas was an important figure in science fiction in three areas: (1) as an author, with such stories as "Shock Treatment," and "Criminal Negligence"; (2) as the coeditor of *Adventures in Time and Space* (New York: Random House, 1946), one of the earliest and most important SF reprint anthologies (as A. J. Budrys has pointed out, this book—and several others edited by Groff Conklin—helped to establish science fiction as a significant branch of literature); and (3) McComas was also the founding coeditor of *The Magazine of Fantasy and Science Fiction,* one of the "big three" of the post–World War II period. His efforts on the magazine were important but almost totally unappreciated, since historians have given their attention only to Anthony Boucher.

McComas the writer has also been underrated, and although his output was small, he produced some memorable stories, including this one. "Brave New Word" is an example of what might be called "prehistoric science fiction," a most interesting subgenre which addresses itself to the question of "how it all began."

The travelers to thc hot country arrived today, carrying many things, so tonight there will be dancing and all the hearts of The People will be good. As ever, when the travelers return, I remember how the thing began with Sleepy Hawk, that great doer of deeds, that laugher, that maker of words.

Most of The People think the matter had its beginning later; but I, whose oldest father had the story from the mouth of Sleepy Hawk himself, think otherwise. The true beginning was when Long Ax, that angry man, had his new ax handle break in his hand the very first time he swung the weapon. Long Ax had chosen the wood with care and knowledge, made it straight with his knife and then, in the chosen way, fixed it to the great stone ax his oldest father had given him.

Then, at the very first trial swing at one of the big trees that grew by the river where The People were camped, the handle had splintered, the great stone head had bounced from the tree to the river water, and Long Ax, a splinter driven into his thumb, danced about, shouting with pain and anger.

Since all this was a very bad sign, the rest of the young men looked very solemn. All, that is, except Sleepy Hawk, who fell on his back and laughed. He laughed so loud and so long that the other four thought he might never stop, but choke himself to death there by the river.

"Why do you laugh?" cried Long Ax. "Now I must make another handle! We can't start until I do!"

"Yes," asked Hungry Dog, who was fat and liked to sit in Long Ax's shadow, "why do you laugh?"

Sleepy Hawk stopped choking himself and said, "I'm sorry. But you looked so—so—" he looked in his head for a word, could not find one and said, "so—laugh-making! One moment you were swinging your great ax, the next moment you were dancing about, a little boy with a splinter in your hand! And the fine new handle for your ax was nothing but wood for the fire!"

At Sleepy Hawk's words, even Mountain Bear, the quiet man, laughed softly deep in his throat.

The face of Long Ax colored the angry red and he said, "How would you like to stay here and laugh while the others follow *me* on our hunt?"

Sleepy Hawk sat up then and looked at the other. His face did look something like that of a hawk that sleeps, with his sharp curved nose and his half-closed eyes. But it was the face of a hawk just waiting to wake and pounce.

"How would you like to try to make me?" he said very softly.

Long Ax was still red with anger but he looked away from Sleepy Hawk, toward the river.

"You have a knife and I have nothing," he growled.

With a move so fast it could barely be seen Sleepy Hawk jumped to his feet, took the knife from his belt and tossed it away.

"Now, I have no knife."

"Enough!" cried Mountain Bear, who was a quiet man but strong like his name animal. "Save your blows for our enemies! Long Ax, I have a stick for a spear, dry and tough. You may have it for your ax. Sleepy Hawk, take up your knife. You know we would not go on a fight or a hunt without you to lead us."

So there was peace but later, while waiting for Long Ax to bind together haft and head of his weapon, Mountain Bear said to Sleepy Hawk, "I cannot understand you. Always you laugh. And there is nothing to smile about in life."

"Yes, there is! Each thing of life, even the worst thing, has a part of it that will make you laugh, if only you will see it."

"Ha! I suppose you laugh even when you are with a woman!"

"Sometimes. If it is the proper woman and her heart is like mine."

But, as I said, most of The People think the matter had its beginning later, there on the ledge of the mountain of the Mud Dwellers, halfway down the great cliff, when the five young men came face to face with six of the little Mud Dwellers and there was no going back for any man.

For, after much thought, the band had decided to go toward the sun and into the mountain of the Mud Dwellers, rather than to the cold mountains and the Dwellers-in-Caves. The young men of The People wanted women. Those Dwellers-in-Caves, who made such queer markings on the walls of their homes, were strong and not easy to surprise. Too, their women were fierce, not kind and pleasing like those of the Mud Dwellers.

So they made a long journey, over a strange country. First, the river had dried into a hot land. After that, they seemed to be in the time of the long sun, come before they had thought, and the skins of animals they wore were hot on their backs. Sleepy Hawk wound into a tight roll his skin of a big cat and wrapped it around his waist. After a while, the others did the same.

Sleepy Hawk looked at them, running slowly along, the water pouring off their bodies, and said, "It is cooler by the side of our river."

Even Long Ax grinned at this although his tongue was swollen in his mouth.

The heat of the long sun fell on them and what little water they found made their hearts sick and their minds weak. So the young men went a day and a night without drinking.

Then, when they felt they could run no longer, they saw before them that great mountain rising straight up from the ground to the sky which held in its heart the little caves of the little men that The People called the Mud Dwellers. They stopped and looked up at the mountain.

"Oo-ee!" cried Hungry Dog. "That will be a hard run!"

But Sleepy Hawk found a trickle of water and they drank it without having their bellies cry out against them.

So the five young men of The People climbed the mountain that day and found its top was broad and flat. They moved carefully across the ground, ducking from tree to tree. Once, they found a pile of rocks that had, in the long ago, been a Mud Dwellers' home, before the wars of The People had driven them down inside the mountain, where the little men thought they might live more safely.

"These do not look like rocks," said Mountain Bear, stopping to look at them.

"They are not rocks," said Sleepy Hawk. "I have heard that the Mud Dwellers mix dried grass with mud, shape this into blocks and let the heat of the sun make the blocks hard. They build their caves with these hard blocks."

"That is a foolish waste of time," said Mountain Bear.

"And we waste time," said Sleepy Hawk. "We must reach the edge of their home place before dark."

So, just before the hiding of the sun, the young hunters came to where the top of the mountain suddenly ended. They crouched down and looked over the edge. There was a great cut, going deep to the heart of the mountain; and down, far down at the bottom of the cut, they could see, moving like bugs on a raw hide, a few of the Mud Dwellers.

"We'll rest here until the first morning light," Sleepy Hawk told them.

"Then climb down as far as we can?" asked Mountain Bear.

Sleepy Hawk nodded.

"Then we should watch another day, I think," said Long Ax.

Sleepy Hawk nodded again.

"We'll have to be quick," said Short Spear.

"Take women only," grunted Long Ax. "Weapons too, if there are any."

"And food!" added Hungry Dog.

"No food!" cried all the others.

"They do not eat," Cat-in-the-Mud told Hungry Dog. "Their food is taken from the ground and it is dirty."

Sleepy Hawk smiled a little at this, but said nothing.

Yet it did not work out as they planned. The five young men waked at the first light and slowly, quietly, they climbed down the steep side of the cut in the mountain. But as they crawled around a high rock to a narrow ledge, six men of the Mud Dwellers came up onto the ledge from the down trail. All stopped suddenly and stared at each other.

Then each side took a step forward, raised their weapons, then stopped again, weapons half lifted in their hands.

"Well," Long Ax growled deep in his throat, "why do we wait?"

"For the same reason they do!" Sleepy Hawk's voice was sharp.

He waved his hand and they all looked quickly about them. There was the long, narrow ledge, with the mountain going straight up from one side and, from the other, straight down in a heart-choking drop. And at each end of the ledge stood a little group of men, angry, uncertain, the length of three steps of a tall man between them.

"Who can win a fight in such a place?" asked Sleepy Hawk.

"We can!" growled Long Ax. "They are but little men!"

"But they are six and we are five, so all is equal."

"Throw spears and after them!" cried Long Ax.

Cat-in-the-Mud and Hungry Dog raised their weapons. As they did so, three of the Mud Dwellers lifted their arms.

"Stop!" cried Sleepy Hawk. Over his shoulder he said to Long Ax, "I am chief here. Now look, all of you. They throw, we throw. None can miss. If any men are left after the throwing, they fight. Perhaps one of all here lives. Then what? If that one is of The People, can he, wounded, alone, ever hope to return to our river? No!"

"You are right," said Mountain Bear.

"They will call for help," warned Cat-in-the-Mud.

"Soon enough to fight then," said Sleepy Hawk. "There is little room for more on this ground."

"True enough," said Mountain Bear.

"Now, quiet, all of you," ordered Sleepy Hawk, "and let me think."

He watched the Mud Dwellers. They were strange little men. Around their waists they wore belts of dried skin, but in these belts were set little pieces of colored stone. They wore smaller belts around their heads, to keep their long hair from falling over their eyes, and these belts, too, had the pieces of stone in them.

Sleepy Hawk liked these colored stones very much. But he did not think he would get any from the Mud Dwellers, who, though small, stood their ground as bravely as did The People, frowning, with knives and spears ready for the fight.

"Look at their spears," Sleepy Hawk said.

"They have two handles!" There was wonder in Cat-in-the-Mud's voice.

"Yes. One goes back from the hand, then joins the other, which goes forward to the head of the spear."

"I don't understand," Mountain Bear said softly.

"Neither do I." Sleepy Hawk frowned. "Two handles . . . I would like a closer look at those strange spears."

"Enough of this women's chatter!" screamed Long Ax. "Let us fight like men!"

Sleepy Hawk shrugged.

"If the rest of you feel that we should get ourselves killed," he said quietly, "and leave our bones here for Mud Dwellers to hang in their caves, why—let Long Ax begin the fight."

None moved.

Long Ax called out again but still no man of the other four moved and Long Ax closed his mouth tightly.

For a time there was silence on the ledge. Sleepy Hawk watched the Mud Dwellers; he had a wish to talk with them, to learn what they might be thinking. Now, like many of The People, Sleepy Hawk had a woman from the Mud Dwellers in his family, and from her had learned a few of their love words, the words that a mother says to a child that pleases her. But that was all. When The People caught a Mud Dweller woman it was her duty to learn their talk, not theirs to learn her noises.

So there was nothing he could say to them. He watched. They, too, stood as did The People, their leader a little in front of them, staring at his enemies, his men behind him, looking about nervously, their knives and strange two-handled spears ready for blood.

It seemed then to Sleepy Hawk that the two groups of men looked like two deer caught in the trap sands of a river. A deer so caught by the water hiding below the quiet-looking sands cannot step forward, nor can it move backward. So it was with the men. Their legs were caught on the rock. They dared not move either up or down. All of them, The People and Mud Dwellers, could only stand still and wait for what would happen.

And thinking of the men trapped like silly deer, Sleepy Hawk laughed aloud.

"Why do you laugh?" snarled Hungry Dog. Fright was in his voice.

Sleepy Hawk was choking again, as he always did when laughing swelled in his throat.

"This is—this is all very—" He choked and his breath flew out between his lips and he made a word.

"What was that?" cried Mountain Bear. "What did you say?"

"I said, *funny*."

"What does *funny* mean?"

"It is a word I have made and it means laugh-making. All this—we and they standing here, of us all none daring to go a step forward or back—it is very laugh-making . . . very *funny!*"

"We have a crazy man for a chief," growled Long Ax. "Or a fool. It takes little to make a fool laugh—"

But Sleepy Hawk was not listening. He was watching the leader of the Mud Dwellers and he was so startled by what that one was doing that he gave no ear to Long Ax's words. For the Mud Dweller was smiling. At first, it was a little smile, on the mouth only, but then, as Sleepy Hawk started to laugh again, the Mud Dweller's smile shone in his eyes, he opened his mouth and laughed as loudly as Sleepy Hawk ever did.

The two of them stood and laughed with each other while their followers looked at them uneasily and Long Ax muttered words of anger that he knew Sleepy Hawk could not hear.

Then, perhaps because his heart was warmed by his laughing, or because he was a great thinker as the later days of his life proved, Sleepy Hawk did a very strange thing. First he put his knife back in his belt, so that his left hand held nothing. Then he dropped his spear from his right hand. Mountain Bear cried out at this, but Sleepy Hawk did not listen. He stepped forward one step and raised his right hand, so that the chief of the Mud Dwellers could see that it was empty.

The Mud Dweller's smile was now on his lips only. He looked very hard at Sleepy Hawk, then he slowly nodded his head. Then he moved his hands slowly so that the two handles of his spear came apart. In one hand, he held a spear with a sharp stone head. In the other, just a simple, harmless stick with a hook at one end. He dropped these to the ground and stepped toward Sleepy Hawk, his right hand raised.

The two of them came close together. Sleepy Hawk said a Mud Dweller word that they all knew, one that a mother uses when her child makes her smile at his play. The Mud Dweller's smile became smaller; the young men saw that he did not like the use of that word between men. So Sleepy Hawk pointed at the young men of The People, then at the Mud Dwellers, making fearful frowns to show each of them angry at the other. Then he pointed to himself and laughed. He pointed to the Mud Dweller and laughed. He swept his arm around the air, pointing at both sides and laughing.

Then, slowly and clearly, Sleepy Hawk said his new word.

The chief of the Mud Dwellers nodded and said it after him.

"*Fun—nee!*" he said.

Sleepy Hawk held out his empty right hand and the Mud Dweller slowly reached out and touched Sleepy Hawk's hand with his.

"Very funny," answered Sleepy Hawk, grinning. Then, hoping the Mud Dweller might know the tongue of The People, he said, "I am Sleepy Hawk."

But the Mud Dweller did not understand. He said some words, in the high bird voice of the Mud Dwellers. Nor did Sleepy Hawk understand the Mud Dweller's words, so the two men just stood there, their right hands touching, smiling.

"Do any of you know any of the Mud Dwellers' words among men?" asked Sleepy Hawk.

The young men shook their heads.

"Never mind. Put down your weapons."

"Is that wise?" asked Mountain Bear.

"It is. Put them down."

So all the young men except Long Ax lowered their spears and put their knives and axes in their belts.

"Long Ax! I command you—" Sleepy Hawk began, but the chief of the Mud Dwellers turned his head and said a few words to his followers and they, slowly, took apart their two-handled spears and set them on the ground and those that had knives in their hands put these back in their belts. So Long Ax, too, let his weapon rest on the ground.

While their men stood, not at peace, but not ready for war, the two chiefs made talk with their hands; and after a while Sleepy Hawk nodded many times and turned to his followers and said, "Now we may go. With no spears in our backs. I have his promise."

"What is that worth!" cried Long Ax. "I do not turn my back on an enemy."

"Stay here, then," answered Sleepy Hawk. He himself waved at the Mud Dweller, turned and took a step back toward the upward trail.

Then he stopped, so suddenly that Mountain Bear, who was behind him, bumped into Sleepy Hawk.

"What is the matter with you?" cried Mountain Bear.

"Let us stay a little longer. I want one of those spears."

Sleepy Hawk looked again at the Mud Dweller, smiled, and very slowly, took the knife from his belt. The Mud Dweller frowned, but made no move when he saw that Sleepy Hawk held the knife by its blade and offered it to him.

"One does not give presents to an enemy," said Hungry Dog.

"This is no present. Watch and see."

The Mud Dweller took Sleepy Hawk's knife and looked at it. It was a good knife, with a blade of sharp flint and a handle made of the polished horn of old humpback. It was easy to see that the Mud Dweller wanted the knife.

Then Sleepy Hawk pointed to the little headbelt with its polished stones. Then he pointed to himself, then to the knife, and finally, to the Mud Dweller.

The Mud Dweller reached behind his head and took off the belt. Its bright-colored stones sparkled in the sun's light. The Mud Dweller handed it to Sleepy Hawk, who fastened it around his head. The Mud Dweller weighed the knife in his hand, nodded twice, and put the knife in the belt around his waist.

"Ha!" said Mountain Bear. "I thought you wanted a spear."

"Be quiet! I shall get one."

"How?"

"You shall see."

Once more Sleepy Hawk made as if to go. And once more he stopped and turned back to the Mud Dweller. That little man watched with sharp eyes. Sleepy Hawk took his rolled-up skin of a mountain cat from around his waist, shook it out so that the Mud Dweller could see, and spread it on the ground.

The Mud Dweller felt of the skin and his fingers saw how soft it was, having been well cured by Sleepy Hawk's oldest mother. Sleepy Hawk looked up at the sun, covered his eyes and shivered. The Mud Dweller watched closely. Sleepy Hawk uncovered his eyes but still shivered. Then he reached for the skin and wrapped it around him. As soon as it covered him all over, he stopped shaking and smiled.

The chief of the Mud Dwellers nodded to show he understood that when the time of little sun came, the skin would keep him warm and dry.

He reached toward Sleepy Hawk for the skin of the big cat.

"Careful!" Mountain Bear called softly.

Sleepy Hawk let the skin fall to the ground. The Mud Dweller reached for it again, but Sleepy Hawk raised his hand, shook his head just a little and walked over to where the two parts of the chief's spear lay on the ground. A Mud Dweller started for Sleepy Hawk, but his chief called out and the man was quiet. Sleepy Hawk picked up the two parts of the weapon but did not take them away. Instead he carried them back to the chief of the Mud Dwellers.

Sleepy Hawk made slow, careful signs. He lifted in his hand the spear that was no spear, but just a harmless stick. He shook it, held each end of it in turn, very close to his eyes, then, shaking his head, he let that stick fall to the ground. Next, Sleepy Hawk looked at the spear that was a proper spear, felt its sharp point with his thumb and nodded. After that, he picked up the other stick and held both parts out toward the Mud Dweller.

The Mud Dweller shook his head.

Sleepy Hawk stirred the cat's skin with his toe.

The Mud Dweller frowned just a little, then nodded. He moved his hand to show that Sleepy Hawk could have the two spears and reached down for the skin. But Sleepy Hawk shook his head and held out the stick part that was not a spear at all.

The Mud Dweller smiled, took both parts from Sleepy Hawk's hands. He looked around him, then moved to the rim of the ledge and stood there, looking upward.

"Now we shall see how a man throws that spear," Sleepy Hawk said softly.

"Surely he will not throw it *up* the mountain," said Mountain Bear.

But that is what the little man did. The Mud Dweller put the pieces together and raised his arm back to throw. One of the shafts went back from his hand. The queer hook at its end held the haft of the true spear. Then the Mud Dweller threw and, as the stick in his hand made his arm twice as long as any man's, so was his throw twice as strong and the spear flew up the mountain, farther than the farthest spear ever thrown by any of The People. It landed beside the trail down which the young men had come and stood there, its point deep in the ground.

"Oo—ee!" whistled Mountain Bear.

"A stick that throws!" cried Sleepy Hawk.

"The stick throws the spear!" said Cat-in-the-Mud. He grinned sourly at Long Ax. "Their weapons are better than ours. Sleepy Hawk is a very wise chief."

And Hungry Dog nodded and moved away from Long Ax.

Then the chief of the Mud Dwellers took up Sleepy Hawk's spear and showed him how to fit it on the throwing stick. He seemed to think of something new, then, for he pointed to his own spear sticking in the ground high up the mountain. He made a sign to keep Sleepy Hawk's spear, then pointed at Sleepy Hawk and to the spear up by the trail.

"A wise man," Sleepy Hawk said to Mountain Bear. "He wants to keep my spear and I will take his as we pass by it."

"Wait!" cried Mountain Bear. "I want one of those spear throwers!"

And he unwrapped his bear's skin from where it was wound around his middle and walked over to one of the Mud Dwellers. After him came the rest of the young men of The People, even the angry Long Ax, and The People and the Mud Dwellers stood beside each other, smiling and talking, even though there was no understanding of what was said.

And all of them laughed when a little, fat Mud Dweller offered Hungry Dog some small, round brown things and made signs that Hungry Dog should eat them. Which Hungry Dog did, of course.

"Good!" he cried with his mouth full, as a man should not. "Eat them! They're good!"

"Now, Hungry Dog," said Sleepy Hawk, "give them some dried meat."

Hungry Dog looked unhappy at this but he took some dried flesh of deer and offered it to the Mud Dwellers. After chewing a little bit, they smiled and rubbed their middles to show that the dried meat was good to their insides.

Now the sun was straight up in the sky. The giving and receiving was finished and the men stood about, tired, hot, but peaceful. Sleepy Hawk made signs to the Mud Dweller chief, pointing up the mountain. That man nodded, but he looked sad. Then Sleepy Hawk looked up at the sun, waved his hand across the sky, pointed down at the ledge, held up his fingers many times. The Mud Dweller smiled.

Sleepy Hawk thought a long time, looking hard at the Mud Dweller, then he said a word. Mountain Bear, who was standing by, had never heard this word before.

Sleepy Hawk pointed to the Mud Dwellers and the young men of The People, at the skins and the weapons, and at the belts with the colored stones.

He said the word again.

The Mud Dweller said the word after Sleepy Hawk.

Sleepy Hawk and the Mud Dweller said the word together.

Then the young men of The People waved to the Mud Dwellers and started the climb back to the top of the mountain.

When they reached the flat top of the mountain and rested awhile, Sleepy Hawk laughed softly and said to Mountain Bear, "You know, I have another, better knife at home. And my cat's skin was old. I shall hunt for another one." He laughed again. "But I have never had a stick that throws spears farther than can a man's arms. And when I seek a wife, I shall give her father some of the colored stones. Even the chief of all our chiefs should then be willing to give me his oldest daughter—the beautiful one."

Mountain Bear hefted the throwing stick. "We are coming back?"

"Yes. I want more throwing sticks. I want many belts with their stones of many colors. Yes, in three hands of suns I will return to . . ."

"To what?" asked Mountain Bear. "I heard you make a word."

"Yes. I made a word to tell of giving one thing to get another. I taught it to that chief of the Mud Dwellers. So, from now on, unless some fool like Long Ax makes trouble, the Mud Dweller and I will not fight. We will *trade*."

And that is why we go peacefully to the land of Mud Dwellers and bring back many things without war. And that is why the youngest young son of Sleepy Hawk, who is like the old man was, is planning to go up the mountains where the Dwellers-in-Caves are. He thinks they will trade us the strange colors they put on the walls of their caves and other things for our throwing sticks and skins and bright stones.

FREDERIK POHL

The Tunnel Under the World

The novels and short stories of Frederik Pohl (some written in collaboration with C. M. Kornbluth) are among the finest and most important in science fiction. His attacks on the institutionalized holders of wealth and power—especially his portrayals of uncontrolled corporate greed and domination—found many admirers and imitators in the fifties and sixties. Pohl's particular concern was the manipulation of human desires through advertising and the resulting drive to consume. He has produced a series of stories (and, with Kornbluth, the seminal novel *The Space Merchants*) on this theme, including "The Midas Plague," "The Man Who Ate the World," "Happy Birthday, Dear Jesus," and the present selection.

Marketing research is an important component of the advertising business and vast sums are expended in efforts to perfect techniques and approaches and to identify the audience for a particular product. Most of this is accomplished through the process called sampling, and it is more effective if one can control the variables affecting the group being sampled. In "The Tunnel Under the World" we enter a closed system, one where the variables are more carefully controlled than usual.

On the morning of June 15, Guy Burckhardt woke up screaming out of a dream.

It was more real than any dream he had ever had in his life. He could still hear and feel the sharp, ripping-metal explosion, the violent heave that had tossed him furiously out of bed, the searing wave of heat.

He sat up convulsively and stared, not believing what he saw, at the quiet room and the bright sunlight coming in the window.

He croaked, "Mary?"

His wife was not in the bed next to him. The covers were tumbled and awry, as though she had just left it, and the memory of the dream was so strong that instinctively he found himself searching the floor to see if the dream explosion had thrown her down.

But she wasn't there. Of course she wasn't, he told himself, looking at the familiar vanity and slipper chair, the uncracked window, the unbuckled wall. It had only been a dream.

"Guy?" His wife was calling him querulously from the foot of the stairs. "Guy, dear, are you all right?"

He called weakly, "Sure."

There was a pause. Then Mary said doubtfully, "Breakfast is ready. Are you sure you're all right? I thought I heard you yelling."

Burckhardt said more confidently, "I had a bad dream, honey. Be right down."

In the shower, punching the lukewarm-and-cologne he favored, he told himself that it had been a beaut of a dream. Still bad dreams weren't unusual, especially bad dreams about explosions. In the past thirty years of H-bomb jitters, who had not dreamed of explosions?

Even Mary had dreamed of them, it turned out, for he started to tell her about the dream, but she cut him off. "You *did?*" Her voice was astonished. "Why, dear, I dreamed the same thing! Well, almost the same thing. I didn't actually *hear* anything. I dreamed that something woke me up, and then there was a sort of quick bang, and then something hit me on the head. And that was all. Was yours like that?"

Burckhardt coughed. "Well, no," he said. Mary was not one of the strong-as-a-man, brave-as-a-tiger women. It was not necessary, he thought, to tell her all the little details of the dream that made it seem so real. No need to mention the splintered ribs, and the salt bubble in his throat, and the agonized knowledge that this was death. He said, "Maybe there really was some kind of explosion downtown. Maybe we heard it and it started us dreaming."

Mary reached over and patted his hand absently. "Maybe," she agreed. "It's almost half-past eight, dear. Shouldn't you hurry? You don't want to be late to the office."

He gulped his food, kissed her and rushed out—not so much to be on time as to see if his guess had been right.

But downtown Tylerton looked as it always had. Coming in on the bus, Burckhardt watched critically out the window, seeking evidence of an explosion. There wasn't any. If anything, Tylerton looked better than it ever had before. It was a beautiful crisp day, the sky was cloudless, the buildings were clean and inviting. They had, he observed, steam-blasted the Power & Light Building, the town's only skyscraper—that was the penalty of having Contro Chemicals' main plant on the outskirts of town; the fumes from the cascade stills left their mark on stone buildings.

None of the usual crowd was on the bus, so there wasn't anyone Burckhardt could ask about the explosion. And by the time he got out at the corner of Fifth and Lehigh and the bus rolled away with a muted diesel moan, he had pretty well convinced himself that it was all imagination.

He stopped at the cigar stand in the lobby of his office building, but Ralph wasn't behind the counter. The man who sold him his pack of cigarettes was a stranger.

"Where's Mr. Stebbins?" Burckhardt asked.

The man said politely, "Sick, sir. He'll be in tomorrow. A pack of Marlins today?"

"Chesterfields," Burckhardt corrected.

"Certainly, sir," the man said. But what he took from the rack and slid across the counter was an unfamiliar green-and-yellow pack.

"Do try these, sir," he suggested. "They contain an anticough factor. Ever notice how ordinary cigarettes make you choke every once in a while?"

Burckhardt said suspiciously, "I never heard of this brand."

"Of course not. They're something new." Burckhardt hesitated, and the man said persuasively, "Look, try them out at my risk. If you don't like them, bring back the empty pack and I'll refund your money. Fair enough?"

Burckhardt shrugged. "How can I lose? But give me a pack of Chesterfields, too, will you?"

He opened the pack and lit one while he waited for the elevator. They weren't bad, he decided, though he was suspicious of cigarettes that had the tobacco chemically treated in any way. But he didn't think much of Ralph's stand-in; it would raise hell with the trade at the cigar stand if the man tried to give every customer the same high-pressure sales talk.

The elevator door opened with a low-pitched sound of music. Burckhardt and two or three others got in and he nodded to them as the door closed. The thread of music switched off and the speaker in the ceiling of the cab began its usual commercials.

No, not the *usual* commercials, Burckhardt realized. He had been exposed to the captive-audience commercials so long that they hardly registered on the outer ear anymore, but what was coming from the recorded program in the basement of the building caught his attention. It wasn't merely that the brands were most unfamiliar; it was a difference in pattern.

There were jingles with an insistent, bouncy rhythm, about soft drinks he had never tasted. There was a rapid patter dialogue between what sounded like two ten-year-old boys about a candy bar, followed by an authoritative bass rumble: "Go right out and get a DELICIOUS Choco-Bite and eat your TANGY Choco-Bite *all up*. That's *Choco-Bite!*" There was a sobbing female whine: "I *wish* I had a Feckle Freezer! I'd do *anything* for a Feckle Freezer!" Burckhardt reached his floor and left the elevator in the middle of the last one. It left him a little uneasy. The commercials were not for familiar brands; there was no feeling of use and custom to them.

But the office was happily normal—except that Mr. Barth wasn't in. Miss Mitkin, yawning at the reception desk, didn't know exactly why. "His home phoned, that's all. He'll be in tomorrow."

"Maybe he went to the plant. It's right near his house."

She looked indifferent. "Yeah."

A thought struck Burckhardt. "But today is June 15! It's quarterly tax-return day—he has to sign the return!"

Miss Mitkin shrugged to indicate that that was Burckhardt's problem, not hers. She returned to her nails.

Thoroughly exasperated, Burckhardt went to his desk. It wasn't that he couldn't sign the tax returns as well as Barth, he thought resentfully. It simply wasn't his job, that was all; it was a responsibility that Barth, as office manager for Contro Chemicals' downtown office, should have taken.

He thought briefly of calling Barth at his home or trying to reach him at the factory, but he gave up the idea quickly enough. He didn't really care much for the people at the factory and the less contact he had with them, the better. He had been to the factory once, with Barth; it had been a confusing and, in a way, a frightening experience. Barring a handful of executives and engineers, there wasn't a soul in the factory—that is, Burckhardt corrected himself, remembering what Barth had told him, not a *living* soul—just the machines.

According to Barth, each machine was controlled by a sort of computer which reproduced, in its electronic snarl, the actual memory and mind of a human being. It was an unpleasant thought. Barth, laughing, had assured him that there was no Frankenstein business of robbing graveyards and implanting brains in machines. It was only a matter, he said, of transferring a man's habit patterns from brain cells to vacuum-tube cells. It didn't hurt the man and it didn't make the machine into a monster.

But they made Burckhardt uncomfortable all the same.

He put Barth and the factory and all his other little irritations out of his mind and tackled the tax returns. It took him until noon to verify the figures—which Barth could have done out of his memory and his private ledger in ten minutes, Burckhardt resentfully reminded himself. He sealed them in an envelope and walked out to Miss Mitkin. "Since Mr. Barth isn't here, we'd better go to lunch in shifts," he said. "You can go first."

"Thanks." Miss Mitkin languidly took her bag out of the desk drawer and began to apply makeup.

Burckhardt offered her the envelope. "Drop this in the mail for me, will you? Uh—wait a minute. I wonder if I ought to phone Mr. Barth to make sure. Did his wife say whether he was able to take phone calls?"

"Didn't say." Miss Mitkin blotted her lips carefully with a Kleenex. "Wasn't his wife, anyway. It was his daughter who called and left the message."

"The kid?" Burckhardt frowned. "I thought she was away at school."

"She called, that's all I know."

Burckhardt went back to his own office and stared distastefully at the unopened mail on his desk. He didn't like nightmares; they spoiled his whole day. He should have stayed in bed, like Barth.

A funny thing happened on his way home. There was a disturbance at the corner where he usually caught his bus—someone was screaming something about a new kind of deep-freeze—so he walked an extra block. He saw the bus coming and started to trot. But behind him, someone was calling his name. He looked over his shoulder; a small, harried-looking man was hurrying toward him.

Burckhardt hesitated, and then recognized him. It was a casual acquaintance named Swanson. Burckhardt sourly observed that he had already missed the bus.

He said, "Hello."

Swanson's face was desperately eager. "Burckhardt?" he asked inquiringly, with an odd intensity. And then he just stood there silently, watching Burckhardt's face, with a burning eagerness that dwindled to a faint hope and died to a regret. He was searching for something, waiting for something, Burckhardt thought. But whatever it was he wanted, Burckhardt didn't know how to supply it.

Burckhardt coughed and said again, "Hello, Swanson."

Swanson didn't even acknowledge the greeting. He merely sighed a very deep sigh.

"Nothing doing," he mumbled, apparently to himself. He nodded abstractedly to Burckhardt and turned away.

Burckhardt watched the slumped shoulders disappear in the crowd. It was an *odd* sort of day, he thought, and one he didn't much like. Things weren't going right.

Riding home on the next bus, he brooded about it. It wasn't anything terrible or disastrous; it was something out of his experience entirely. You live your life, like any man, and you form a network of impressions and reactions. You *expect* things. When you open your medicine chest, your razor is expected to be on the second shelf; when you lock your front door, you expect to have to give it a slight extra tug to make it latch.

It isn't the things that are right and perfect in your life that make it familiar. It is the things that are just a little bit wrong—the sticking latch, the light switch at the head of the stairs that needs an extra push because the spring is old and weak, the rug that unfailingly skids underfoot.

It wasn't just that things were wrong with the pattern of Burckhardt's life; it was that the *wrong* things were wrong. For instance, Barth hadn't come into the office, yet Barth *always* came in.

Burckhardt brooded about it through dinner. He brooded about it, despite his wife's attempt to interest him in a game of bridge with the neighbors, all through the evening. The neighbors were people he liked—Anne and Farley Dennerman. He had known them all their lives. But they were odd and brooding, too, this night and he barely listened to Dennerman's complaints about not being able to get good phone service or his wife's comments on the disgusting variety of television commercials they had these days.

Burckhardt was well on the way to setting an all-time record for continuous abstraction when, around midnight, with a suddenness that surprised him—he was strangely *aware* of it happening—he turned over in his bed and, quickly and completely, fell asleep.

On the morning of June 15, Burckhardt woke up screaming.

It was more real than any dream he had ever had in his life. He could still hear the explosion, feel the blast that crushed him against a wall. It did not seem right that he should be sitting bolt upright in bed in an undisturbed room.

His wife came pattering up the stairs. "Darling!" she cried. "What's the matter?"

He mumbled, "Nothing. Bad dream."

She relaxed, hand on heart. In any angry tone, she started to say: "You gave me such a shock—"

But a noise from outside interrupted her. There was a wail of sirens and a clang of bells; it was loud and shocking.

The Burckhardts stared at each other for a heartbeat, then hurried fearfully to the window.

There were no rumbling fire engines in the street, only a small panel truck, cruising slowly along. Flaring loudspeaker horns crowned its top. From them issued the screaming sound of sirens, growing in intensity, mixed with the rumble of heavy-duty engines and the sound of bells. It was a perfect record of fire engines arriving at a four-alarm blaze.

Burckhardt said in amazement, "Mary, that's against the law! Do you know what they're doing? They're playing records of a fire. What are they up to?"

"Maybe it's a practical joke," his wife offered.

"Joke? Waking up the whole neighborhood at six o'clock in the morning?" He shook his head. "The police will be here in ten minutes," he predicted. "Wait and see."

But the police weren't—not in ten minutes, or at all. Whoever the pranksters in the car were, they apparently had a police permit for their games.

The car took a position in the middle of the block and stood silent for a few minutes. Then there was a crackle from the speaker, and a giant voice chanted:

Feckle Freezers!
Feckle Freezers!
Gotta have a
Feckle Freezer!
Feckle, Feckle, Feckle,
Feckle, Feckle, Feckle—

It went on and on. Every house on the block had faces staring out of windows by then. The voice was not merely loud; it was nearly deafening.

Burckhardt shouted to his wife, over the uproar, "What the hell is a Feckle Freezer?"

"Some kind of a freezer, I guess, dear," she shrieked back unhelpfully.

Abruptly the noise stopped and the truck stood silent. It was still misty morning; the sun's rays came horizontally across the rooftops. It was impossible to believe that, a moment ago, the silent block had been bellowing the name of a freezer.

"A crazy advertising trick," Burckhardt said bitterly. He yawned and turned away from the window. "Might as well get dressed. I guess that's the end of—"

The bellow caught him from behind; it was almost like a hard slap on the ears. A harsh, sneering voice, louder than the archangel's trumpet, howled:

"Have you got a freezer? *It stinks!* If it isn't a Feckle Freezer, *it stinks!* If it's a last year's Feckle Freezer, *it stinks!* Only this year's Feckle Freezer is any good at all! You know who owns an Ajax Freezer? Fairies own Ajax Freezers! You know who owns a Triplecold Freezer? Commies own Triplecold Freezers! Every freezer but a brand-new Feckle Freezer *stinks!*"

The voice screamed inarticulately with rage. "I'm warning you! Get out and buy a Feckle Freezer right away! Hurry up! Hurry for Feckle! Hurry for Feckle! Hurry, hurry, hurry, Feckle, Feckle, Feckle, Feckle, Feckle, Feckle . . ."

It stopped eventually. Burckhardt licked his lips. He started to say to his wife, "Maybe we ought to call the police about—" when the speaker erupted again. It caught him off guard; it was intended to catch him off guard. It screamed:

"Feckle, Feckle, Feckle, Feckle, Feckle, Feckle, Feckle, Feckle. Cheap freezers ruin your food. You'll get sick and throw up. You'll get sick and die. Buy a Feckle, Feckle, Feckle, Feckle! Ever take a piece of meat out of the freezer you've got and see how rotten and moldy it is? Buy a Feckle, Feckle, Feckle, Feckle, Feckle. Do you want to eat rotten, stinking food? Or do you want to wise up and buy a Feckle, Feckle, Feckle—"

That did it. With fingers that kept stabbing the wrong holes, Burckhardt finally managed to dial the local police station. He got a busy signal—it was apparent that he was not the only one with the same idea—and while he was shakily dialing again, the noise outside stopped.

He looked out the window. The truck was gone.

Burckhardt loosened his tie and ordered another Frosty-Flip from the waiter. If only they wouldn't keep Crystal Cafe so *hot!* The new paint job—searing reds and blinding yellows—was bad enough, but someone seemed to have the delusion that this was January instead of June; the place was a good ten degrees warmer than outside.

He swallowed the Frosty-Flip in two gulps. It had a kind of peculiar flavor, he thought, but not bad. It certainly cooled you off, just as the waiter had promised. He reminded himself to pick up a carton of them on the way home; Mary might like them. She was always interested in something new.

He stood up awkwardly as the girl came across the restaurant toward him. She was the most beautiful thing he had ever seen in Tylerton. Chin-height, honey-blonde hair and a figure that—well, it was all hers. There was no doubt in the world that the dress that clung to her was the only thing she wore. He felt as if he were blushing as she greeted him.

"Mr. Burckhardt." The voice was like distant tom-toms. "It's wonderful of you to let me see you, after this morning."

He cleared his throat. "Not at all. Won't you sit down, Miss—"

"April Horn," she murmured, sitting down—beside him, not where he had pointed on the other side of the table. "Call me April, won't you?"

She was wearing some kind of perfume, Burckhardt noted with

what little of his mind was functioning at all. It didn't seem fair that she should be using perfume as well as everything else. He came to with a start and realized that the waiter was leaving with an order for filets mignons for two.

"Hey!" he objected.

"Please, Mr. Burckhardt." Her shoulder was against his, her face was turned to him, her breath was warm, her expression was tender and solicitous. "This is all on the Feckle Corporation. Please let them—it's the *least* they can do."

He felt her hand burrowing into his pocket.

"I put the price of the meal into your pocket," she whispered conspiratorially. "Please do that for me, won't you? I mean I'd appreciate it if you'd pay the waiter—I'm old-fashioned about things like that."

She smiled meltingly, then became mock-businesslike. "But you must take the money," she insisted. "Why, you're letting Feckle off lightly if you do! You could sue them for every nickel they've got, disturbing your sleep like that."

With a dizzy feeling, as though he had just seen someone make a rabbit disappear into a top hat, he said, "Why, it really wasn't so bad, uh, April. A little noisy, maybe, but—"

"Oh, Mr. Burckhardt!" The blue eyes were wide and admiring. "I *knew* you'd understand. It's just that—well, it's such a *wonderful* freezer that some of the outside men get carried away, so to speak. As soon as the main office found out about what happened, they sent representatives around to every house on the block to apologize. Your wife told us where we could phone you—and I'm so very pleased that you were willing to let me have lunch with you, so that I could apologize, too. Because truly, Mr. Burckhardt, it is a *fine* freezer.

"I shouldn't tell you this, but—" the blue eyes were shyly lowered— "I'd do almost anything for Feckle Freezers. It's more than a job to me." She looked up. She was enchanting. "I bet you think I'm silly, don't you?"

Burckhardt coughed. "Well, I—"

"Oh, you don't want to be unkind!" She shook her head. "No, don't pretend. You think it's silly. But really, Mr. Burckhardt, you wouldn't think so if you knew more about the Feckle. Let me show you this little booklet—"

Burckhardt got back from lunch a full hour late. It wasn't only the girl who delayed him. There had been a curious interview with a little man named Swanson, whom he barely knew, who had stopped him with desperate urgency on the street—and then left him cold.

But it didn't matter much. Mr. Barth, for the first time since Burckhardt had worked there, was out for the day—leaving Burckhardt stuck with the quarterly tax returns.

What did matter, though, was that somehow he had signed a purchase order for a twelve-cubic-foot Feckle Freezer, upright model, self-defrosting, list price $625, with a ten percent "courtesy" discount—"Because of that *horrid* affair this morning, Mr. Burckhardt," she had said.

And he wasn't sure how he could explain it to his wife.

He needn't have worried. as he walked in the front door, his wife said almost immediately, "I wonder if we can't afford a new freezer, dear. There was a man here to apologize about that noise and—well, we got to talking and—"

She had signed a purchase order, too.

It had been the damnedest day. Burckhardt thought later, on his way up to bed. But the day wasn't done with him yet. At the head of the stairs, the weakened spring in the electric light switch refused to click at all. He snapped it back and forth angrily and, of course, succeeded in jarring the tumbler out of its pins. The wires shorted and every light in the house went out.

"Damn!" said Guy Burckhardt.

"Fuse?" His wife shrugged sleepily. "Let it go till the morning, dear."

Burckhardt shook his head. "You go back to bed. I'll be right along."

It wasn't so much that he cared about fixing the fuse, but he was too restless for sleep. He disconnected the bad switch with a screwdriver, tumbled down into the black kitchen, found the flashlight and climbed gingerly down the celllar stairs. He located a spare fuse, pushed an empty trunk over to the fuse box to stand on and twisted out the old fuse.

When the new one was in, he heard the starting click and steady drone of the refrigerator in the kitchen overhead.

He headed back to the steps, and stopped.

Where the old trunk had been, the cellar floor gleamed oddly bright. He inspected it in the flashlight beam. It was metal!

"Son of a gun," said Guy Burckhardt. He shook his head unbelievingly. He peered closer, rubbed the edges of the metallic patch with his thumb and acquired an annoying cut—the edges were *sharp*.

The stained cement floor of the cellar was a thin shell. He found a hammer and cracked it off in a dozen spots—everywhere was metal.

The whole cellar was a copper box. Even the cement-brick walls were false fronts over a metal sheath!

Baffled, he attacked one of the foundation beams. That, at least, was real wood. The glass in the cellar windows was real glass.

He sucked his bleeding thumb and tried the base of the cellar stairs. Real wood. He chipped at the bricks under the oil burner. Real bricks. The retaining walls, the floor—they were faked.

It was as though someone had shored up the house with a frame of metal and then laboriously concealed the evidence.

The biggest surprise was the upside-down boat hull that blocked the rear half of the cellar, relic of a brief home-workshop period that Burckhardt had gone through a couple of years before. From above, it looked perfectly normal. Inside, though, where there should have been thwarts and seats and lockers, there was a mere tangle of braces, rough and unfinished.

"But I *built* that!" Burckhardt exclaimed, forgetting his thumb. He leaned against the hull dizzily, trying to think this thing through. For reasons beyond his comprehension, someone had taken his boat and his cellar away, maybe his whole house, and replaced them with a clever mock-up of the real thing.

"That's crazy," he said to the empty cellar. He stared around in the light of the flash. He whispered, "What in the name of heaven would anybody do that for?"

Reason refused an answer; there wasn't any reasonable answer. For long minutes, Burckhardt contemplated the uncertain picture of his own sanity.

He peered under the boat again, hoping to reassure himself that it was a mistake, just his imagination. But the sloppy, unfinished bracing was unchanged. He crawled under for a better look, feeling the rough wood incredulously. Utterly impossible!

He switched off the flashlight and started to wriggle out. But he didn't make it. In the moment between the command to his legs to move and the crawling out, he felt a sudden draining weariness flooding through him.

Consciousness went—not easily, but as though it were being taken away, and Guy Burckhardt was asleep.

On the morning of June 16, Guy Burckhardt woke up in a cramped position huddled under the hull of the boat in his basement—and raced upstairs to find it was June 15.

The first thing he had done was to make a frantic, hasty inspection of the boat hull, the faked cellar floor, the imitation stone. They were all as he had remembered them, all completely unbelievable.

The kitchen was its placid, unexciting self. The electric clock was purring soberly around the dial. Almost six o'clock, it said. His wife would be waking at any moment.

Burckhardt flung open the front door and stared out into the quiet street. The morning paper was tossed carelessly against the steps, and as he retrieved it, he noticed that this was the fifteenth day of June.

But that was impossible. *Yesterday* was the fifteenth of June. It was not a date one would forget, it was quarterly tax-return day.

He went back into the hall and picked up the telephone; he dialed for Weather Information, and got a well-modulated chant: "—and cooler, some showers. Barometric pressure thirty point zero four, rising . . . United States Weather Bureau forecast for June 15. Warm and sunny, with high around—"

He hung the phone up. June 15.

"Holy Heaven!" Burckhardt said prayerfully. Things were very odd indeed. He heard the ring of his wife's alarm and bounded up the stairs.

Mary Burckhardt was sitting upright in bed with the terrified, uncomprehending stare of someone just waking out of a nightmare.

"Oh!" she gasped, as her husband came in the room. "Darling, I just had the most *terrible* dream! It was like an exposion and—"

"Again?" Burckhardt asked, not very sympathetically. "Mary, something's funny! I *knew* there was something wrong all day yesterday and—"

He went on to tell her about the copper box that was the cellar, and the odd mock-up someone had made of his boat. Mary looked astonished, then alarmed, then placatory and uneasy.

She said, "Dear, are you *sure?* Because I was cleaning that old trunk out just last week and I didn't notice anything."

"Positive!" said Guy Burckhardt. "I dragged it over to the wall to step on it to put a new fuse in after we blew the lights out and—"

"After we what?" Mary was looking more than merely alarmed.

"After we blew the lights out. You know, when the switch at the head of the stairs stuck. I went down to the cellar and—"

Mary sat up in bed. "Guy, the switch didn't stick. I turned out the lights myself last night."

Burckhardt glared at his wife. "Now I *know* you didn't! Come here and take a look!"

He stalked out to the landing and dramatically pointed to the bad switch, the one that he had unscrewed and left hanging the night before. . . .

Only it wasn't. It was as it had always been. Unbelieving, Burckhardt pressed it and the lights sprang up in both halls.

Mary, looking pale and worried, left him to go down to the kitchen and start breakfast. Burckhardt stood staring at the switch for a long time. His mental processes were gone beyond the point of disbelief and shock; they simply were not functioning.

He shaved and dressed and ate his breakfast in a state of numb introspection. Mary didn't disturb him; she was apprehensive and soothing. She kissed him good-bye as he hurried out to the bus without another word.

Miss Mitkin, at the reception desk, greeted him with a yawn. "Morning," she said drowsily. "Mr. Barth won't be in today."

Burckhardt started to say something, but checked himself. She would not know that Barth hadn't been in yesterday, either, because she was tearing a June 14 pad off her calendar to make way for the "new" June 15 sheet.

He staggered to his own desk and stared unseeingly at the morning's mail. It had not even been opened yet, but he knew that the Factory Distributors envelope contained an order for twenty thousand feet of the new acoustic tile, and the one from Finebeck & Sons was a complaint.

After a long while, he forced himself to open them. They were.

By lunchtime, driven by a desperate sense of urgency, Burckhardt made Miss Mitkin take her lunch hour first—the June-15-that-was-yesterday, *he* had gone first. She went, looking vaguely worried about his strained insistence, but it made no difference to Burckhardt's mood.

The phone rang and Burckhardt picked it up abstractedly. "Contro Chemicals Downtown, Burckhardt speaking."

The voice said, "This is Swanson," and stopped.

Burckhardt waited expectantly, but that was all. He said, "Hello?"

Again the pause. Then Swanson asked in sad resignation, "Still nothing, eh?"

"Nothing what? Swanson, is there something you want? You came up to me yesterday and went through this routine. You—"

The voice crackled: "Burckhardt! Oh, my good heavens, *you remember!* Stay right there—I'll be down in half an hour!"

"What's this all about?"

"Never mind," the little man said exultantly. "Tell you about it when I see you. Don't say any more over the phone—somebody may be listening. Just wait there. Say, hold on a minute. Will you be alone in the office?"

"Well, no. Miss Mitkin will probably—"

"Hell. Look, Burckhardt, where do you eat lunch? Is it good and noisy?"

"Why, I suppose so. The Crystal Cafe. It's just about a block—"

"I know where it is. Meet you in half an hour!" And the receiver clicked.

The Crystal Cafe was no longer painted red, but the temperature was still up. And they had added piped-in music interspersed with commercials. The advertisements were for Frosty-Flip, Marlin Cigarettes—"They're sanitized," the announcer purred—and something called Choco-Bite candy bars that Burckhardt couldn't remember ever having heard of before. But he heard more about them quickly enough.

While he was waiting for Swanson to show up, a girl in the cellophane skirt of a nightclub cigarette vendor came through the restaurant with a tray of tiny scarlet-wrapped candies.

"Choco-Bites are *tangy,*" she was murmuring as she came close to his table. "Choco-Bites are *tangier* than tangy!"

Burckhardt, intent on watching for the strange little man who had phoned him, paid little attention. But as she scattered a handful of the confections over the table next to his, smiling at the occupants, he caught a glimpse of her and turned to stare.

"Why, Miss Horn!" he said.

The girl dropped her tray of candies.

Burckhardt rose, concerned over the girl. "Is something wrong?"

But she fled.

The manager of the restaurant was staring suspiciously at Burckhardt, who sank back in his seat and tried to look inconspicuous. He hadn't insulted the girl! Maybe she was just a very strictly reared young lady, he thought—in spite of long bare legs under the cellophane skirt—and when he addressed her, she thought he was a masher.

Ridiculous idea. Burckhardt scowled uneasily and picked up his menu.

"Burckhardt!" It was a shrill whisper.

Burckhardt looked up over the top of his menu, startled. In the seat across from him, the little man named Swanson was sitting, tensely poised.

"Burckhardt!" the little man whispered again. "Let's get out of here! They're on to you now. If you want to stay alive, come on!"

There was no arguing with the man. Burckhardt gave the hovering manager a sick, apologetic smile and followed Swanson out. The little man seemed to know where he was going. In the street, he clutched Burckhardt by the elbow and hurried him off down the block.

"Did you see her?" he demanded. "That Horn woman, in the phone booth? She'll have them here in five minutes, believe me, so hurry it up!"

Although the street was full of people and cars, nobody was paying any attention to Burckhardt and Swanson. The air had a nip in it—more like October than June, Burckhardt thought, in spite of the weather bureau. And he felt like a fool, following this mad little man down the street, running away from some "them" toward—toward what? The little man might be crazy, but he was afraid. And the fear was infectious.

"In here!" panted the little man.

It was another restaurant—more of a bar, really, and a sort of second-rate place that Burckhardt had never patronized.

"Right straight through," Swanson whispered; and Burckhardt, like a biddable boy, sidestepped through the mass of tables to the far end of the restaurant.

It was L-shaped, with a front on two streets at right angles to each other. They came out on the side street, Swanson staring coldly back at the question-looking cashier, and crossed to the opposite sidewalk.

They were under the marquee of a movie theater. Swanson's expression began to relax.

"Lost them!" he crowed softly. "We're almost there."

He stepped up to the window and bought two tickets. Burckhardt trailed him into the theater. It was a weekday matinee and the place was almost empty. From the screen came sounds of gunfire and horses' hooves. A solitary usher, leaning against a bright brass rail, looked briefly at them and went back to staring boredly at the picture as Swanson led Burckhardt down a flight of carpeted marble steps.

They were in the lounge and it was empty. There was a door for men and one for ladies; and there was a third door, marked "MANAGER" in gold letters. Swanson listened at the door, and gently opened it and peered inside.

"Okay," he said, gesturing.

Burckhardt followed him through an empty office, to another door—a closet, probably, because it was unmarked.

But it was no closet. Swanson opened it warily, looked inside, then motioned Burckhardt to follow.

It was a tunnel, metal-walled, brightly lit. Empty, it stretched vacantly away in both directions from them.

Burckhardt looked wonderingly around. One thing he knew and knew full well:

No such tunnel belonged under Tylerton.

There was a room off the tunnel with chairs and a desk and what looked like television screens. Swanson slumped in a chair, panting.

"We're all right for a while here," he wheezed. "They don't come here much anymore. If they do, we'll hear them and we can hide."

"Who?" demanded Burckhardt.

The little man said, "Martians!" His voice cracked on the word and the life seemed to go out of him. In morose tones, he went on: "Well, I think they're Martians. Although you could be right, you know; I've had plenty of time to think it over these last few weeks, after they got you, and it's possible they're Russians after all. Still—"

"Start from the beginning. Who got me when?"

Swanson sighed. "So we have to go through the whole thing again. All right. It was about two months ago that you banged on my door, late at night. You were all beat up—scared silly. You begged me to help you—''

''*I* did?''

''Naturally you don't remember any of this. Listen and you'll understand. You were talking a blue streak about being captured and threatened, and your wife being dead and coming back to life, and all kinds of mixed-up nonsense. I thought you were crazy. But—well, I've always had a lot of respect for you. And you begged me to hide you and I have this darkroom, you know. It locks from the inside only. I put the lock on myself. So we went in there—just to humor you—and along about midnight, which was only fifteen or twenty minutes after, we passed out.''

''Passed out?''

Swanson nodded. ''Both of us. It was like being hit with a sandbag. Look, didn't that happen to you again last night?''

''I guess it did.'' Burckhardt shook his head uncertainly.

''Sure. And then all of a sudden we were awake again, and you said you were going to show me something funny, and we went out and bought a paper. And the date on it was June 15.''

''June 15? But that's today! I mean—''

''You got it, friend. It's *always* today!''

It took time to penetrate.

Burckhardt said wonderingly, ''You've hidden out in that darkroom for how many weeks?''

''How can I tell? Four or five, maybe, I lost count. And every day the same—always the fifteenth of June, always my landlady, Mrs. Keefer, is sweeping the front steps, always the same headline in the papers at the corner. It gets monotonous, friend.''

It was Burckhardt's idea and Swanson despised it, but he went along. He was the type who always went along.

''It's dangerous,'' he grumbled worriedly. ''Suppose somebody comes by? They'll spot us and—''

''What have we got to lose?''

Swanson shrugged. ''It's dangerous,'' he said again. But he went along.

Burckhardt's idea was very simple. He was sure of only one thing—the tunnel went somewhere. Martians or Russians, fantastic plot or crazy hallucination, whatever was wrong with Tylerton had an explanation, and the place to look for it was at the end of the tunnel.

They jogged along. It was more than a mile before they began to see an end. They were in luck—at least no one came through the tunnel to spot them. But Swanson had said that it was only at certain hours that the tunnel seemed to be in use.

Always the fifteenth of June. Why? Burckhardt asked himself. Never mind the how. *Why?*

And falling asleep, completely involuntarily—everyone at the same time, it seemed. And not remembering, never remembering anything—Swanson had said how eagerly he saw Burckhardt again, the morning after Burckhardt had incautiously waited five minutes too many before retreating into the darkroom. When Swanson had come to, Burckhardt was gone. Swanson had seen him in the street that afternoon, but Burckhardt had remembered nothing.

And Swanson had lived his mouse's existence for weeks, hiding in the woodwork at night, stealing out by day to search for Burckhardt in pitiful hope, scurrying around the fringe of life, trying to keep from the deadly eyes of *them.*

Them. One of "them" was the girl named April Horn. It was by seeing her walk carelessly into a telephone booth and never come out that Swanson had found the tunnel. Another was the man at the cigar stand in Burckhardt's office building. There were more, at least a dozen that Swanson knew of or suspected.

They were easy enough to spot, once you knew where to look, for they alone in Tylerton changed their roles from day to day. Burckhardt was on that 8:51 bus, every morning of every day-that-was-June-15, never different by a hair or a moment. But April Horn was sometimes gaudy in the cellophane skirt, giving away candy or cigarettes; sometimes plainly dressed; sometimes not seen by Swanson at all.

Russians? Martians? Whatever they were, what could they be hoping to gain from this mad masquerade?

Buckhardt didn't know the answer, but perhaps it lay beyond the door at the end of the tunnel. They listened carefully and heard distant sounds that could not quite be made out, but nothing that seemed dangerous. They slipped through.

And, through a wide chamber and up a flight of steps, they found they were in what Burckhardt recognized as the Contro Chemicals plant.

Nobody was in sight. By itself, that was not so very odd; the automatized factory had never had very many persons in it. But Burckhardt remembered, from his single visit, the endless, ceaseless busyness of the plant, the valves that opened and closed, the vats that emptied themselves and filled themselves and stirred and cooked and chemically tasted the bubbling liquids they held inside themselves. The plant was never populated, but it was never still.

Only now it *was* still. Except for the distant sounds, there was no breath of life in it. The captive electronic minds were sending out no commands; the coils and relays were at rest.

Burckhardt said, "Come on." Swanson reluctantly followed him through the tangled aisles of stainless-steel columns and tanks.

They walked as though they were in the presence of the dead. In a way, they were, for what were the automatons that once had run the factory, if not corpses? The machines were controlled by computers that were really not computers at all, but the electronic analogues of living brains. And if they were turned off, were they not dead? For each had once been a human mind.

Take a master petroleum chemist, infinitely skilled in the separation of crude oil into its fractions. Strap him down, probe into his brain with searching electronic needles. The machine scans the patterns of the mind, translates what it sees into charts and sine waves. Impress these same waves on a robot computer and you have your chemist. Or a thousand copies of your chemist, if you wish, with all of his knowledge and skill, and no human limitations at all.

Put a dozen copies of him into a plant and they will run it all, twenty-four hours a day, seven days of every week, never tiring, never overlooking anything, never forgetting.

Swanson stepped up closer to Burckhardt. "I'm scared," he said.

They were across the room now and the sounds were louder. They were not machine sounds, but voices; Burckhardt moved cautiously up to a door and dared to peer around it.

It was a smaller room, lined with television screens, each one—a dozen or more, at least—with a man or woman sitting before it, staring into the screen and dictating notes into a recorder. The viewers dialed from scene to scene; no two screens ever showed the same picture.

The pictures seemed to have little in common. One was a store, where a girl dressed like April Horn was demonstrating home freezers. One was a series of shots of kitchens. Burckhardt caught a glimpse of what looked like the cigar stand in his office building.

It was baffling and Burckhardt would have loved to stand there and puzzle it out, but it was too busy a place. There was the chance that someone would look their way or walk out and find them.

They found another room. This one was empty. It was an office, large and sumptuous. It had a desk, littered with papers. Burckhardt stared at them, briefly at first—then, as the words on one of them caught his attention, with incredulous fascination.

He snatched up the topmost sheet, scanned it, and another, while Swanson was frenziedly searching through the drawers.

Burckhardt swore unbelievingly and dropped the papers to the desk.

Swanson, hardly noticing, yelped with delight: "Look!" He dragged a gun from the desk. "And it's loaded, too!"

Burckhardt stared at him blankly, trying to assimilate what he had read. Then, as he realized what Swanson had said, Burckhardt's eyes sparked. "Good man!" he cried. "We'll take it. We're getting out of here with that gun, Swanson. And we're not going to the police! Not the cops in Tylerton, but the FBI, maybe. Take a look at this!"

The sheaf he handed Swanson was headed: "Test Area Progress Report. Subject: Marlin Cigarettes Campaign." It was mostly tabulated figures that made little sense to Burckhardt and Swanson, but at the end was a summary that said:

> Although Test 47-K3 pulled nearly double the number of new users of any of the other tests conducted, it probably cannot be used in the field because of local sound-truck control ordinances.
>
> The tests in the 47-K12 group were second best and our recommendation is that retests be conducted in this appeal, testing each of the three best campaigns with and without the addition of sampling techniques.
>
> An alternative suggestion might be to proceed directly with the top appeal in the K12 series, if the client is unwilling to go to the expense of additional tests.
>
> All of these forecast expectations have an 80% probability of being within one-half of one percent of results forecast, and more than 99% probability of coming within 5%.

Swanson looked up from the paper into Burckhardt's eyes. "I don't get it," he complained.

Burckhardt said, "I don't blame you. It's crazy, but it fits the facts, Swanson, *it fits the facts.* They aren't Russians and they aren't Martians. These people are advertising men! Somehow—heaven knows how they did it—they've taken Tylerton over. They've got us, all of us, you and me and twenty or thirty thousand other people, right under their thumbs.

"Maybe they hypnotize us and maybe it's something else; but however they do it, what happens is that they let us live a day at a time. They pour advertising into us the whole damned day long. And at the end of the day, they see what happened—and then they wash the day out of our minds and start again the next day with different advertising."

Swanson's jaw was hanging. He managed to close it and swallow. "Nuts!" he said flatly.

Burckhardt shook his head. "Sure, it sounds crazy, but this whole thing is crazy. How else would you explain it? You can't deny that most of Tylerton lives the same day over and over again. You've *seen* it! And that's the crazy part and we have to admit that that's true—unless *we* are the crazy ones. And once you admit that somebody, somehow, knows how to accomplish that, the rest of it makes all kinds of sense.

"Think of it, Swanson! They test every last detail before they spend a nickel on advertising! Do you have any idea what that means? Lord knows how much money is involved, but I know for a fact that some companies spend twenty or thirty million dollars a year on advertising. Multiply it, say, by a hundred companies. Say that every one of them learns how to cut its advertising cost by only ten percent. And that's peanuts, believe me!

"If they know in advance what's going to work, they can cut their costs in half—maybe to less than half, I don't know. But that's saving two or three hundred million dollars a year—and if they pay only ten or twenty percent of that for the use of Tylerton, it's still dirt cheap for them and a fortune for whoever took over Tylerton."

Swanson licked his lips. "You mean," he offered hesitantly, "that we're a—well, a kind of captive audience?"

Burckhardt frowned. "Not exactly." He thought for a minute. "You know how a doctor tests something like penicillin? He sets up a series of little colonies of germs on gelatin disks and he tries the stuff on one after another, changing it a little each time. Well, that's us—we're the germs, Swanson. Only it's even more efficient than that. They don't have to test more than one colony, because they can use it over and over again."

It was too hard for Swanson to take in. He only said, "What do we do about it?"

"We go to the police. They can't use human beings for guinea pigs!"

"How do we get to the police?"

Burckhardt hesitated. "I think—" he began slowly. "Sure. This is the office of somebody important. We've got a gun. We'll stay right here until he comes along. And he'll get us out of here."

Simple and direct. Swanson subsided and found a place to sit, against the wall, out of sight of the door. Burckhardt took up a position behind the door itself—

And waited.

The wait was not as long as it might have been. Half an hour, perhaps. Then Burckhardt heard approaching voices and had time for a swift whisper to Swanson before he flattened himself against the wall.

It was a man's voice, and a girl's. The man was saying, "—reason why you couldn't report on the phone? You're ruining your whole day's tests! What the devil's the matter with you, Janet?"

"I'm sorry, Mr. Dorchin," she said in a sweet, clear tone. "I thought it was important."

The man grumbled, "Important! One lousy unit out of twenty-one thousand."

"But it's the Burckhardt one, Mr. Dorchin. Again. And the way he got out of sight, he must have had some help."

"All right, all right. It doesn't matter, Janet; the Choco-Bite program is ahead of schedule anyhow. As long as you're this far, come on in the office and make out your worksheet. And don't worry about the Burckhardt business. He's probably just wandering around. We'll pick him up tonight and—"

They were inside the door. Burckhardt kicked it shut and pointed the gun.

"That's what you think," he said triumphantly.

It was worth the terrified hours, the bewildered sense of insanity, the confusion and fear. It was the most satisfying sensation Burckhardt had ever had in his life. The expression on the man's face was one he had read about but never actually seen: Dorchin's mouth fell open and his eyes went wide, and though he managed to make a sound that might have been a question, it was not in words.

The girl was almost as surprised. And Burckhardt, looking at her, knew why her voice had been so familiar. The girl was the one who had introduced herself to him as April Horn.

Dorchin recovered himself quickly. "Is this the one?" he asked sharply.

The girl said, "Yes."

Dorchin nodded. "I take it back. You were right. Uh, you—Burckhardt. What do you want?"

Swanson piped up, "Watch him! He might have another gun."

"Search him then," Burckhardt said. "I'll tell you what we want, Dorchin. We want you to come along with us to the FBI and explain to them how you can get away with kidnapping twenty thousand people."

"Kidnapping?" Dorchin snorted. "That's ridiculous, man! Put that gun away; you can't get away with this!"

Burckhardt hefted the gun grimly. "I think I can."

Dorchin looked furious and sick—but oddly, not afraid. "Damn it—" he started to bellow, then closed his mouth and swallowed. "Listen," he said persuasively, "you're making a big mistake. I haven't kidnapped anybody, believe me!"

"I don't believe you," said Burckhardt bluntly. "Why should I?"

"But it's true! Take my word for it!"

Burckhardt shook his head. "The FBI can take your word if they like. We'll find out. Now how do we get out of here?"

Dorchin opened his mouth to argue.

Burckhardt blazed, "Don't get in my way! I'm willing to kill you if I have to. Don't you understand that? I've gone through two days of hell and every second of it I blame on you. Kill you? It would be a pleasure and I don't have a thing in the world to lose! Get us out of here!"

Dorchin's face went suddenly opaque. He seemed about to move, but the blonde girl he had called Janet slipped between him and the gun.

"Please!" she begged Burckhardt. "You don't understand. You mustn't shoot!"

"Get out of my way!"

"But, Mr. Burckhardt—"

She never finished. Dorchin, his face unreadable, headed for the door. Burckhardt had been pushed one degree too far. He swung the gun, bellowing. The girl called out sharply. He pulled the trigger. Closing on him with pity and pleading in her eyes, she came again between the gun and the man.

Burckhardt aimed low instinctively, to cripple, not to kill. But his aim was not good.

The pistol bullet caught her in the pit of the stomach.

Dorchin was out and away, the door slamming behind him, his footsteps racing into the distance.

Burckhardt hurled the gun across the room and jumped to the girl.

Swanson was moaning. "That finishes us, Burckhardt. Oh, why did you do it? We could have got away. We could have gone to the police. We were practically out of here! We—"

Burckhardt wasn't listening. He was kneeling beside the girl. She lay flat on her back, arms helter-skelter. There was no blood, hardly any sign of the wound; but the position in which she lay was one that no living human being could have held.

Yet she wasn't dead.

She wasn't dead—and Burckhardt, frozen beside her, thought: *She isn't alive, either.*

There was no pulse, but there was a rhythmic ticking of the outstretched fingers of one hand.

There was no sound of breathing, but there was a hissing, sizzling noise.

The eyes were open and they were looking at Burckhardt. There was neither fear nor pain in them, only a pity deeper than the Pit.

She said, through lips that writhed erratically, "Don't—worry, Mr. Burckhardt. I'm—all right."

Burckhardt rocked back on his haunches, staring. Where there should have been blood, there was a clean break of a substance that was not flesh, and a curl of thin golden-copper wire.

Burckhardt moistened his lips.

"You're a robot," he said.

The girl tried to nod. The twitching lips said, "I am. And so are you."

Swanson, after a single inarticulate sound, walked over to the desk and sat staring at the wall. Burckhardt rocked back and forth beside the shattered puppet on the floor. He had no words.

The girl managed to say, "I'm—sorry all this happened." The lovely lips twisted into a rictus sneer, frightening on that smooth young face, until she got them under control. "Sorry," she said again. "The—nerve center was right about where the bullet hit. Makes it difficult to—control this body."

Burckhardt nodded automatically, accepting the apology. Robots. It was obvious, now that he knew it. In hindsight, it was inevitable. He thought of his mystic notions of hypnosis or Martians or something stranger still—idiotic, for the simple fact of created robots fitted the facts better and more economically.

All the evidence had been before him. The automatized factory, with its transplanted minds—why not transplant a mind into a humanoid robot, give it its original owner's features and form?

Could it know that it was a robot?

"All of us," Burckhardt said, hardly aware that he spoke out loud. "My wife and my secretary and you and the neighbors. All of us the same."

"No." The voice was stronger. "Not exactly the same, all of us. I chose it, you see. I—" This time the convulsed lips were not a random contortion of the nerves— "I was an ugly woman, Mr. Burckhardt, and nearly sixty years old. Life had passed me. And when Mr. Dorchin offered me the chance to live again as a beautiful girl, I jumped at the opportunity. Believe me, I *jumped,* in spite of its disadvantages. My flesh body is still alive—it is sleeping, while I am here. I could go back to it. But I never do."

"And the rest of us?"

"Different, Mr. Burckhardt. I work here. I'm carrying out Mr. Dorchin's orders, mapping the results of the advertising tests, watching you and the others live as he makes you live. I do it by choice, but you have no choice. Because, you see, you are dead."

"Dead?" cried Burckhardt; it was almost a scream.

The blue eyes looked at him unwinkingly and he knew that it was no lie. He swallowed, marveling at the intricate mechanisms that let him swallow, and sweat, and eat.

He said: "Oh. The explosion in my dream."

"It was no dream. You are right—the explosion. That was real and this plant was the cause of it. The storage tanks let go and what the blast didn't get, the fumes killed a little later. But almost everyone died in the blast, twenty-one thousand persons. You died with them and that was Dorchin's chance."

"The damned ghoul!" said Burckhardt.

The twisted shoulders shrugged with an odd grace. "Why? You were gone. And you and all the others were what Dorchin wanted—a whole town, a perfect slice of America. It's as easy to transfer a pattern from a dead brain as a living one. Easier—the dead can't say no. Oh, it took work and money—the town was a wreck—but it was possible to rebuild it entirely, especially because it wasn't necessary to have all the details exact.

"There were the homes where even the brain had been utterly destroyed, and those are empty inside, and the cellars that needn't be too perfect, and the streets that hardly matter. And anyway, it only has to last for one day. The same day—June 15—over and over again; and if someone finds something a little wrong, somehow, the discovery won't have time to snowball, wreck the validity of the tests, because all errors are canceled out at midnight."

The face tried to smile. "That's the dream, Mr. Burckhardt, that day of June 15, because you never really lived it. It's a present from Mr. Dorchin, a dream that he gives you and then takes back at the end of the day, when he has all his figures on how many of you respond to what variation of which appeal, and the maintenance crews go down the tunnel to go through the whole city, washing out the new dream with their little electronic drains, and then the dream starts all over again. On June 15.

"Always June 15, because June 14 is the last day any of you can remember alive. Sometimes the crews miss someone—as they missed you, because you were under your boat. But it doesn't matter. The ones who are missed give themselves away if they show it—and if they don't, it doesn't affect the test. But they don't drain us, the ones of us who work for Dorchin. We sleep when the power is turned off, just as you do. When we wake up, though, we remember." The face contorted wildly. "If I could only forget!"

Burckhardt said unbelievingly, ''All this to sell merchandise! It must have cost millions!''

The robot called April Horn said, ''It did. But it has made millions for Dorchin, too. And that's not the end of it. Once he finds the master words that make people act, do you suppose he will stop with that? Do you suppose—''

The door opened, interrupting her. Burckhardt whirled. Belatedly remembering Dorchin's flight, he raised the gun.

''Don't shoot,'' ordered the voice calmly. It was not Dorchin; it was another robot, this one not disguised with the clever plastics and cosmetics, but shining plain. It said metallically, ''Forget it, Burckhardt. You're not accomplishing anything. Give me that gun before you do any more damage. Give it to me *now*.''

Burckhardt bellowed angrily. The gleam on this robot torso was steel; Burckhardt was not at all sure that his bullets would pierce it, or do much harm if they did. He would have put it to the test—

But from behind him came a whimpering, scurrying whirlwind: its name was Swanson, hysterical with fear. He catapulted into Burckhardt and sent him sprawling, the gun flying free.

''Please!'' begged Swanson incoherently, prostrate before the steel robot. ''He would have shot you—please don't hurt me! Let me work for you, like that girl. I'll do anything, anything you tell me—''

The robot voice said, ''We don't need your help.'' It took two precise steps and stood over the gun—and spurned it, left it lying on the floor.

The wrecked blonde robot said, without emotion, ''I doubt that I can hold out much longer, Mr. Dorchin.''

''Disconnect if you have to,'' replied the steel robot.

Burckhardt blinked. ''But you're not Dorchin!''

The steel robot turned deep eyes on him. ''I am,'' it said. ''Not in the flesh—but this is the body I am using at the moment. I doubt that you can damage this one with the gun. The other robot body was more vulnerable. Now will you stop this nonsense? I don't want to have to damage you; you're too expensive for that. Will you just sit down and let the maintenance crews adjust you?''

Swanson groveled. ''You—you won't punish us?''

The steel robot had no expression, but its voice was almost surprised. ''Punish you?'' it repeated on a rising note. ''How?''

Swanson quivered as though the word had been a whip, but Burckhardt flared: "Adjust *him,* if he'll let you—but not me! You're going to have to do me a lot of damage, Dorchin. I don't care what I cost or how much trouble it's going to be to put me back together again. But I'm going out of that door! If you want to stop me, you'll have to kill me. You won't stop me any other way!"

The steel robot took a half-step toward him, and Burckhardt involuntarily checked his stride. He stood poised and shaking, ready for death, ready for attack, ready for anything that might happen.

Ready for anything except what did happen. For Dorchin's steel body merely stepped aside, between Burckhardt and the gun, but leaving the door free.

"Go ahead," invited the steel robot. "Nobody's stopping you."

Outside the door, Burckhardt brought up sharp. It was insane of Dorchin to let him go! Robot or flesh, victim or beneficiary, there was nothing to stop him from going to the FBI or whatever law he could find away from Dorchin's sympathetic empire, and telling his story. Surely the corporations who paid Dorchin for test results had no notion of the ghoul's technique he used; Dorchin would have to keep it from them, for the breath of publicity would put a stop to it. Walking out meant death, perhaps, but at that moment in his pseudolife, death was no terror for Burckhardt.

There was no one in the corridor. He found a window and stared out of it. There was Tylerton—an ersatz city, but looking so real and familiar that Burckhardt almost imagined the whole episode a dream. It was no dream, though. He was certain of that in his heart and equally certain that nothing in Tylerton could help him now.

It had to be the other direction.

It took him a quarter of an hour to find a way, but he found it—skulking through the corridors, dodging the suspicion of footsteps, knowing for certain that his hiding was in vain, for Dorchin was undoubtedly aware of every move he made. But no one stopped him, and he found another door.

It was a simple enough door from the inside. But when he opened it and stepped out, it was like nothing he had ever seen.

First there was light—brilliant, incredible, blinding light. Burckhardt blinked upward, unbelieving and afraid.

He was standing on a ledge of smooth, finished metal. Not a dozen yards from his feet, the ledge dropped sharply away; he hardly dared approach the brink, but even from where he stood he could see no bottom to the chasm before him. And the gulf extended out of sight into the glare on either side of him.

No wonder Dorchin could so easily give him his freedom! From the factory there was nowhere to go. But how incredible this fantastic gulf, how impossible the hundred white and blinding suns that hung above!

A voice by his side said inquiringly, "Burckhardt?" And thunder rolled the name, mutteringly soft, back and forth in the abyss before him.

Burckhardt wet his lips. "Y-yes?" he croaked.

"This is Dorchin. Not a robot this time, but Dorchin in the flesh, talking to you on a hand mike. Now you have seen, Burckhardt. Now will you be reasonable and let the maintenance crews take over?"

Burckhardt stood paralyzed. One of the moving mountains in the blinding glare came toward him.

It towered hundreds of feet over his head; he stared up at its top, squinting helplessly into the light.

It looked like—

Impossible!

The voice in the loudspeaker at the door said, "Burckhardt?" But he was unable to answer.

A heavy rumbling sigh. "I see," said the voice. "You finally understand. There's no place to go. You know it now. I could have told you, but you might not have believed me, so it was better for you to see it yourself. And after all, Burckhardt, why would I reconstruct a city just the way it was before? I'm a businessman; I count costs. If a thing has to be full-scale, I build it that way. But there wasn't any need to in this case."

From the mountain before him, Burckhardt helplessly saw a lesser cliff descend carefully toward him. It was long and dark, and at the end of it was whiteness, five-fingered whiteness . . .

"Poor little Burckhardt," crooned the loudspeaker, while the echoes rumbled through the enormous chasm that was only a workshop. "It must have been quite a shock for you to find out you were living in a town built on a tabletop."

It was the morning of June 15, and Guy Burckhardt woke up screaming out of a dream.

It had been a monstrous and incomprehensible dream, of explosions and shadowy figures that were not men and terror beyond words.

He shuddered and opened his eyes.

Outside his bedroom window, a hugely amplified voice was howling.

Burckhardt stumbled over to the window and stared outside. There was an out-of-season chill to the air, more like October than June; but the scene was normal enough—except for a sound truck that squatted at curbside halfway down the block. Its speaker horns blared:

"Are you a coward? Are you a fool? Are you going to let crooked politicians steal the country from you? NO! Are you going to put up with four more years of graft and crime? NO! Are you going to vote straight Federal Party all up and down the ballot? YES! *You just bet you are!*"

Sometimes he screams, sometimes he wheedles, threatens, begs, cajoles . . . but his voice goes on and on through one June 15 after another.

ANN WARREN GRIFFITH

Captive Audience

Ann Warren Griffith was one of the neglected female pioneers of fantasy and science fiction, largely because her output was small. This story is her finest and was immediately recognized as an important work at the time of its publication in *The Magazine of Fantasy and Science Fiction* in the early fifties, but it seems to have been mostly forgotten since then.

It is a disturbing story, both because of its implications and because much of what it warned against has already happened. All of us are victims of the "admass culture," our senses constantly enticed or affronted by the sights and sounds from Madison Avenue. Ms. Griffith presents a society in which government has surrendered to the interests of corporate capitalism, a society in which the Master Ventriloquism Corporation of America pulls the strings on human puppets.

Mavis Bascom read the letter hastily and passed it across the breakfast table to her husband, Fred, who read the first paragraph and exclaimed, "She'll be here this afternoon!" but neither Mavis nor the two children heard him because the cereal box was going "Boom! Boom!" so loudly. Presently it stopped and the bread said urgently, "One good slice deserves another! How about another slice all around, eh, Mother?" Mavis put four slices into the toaster, and then there was a brief silence. Fred wanted to discuss the impending visit, but his daughter Kitty got in ahead of him, saying,

"Mom, it's my turn to choose the next cereal, and this shot-from-a-cannon stuff is almost gone. Will you take me to the store this afternoon?"

"Yes, dear, of course. I must admit I'll be glad when this box is gone. 'Boom, boom, boom,' that's all it ever says. And some of the others have such nice songs and jingles. I don't see whyever you picked it, Billy."

Billy was about to answer when his father's cigarette package interrupted, "Yessir, time to light up a Chesterfield! Time to enjoy that first mild, satisfying smoke of the day."

Fred lit a cigarette and said angrily, "Mavis, you know I don't like you to say such things in front of the children. It's a perfectly good commercial, and when you cast reflections on one, you're undermining all of them. I won't have you confusing these kids!"

"I'm sorry, Fred," was all Mavis had time to answer, because the salt box began a long and technically very interesting talk on iodization.

Since Fred had to leave for the office before the talk was over, he telephoned back to Mavis about her grandmother's visit. "Mavis," he said, "she can't stay with us! You'll have to get her out just as soon as possible."

"All right, Fred. I don't think she'll stay very long anyway. You know she doesn't like visiting us any more than you like having her."

"Well, the quicker she goes the better. If anybody down here finds out about her I'll be washed up with MV the same day!"

"Yes, Fred, I know. I'll do the best I can."

Fred had been with the Master Ventriloquism Corporation of America for fifteen years. His work had been exceptional in every respect and, unless word leaked out about Mavis's grandmother, he could expect to remain with it for the rest of his life. He had enjoyed every step of the way from office boy to his present position as Assistant Vice-President in Charge of Sales, though he sometimes wished he could have gone into the technical end of it. Fascinating, those huge batteries of machines pouring out their messages to the American people. It seemed to him almost miraculous, the way the commercials were broadcast into thin air and picked up by the tiny discs embedded in the bottle or can or box or whatever wrapping contained the product, but he knew it involved some sort of electronic process that he couldn't understand. Such an incredibly complex process, yet unfailingly accurate! He had never heard of the machines making a mistake; never, for instance, had they thrown a shoe polish commercial so that it came out of a hair tonic bottle. Intrigued though he was by the mechanical intricacies of Master Ventriloquism, however, he had no head for that sort of thing, and was content to make his contribution in the sales end.

And quite a contribution it was. Already in the two short years since his promotion to Assistant Vice-President he had signed up two of the toughest clients that had ever been brought into the MV camp. First had been the telephone company, now one of the fattest accounts on the Corporation's books. They had held out against MV for years, until he, Fred, hit upon the idea that sold them—a simple message to come from every telephone, at fifteen-minute intervals throughout the MV broadcasting day, reminding people to look in the directory before dialing information. After the telephone company coup, Fred became known around the Corporation as a man to watch. He hadn't rested on his laurels. He had, if anything, topped his telephone performance. MV had pretty much given up hope of selling its services to the dignified, the conservative *New York Times*. But Fred went ahead and did it. He'd kept the details a secret from Mavis. She'd see it for the first time tomorrow morning. Tomorrow morning! Damn! Grandmother would be here. You could bet she'd make some crack and spoil the whole thing.

Fred honestly didn't know if he would have gone ahead and married Mavis if he'd known about her grandmother.

For the sad fact of the matter was that Grandmother had never adjusted to MV. She was the only person he and Mavis knew who still longed for the "good old days," as she called them, the days before MV, and she yapped about them *ad nauseam*. She and her "A man's home is his castle"—if he'd heard her say it once he'd heard her say it 500 times. Unfortunately, it wasn't just that Grandmother was a boring old fool who refused to keep up with the times. The sadder fact of the matter was that she had broken the law, and today was finishing a five-year prison term. Did any other man here at MV have such a cross to bear?

Again and again he and Mavis had warned Grandmother that her advanced years would not keep her from being clapped into jail, and they hadn't. She'd gone absolutely wild on the day the Supreme Court had handed down the Earplug Decision. It was the climax of a long and terribly costly fight by the MV Corporation. The sale of earplugs had grown rapidly during the years MV was expanding, and just at a peak period, when MV had over 3000 accounts, National Earplug Associates, Inc. had boldly staged a country-wide campaign advertising earplugs as the last defense against MV. The success of the campaign was such that the Master Ventriloquism Corporation found itself losing hundreds of accounts. MV sued immediately and the case dragged through the courts for years. Judges had a hard time making up their minds. Some sections of the press twaddled about "captive audiences." The MV Corporation felt reasonably certain that the Supreme Court justices were sensible men, but with its very existence at stake there was nerve-racking suspense until the decision was made. National Earplug Associates, Inc. was found guilty of Restraint of Advertising, and earplugs were declared unconstitutional.

Grandmother, who was visiting Fred and Mavis at the time, hit the ceiling. She exhausted herself and them with her tirades, and swore that never never never would she give up her earplugs.

MV's representatives in Washington soon were able to get Congress to put teeth into the Supreme Court's decision, and eventually, just as Fred and Mavis predicted, Grandmother joined the ridiculous band who went to jail for violating the law prohibiting the use or possession of earplugs.

That was some skeleton for anybody, let alone an executive of MV, to have in his closet! Luckily, it had, up to now, remained in the closet, for at no time during her trial or afterward did Grandmother mention having a relative who worked for the Corporation. But they had been lulled into a false sense of security. They assumed that Grandmother would die before finishing her prison term and that the problem of Grandmother was, therefore, solved. Now they were faced with it all over again. How were they going to keep her from shooting off her mouth before their friends and neighbors? How persuade her to go away and live in some distant spot?

Fred's secretary broke in on these worrisome thoughts, bringing him an unusually large batch of morning mail. "Seems there's kind of an unfavorable reaction to the new Pratt's Airotsac campaign. Forty-seven letters of protest already—read 'em and weep," she said saucily, and returned to her own office.

Fred picked a letter out of the pile and read:

Dear Sirs,

Like most mothers, I give my baby Pratt's Airotsac every time she cries for it. For the past few days, however, it has seemed to me that she has cried for it much more often than usual. Then I heard about the new Pratt's Airotsac commercial, and caught on that part of the time it wasn't my baby but the MV baby crying. I think it's a very cute idea, but am wondering if you could possibly use another baby because the one you have now sounds so much like mine and I cannot tell them apart so that I do not know when my baby is actually crying for Pratt's Airotsac and when it's the MV baby.

Thanking you in advance for anything you can do about this, and with all good wishes for your continued success, I am,

Mrs. Mona P. Hayes.

Fred groaned and flipped through some of the other letters. The story was the same—mothers not knowing whether it was their own baby or the MV baby and consequently confused as to when to administer the medicine. Dopes! Why didn't they have sense enough to put the Airotsac bottle at the other end of the house from the baby, and then they could tell by the direction the sound came from whether it was a bona fide baby or an advertising baby! Well, he'd have to figure out some way to change it, since many of the letters reported babies getting sick from overdoses. The Master Ventriloquism Corporation certainly didn't want to be responsible for that sort of thing.

Underneath the forty-seven complaints was a memo from the Vice-President in Charge of Sales congratulating Fred on his brilliant handling of the *New York Times*. Ordinarily, this would have made it a red-letter day, but what with Grandmother and Pratt's, Fred's day was already ruined.

Mavis's day was not going well, either.

She felt uneasy, out-of-sorts, and in the lull between the Breakfast Commercials and the Cleaning Commercials she tried to analyze her feelings. It must be Grandmother. Perhaps it was true, as Fred said, that Grandmother was a bad influence. It wasn't that she was *right*. Mavis believed in Fred, because he was her husband, and believed in the MV Corporation, because it was the largest corporation in the entire United States. Nevertheless, it upset her when Fred and Grandmother argued, as they almost always did when they were together.

Anyway, maybe this time Grandmother wouldn't be so troublesome. Maybe jail had taught her how wrong it was to try to stand in the way of progress. On this hopeful note her thinking ended, for the soap powder box cried out, "Good morning, Mother! What say we go after those breakfast dishes and give our hands a beauty treatment at the same time? You know, Mother, no other soap gives you a beauty treatment *while* you wash your dishes. Only So-Glow, So-Glow, right here on your shelf, waiting to help *you*. So let's begin, shall we?''

While washing the dishes, Mavis was deciding what dessert to prepare. She'd bought several new ones the day before, and now they all sounded so good she couldn't make up her mind which to use first. The commercial for the canned apple pie ingredients was a little playlet, about a husband coming home at the end of a long hard day, smelling the apple pie, rushing out to the kitchen, sweeping his wife off her feet, kissing her saying, ''That's my girl!'' It sounded promising to Mavis, especially when the announcer said any housewife who got to work right this minute and prepared that apple pie could be almost certain of getting that reaction from her husband.

Then there was a cute jingle from the devil's food cake mix, sung by a trio of girls' voices with a good swing band in the background. If she'd made the mistake of buying only one box, it said, she ought to go out and buy another before she started baking because one of these luscious devil's food cakes would not be enough for her hungry family. It was peppy and made Mavis feel better. She checked her shelves and, finding she had only one box, jotted it down on her shopping list.

Next, from the gingerbread mix box, came a homey-type commercial that hit Mavis all wrong with its: ''MMMMMMMMM, yes! Just like Grandmother used to make!''

After listening to several more, she finally decided to use a can of crushed pineapple. ''It's quick! It's easy! Yes, Mother, all you do is chill and serve.'' That was what she needed, feeling the way she did.

She finished the dishes and was just leaving the kitchen when the floor wax bottle called out, ''Ladies, look at your floors! You know that others judge you by your floors. Are you proud of yours? Are they ready—spotless and gleaming for the most discerning friend who might drop in?'' Mavis looked at her floors. Definitely, they needed attention. She gave them a hasty going-over with the quick-drying wax, grateful, as she so often was, to MV for reminding her.

In rapid succession, then, MV announced that now it was possible to polish her silverware to a higher, brighter polish than ever before; wondered if she weren't perhaps guilty of ''H.O.—Hair Odor,'' and shouldn't perhaps wash her hair before her husband came home; told her at three different times to relax with a glass of cola; suggested that she had been neglecting her nails and might profit from a new coat of enamel; asked her to give a thought to her windows; and reminded her that her home permanent neutralizer would lose its wonderful effectiveness the longer it was kept. By early afternoon she had done the silver and the windows, given herself a shampoo and a manicure, determined to give Kitty a home permanent that very afternoon, and was full of cola. But she was exhausted.

It *was* a responsibility to be the wife of an MV executive. You had to be sort of an example to the rest of the community. Only sometimes she got so tired! Passing the bathroom, she was attracted by a new bottle of pills that Fred had purchased. It was saying. "You know, folks, this is the time of day when you need a lift. Yessir, if you're feeling listless, tired, run down, put some iron back in your backbone! All you do is take off my top, take out one tablet, swallow it, and feel your strength return!" Mavis was about to do so when an aspirin bottle called out, "I go to work instantly!" and then another aspirin bottle (Why *did* Fred keep buying new ones before they'd finished up the old ones? It made things so confusing!) said, "I go to work twice as fast!" Aspirin, Mavis suddenly realized, was what she needed. She had a splitting headache, but heavens, how did one know which to take? One of each seemed the only fair solution.

When the children came home from school, Kitty refused to have her hair permanented until her mother took her to the store, as promised. Mavis felt almost unable to face it. What was it Grandmother used to call their supermarket? Hell on earth, hell on wheels, something like that. Mavis, of course, understood that simultaneous MV messages were necessary in the stores in order to give every product a chance at its share of the consumer dollar, but just this afternoon she did wish she could skip it.

Having promised, though, there was nothing to do but get it over with. Billy had to come along too, naturally—both the children loved visiting the supermarket more than most anything else. They made their way down the aisles through a chorus of "Try me . . . Try me . . . Here is the newer, creamier . . . Mother, your children will . . . Kiddies, ask Mom to pick the bright green and red package . . . Here I am, right here, the shortening all your friends have been telling you about. . . ."

Billy listened to as many as he could while they were passing by, and for the thousandth time wished that he could hear the store-type commercials at home. Why, some of them were just as good as the home-type! He always tried to talk the supermarket checkers out of tearing off the Buy-Me-Discs, but they always grumbled that them was their orders and they didn't have no time to bother with him. That was one of the reasons Billy had long since decided to be a supermarket checker himself when he grew up. Think of it! Not only would you hear the swell home-type commercials all day while you worked, and be hep to the very latest ones, but you'd get to hear all the store commercials too. And what with the thousands of Buy-Me-Discs he'd be tearing off, as a checker, he bet he could slip some into his pockets from time to time, and then wouldn't his friends envy him, being able to receive store-type commercials at home!

They reached the cereal area, and as always the children were entranced. Their faces shone with excitement as they picked up one box after another, to hear the commercials more clearly. There were sounds of gunfire; all kinds of snapping, crackling, and popping; there were loud shouts of "CRISPIER! NUTTIER! YUMMIER!" There were more modulated appeals, addressed to Mother, about increased nourishment and energy-building; there were the voices of athletes, urging the kids to come on and be one of the gang; there were whinnies of horses and explosive sounds of jets and rockets; there were cowboy songs and hillbilly songs and rhymes and jingles and bands and quartets and trios! Poor Kitty! How could she ever choose?

Mavis waited patiently for twenty minutes, enjoying the children's pleasure even though her headache was growing worse, and then told Kitty that she really must make up her mind.

"OK, Mom, I'll take this one this time," said Kitty. She held the box close to her mother's ear. "Listen to it, Mom, isn't it swell?" Mavis heard a shattering command, "FORWARD, MARCH!" and then what sounded like a thousand marching men. "Crunch, crunch, crunch, crunch," they were shouting in unison, above the noise of their marching feet, and a male chorus was singing something about Crunchies were marching to your breakfast table, right into your cereal bowl. Suddenly inexplicably, Mavis felt she couldn't stand this every morning. "No, Kitty," she said, rather harshly, "you can't have that one. I won't have all that marching and shouting at breakfast!" Kitty's pretty face turned to a thundercloud, and tears sprang into her eyes. "I'll tell Daddy what you said! I'll tell Daddy what you said! I'll tell Daddy if you don't let me have it!" Mavis came to her senses as quickly as she had taken leave of them. "I'm sorry, dear, I don't know what came over me. Of course you can have it. It's a very nice one. Now let's hurry on home so we can give you your permanent before Grandmother comes."

Grandmother arrived just in time for dinner. She kissed the children warmly, though they didn't remember her, and seemed glad to see Mavis and Fred. But it soon became clear that she was the same old Grandmother. She tried, at table, to shout above the dinner commercials, until Mavis had to shush her or the family would have missed them, and she nearly succeeded in spoiling their pleasure in the new Tummys' campaign, which they had been eagerly looking forward to for several days.

Fred knew the kids were going to like it. He had a brand-new roll of Tummys in his pocket, all ready to receive it. It was nicely timed—just as Fred was finishing his pineapple came a loud and unmistakable belch. The children looked startled and then burst into laughter. Mavis looked shocked, and then joined the laughter as a man's voice said, "Embarrassing, isn't it? Supposing that had been *you!* But what's worse is the distress of suppressing somach gases. Why risk either the embarrassment or the discomfort? Take a Tummy after each meal and avoid the risk of [the belch was repeated, sending the children into fresh gales of laughter]. Yes, folks, be sure it doesn't happen to YOU."

Fred handed Tummys to all of them amidst exclamations from the children, "Gee, Daddy, that's the best yet," and "I can't wait for tomorrow night to hear it again!" Mavis thought it was "very good, very effective." Grandmother, however, took her Tummy tablet, dropped it on the floor, and ground it to powder with her foot. Fred and Mavis exchanged despairing glances.

That evening the children were allowed to sit up late so they could talk to their great-grandmother after the MV went off at eleven. They had been told she'd just returned from a "trip," and when they asked her about it now she made up stories of faraway places where she'd been, where there wasn't any MV. Then she went on, while they grew bored, to tell them stories of her girlhood, before MV was invented, long before, as she said, "that fatal day when the Supreme Court opened the door to MV by deciding that defenseless passengers on buses had to listen to commercials whether they wanted to or not."

"But didn't they *like* to hear the commercials?" Billy asked.

Fred smiled to himself. Sound kid. Sound as a dollar. Grandmother could talk herself cross-eyed but Billy wouldn't fall for that stuff.

"No," Grandmother said, and she seemed very sad, "they didn't like them." She made a visible effort to pull herself together. "You know, Fred, the liquor business is missing a big opportunity. Why, if there were a bottle of Old Overholt here right now, saying, 'Drink me, drink me,' I'd do it!"

Fred took the hint and mixed three nightcaps.

"As a matter of fact," Mavis said, looking proudly at her husband, "Fred can claim a lot of the credit for that. All those liquor companies begged and pleaded with him for time, offered piles of money and everything, but Fred didn't think it would be a good influence in the home, having bottles around telling you to drink them, and I think he's right. He turned down a whole lot of money!"

"That was indeed splendid of Fred. I congratulate him." Grandmother drank her drink thirstily and looked at her watch. "We'd all better get to bed. You look tired, Mavis, and one must, I assume, especially in this household, be up with the MV in the morning."

"Oh, yes, we usually are, and tomorrow," Mavis said excitedly, "Fred has a wonderful surprise for us. Some big new account he's gotten and he won't tell us what it is, but it's going to start tomorrow."

Next morning as the Bascoms and Grandmother were sitting down to breakfast there was a loud knock at the door.

"That's it!" shouted Fred. "Come on, everybody!"

They all ran to the door and Fred threw it open. Nobody was there, but a copy of the *New York Times* was lying on the doorstep, saying,

"Good morning, this is your *New York Times!* Wouldn't you like to have me delivered to your door *every* morning? Think of the added convenience, the added . . ." Mavis pulled Fred out onto the lawn where he could hear her. "Fred! she cried, "the *New York Times*—you sold the *New York Times!* However did you do it?"

The children crowded around, congratulating him. "Gosh, Dad, that's really something. Did that knocking come right with the message?"

"Yep," said Fred with justifiable pride, "it's part of the message. Look, Mavis," he waved his hand up and down the street. In both directions, as far as they could see, families were clustered around their front doors, listening to *New York Timeses.*

When it was over, the nearer neighbors shouted, "That your idea, Fred?"

" 'Fraid I'll have to admit it is," Fred called back, laughing.

From all sides came cries of "Great work, Fred," and "Swell stuff, Fred," and "Say, you sure are on the ball, Fred." Probably only he and Mavis, though, fully realized what it was going to mean in terms of promotion.

Unnoticed, Grandmother had gone into the house, into her room, and extracted a small box from one of her suitcases. Now she came out of the house again and crossed to the family group on the lawn.

"While you're out here where we can talk, I've something to tell you. It might be better if you sent the children into the house."

Mavis asked Kitty if she weren't afraid of missing her new Crunchies commercial, and the children raced inside.

"I can't stand another day of it," Grandmother said. "I'm sorry, but I've got to leave right now."

"Why, Grandmother, you can't—you don't even know where you're going!"

"Oh, I do know where I'm going. I'm going back to jail. It's really the only sensible place for me. I have friends there, and it's the quietest place I know."

"But you can't . . ." Fred began.

"But I can," Grandmother replied. She opened her hand and showed them the little box.

"Earplugs! Grandmother! Put them out of sight, quickly. Wherever did you get them?"

Grandmother ignored Mavis's question. "I'm going to telephone the police and ask them to come and get me." She turned and started into the house.

"She can't do that," Fred said wildly.

"Let her go, Fred. She's right, and besides it solves the whole problem."

"But, Mavis, if she calls the police here it'll be all over town. I'll be ruined! Stop her and tell her we'll drive her to some other police station!"

Mavis reached her grandmother before Grandmother reached the police, and explained Fred's predicament. A wicked gleam appeared in Grandmother's eye, but it was gone in a second. She looked at

Mavis with some tenderness and said all right, just as long as she got back to the penitentiary as quickly as possible.

They all had breakfast. The children, humming the new Crunchies song, marched off to school—they would be told at night that Grandmother had suddenly gone on another "trip"—and Mavis and Fred drove to a town fifty miles away, with Grandmother and her luggage in the back seat. Grandmother was happy and at peace, thinking, as she listened to the gas tanks yelling to be filled up, the spark plugs crying to be cleaned, and all the other parts asking to be checked, or repaired, or replaced, that she was hearing MV for the last time.

But as the Bascoms were driving back home, after depositing Grandmother, it hit Fred all of a sudden. He fairly shouted in his excitement. "Mavis! We've all been blind as bats!"

"How do you mean, dear?"

"Blind, I tell you, blind! I've been thinking about Grandmother in prison, and all the thousands of people in jail and prison, *without MV*. They don't buy any products, so they don't get any MV. Can you imagine what that does to their buying habits?"

"Yes, you're right, Fred—five or ten or twenty years without it, they probably wouldn't *have* any buying habits after all that time." She laughed. "But I don't see what you can do about it."

"Plenty, Mavis, and not just about prisons. This is going to revolutionize the Corporation! Do you realize that ever since MV was invented we've just assumed that the discs had to be right with the products? Why? In the name of heaven, why? Take a prison, for instance. Why couldn't we, say, have a little box in each cell where the discs could be kept and that way the prisoners could still hear the MV and it would sort of preserve their buying habits and then when they got out they wouldn't be floundering around?"

"I wonder, Fred, about the prison authorities. You'd have to get their cooperation; I mean they'd have to distribute the discs, wouldn't they?"

Fred was way ahead of her. "We make it a public service, Mavis. Besides the regular MV, we get a few sponsors with vision, some of those big utilities people that like to do good, and they'll be satisfied with just a short plug for their product and then the rest of the message can be for the benefit of the prisoners, like little talks on honesty is the best policy and how we expect them to behave when they get out of jail—things that'll really help prepare them for life on the outside again."

Impulsively, Mavis put her hand on his arm and squeezed it. No wonder she was so proud of her Fred! Who but Fred—Mavis blinked to keep back the tears—who but Fred would think right off, first thing, not just of the moneymaking side, but of the welfare and betterment of all those poor prisoners!

JOHN JAKES

The Sellers of the Dream

John Jakes is one of a number of science fiction writers (including Frank Robinson, John D. MacDonald, and Tom Scortia) who have been successful in other areas of literature. Jakes had produced hundreds of stories and novels in the mystery, Western, and historical fiction genres before his massive success with a series of historical novels on Bicentennial themes during 1975 and 1976.

In science fiction, he is best known as the author of a number of excellent short stories. In "The Sellers of the Dream" Jakes constructs yet another social system dominated by advertising. But this story is not derivative—it is in many ways a classic treatment of the theme of choice eradication. We are all familiar with the way in which the automobile industry appeals to millions of consumers by yearly changing the design or other features—changes which are often minor and not necessarily improvements—of its major lines. Jakes takes this one step further to a time when human personalities can be changed at "will," and new models are introduced each year in much the same way that new cars are brought onto the market. The sellers in this case are marketing the dream of "the new you" and regard their mission in life as keeping the masses consuming. How they go about it in this story makes it required reading for many businesses and the people who support them.

I

His gaudy wristwatch showed thirty minutes past nine, sixth July. It was time. From here on it was do the job right or be ruined. If not physically, then professionally.

Finian Smith dug for tools in the pouches of his imitation stomach. The left eye of the watch's moon face gave a ludicrous wink to complete the time signal. Finian hated the watch. He'd got used to the confines of the camouflaged polymer leech clinging to the keel of the hydrofoiler. He'd got used to performing necessary bodily functions in intimate contact with the leech's servomechanisms for thirty-six hours. But the watch—never.

It was effete, like his clothes. Effeteness was big this year. Next year it would be hand-loomed woolens. But he wasn't being paid to inherit the soul of the man he was impersonating, after all. He applied the first of his meson torches to the thick hull. His long, pleasantly ugly face began to bead with perspiration.

He had precisely four minutes to cut through.

His face was half shadowed by the hull as he worked, half washed in flickering sunlight through anemone and brain coral. He defused a large U-shaped section and replaced the torch with a pistol unit fitted with a round cup at the muzzle. This cup he applied to the hull. A blue whine of power—he forced the hull inward far enough to accommodate entry to the fuel baffle chamber.

He set a small black box to blow the polymer leech off the hull in fifty seconds, glad that he'd spent a full twenty nights under the hypnolearner. The penetration plan was drummed so deeply into his skull he could operate like an automaton.

With a last tool he resealed the hull, touched a stud and watched the tool collapse to gritty pumice. Right now the leech should be quietly disintegrating, without so much as a murmur to disturb the TTIC spy radar. It took a lot of money to arrange this penetration, Finian thought. Knowing how much made him nervous.

Finian hurried up a lonely companionway. Before stepping to the yacht's deck he dusted his pleatless puce satin pantaloons and also made sure the precision camera, a combined effort of G/S dental technicians and optics men, was in place where his right front incisor had once been. The blade shutter's release was a knob on the tooth's inner surface, triggered by tongue pressure. Fake enamel would fly aside a microinstant and TTIC secrets would be recorded for posterity, not to mention G/S market analysts.

On deck, Finian adjusted his identification badge.

Beneath his picture it said *Woodrow Howslip, Missoula, Mont., Upper North American Distributorship*. Finian hoped Woodrow Howslip was still lost in the Mojave Desert. If so, the only thing Finian had to worry over was his old enemy.

Every few yards along the deck armed TTIC security men stood at attention: TTIC seemed to have innumerable armed guards. So did

G/S for that matter. Finian often wondered why. No one got angry anymore, why have armed guards?

"Hi, there, I'm Woody Howslip."

"Morning, sir." The guard stared into the Pacific's cobalt swell.

"Say, fella. Last year when I came to see the new models innerduced, I ran into a hell of a swell person—Spool or Stool. Sure like to buy him a drink. Is he on board?"

"I don't believe so, sir."

"Oh, too bad. Maybe he'll show up. They always have the top dogs at these distributor shows. I hear Stool's a top dog. Chief of company spies or something."

The guard concealed irritation.

"*Sprool,* sir. Chief of industrial investigation."

Finian gigged the man's ribs. "Keep those Goods/Services jerks hopping, huh? Well, sorry Sprool isn't around. Maybe later. See you in the videofunnies—"

Overdoing it, Finian thought as he hurried along. Still, it was reassuring to know the intelligence was correct: Sprool was in Bombay. Finian had run up against him most recently when TTIC tried to steal G/S designs for the midyear hairdo changes during the 2004–5 season.

Finian joined a crowd of distributors hurrying into an auditorium beneath a banner reading:

WELCOME
Things to Come Incorporated
World Distributors
"Last Year's Woman Is This
Year's Consumer"

As he took a seat in the shadowy hall he listened to voices all around:

"It's rumored she's of the Grecian mode," said the European Common Market distributor.

"What? Copy the tripe G/S peddled two years ago?" That was the White/Blue Nile man.

The Chinese distributor protested: "Last year, too severe. Humble percent of market drop severely. Five thousand years in fields, China women do not desire box haircut, woolen socks."

"Hope it's a real smasher this time," said the British Empire distributor, a seedy fellow wearing cologne. One run-down warehouse in

Jamaica comprised the Empire anymore. TTIC or G/S could buy or sell the Empire a thousand times. Or any other country. Finian was sweating. No wonder the stakes were so high.

On an austere platform up front sat three men. One was a florid old gentleman with dewlaps and blue, vaguely crossed eyes. Another—a spindly type with a flower at each cuff—rose and was introduced by a loudspeaker as Corporate Director of Sales, Northcote Hastings.

"Thank you, thank you. I won't waste time, gentlemen. You've traveled thousands of miles in secrecy and we appreciate it. We trust you also appreciate why we must maintain the mobility of our personality design center. One never knows when the—ah—competition might infiltrate a permanent site. They can't match our sales in new personalities, so they try to outfight us with punches below the belt."

He fingered his, of ermine, to illustrate. Finian joined the laughter, but meant his.

"After luncheon, gentlemen, you're scheduled for individual sessions with our designers, psychiatrists, plastic surgeons and sociability coordinators, not to mention apparel teams and accessory experts."

Hastings glanced at the old gentleman with the vaguely crossed eyes.

"Before we proceed, however, I should like to introduce TTIC's beloved chairman of the board, Mr. Alvah Loudermilk. Stand up, Mr. Loudermilk." The sales manager was plainly annoyed by having to make the introduction. The old dodderer took a step toward the podium. Hastings let a tolerant smile be seen by the distributors but did not relinquish the mike.

"You can talk with Mr. Loudermilk personally later, gentlemen."

The florid old gentleman sat down again, as though no one appreciated him. Smoothly Hastings continued, "Let me get on by bringing forward the great design chief of Things to Come Incorporated—" He flung out a hand. "Dr. Gerhard Krumm."

The famed Krumm, an obese toad with the inevitable disarrayed look of the corporate intellectual, walked to the podium. His apricot slippers, pantaloons and bolero jacket seemed to have come from a dustbin. Behind Krumm stage blowers whirred. They were readying curtains and screen.

Finian slid his tongue near his tooth.

"Gentlemen," Krumm said, "first the bad news."

At the unhappy grumble he held up his hand. ''Next year—I promise!—TTIC will absolutely and without qualification be ready to introduce the concept of the obsolescent male personality, exactly as we did in the female market ten years ago. I can only emphasize again the tremendous physical problems confronting us, and point to the lag in male fashion obsolescence that was not finally overcome until the late twentieth century, by the sheer weight of promotion. Men, unlike women, accept new decorative concepts slowly. TTIC has a lucrative share of the semiannual male changeover, but we are years behind the female personality market. Next year we catch up.''

''May we see what you have for the girls, old chap?'' someone asked. ''Then we'll decide whether we're happy.''

''Very well.'' Krumm began to read from a promotion script: ''This year we steal a leaf from yesterday's—uh—scented album.'' The lights dimmed artfully. Perfume sprayed the chamber from hidden ducts. A stereo orchestra swelled. The curtains parted. Finian's upper lip was rolled back as far as possible.

A nostalgic solido view of New York when it was once populated by people flashed on the screen. Violins throbbed thrillingly.

''Remember the sweet, charming girl of yesteryear? We capture her for you—warm, uncomplicated, reveling in—uh, let's see—sunlight and outdoor sports.''

A series of solido slides, illustrating Krumm's points with shots of nuclear ski lifts or the Seine, merged one into another.

''Gone is the exaggerated IQ of this year, gone the modish clothing. A return of softness. A simple mind, clinging, sweet. The stuff of everyman's dreams. Gentlemen, I give you—''

Hidden kettledrums swelled. The name flashed on the screen:

DREAM DESIRE.

''Dream Desire! New Woman of the 2007–08 market year!''

Over enthusiastic applause Krumm continued: ''At our thirty thousand personality alteration centers over the world, every woman will be able to change her body and mind, by means of surgical and psychological techniques of which TTIC is the acknowledged master, to become Dream Desire. Backed by the most intensive promotion program in history, we promise that more women will become Dream Desire than have ever become one of our previous models. Because, gentlemen, no woman could possibly resist becoming—this.''

Sitting forward with tooth ready to shoot, Finian was unprepared for the shock that awaited him.

On the screen slid the naked figure of a girl. Only her back was exposed. Nothing could be seen of her face. Her hair was yellow, that was all. The flesh itself was tanned, in sharp contrast to the pale library look currently being merchandised. The proportions of the girl's buttocks had been surgically worked out to be almost the apex of voluptuousness. But what shook Finian to the soles of his mink slippers was a star-shaped raspberry mark on the new model's left rear.

That isn't Dream Desire, he thought wildly. *That's—that's—*

"We begin with the, uh, rear elevation," said Krumm. "In that colorful mark you see TTIC marketing genius. That mark will stamp the woman who buys this new personality as a genuine Dream Desire, not a shoddy G/S counterfeit. To be frank, adoption of this unique—ah—signature, was not planned. When we sought a girl for our prototype, we discovered the girl we chose was blessed with such a mark. It inspired serendipity. But this is just the beginning. See what we have done with the face."

Only just in time did Finian remember to trigger his tooth and take a shot of the rear elevation before the front view flashed on. The girl, naked and coy on a divan, had pink cheeks, red lips, china-blue doll eyes. Pretty, in a cuddlesome, vapid way.

Quickly he exposed two more frames. He was falling apart, muffing the job. Krumm's voice became a drone detailing the surgical and analytical procedures necessary for a woman to buy the appearance and personality of Dream Desire. Finian didn't hear a thing about price schedules or what lower-priced models were contemplated. He photographed each slide mechanically, thinking of the raspberry mark.

It's not Dream Desire, he said to himself. *My God—it's Dolly Novotny.*

Not the face, not the breasts. But *there,* far down in the eyes. They weren't even brown anymore. But colored contacts could change eyes so easily.

Never had he been more profoundly shocked. His own sweet lost Dolly!

A heavy hand seized his shoulder.

"Here he is!"

Finian was dragged from his seat. A searing light flashed in his face.

"Well, well. Finian Smith. When you took hold of that rail coming into the hall, you should have recalled we have sweat prints for all you G/S boys. Give me the camera and come along quietly," finished Sprool.

II

"I thought you were in Bombay," said Finian. "I got bum information."

Sprool smiled somewhere in the depths of his almost colorless eyes. His pale, saturnine face, however, was devoid of humor.

"Never trust Lyman Pushkyn for information, Fin. Since when is an advertising man qualified to supervise an industrial investigation program?"

"You're right. I tried to get them to give me the post once."

"Did you? I didn't realize that. When?"

"Right after I was cashiered by the DOCs and finished my first case for G/S." He couldn't repress a smile. "The time I stole your men's changeover layouts by disguising myself as part of the lavatory wall. When you still had the design center on land, out in California."

Sprool chuckled flatly. "We've been friendly enemies quite a while, haven't we, Fin?"

"You never put one over on me like this, though."

"Shame you forgot sweat prints."

"My own damned fault." Finian thrust out his jaw. "I'll take what's coming. I was counting on this play to cut through all that stupid bureaucracy at the top of G/S and maybe net me the chief investigator's post." Finian scowled out of the office porthole to the heaving blue Pacific. Sprool smoothed thinning hair.

"Might as well give me the camera."

Finian made a show of dipping into his artificial paunch. He came up with a palm-sized micro 35mm. and snapped open the case release. He pulled the leader on the cassette all the way out, exposing the film. Chuckling, Sprool picked up the cylinder.

"Very nice, Finian. May I now have the real camera?"

"Ah, you slick bastard," grumbled Finian. This time he took a piece of equipment from beneath his singlet. Sprool dropped it down a hissing disposal tube.

"You look positively vengeful, Fin."

"I could smash a few heads right now. That damn G/S Comptroller Central makes investigators do their own penetration workups. They're nickel-nursers besides. I *thought* of sweat prints. They said the corrective was too expensive. I wasn't positive you had the index on file, so—"

"Fin, please don't bristle. Remember we have telephotos on you at this very moment. In that bust of Loewy, for instance. His collar button is watching you. Don't fight me and you won't get hurt. TTIC is a business operation just like G/S. Firm but paternalistic. When we dispose of an irritant, we do it with flexibility and permanence, but no physical pain."

"That's nice to know, considering you'll probably ruin my career."

"Were you ever really cut out for business, Fin?"

"If I wasn't *what* the hell was I cut out for? Not the DOCs."

Sprool raised a chiding finger. "See? That burst of temper is all too typical of you. People simply don't rock the boat these days, Fin. Why, if either G/S or TTIC went for more than a fifty percent share of the renewal personality market—plus or minus the two percent gain or loss as a result of spying, design leaks and so forth—the UN would have its economic cycle theorists down on us instantly."

"God, Sprool, I try and try. I guess I just wasn't meant to be a twenty-first-century man. I never had the proper education, like those reading primers written by the market boys from—where was it?—BBDO? I went to private school. On my pop's knee."

"Then your attitudes are understandable. How can you expect to be anything but yourself when your father was a Galbraither? Perhaps the last of that persuasion allowed to teach economics in public universities? Your father was dead set against the kind of obsolescence practiced by the corporations we both represent. The two largest corporations in the world!"

"Pop wanted consumer money spent on libraries, schools, highways, pretty, green, roadside picnic parks."

"None of which contributes very much to keeping the world plant running at top output. None of which provides the millions of jobs needed to give black and yellow and white alike ample opportunity for the good life. If you'd only understand yourself, how you fit the scheme of things."

"I don't. That's the trouble. What the hell am I supposed to do, join the prisoners in New York? I keep quiet about what I think. I call it well enough to be an operative for the Department of Obsolescence Control. I was doing all right until—''

Memory clouded his brow. He wriggled deep down in the foam of his chair. He wished he were free of this hellish interview, free to think on the problem of Dream Desire who was not Dream Desire at all but Dolly.

''Until what? I never really knew.''

''Until I rocked the boat, God damn it! I was chief of the Indiana bureau. I tried to stop a car-smash rally a week before the new models came out. The district supervisor was there, making a speech. I thought I saw a kid inside one of the levacars the crowd was pushing into the Wabash River. I went to see, hold back the crowd. The district supervisor told me to stop. I hit him. *I hit him.* You know what happens when you hit an executive.''

Finian pinched the bridge of his nose to shut out the ugly memory. At length he added, ''In case you never heard the rest of the story either, a wreck crew examined the levacar afterward. There was no kid inside. Only a big mechanical doll somebody had forgotten to take out before the smash.''

''Very touching,'' said Sprool emptily.

''Come on, Sprool. Let's get this over.''

''Of course. But let me make one more point. Do you know why I'm here, not in Bombay?''

''The mental riot at the TTIC nylon plant was a fake.''

''Not at all. The rioters were manning the controls of the motorized strike gangs day and night, from their homes. The moment TTIC cabled agreement to their demand for two extra holidays, before and after Nehru's birthday, they gave up all their other requests—for free anticigarette immunization and the like. People are soft, Fin. They cooperate. It must be so, or the plant would stop functioning. How many billions do G/S and TTIC employ? Put those people out of work—disaster! Hunger, pestilence, *real* rioting. The people also have another role to fill, as consumers. If they're unhappy, they respond less adequately to advertising. The plant slows down. Why, until TTIC conceived the idea of introducing new female personalities every year, not just new clothes but complete new mental patterns, the world was headed for ruin. We ran out of new gadgets long ago.''

''Don't kid me,'' Finian said cynically. ''Personality obsolescence was thought up by Old Man Pharoh of G/S. His granddad told him a story about the Kennedy lady's mushroom hair changing the style overnight and it started him thinking.''

''He had considerable help from Alvah Loudermilk.''

''Who cares? All I say is, it's a hell of a shame the Triple Play War didn't end in something besides a stalemate. We wouldn't have had everybody palsy-walsy, black and white and yellow. And this damned population problem—the first rockets rusting on the moon and nobody interested in following them in person. Everybody's a consumer and a worker and—and damn it, soft as Jell-O. And it's a miserable mess from top to bottom.''

Sprool was genuinely shocked.

''Fin, are you seriously advocating periodic wars?''

Finian shielded his eyes from the sun falling through the port.

''Oh, no. I can't think of anything else, that's all. Fatness or fighting, fighting or fatness. In my book they're both lousy. I wish there were a third way. I can't think of one. Maybe if I were smart like you—'' Finian stopped, bitterly.

Sprool dialed a magenta visorphone. ''Really, Fin, this is becoming pointless temperament.'' Into the phone he said, ''We're ready, Doctor.'' To Finian again: ''Please don't try to reform our delicately balanced world, my friend. At least not until we scrub your mind clean of what you saw in the auditorium.''

A shiver crawled on Finian's spine.

''Scrub—?''

Too late. Pneumatic doors slid aside. Two unsavory specimens in white smocks bordered with lace wheeled a rubber-tired mechanism into the room. Before Finian could move they adjusted several wing nuts and lowered a bowl device over his head. He tried to stand up, cursing. He was quickly but painlessly pinioned by sleek tubular metal arms clasping him from the back of the chair.

''The worst damage you did was on film,'' Sprool said, striding back and forth, dry-washing his hands. ''I naturally assume that in your heightened nervous state, what you saw with your eyes didn't make much of an impression. But we'll be sure. Give him a mild jolt to start, boys.''

Several sinister cathode tubes began to hiss at various points on the machine. Finian felt a tingle on his scalp, similar to a healthful massage. He closed his eyes and tried to remember the rear elevation of Dream Desire.

He panicked.

Almost as though there were a mental vacuum cleaner in his head, certain synapses were blocked, certain memory receptors temporarily sucked dry. The technique was a portion of that employed in changing the female consumer's intelligence quotient from year to year to conform to the new personality design she purchased. It made Finian fume to think of them tampering with his skull. He was no rotten Metropolis wife merchandised into adopting the latest fashion trend. He writhed ferociously. Sprool looked on with disapproval.

Try as he might, Finian could not remember what—*good Lord!* He'd forgotten the name!

What did she look like? *What?*

He had a blurry recollection of colors on a screen, little else. The laboratory cretins unhooded him. The chair relaxed. Sprool assisted him to his feet.

"Feeling better? Free of unpleasant memories?"

"You've no business tampering—"

Dolly Novotny had a raspberry mark.

So did Dream Desire.

"Yeah, Yeah. I'm okay."

It took all Finian's strength to keep from revealing that the mental dike had just burst.

He wasn't really surprised. Dolly Novotny had once meant far more to him than assignment could. She would again, when he learned how and why she—

He laughed inwardly. Poor Sprool. He'd stolen a march. Two. Finian still had the tooth camera. And how could Sprool know Finian wanted to—*must*—remember Dolly Novotny, because she was the only creature he ever really loved?

Dolly was the girl to whom he'd been engaged, before her parents broke it off after he was cashiered from the DOCs. An ex-DOC who became an industrial investigator was little more than a low-life spy in their estimations. Finian had been away so much, on assignment. Dolly had tried to resist her parents, but they held the cash-box for a modeling career. She tried; she loved him. But one day when he came back to Bala-Cynwyd she was gone. The whole family had moved.

Finian received one final letter. He thought from the words, or rather what was between them, really, that she still loved him. The words were obviously parentally ghosted.

Blinking at Sprool now, scratching his scalp to relieve the prickle, Finian realized anew the rather disheartening truth. He was a maverick. Pop had made him so, against his mother's shrill protests. So be it. Especially since someone—the system, maybe, he didn't know, cared less because a man couldn't really fight a system, not an ordinary man anyway—had corrupted the flesh he loved so well.

Finian was vaguely aware of Sprool, bland, pointing.

"Up that stairway, Fin. Directly to the vertijet takeoff stage. Spare you the embarrassment of going on deck." He extended his hand. "Luck, Fin. I hope the sacking isn't too bad."

Finian slipped the hand aside. He grinned. If you had to be a loony, why not enjoy it?

"Thanks for nothing, pal."

He marched defiantly up the stairs into sunlight.

Who had Sprool been kidding about paternalism? Three hours later the vertijet hovered six inches from Lyman Pushkyn's green front door, the lawn of Panpublix on the outskirts of the Eastern metropolis. Finian was rudely pushed out. The vertijet climbed a white column of vapor into the sky.

Finian picked fresh-cut grass from his pantaloons. Oh, that kind, gentle Sprool. On his instructions the vertijet pilot had beamed an anonymous message on the Panpublix band, announcing that Finian Smith was being returned to continental U.S. by a TTIC skycraft. Still, Finian had one ace to stave off financial disaster.

Five minutes later he lost it.

A squad of G/S industrial guards boiled onto the lawn and hustled Finian to a cold tile room in the personnel wing. There he discovered two astonishing things. One, the corporation was not quite so paternalistic as it masked itself to appear. The policemen roughed him as they stripped him. Two, the vast G/S industrial police force was not the harmless, aimless body it looked to be from outside. Apparently the guards were paid so well because they had to move savagely if a bubble boiled up the bland surface of the world stew.

In fact, their professionalism with the see-rays in the personnel lab relieved him, howling and kicking and pummeling, of the precious tooth camera, just before he was hustled to Pushkyn's floor.

III

Panpublix was the wholly owned internal advertising agency for G/S. The building loomed forty stories. Within its curtain walls quite a few thousand communicators devoted themselves to the task of planning and executing campaigns to move the bodies, as the expression went. The fortieth, or solarium, floor belonged to the agency's executive officer, Pushkyn, into whose presence Finian was unceremoniously thrust.

"You miserable creep," Lyman said, as he shooed away his masseuse and beetled his thick Ukrainian brows. "You bumbler, you! We heard all about your incredible performance from Sprool's agents. You're fired. Blackballed. Eradicated. *Kapoosht.*"

Finian had a hard light in his eyes. He sat down, tilted his feet to the chaise footrest and dialed the arm for a B-complex cocktail. "Lyman, those goonies of yours messed me up. I never knew they were more than window dressing. I didn't know they were supposed to fight."

Pudgy Pushkin snapped the elastic of his old rose knickerbockers. His stomach, lumpy and white as the rest of him, hung out unglamorously.

"Rock the boat some more, creepnik. You'll find out how they can fight."

"Oh, shut up. I delivered your pictures. Even if your men did take them by force."

Pushkyn turned his back. "Peddle it another place, jerk. You're through."

"You can't talk to me that way. If you hadn't chintzed about a lousy sweat-print job—"

Pushkyn squinted around. "So *that's* how. That Sprool, he's a regular fiend."

"Damn it, Lyman—"

Extending a trembling sausage finger Pushkyn breathed, "*You* we ought to have psyched, deep and permanent. What a fool I was to string along with you for years! A stumblebum private cop dignifying himself by calling himself an industrial investigator. Come in here storming, cursing—no wonder the DOCs kicked you out!"

Momentarily bewildered, Finian countered, "Lyman, your own guards—"

"Quiet! We'll get a nice fat rap in the public image when the investigator trade journals pick up the story of how G/S flopped."

Glowering, Finian stalked him. "Regardless of that, I delivered. I want my fee."

"I'll be damned if I—"

Conflict was temporarily forestalled by the arrival of a thin assistant art director, carrying a square item masked in gray silk. Finian stared moodily at the G/S model announcement layouts in the wall display racks. The trade name of the new G/S woman and her figure were greeked; but from the woodcut and steel-engraving technique of the gatefold and bleed comps, Finian suspected G/S was going to market a bit of nostalgia even older than the kind chosen by TTIC. Bustless, mandolins and stereopticons by gaslight? Finian had a prepossessing urge to throw up.

"Want to see this, chief?" said the assistant art director.

He whipped off the silk, revealing an oil painting in a platinum frame.

"What the rinkydink hell is that?" Pushkyn cried.

The art director blanched. "Why, chief, it's R. R. Pharoh III!"

"Of course, of course, jerkola. You think I don't know? I haven't seen the old smeller in three years maybe, but think I don't know the chairman of my own bread and butter? Why the fancy-fancy oil treatment? You do it?"

"Spare time, only, chief," trembled the art director. "Got a memo. Salinghams—you know, the audiotonal effects veep—memoized Pharoh. Wanted a personal portrait of his leader. Pharoh memoized me, okaying having his picture done. I patched together this little work from the descriptive PR biog. There aren't any good portraits extant."

"Why bring it to me?"

"But, chief! You memoized me when I memoized you that—"

"I did? Oh, yeah. Well, I'm busy. Take it to Salinghams."

The art director veiled his creation and disappeared down the tube. Pushkyn was about to speak to Finian when he noted the gray sweat patina on Finian's face. He demanded to know whether Finian was ill.

"Nothing, nothing's wrong," said Finian, shivering, wildly curious. The image in the portrait burned into Finian's skull. It was that of a florid old gentleman with dewlaps and blue, vaguely crossed eyes.

Tightening his nerves, Finian said, "Pushkyn, let me lay it out. I got to have the fee. I need it to find the prototype of the TTIC girl. I used to know her."

A visorphone glowed. Pushkyn slapped the command button. A pale man danced up and down on the screen.

"Chief, chief, it's a breakthrough, a breakthrough! We turned up the TTIC pilot plant just an hour ago. Molecular triangulation. My God, sir, it's a miracle of deception. Manhattan! The prison! An old, run-down distillery company building in the worst stews of—" He consulted a paper. "Parkave, that's the place."

Listening transfixed, Pushkyn started, slid his gaze to Finian and snarled at the screen, "Oh, boy, is *your* fat in the fire. Call me back." He shut off and squinted at Finian, whose mind churned. "You were talking?"

Finian swallowed hard. "Pushkyn, I must find out what's happened to the girl they made into the TTIC prototype. If they've changed her they've done wrong. She was sweet and desirable. They've made her all soft and disgusting. Like marshmallow."

"The new TTIC broad? You were hot for her once, that it?"

"That's it. I was only holding back the camera so you'd pay me. Give me a chance!"

"Think we run a sniveling charity?" Pushkyn's sweeping gesture encompassed the heavens and the pulsing, overpopulated smog banks beneath. "We gotta keep the plant running! Create demand every minute! Off with the old woman! On with the new! The old woman, she smells, she's out of date! We got a crusade here at Panpublix! We got a holy mission! You want the plant wheels to stop like they put sand in them? While we take care of your *personal* problems? Don't be a jerkola. Like to argue about the fee? I'll call up the guards again."

Something akin to a cool rush of air swept Finian's brain.

"Then I'll find her without the fee, Lyman."

"Hah-hah, sure. Big independent operator, big millionaire. Go get psyched and lose those hostile tendencies. Don't rock the world, she don't rock so good. Everybody's happy, you be happy. Go grub and be happy."

"I'm not happy. All of a sudden I'm not happy, if people like you make the only girl I ever fell in love with obsolete."

"Get out, chummo. I don't like you anymore. You're dangerous."

Finian Smith nodded crisply. "I could very well be." And left.

As Finian left the Panpublix building he heard a menacing hiss. He tried to dodge the rainbow spray. Too late.

His clothing was soon soaked with a noxious admixture of water, special nitrites and phosphorous compounds shot into the air by the underground sprinkler system.

At the levacar station he finally controlled his anger. How petty they could be, to order the lawns sprinkled just then.

Waiting passengers moved away and made rude remarks about his smell. Finian found himself sole occupant of the front car on the ride down the Philadelphia spur.

The enforced loneliness gave him a chance to organize his muddled thoughts and decide what course of action he had to pursue concerning Dolly Novotny.

Two facts he possessed. What they meant, he didn't know.

A likely place to find her was the TTIC pilot plant on Manhattan, the prison island. Still, he was certain to have a rough time getting onto the island and into the plant after that. With few resources at his disposal it might be better to pursue the other thread a bit.

Its significance left him even more muddled. Alvah Loudermilk, TTIC chairman, had appeared at the dealer presentation, somewhat to the annoyance of his inferiors. And R. R. Pharoh, top G/S executive, hadn't been acting quite sensibly either when he permitted an oil portrait of himself to be painted. Finian had never seen a public photo of either man. Both executives were practically legendary.

Then why in the name of Galbraith did they look so much like each other?

When Finian thought on it, one cold, unpleasant word gnawed his head. *Conspiracy.*

A moment later his professional memory dredged up a source of proving or disproving his odd theory. What he intended to do with evidence, if any existed, he couldn't say. But he had a vague desire to be armed with a little more certainty before he sought Dolly.

An achingly musical name. *Dolly, Dolly—*

He remembered her so well, from summer evenings on the back

porch before Bala-Cynwyd, like the other suburbs, was swallowed in the fester of the metropolis.

Her dark hair. Her gentle eyes. Her animated mouth. And the raspberry mark, one night during an electrical storm.

She'd tentatively shared Finian's inherited ideas about their constantly obsolete world, ideas long suppressed in him and now flooding back under the double stimulus of Sprool's lecture and Pushkyn's vindictive parsimony. Dolly hadn't exactly been sympathetic. The philosophy of enduring worth was too daring even then. (Today it was sheer lunacy.) But neither had she been as adamant as most citizens. As her parents, for example. They replaced their furniture monthly with the latest G/S fiberboard laminate imitation Finnish modern modes. Good consumers, both. Then came his dismissal from the DOCs, the enforced breakup—

The levacar slowed for Bala Cynwyd. In the abstract, remodeling a woman's mind to make her the pattern to which nearly all other women in the world could conform was acceptable to Finian. When it came to the specific of changing Dolly to the marshmallow-trumpery creature looming on the screen behind Krumm, that was too much.

As he stepped off at Bala-Cynwyd, it began to rain. He hurried along beneath warped building fronts of chartreuse and electric blue extruded plastic. From a doorway a hapless bum in last year's pseudo-cotton sport clothes begged for three dollars for a tube of model cement to sniff. Finian shuddered and walked faster. He stopped at Abe Kane's Autosuiter, the last shop left open on the block, selected a few new clothes from the plastic catalog sheets fastened to the walls and fed his universal credit card into the slot after punching out his measurements.

A red lucite sign blinked on: *Credit N.G.*

Finian frowned, hit the cancel lever and tried again. The third time he tried his card was not returned.

Pushkyn! Damn the vindictive bastard.

He trudged on through the rain, never having felt so alone in his life. It was a queer sensation, the total absence of credit. Once, he remembered dimly, Pop had brought home a suit of clothes purchased with cash. It had caused a near-riot among Bala-Cynwyd burghers.

Reaching his shabby apartment, Finian changed from the effete suit, scrubbed up as best he could, packed his few belongings into a satchel and walked back into the rain. He passed a crowd of workers from the local G/S visorphone plant. It specialized in treating receiver parts with reagents that would crack the plastic precisely eight months after installation.

A little smog had mixed with the rain, turning the street ghostly. At a corner booth Finian used his last few coins to make a toll call to the House of Sinatra in Los Angeles.

A sound truck rolled past, repeating over and over, *"Gee-ess, Gee-ess, don't guess, it's bess—Take free shuttle at Exit 5–6 to the G/S Plaza—Gee-ess, don't—"*

A dapper young man appeared on the screen, snapping his fingers. "Hiyah. What can this gasser of a full-service bank do for you, Clyde?"

Finian showed his bank identification card.

"I'd like to withdraw my balance."

The banker came back into view a moment later. "Get lost. Your balance is nonesville. Garnisheed at noon. Unperformance and nonfulfilling of verbal contract, with waiver of cooperation. You signed it, Charlie."

"Damn it, I performed—" Finian began.

The screen had already blacked.

He staggered into the drifting smog. So Pushkyn had gone that far. Just for the sake of meanness. Well, Finian Smith would show the whole rotten bunch. They had angered him now. He wasn't quite witless, not yet.

Gee-ess, Gee-ess, it's bess came a lonely bellow. The polluted smog made Finian cough. His eyes smarted as he turned his pockets inside out.

A dollar left. Enough for a cup of coffee. No transportation. Just a single walking man in a cloud of industrial fumes and a long, empty night for thinking of Dolly.

Resolutely Finian hefted his satchel and started out to walk to Missouri.

IV

Thirty-six days later Finian staggered into the National Record Office in Rolla. Thirty-six frightening, alarming, eye-opening, solitary, transfiguring days they had been, too.

Days of dodging robot levacars whose spot beams hunted him in the shadows beneath the elevated turnpikes, seeking to arrest him for pedestrianship.

Days of remembering his pop. And nights too. Especially nights, thinking as he lay under a berry bush half-starved and chilly, how Pop had enjoyed prizefights, antisocial, uncooperative prizefights. How young Finian had been dragged to lonely boxcars or dim garages where furtive men watched the sport before it was finally stamped out in the name of bland humanity.

The world too was one bland custard, blandly happy. Except not really, as Finian, horrified, discovered.

No plant could function at total efficiency, at complete peak year after year. A low percentage of chronic unemployment had never been whipped by the cyclic theorists. Strange wild caravans of men and wives and children, human wolves almost, passed Finian occasionally on red-leafed back roads in Pennsylvania and Ohio. He almost fell into the hands of one such band. Thereupon he decided he must possess a weapon of self-defense at all costs. His belly he could protect by shoveling in wild berries and an occasional stolen chunk of honeycomb. But his life, against such a seething pack of wild creatures as he had fled from on that lonely road, needed more dependable protection.

Difficult problem. Under law, weapons were prohibited except upon special occasions. What necessity for weapons when all was pleasant cooperation?

Yet the G/S guards carried weapons. So did the TTIC internal force. Finian was beginning to believe he knew why that might be so. Too early to tell, however. And the other problem pressed him to concentration upon it.

Weapon devotees were even more suspect than pedestrians in the lonely country between metropolises. Occasionally Finian glimpsed a wire compound, acres and acres, against the sunburned horizon. Manhattan Prison was too far for local DOCs to send recalcitrant Hoosier or Buckeye antiobsols, so they were thrown into smaller country compounds, together with those few madmen who settled disputes with fists. Such compound inmates were described as juves, Finian remembered, passing one such wire enclosure on a white moonlit night and shuddering. He didn't recognize the term juve, but it obviously meant the middle-aged or geriatric specimens huddled within the cages, a few defiantly wearing ancient gaudy jackets with mottoes stitched on them, forgotten anarchist slogans like Pfluger's Idle Hour Pin Barons.

On the outskirts of South Bend, Finian luckily came upon an obsolescence carnival.

Several thousand people swarmed across a treeless terrain in a housing project smash. Motorized work gangs stood at the development's fringe, waiting to set up new prefab Moorish Manors to replace obsolete Five-Bedroom Geneva Châteaux.

Finian infiltrated the wild carnival crowd, ripping draperies and smashing furniture with feigned laughter ringing from his lips. When the carnival wore itself out near dawn and the work gangs rolled in through clouds of soy-fuel smoke, Finian filched a shiny flick-blade knife from a Boy Scout chopping up a last slab of plastic plaster and lath.

The Scout shrieked for the DOCs on duty. Finian was away and running through a hydroponic cornfield before he could be caught.

Now, dressed in his only presentable suit, last year's G/S Nubby Oppenheimer, he flashed his personal identification card before the computer grid in the empty green marble rotunda of the National Record Office. Personal identity was one quantity Pushkyn couldn't revoke.

Finian felt his fingers tingle as the grid scanned the card.

"Investigator Smith, Bond Number PA-5006, you are recognized."

"Permission to examine ownership statements for corporations over one billion, please."

"What year?" buzzed the mechanical voice.

"Not certain," Finian replied. "Could be as far back as 1980 or even 1970."

"Second tier from lowest level. Tube nine, your left."

It gave Finian a weird sensation, plummeting in the airtube and realizing he was dropping eighty stories into the depths of the nation's largest insane asylum. But legal transactions had proliferated so in the past decades, as had neurotic behavior, that only a combined institution and record office was feasible for saving space and offering a less-than-fatal end for hopeless maniacs.

The reading room below ground smelled of mold. Gray block walls heightened the unpleasant mood. Finian sat at the call-out console. He manipulated the controls and spoke into the unit:

"Let me have the volume covering Goods/Service corporation for—ah—1974, please."

Several minutes passed. A door slid aside. A white male, perhaps seventy, with yellow-rimmed lackluster eyes and a lantern jaw, shuffled in and waited with docile manner. The creature wore a seedy twill uniform, anciently cut.

"What do you have on any asset transfers for Goods/Services, please?" Finian asked.

The elderly gentleman did not so much as blink. He hesitated only a moment as the index system in his sick skull, instilled by hypnolearning, turned over record after invisible record. Finally he said vacantly, "No asset transfers."

"Nothing in the way of stock, even?"

"No asset transfers, no asset transfers."

"Thank you, that's all."

But the man had already departed, needing no thanks. Finian turned to the console again, wondering whether he could endure as many days as it might take:

"Let me have the volume covering Goods/Services corporation for 1975."

A total of eighteen hours went by, relieved only by three short naps above ground, Finian sleeping in a magnolia bush on Rolla's outskirts, before he found what he wanted.

He'd worked through Goods/Services from its 1969 inception to 1997, interviewing assorted madmen and women who shuffled in, reeled off figures and names or lack of them, then shuffled back out. Asset transfers exhausted itself as a lead. He tried register of directorship as well as deposition of tangible real-estate sale. Useless, useless. Only then did it slip back.

In some dim time in the past—Pushkyn had mentioned it once—public stock of G/S had been called off the market.

Once more he began with a different set of volumes, working his way down the years. In 1992 he located it: All certificates dedeemed.

The scent overpowered the must of the underground box like the smell of blood. He called out the volume covering Things to Come Incorporated for the same year. It was a naturalized Japanese weighing close to three hundred pounds.

One month after the G/S redemption came a callback by the board of TTIC. Finian almost wished the poor Japanese could appreciate tea. He'd have bought him a bucket, had he the money.

Tensely his fingers flew to the console.

"Two volumes, please. For 1992 and 1993. Covering Flotations without tangible assets."

When 1992 arrived (a mulatto with his face fixed in a perpetual grin) Finian was disappointed. Nothing. The volume for 1993 (a strikingly voluptuous red-haired girl who had eyes that made him think hauntingly of Dolly) was another case entirely. Finian trembled:

"Give me what you have on holding companies, please."

The third was it, the redhead staring through him:

"Holders Limited. Ten thousand shares privately issued."

Finian was on his feet, sweating, his empty belly achurn. "Officers, please."

"Chairman of the board, Alvah Pharoh."

"There must be some mistake. Uh—recheck, please. What is the name?"

"Full legal name Alvah Robert Loudermilk Pharoh."

A florid old gentleman with dewlaps and blue, vaguely crossed—by heaven!

Finian almost forgot to return the volume to its detention cell after he got the names of the other registered corporate executives, which meant nothing to him. But Alvah Robert Loudermilk Pharoh most certainly did.

Finian wondered, as he left the National Record building and turned his face east again, what had possessed the old man to think it safe to appear occasionally as head of both companies. Not that he appeared often, mind you. The painting *must* have been a slip. So too the appearance on the hydrofoiler, displeasing his underlings. Senility? Senility and a strength that had refused to completely drain away, as the dewlaps lengthened?

Hungry and tattered though he was, Finian felt renewed as he threw himself into the weary tramp back to Manhattan. The flick-blade knife armed him. So did the knowledge that even the most mighty, even those who kept the plant running at all costs, including the cost of sloth, could occasionally slip.

And they still had Dolly.

V

Ahead in the gloomy purple twilight, giant rats were squealing after blood.

Quickening his step, Finian unshipped the flick knife. Making headway was hard. This particular section of the Hudson Bluffs National Dump was a miniature mountain range of discarded but eminently serviceable—except for the usual engineered-to-fail tubes and cracked cabinets—solido sets. To the east behind the rubble the towers of Manhattan Prison thrust into the darkening sky.

Finian walked rapidly away from the squee-squee of the rats. He'd glimpsed a pack of them earlier, down by the Tunnel at the far end of the hundred-thousand-acre junk tract. They were nearly three feet long from drinking the waste spewed out by the pharmaceutical factories upriver. Hoping to avoid a meeting with needly fangs, Finian was suddenly arrested by a fresh sound.

A human voice, in fright.

He doubled back in his tracks, cold sweat all over him. The vitaminized beasts were attacking a real person!

Finian rounded a solido heap. A little wisp-haired balloon of a man in a ragged gray smock was backed against a trash peak, trying vainly to swing at three of the rats, armed only with a plastic leg broken from a solido console. The man's left trouser leg was shredded, black-shining with blood. The blood maddened the rats. They danced and snapped and squee-squeed and made the little man even more pale.

Finian snatched up a solido cabinet and heaved. One of the rats yipped, turned and scuttled at Finian like a small furry tank. Shaking, Finian stood his ground. He tried to dodge the creature's leap but was not agile enough. Hellish teeth sank into his arm.

Finian jammed his flick knife into the smelly hair at the base of the rat's brain. Squirting blood like a fountain, the rat flipped over in the air and gave a death squee. Its comrades received solid whacks between the eyes from the other man. They turned tail and vanished.

"Let me see that arm," said the man, a filthy specter with moist, disappointed eyes. "Oh, not good at all. Come along. I'm a doctor. Humphrey Cove."

Finian gaped as he was led along the bluff. "A doctor? In the National Dump?"

"I live here. Never mind, I'll explain later. I have a shack. Hurry, we don't want those rat toxins to run through you. I think I have immunization. Oh, I was really done for until you came along."

The small doctor giggled as he hustled Finian along. Finian was not too sure he approved of his would-be savior. In spite of Dr. Cove's rather pitiful mien, there was a certain unsteadiness in his wet eyes. He clucked and talked to himself as he led the way to a ramshackle structure nearly the size of a small private dwelling, constructed solely of panels from solido consoles jerry-rigged together with wire and other scrap materials.

"No one comes here. No humans. Only the littersweep convoys from up and down the coast, all mech-driven. The only people I ever talk with are the poor juves in the prison. What's your name? What are you doing here?"

At the hovel entrance Cove suddenly halted, stared at Finian and turned pale.

"Did you come to arrest—?"

Finian shook his head. "I came to get into Manhattan."

"Via the Dumps?" Cove blinked suspiciously. "There's the Tunnel."

"To use the Tunnel, you have to be a priest going in for last rites. Or a coroner or a psychiatry student. Or have a DOC pass. I watched the Tunnel three hours." Suddenly Finian had an impulse to trust this odd little person: "I have no pass. I'll be entering the prison illegally."

"Well, then! Come inside, do come inside!"

Names were exchanged again, Cove having forgotten he'd given his. From behind a triple stack of ancient medical texts Cove said he'd rescued from dump piles, the doctor produced a frowsy leather-plas diagnostic kit. He clamped the analyzer to Finian's upper arm and switched on the battery. A whir. A moment later the proper medication had been pressure-sprayed through Finian's epidermal cells.

Cove watched with proud glowing eyes, saying as he unstrapped the unit:

"A miracle I found this kit, I'll tell you. Three years ago. The only persons who use it are the poor juves. No regular medical help for them, I'm afraid. So I've a skiff. Actually an old levacar inverted. I paddle across once a month after dark." He giggled. "The DOCs at the Tunnel post would psych me if I got caught. But I feel I'm doing my bit to keep the antiobsols content in their unhappiness."

Through a rift in the wall Cove's moist eyes sought the darkening towers. His voice was quickly vengeful.

"I'd like to see those buildings fall to ash. Margarita, ah, poor Margarita." He whipped his head around, eyes almost as vicious as those of the rats. "Who are you? If this is all a clever trap to smoke me out—"

"No trap," Finian assured him. "I'll tell you about it. But do you have any food?"

Cove nodded and fetched a brown gallon pharmaceutical bottle, instructing Finian to drink.

"Protein and vitamins. Distill it myself from the drug sludge in the river. After you drink I may or may not give you one of the soy bars I get from the juves. When their wives bear children, it's the only way they can pay, you know. They're very proud, always pay."

Cove squatted with difficulty, an oddly savage little man in the fading light.

"Whether I let you have a soy bar depends on your story. If you're an enemy, I can run away and leave you to wander the Dumps at night. You won't last long with the rats, being a stranger."

"There's a woman over on that island I have to find," said Finian and launched out.

As he recounted his tale, careful not to become too emotional about it, he noticed a growing excitement in Cove's damp eyes. Finally, when he had concluded, Cove leaped up.

"Capital, Smith, that's capital. Let me help. Let me ferry you across."

Finian smiled grudgingly. "Okay. I was prepared to swim it."

"The sludge would poison you before you got halfway."

"What's your stake in this, Cove? I mean, this food pays me back for the rats."

Cove's little eyes were miserable.

"Margarita. My wife. She died over there."

Painfully the story came out, dredged from an unhappy past:

Cove had been a plastic surgeon by specialty, in the employ of TTIC at its Bangor Personality Salon. But a quirk in his nature made him rebel against the work, permitted him to fall prey to dangerous Galbraither notions. His wife had informed on him.

Cove discovered it before the TTIC police could arrest him. He fled to the outskirts of Bangor, hiding there in the woods while a few reluctant friends supplied him with food. TTIC industrial police combed the woods with talk horns, threatening to psych his wife into antiobsol attitudes if he didn't surrender.

"The filth!" Cove rocked on his haunches. "I thought it was a trick, a lever. I ran away. Margarita, poor thing, was on their side. She couldn't help what she did. She came of a respected family. TTIC middle management. But a year later I found out. They did it anyway. Oh, they smile and smile and treat the mob kindly. But underneath, when they're opposed—I learned Margarita had been sentenced to Manhattan. It took me another nine months to get here and find means of crossing. By that time she'd died of pneumonia. No antibiotics allowed the juves, you see. Juves are worthless. She died." Cove rocked and rocked, wild-eyed. "Died, died."

"Dr. Cove, will you help me get across?"

"Of course, of course. But to hunt that pilot plant, a knife won't be much good. The moment you're discovered they'll set on you like wild dogs."

"Then I'll need something else."

Finian's brain ran rapidly with his career with G/S. He recalled Leveranz, an unfortunate operative charged with a dangerous penetration of the TTIC Marketing Office in Beirut.

"I knew a man once who was bombed. Is there anything here—?" Finian's gesture swept the shack and dump beyond. "Do you remember enough, even if we could find an explosive source, to bomb me?"

The moist eyes of Cove widened with malicious delight. "Blow them up?"

Now Finian himself felt hard and cold.

"I just might, if they've hurt her."

"Possibly we could use the charger pack from an old solido." Cove was warming to the challenge. "Yes, we very well might. Extremely miniaturized. I'd have to check the formula but I think I have a chem text in that pile. And a military medicine volume, too.'' He began to tear through the books. ''No anesthesia, or precious little. Perhaps I could knock you out.''

''What for a trigger?'' Finian questioned. He showed his mouth. ''I have this empty socket where I carried a camera once.''

Chortling, Cove scuffled among his belongings and produced a cardboard carton full of ivory chips of all sizes.

''Why, that ought to work, Smith. The miserable juves aren't fluoridated either. I do quite a few extractions. Imagine a plastic surgeon doing extractions! Let's see, give me a minute to find the chem text . . .''

Dr. Humphrey Cove unearthed the text in two minutes. The rest took four days.

Finian suffered excruciatingly, especially during the operation. Cove kept smacking him on the head with a solido leg when the pain grew too hideous. Finian dug his nails into his palms and thought of murmurous summer evenings on the back porch in Bala-Cynwyd, and vowed in his pain-streaked mind the hurt was worth it if only he had a means to strike at them if they'd hurt Dolly, his own Dolly.

When he was ready to enter the prison, his left foot flesh carried a small capsule that would detonate an explosive force when the yellowing tooth in his dead socket was turned a proper one-half turn in its clumsily hand-chiseled housing.

An old trick, bombing. A relic of the Triple Play War. But it gave Finian a little more courage to go hunting death.

In an unpleasant mist-clammy midnight, Dr. Cove paddled the improvised skiff through the sticky penicillin waste forming a crust on the Hudson, to the dilapidated pier that once belonged to the Cunard division of G/S. Off down black, ruined streets distant reddish lights pulsed. Cove shook his hand fervently. ''I hope you kill them. I hope you don't cooperate and kill them all.''

Then the skiff slithered away into the smelly broth. Finian shivered and walked.

Three blocks from the pier a ragged band of thirty-odd men and women, with a couple of malnourished youngsters hanging at the fringes, slipped out of an alley and closed around him.

They hissed and backed a terrified Finian against a polybrick wall.

The leader of the juve pack, an oldster of eighty in tapered blue denim trousers and an antiquarian jacket spangled with fake platinum stars and buckles swaggered up and down, thumbs hooked in a six-inch belt.

"Sending DOCs into the streets these days, are they, sonny?"

"I'm no DOC." Finian searched the hostile eyes for succor. There was none.

"We eat DOCs alive in the prison. They step off the guard post, we swallow 'em up and chew 'em to pieces, sonnyboy."

"A DOC stew tonight! Oh, wunnerful!" piped a seven-year-old.

"Scream a little for us, will you please?" said the aging juve with a smile, shuffling forward.

Finian thought of the flick knife and whipped it out. Another sibilant hiss ran from mouth to mouth as the blade caught the distant red glow.

"Look, don't kill me. See this? It's a knife, a real knife. You people can recognize a genuine useful antique twentieth-century artifact, can't you? Nonobsolescent. Nonobsolescent, see? Still works?"

A touched stud and the blade retracted. Another touch and it sprang out.

"Would I be a DOC and carry this?"

The juve leader had an almost religious expression on his face. His hand shook as he extended it.

"Uh—could you—leave me see?"

Finian thrust it into his hand.

"Yours. Listen, take it." A dark, malicious streak forced out the next words. "Could you make more? Why don't you try? Now you have a pattern. Then you wouldn't have to wait for the DOCs to leave the guard post. Then a lot of you could pay them a visit."

Whispering over their icon, the juves melted into the night.

VI

Keeping to back streets, Finian crossed Bway several blocks above a strange complex of glittering red lights. Cove had told him it was the prison recreation area, a kind of open plaza known, unpronounceably, as Timesq. Hurrying on, he reached Parkave.

Several blocks south he saw a white chain working its way across the ruined thoroughfare. Approaching in the cover of shadows, he gazed up at a glistening glass structure with windows painted over. Then he looked down to the street again.

The white chain came apart into individual females, double-timing along between a cordon of TTIC industrial guards. One chain rushed west, another east, vanishing into the building. Finian skulked, grinning mirthlessly, estimating the time to be somewhere in the neighborhood of eleven at night. Protected, the pilot plant nursing staff was changing shift. Cove had told Finian about the nurses, and also what might be done. He hurried back toward Bway.

The recreation area was curiously deserted of juves at this hour. Finian wondered whether the flick knife was really that much of a talisman. It must be, since he'd seen no juves after the first encounter. Cove said there were several hundred thousand on the island. Perhaps they'd gone underground to the ruined transportation tubes.

Timesq featured open shops subsidized out of national taxes as a sop to the theory of rehabilitation . . . antiques, genuine meatburgers, bizarre novelty stores where articles were actually displayed on open counters instead of behind automated windows. But the shops were actually intended to pander to the vices of the juves. Else why would Finian have been able to slip so easily into a deserted costumer's?

Half starved, his shanks frozen by wind whistling under the ancient white uniform and the musty gray wig prickling his ears, Finian dozed the daylight hours away in an alley, blearily on the alert for juves. He saw one large pack passing a block away, several hundred on the run. They didn't see him. Otherwise he was undisturbed until night fell again.

Midway between the hotel which apparently served as nurses' quarters and the ruined liquor building, Finian ducked into one of the double-timing white chains as the eleven o'clock shift changed. He hoped his male shoes wouldn't be too noticeable But the street was dark. The hundred or so nurses were on dangerous extra-pay duty from the way they rushed along between the guard cordons, not speaking, intent only on gaining the safety of the pilot plant.

As in all hospitals, lights burned low in the marble mausoleum of a lobby as the nurses fanned out to the various tube banks. Finian spied a rest room next to a boarded-up newsstand, slipped inside and waited half an hour out of sight.

Then he returned to the lobby. A late nurse was hurrying to the tubes. Outside, the TTIC guard cordons were no more. Finian ran up behind the nurse, thinking smugly that it had been easy so far. He'd remembered to touch no doors, in case there was a sweat-print check.

The nurse gave a frightened *kkk* sound as Finian looped his elbow around her neck.

"Where's the prototype kept, lady? Tell me or I'll crack you in half."

"Tw-twelve," came the panicky answer. "I can't breathe!"

"You won't ever again unless you take me up there."

"It's not my floor—"

"With lights out, who'll know? There's the tube. Inside! Don't speak to anyone. Don't even raise an eyebrow, or I'll throttle you."

In the deserted tube the alarmed woman, elderly, eyed Finian's wig, all too obvious in the full illumination.

"What are you, some kind of degenerate?"

"Yes, but not the kind you think."

Finian laughed, feeling frightened and brave all at once.

On twelve, isolated pools of radiance interspersed vast islands of aseptic black. Three nurses clustered at a floor desk to the right. Finian's terrified victim led him to the left.

Double doors loomed at the far corridor end. Why was it so easy? Finian felt vague alarm as he shoved the old lady through the doors. The isolation, that must be it, he reasoned. The improbable isolation here on Manhattan where no investigator would dream of looking for a pilot plant.

Still, Pushkyn's people had discovered it by molecular-triangulation sonics. Were they penetrating even now?

In the chamber a white blur stretched naked in the warm, purified air. Finian held tight to the old nurse's arm and approached the dreaming girl. The raspberry mark stood out black in the faint gleam from the half-open door of an attached dispensary. There encephalographs and other equipment winked, chromed and cold.

"Dolly?" Finian's lips felt like shreds of paper, crinkled dry. "Dolly, hear me?"

A vacuous mewing sound came from the girl. She twisted deeper in silk coverlets. "Wake her," Finian ordered.

"You're a madman! I don't know how. I'm on six, neurosearch."

He shoved her rudely. "There must be a chart in the dispensary."

Finian had to threaten to cuff her several times before she tremblingly translated the medical Latin in the last twelve thick casebooks on the dispensary shelf. From the section marked *Emergency Antidotal Procedures* she read out the correct mix of ampoules from the wall-wide freezer.

Finian was acutely conscious of the silence of the great dark room, the whisper of Dolly's breathing from the bed, the rush of controlled air in and out of blowers. Time was moving inexorably. What he would do when and if he wakened Dolly he was not precisely sure. All he could tell was that he must talk to her. Talking to her once was what he had worked and tramped and almost died for.

The pressuredermic barrel gleamed in the light. Finian snatched it from the nurse.

"If you've tricked me—I don't take to hurting women, but I will!"

"I swear to Loudermilk I didn't. Only please don't hurt me."

"In there," Finian instructed. He latched the dispensary door behind her. There was no visorphone inside. He would be safe a moment longer.

With shaking hands he pressed the instilling cup near the raspberry mark, and plunged.

Slowly, slowly, the naked girl rolled over, lids fluttering drowsily. Finian crouched by the bed. His hand knotted up in the silken sheets. He'd turned up a rheostat to provide a gleam for judging her eyes. Doll-blue, they flew open—

Blank, unknowing.

"Why, hello there." The voice tormented him. It was so slow, so silly. "Whatever are you doing in Dream's bedroo— Dream's bed—"

Like a broken mechanism the voice ran down. One of her voluptuous hands crept tentatively toward his. *"Finian?"*

"Oh, my God, my God, Dolly."

He buried his head on her shoulder, almost crying.

When he had controlled himself sufficiently to talk, he asked her what it was like.

"Not too terrible." Dolly's voice now, not her body but for the mark, only her voice trying painfully to re-form old associations. "When we moved . . . Well, it was luck and a little moral compromise that snared me a chance to be the prototype."

"Do you remember anything? I mean, when you're under?"

"A little. A very little. Far down in my head, like the bottom of a well. I won't in a week or two, so they say."

"It's wrong, Dolly! It's wrong for them to change you!"

She laughed tolerantly, not a little sadly.

"Those wild old ideas of yours again."

"I love you, Dolly. I want you the way you were."

"Impossible, Fin. My body's changed." One hand lifted the hem of the sheet. "It's part of the price for being the prototype. I nearly died when my parents made us move. I wasn't strong. I'm not much stronger now. This"—a gesture to the room—"when they're finished with me, in a week or two, I'll never be able to go back. The prototype can't. Other women can, the change isn't so deep when it's purchased. But in return I'll receive more money than most women ever see. I wish you hadn't come here, Fin. I'd nearly got over you."

"Take out the contacts, Dolly. Then tell me it's all over."

"Fin, I can't. They're permanent." She clutched his arm. "If you're caught here—"

Rapidly he told her of what he'd learned at the National Record Office. "Some kind of conspiracy, Dolly. Awful, awful. Hell, I'm not bright enough to fathom what it means. Maybe Pop could have. I'm just certain I want you out before this crazy double cross blows right up."

Dolly hesitated. "I'm not sure. My mind's full of someone else—"

"Don't let him frighten you," said a voice. "He's done anyway."

Caught, heartbeat wild and racing, Finian turned as all the lights blazed up in the room. Dolly shrieked and burrowed under the sheet.

Outside the closing panel Finian glimpsed a phalanx of armed TTIC police. The three men inside moved swiftly toward him. Sprool and Pushkyn shoulder to shoulder, and shuffling behind, Alvah Robert Loudermilk Pharoh with his dewlaps jiggling and his blue, vaguely crossed eyes filled with fright.

"We should of killed the jerko," Pushkyn offered.

"Be quiet." Sprool breathed tightly, thinking hard.

"No one listens to me," Alvah Robert Loudermilk Pharoh whined. "No one listens anymore even though I'm the chief executive of Holders."

"You simpleton!" Sprool spun on him, barely able to control his fury. "You incredible wreck! I wish Pushkyn and I had retired you to a senility farm long ago. If your addled brain could have understood it wasn't safe for you to go around making public appearances! Having your portrait painted!''

''Holders is my firm!''

''It *was*. Before your brains turned to mashed potatoes,'' said Pushkyn.

''You wouldn't have penetrated the pilot plant, would you, Pushkyn?'' Finian was suddenly enraged, and beginning to understand. ''Even though you knew where it was.''

Pushkyn sneered. ''Whaddya think, put sand in the wheels? Always the funny finko, huh? If it wasn't for me, Sprool and a few others on both sides, running the show while this old bonebag sits on the Holders board—''

''He means to say,'' Sprool put in, somewhat sadly, ''we have done our best to keep the plant running. You, Fin, have done your best to stop it.''

''How did you find me?'' Finian demanded.

Sprool shrugged. ''See-ray.''

''I never touched a doorknob anyplace!''

''There is a false socket in your head. Every person entering or leaving this plant is rayed for dental coding. Yours failed to check. It took a few minutes to collect Pushkyn. And the old man. I want him to see the fruits of his senility. We vertijetted.''

''Ah, damn,'' said Finian, impotently.

''I very nearly admire you,'' Sprool told him. ''In proper circumstances you might have filled a responsible position with Holders. Do you realize what a difficult and exciting enterprise it is to run this world, Fin?''

''I realize you sold everybody a bill of goods, kept them soft, sucked their guts out.''

''Would you rather have howling millions out of work and rioting?''

''Yes! Yes. I mean, no. I don't want people to starve, but this way—I'd rather have some guts in life. Trouble and guts.''

''Trouble we have, Finian,'' Sprool returned with a sigh. ''Do you know what we saw as we came over the Tunnel in the vertijet? The DOC post in ruins. The juves are breaking out, Fin, actually breaking out. Most of them are dead, of course. But several hundred escaped. There's a pitched battle going on in Jersey this minute. The juves will die as soon as I give the mobilization order. A few may get away and start in other cities, inciting riot, pulling down what we've built so carefully to ensure everyone a decent life. Both TTIC and G/S are alerting industrial guards for trouble such as this. We'll also have to apply considerable pressure for the DOCs to move. But we'll win. We gave up war long ago, Fin. We won't permit another to start."

"The creeps had knives!" Pushkyn bellowed. "Real knives! You stupid, did you—?"

"I think so," Finian looked up. "I hope so."

Again Sprool sighed, almost sympathetically.

"Fin, Fin. You seem to think we're evil men. We're not. We're *businessmen*. We didn't begin the system. We only inherited it. But you've never understood, have you? Always, I think, you resented us as a result of what your father taught you." Sprool was white now, impassioned. "We had no choice! Either we maintained calm or—"

"You changed Dolly! I don't understand your theories beyond that!"

Sprool outshouted him: "The alternative to a rocked boat is *chaos!*"

"There's got to be another way."

"Go to the guard post! See the mangled bodies and then say that."

"I don't *care,* Sprool! I'm taking Dolly off the island."

"Creep, you won't set one foot from here."

Finian peeled his lips back.

"Look at the tooth, Lyman. You know what was there before." He waggled his left foot. "I'm bombed. The tooth will set it off. Either instantaneously or on timed delay. Stop me from walking out with Dolly and find out."

"Salinghams wanted my portrait—" the florid old gentleman began.

"Bluffer! Lousy, rotten bluffer!" Screaming, Pushkyn rushed forward.

Sprool's hand flew up.

"Don't! I believe him."

For the first time Finian Smith saw Sprool perspiring.

"He's the kind to do it, Pushkyn. I don't want slaughter here, too. So you keep quiet and remember who's senior troubleshooter."

Cold, shrewd lights glittered in Sprool's eyes. "Fin, what guarantee can you offer if we release this woman to you, allow her to go with you under duress?"

"No."

Heads swung, startled. Dolly went on slowly:

"I think—I want—"

A disgusted sigh came from Sprool's lips. He controlled himself. "Very well, Fin. If we permit you to leave, what guarantees do you offer that you'll cause no further trouble? We'll have our hands full quelling the disturbances the juves will start. It hasn't got too far out of hand yet. But if I don't give the mobilization order, it could go nationwide. Even to other countries. I have to be around to stop it. It can be done, even though I don't much like removing the velvet glove."

"Guarantees?" said Finian. "My word. That's all."

Sprool walked quickly to the door and opened it. The threatening knot of industrial police still waited in the shadows. Finian bundled Dolly into the bedclothes and moved her toward the entrance as Sprool said, "Let him pass."

"I won't stand for it!" Pushkyn leaped forward and landed a solid one that rocked Finian on his heels. Then Sprool snapped his fingers. The TTIC police carried the foam-lipped Pushkyn into the dispensary.

Trembling, suddenly cold and trembling clear through, Finian made an effort to keep his face an inflexible mask as he guided Dolly through the aisle between the guards. He hoped she wouldn't question him, wouldn't relent until they were free. Sick fear engulfed him as he touched the tip of his tongue gingerly to the fake tooth while the tube shot down.

Dolly leaned on his shoulder, her hair warm. She made frightened mewing sounds. Finian shepherded her into the night, began the long, terrible walk to the Tunnel, hoping she wouldn't come to her senses until they reached the opposite shore. In time she'd be herself again. That much he could give her even if his search had been all for nothing.

The DOC post at the Tunnel entrance was afire. Juve corpses sprawled everywhere.

Midway along the empty tunnel Finian halted. A figure capered toward them.

"Capital, oh, marvelous!" Humphrey Cove trilled, stepping over a dead DOC's openmouthed head. "Three hundred of them got out, running for their lives. I think it will spread this time. The local camps, the jobless—full-scale! There are so many really lovely pockets of resistance!"

"Shut up and walk." Finian pushed Cove back toward the Jersey side.

"What in heaven's name is wrong with you, Smith?"

"Armed." Finian whispered it so Dolly couldn't hear. "A guy hit me, I'm armed. Can't have more than half an hour before I blow. Cove, don't you say anything. When we're outside, you take care of this girl, understand? Watch out for her until she recovers. She's free of them, I bought her that much."

They passed a shrilling visorphone in a lighted kiosk at the far Tunnel mouth. A DOC alert was being scheduled for Philadelphia. Juve gangs were forming in the streets there, handmade knives were appearing. The mask was off. Full mobilization of combined TTIC and G/S industrial police was being ordered by Sprool. Cove clapped his hands.

Rain was falling as Finian led Dolly out of the Tunnel. Three DOC vertijets from the south were homing on Manhattan, agleam with emergency lights. Dolly murmured. Finian lifted her chin and stared into the doll-blue eyes a moment, conscious of the bomb working, working toward detonation in the flesh of his foot. He couldn't even feel the death seed. Wasn't that a joke?

"Cove'll take care of you," Finian said. He kissed her. Bewildered, Dolly called for him as he turned and walked rapidly away, not seeing the rain or the littered bodies.

He had gone but a dozen steps when something felled him and brought the dark.

Pain, incredible pain was his first sensation.

Then a warmth of flesh. Dolly bending over him. Through a slatted section of solido panel he saw vertijets winking over Manhattan. Finian wriggled, then struggled up, screaming:

"My leg . . . *what happened?*"

Crying, Dolly pressed him down.

"Cove did it. Cove operated. He hates them, Fin. He hates TTIC. Something about his wife. He said you ought to live, even with—I wish my mind would straighten out. I can't say things all right yet."

Finian fought the terror, the dull-fire agony. "Where is he?"

Dolly shuddered. "He packed it in a valise and ran for the Tunnel."

In a burst of fire the center of Manhattan Prison blew up.

When the reverberations and Dolly's screams had stopped, the two of them clung together, listening to the hysterical automatic sirens at both ends of the island wailing as they hadn't wailed since the Triple Play War. Confused, hurting, glad of life, guilty and fearsomely glad and yet sickened by the suddenly swarming sky full of vertijets, their flaring emergency lights promising violence across the land, violence maybe everywhere, Finian clutched the girl to his shoulder and stared at the inferno of the prison island.

"My God, I think I started a war, Dolly. Sprool said—I didn't mean to start—"

The words tore out of him, almost animal: *"Is this the only way?"*

Dolly sobbed. There wasn't any other answer, except the sirens multiplying all around in the disrupted night.

J. G. BALLARD

The Subliminal Man

J. G. Ballard is a British writer who has been called a "poet of death." But Ballard, especially in the early part of his career, also wrote excellent extrapolative science fiction on social themes, and this haunting story is one of his finest.

Here Ballard speaks of the enslavement of the unconscious, of an economic system that forces people to consume against their will through the use of technology. Ballard makes an important assumption—the belief (at least implicitly) that people would not want to consume at high rates if they were not "forced" to do so. In a profound sense, "The Subliminal Man" is a basic critique of the underlying dichotomy that pervades the concept of advertising—that of needs versus wants. We all have basic needs like food, sex, clothing, and shelter. Almost everything else (including the book you are now reading) is wants, often artificially created by the culture in which we live. Think how much more difficult resistance would become if the technology of subliminal advertising were forced upon us. This threat goes beyond the financial difficulties that families would be in. We would also be threatened with dehumanization, for it is the ability to think and chose that separates us from the rest of the animal world.

Ballard's story also assumes that industry will continue to manufacture products that will easily and quickly wear out, or if this is not the case, then it will find ways to make us dissatisfied with the products we now have. There is little evidence that things will change for the better.

"The signs, Doctor! Have you see the signs?"

Frowning with annoyance, Dr. Franklin quickened his pace and hurried down the hospital steps toward the line of parked cars. Over his shoulder he caught a glimpse of a thin, scruffy young man in ragged sandals and lime-stained jeans waving to him from the far side of the drive, then break into a run when he saw Franklin try to evade him.

"Dr. Franklin! The signs!"

Head down, Franklin swerved around an elderly couple approaching the outpatients department. His car was over a hundred yards away. Too tired to start running himself, he waited for the young man to catch him up.

"All right, Hathaway, what is it this time?" he snapped irritably. "I'm getting sick of you hanging around here all day."

Hathaway lurched to a halt in front of him, uncut black hair like an awning over his eyes. He brushed it back with a clawlike hand and turned on a wild smile, obviously glad to see Franklin and oblivious of the latter's hostility.

"I've been trying to reach you at night, Doctor, but your wife always puts the phone down on me," he explained without a hint of rancor, as if well used to this kind of snub. "And I didn't want to look for you inside the Clinic." They were standing by a privet hedge that shielded them from the lower windows of the main administrative block, but Franklin's regular rendezvous with Hathaway and his strange messianic cries had already been the subject of amused comment.

Franklin began to say: "I appreciate that—" but Hathaway brushed this aside. "Forget it, Doctor, there are more important things happening now. They've started to build the first big signs! Over a hundred feet high, on the traffic islands just outside town. They'll soon have all the approach roads covered. When they do we might as well stop thinking."

"Your trouble is that you're thinking too much," Franklin told him. "You've been rambling about these signs for weeks now. Tell me, have you actually seen one signaling?"

Hathaway tore a handful of leaves from the hedge, exasperated by this irrelevancy. "Of course I haven't, that's the whole point, Doctor." He dropped his voice as a group of nurses walked past, watching him uneasily out of the corners of their eyes. "The construction gangs were out again last night, laying huge power cables. You'll see them on the way home. Everything's nearly ready now."

"They're traffic signs," Franklin explained patiently. "The flyover has just been completed. Hathaway, for God's sake, relax. Try to think of Dora and the child."

"I *am* thinking of them!" Hathaway's voice rose to a controlled scream. "Those cables were 40,000-volt lines, Doctor, with terrific switch gear. The trucks were loaded with enormous metal scaffolds. Tomorrow they'll start lifting them up all over the city, they'll block off half the sky! What do you think Dora will be like after six months of that? We've got to stop them, Doctor, they're trying to transistorize our brains!"

Embarrassed by Hathaway's high-pitched shouting, Franklin had momentarily lost his sense of direction and helplessly searched the sea of cars for his own. "Hathaway, I can't waste any more time talking to you. Believe me, you need skilled help; these obsessions are beginning to master you."

Hathaway started to protest, and Franklin raised his right hand firmly. "Listen. For the last time, if you can show me one of these new signs, and prove that it's transmitting subliminal commands, I'll go to the police with you. But you haven't got a shred of evidence, and you know it. Subliminal advertising was banned thirty years ago, and the laws have never been repealed. Anyway, the technique was unsatisfactory; any success it had was marginal. Your idea of a huge conspiracy with all these thousands of giant signs everywhere is preposterous."

"All right, Doctor." Hathaway leaned against the bonnet of one of the cars. His moods seemed to switch abruptly from one level to the next. He watched Franklin amiably. "What's the matter—lost your car?"

"All your damned shouting has confused me." Franklin pulled out his ignition key and read the number off the tag: "NYN 299-566-367-21—can you see it?"

Hathaway leaned around lazily, one sandal up on the bonnet, surveying the square of a thousand or so cars facing them. "Difficult, isn't it, when they're all identical, even the same color? Thirty years ago there were about ten different makes, each in a dozen colors."

Franklin spotted his car, began to walk toward it. "Sixty years ago there were a hundred makes. What of it? The economies of standardization are obviously bought at a price."

Hathaway drummed his palm lightly on the roofs. "But these cars aren't all that cheap, Doctor. In fact, comparing them on an average income basis with those of thirty years ago they're about forty percent more expensive. With only one make being produced you'd expect a substantial reduction in price, not an increase."

"Maybe," Franklin said, opening his door. "But mechanically the cars of today are far more sophisticated. They're lighter, more durable, safer to drive."

Hathaway shook his head skeptically. "They *bore* me. The same model, same styling, same color, year after year. It's a sort of communism." He rubbed a greasy finger over the windshield. "This is a new one again, isn't it, Doctor? Where's the old one—you only had it for three months?"

"I traded it in," Franklin told him, starting the engine. "If you ever had any money you'd realize that it's the most economical way of owning a car. You don't keep driving the same one until it falls apart. It's the same with everything else—television sets, washing machines, refrigerators. But you aren't faced with the problem—you haven't got any."

Hathaway ignored the gibe, and leaned his elbow on Franklin's window. "Not a bad idea, either, Doctor. It gives me time to think. I'm not working a twelve-hour day to pay for a lot of things I'm too busy to use before they're obsolete."

He waved as Franklin reversed the car out of its line, then shouted into the wake of exhaust: "Drive with your eyes closed, Doctor!"

On the way home Franklin kept carefully to the slowest of the four-speed lanes. As usual after his discussions with Hathaway he felt vaguely depressed. He realized that unconsciously he envied Hathaway his footloose existence. Despite the grimy cold-water apartment in the shadow and roar of the flyover, despite his nagging wife and their sick child, and the endless altercations with the landlord and the supermarket credit manager, Hathaway still retained his freedom intact. Spared any responsibilities, he could resist the smallest encroachment upon him by the rest of society, if only by generating obsessive fantasies such as his latest one about subliminal advertising.

The ability to react to stimuli, even irrationally, was a valid criterion of freedom. By contrast, what freedom Franklin possessed was peripheral, sharply demarked by the manifold responsibilities in the center of his life—the three mortgages on his home, the mandatory rounds of cocktail and TV parties, the private consultancy occupying most of Saturday which paid the installments on the multitude of household gadgets, clothes and past holidays. About the only time he had to himself was driving to and from work.

But at least the roads were magnificent. Whatever other criticisms might be leveled at the present society, it certainly knew how to build roads. Eight-, ten- and twelve-lane expressways interlaced across the continent, plunging from overhead causeways into the giant car parks in the center of the cities, or dividing into the great suburban arteries with their multiacre parking aprons around the marketing centers. Together the roadways and car parks covered more than a third of the country's entire area, and in the neighborhood of the cities the proportion was higher. The old cities were surrounded by the vast, dazzling abstract sculptures of the cloverleafs and flyovers, but even so the congestion was unremitting.

The ten-mile journey to his home in fact covered over twenty-five miles and took him twice as long as it had done before the construction of the expressway, the additional miles contained within the three giant cloverleafs. New cities were springing from the motels, cafés and car marts around the highways. At the slightest hint of an intersection a shantytown of shacks and filling stations sprawled away among the forest of electric signs and route indicators, many of them substantial cities.

All around him cars bulleted along, streaming toward the suburbs. Relaxed by the smooth motion of the car, Franklin edged outward into the next speed lane. As he accelerated from 40 to 50 mph a strident, ear-jarring noise drummed out from his tires, shaking the chassis of the car. Ostensibly as an aid to lane discipline, the surface of the road was covered with a mesh of smaller rubber studs, spaced progressively farther apart in each of the lanes so that the tire hum resonated exactly on 40, 50, 60 and 70 mph. Driving at an intermediate speed for more than a few seconds became physiologically painful, and soon resulted in damage to the car and tires.

When the studs wore out they were replaced by slightly different patterns, matching those on the latest tires, so that regular tire changes were necessary, increasing the safety and efficiency of the expressway. It also increased the revenues of the car and tire manufacturers, for most cars over six months old soon fell to pieces under the steady battering, but this was regarded as a desirable end, the greater turnover reducing the unit price and making more frequent model changes, as well as ridding the roads of dangerous vehicles.

A quarter of a mile ahead, at the approach to the first of the cloverleafs, the traffic stream was slowing, huge police signs signaling "Lanes Closed Ahead" and "Drop Speed by 10 mph." Franklin tried to return to the previous lane, but the cars were jammed bumper to bumper. As the chassis began to shudder and vibrate, jarring his spine, he clamped his teeth and tried to restrain himself from sounding the horn. Other drivers were less self-controlled and everywhere engines were plunging and snarling, horns blaring. Road taxes were now so high, up to 30 percent of income (by contrast, income taxes were a bare 2 percent), that any delay on the expressways called for an immediate government inquiry, and the major departments of state were concerned with the administration of the road systems.

Nearer the cloverleaf the lanes had been closed to allow a gang of construction workers to erect a massive metal sign on one of the traffic islands. The palisaded area swarmed with engineers and surveyors and Franklin assumed that this was the sign Hathaway had seen unloaded the previous night. His apartment was in one of the gimcrack buildings in the settlement that straggled away around a nearby flyover, a low-rent area inhabited by service station personnel, waitresses and other migrant labor.

The sign was enormous, at least 100 feet high, fitted with heavy concave grilles similar to radar bowls. Rooted in a series of concrete caissons, it reared high into the air above the approach roads, visible for miles. Franklin craned up at the grilles, tracing the power cables from the transformers up into the intricate mesh of metal coils that covered their surface. A line of red aircraft-warning beacons was already alight along the top strut, and Franklin assumed that the sign was part of the ground approach system of the city airport ten miles to the east.

Three minutes later, as he accelerated down the two-mile link of straight highway to the next cloverleaf, he saw the second of the giant signs looming up into the sky before him.

Changing down into the 40 mph lane, Franklin uneasily watched the great bulk of the second sign recede in his rearview mirror. Although there were no graphic symbols among the wire coils covering the grilles, Hathaway's warnings still sounded in his ears. Without knowing why, he felt sure that the signs were not part of the airport approach system. Neither of them was in line with the principal air lanes. To justify the expense of siting them in the center of the expressway—the second sign required elaborate angled buttresses to support it on a narrow island—obviously meant that their role related in some way to the traffic streams.

Two hundred yards away was a roadside auto mart, and Franklin abruptly remembered that he needed some cigarettes. Swinging the car down the entrance ramp, he joined the queue slowly passing the self-service dispenser at the far end of the rank. The auto mart was packed with cars, each of the five purchasing ranks lined with tired-looking men hunched over their wheels.

Inserting his coins (paper money was no longer in circulation, unmanageable by the automats) he took a carton from the dispenser. This was the only brand of cigarettes available—in fact there was only one brand of everything—though giant economy packs were an alternative. Moving off, he opened the dashboard locker.

Inside, still sealed in their wrappers, were three other cartons.

A strong fishlike smell pervaded the house when he reached home, steaming out from the oven in the kitchen. Sniffing it uneagerly, Franklin took off his coat and hat, and found his wife crouched over the TV set in the lounge. An announcer was dictating a stream of numbers, and Judith scribbed them down on a pad, occasionally cursing under her breath. "What a muddle!" she snapped finally. "He was talking so quickly I took only a few things down."

"Probably deliberate," Franklin commented. "New panel game?"

Judith kissed him on the cheek, discreetly hiding the ashtray loaded with cigarette butts and chocolate wrappings. "Hullo, darling, sorry not to have a drink ready for you. They've started this series of Spot Bargains, they give you a selection of things on which you get a 90 percent trade-in discount at the local stores, if you're in the right area and have the right serial numbers. It's all terribly complicated."

"Sounds good, though. What have you got?"

Judith peered at her checklist. "Well, as far as I can see the only thing is the infrared barbecue spit. But we have to be there before eight o'clock tonight. It's seven-thirty already."

"Then that's out. I'm tired, angel, I need something to eat." When

Judith started to protest he added firmly: "Look, I don't want a new infrared barbecue spit, we've only had this one for two months. Damn it, it's not even a different model."

"But, darling, don't you see, it makes it cheaper if you keep buying new ones. We'll have to trade ours in at the end of the year anyway, we signed the contract, and this way we save at least twenty dollars. These Spot Bargains aren't just a gimmick, you know. I've been glued to that set all day." A note of irritation had crept into her voice, but Franklin sat his ground, doggedly ignoring the clock.

"Right, we lose twenty dollars. It's worth it." Before she could remonstrate he said: "Judith, please, you probably took the wrong number down anyway." As she shrugged and went over to the bar he called: "Make it a stiff one. I see we have health foods on the menu."

"They're good for you, darling. You know you can't live on ordinary foods all the time. They don't contain any proteins or vitamins. You're always saying we ought to be like people in the old days and eat nothing but health foods."

"I would, but they smell so awful." Franklin lay back, nose in the glass of whiskey, gazing at the darkened skyline outside.

A quarter of a mile away, gleaming out above the roof of the neighborhood supermarket, were the five red beacon lights. Now and then, as the headlamps of the Spot Bargainers swung up across the face of the building, he could see the square massive bulk of the giant sign clearly silhouetted against the evening sky.

"Judith!" He went into the kitchen and took her over to the window. "That sign, just behind the supermarket. When did they put it up?"

"I don't know." Judith peered at him curiously. "Why are you so worried, Robert? Isn't it something to do with the airport?"

Franklin stared thoughtfully at the dark hull of the sign. "So everyone probably thinks."

Carefully he poured his whiskey into the sink.

After parking his car on the supermarket apron at seven o'clock the next morning, Franklin carefully emptied his pockets and stacked the coins in the dashboard locker. The supermarket was already busy with early-morning shoppers and the line of thirty turnstiles clicked and slammed. Since the introduction of the "24-hour spending day" the shopping complex was never closed. The bulk of the shoppers were discount buyers, housewives contracted to make huge volume purchases of food, clothing and appliances against substantial overall price cuts, and forced to drive around all day from supermarket to supermarket, frantically trying to keep pace with their purchase schedules and grappling with the added incentives inserted to keep the schemes alive.

Many of the women had teamed up, and as Franklin walked over to the entrance a pack of them charged toward their cars, stuffing their pay slips into their bags and gesticulating at each other. A moment later their cars roared off in a convoy to the next marketing zone.

A large neon sign over the entrance listed the latest discount—a mere 5 percent—calculated on the volume of turnover. The highest discounts, sometimes up to 25 percent, were earned in the housing estates where junior white-collar workers lived. There, spending had a strong social incentive, and the desire to be the highest spender in the neighborhood was given moral reinforcement by the system of listing all the names and their accumulating cash totals on a huge electric sign in the supermarket foyers. The higher the spender, the greater his contribution to the discounts enjoyed by others. The lowest-spending were regarded as social criminals, free-riding on the backs of others.

Luckily this system had yet to be adopted in Franklin's neighborhood. Not because the professional men and their wives were able to exercise more discretion, but because their higher incomes allowed them to contract into more expensive discount schemes operated by the big department stores in the city.

Ten yards from the entrance Franklin paused, looking up at the huge metal sign mounted in an enclosure at the edge of the car park. Unlike the other signs and billboards that proliferated everywhere, no attempt had been made to decorate it, or disguise the gaunt bare rectangle of riveted steel mesh. Power lines wound down its sides, and the concrete surface of the car park was crossed by a long scar where a cable had been sunk.

Franklin strolled along, then fifty feet from the sign stopped and turned, realizing that he would be late for the hospital and needed a new carton of cigarettes. A dim but powerful humming emanated from the transformers below the sign, fading as he retraced his steps to the supermarket.

Going over to the automats in the foyer, he felt for his change, then whistled sharply when he remembered why he had deliberately emptied his pockets.

"The cunning thing!" he said, loud enough for two shoppers to stare at him. Reluctant to look directly at the sign, he watched its reflection in one of the glass door panes, so that any subliminal message would be reversed.

Almost certainly he had received two distinct signals—"Keep Away" and "Buy Cigarettes." The people who normally parked their cars along the perimeter of the apron were avoiding the area under the enclosure, the cars describing a loose semicircle fifty feet around it.

He turned to the janitor sweeping out the foyer. "What's that sign for?"

The man leaned on his broom, gazing dully at the sign. "Dunno," he said, "must be something to do with the airport." He had an almost fresh cigarette in his mouth, but his right hand reached unconsciously to his hip pocket and pulled out a pack. He drummed the second cigarette absently on his thumbnail as Franklin walked away.

Everyone entering the supermarket was buying cigarettes.

Cruising quietly along the 40 mph lane, Franklin began to take a closer interest in the landscape around him. Usually he was either too tired or too preoccupied to do more than think about his driving, but now he examined the expressway methodically, scanning the roadside cafés for any smaller versions of the new signs. A host of neon displays covered the doorways and windows, but most of them seemed innocuous, and he turned his attention to the larger billboards erected along the open stretches of the expressway. Many of these were as high as four-story houses, elaborate three-dimensional devices in which giant, glossy-skinned housewives with electric eyes and teeth jerked and postured around their ideal kitchens, neon flashes exploding from their smiles.

The areas of either side of the expressway were wasteland, continuous junkyards filled with cars and trucks, washing machines and refrigerators, all perfectly workable but jettisoned by the economic pressure of the succeeding waves of discount models. Their intact chrome hardly tarnished, the mounds of metal shells and cabinets glittered in the sunlight. Nearer the city the billboards were sufficiently close together to hide them, but now and then, as he slowed to approach one of the flyovers, Franklin caught a glimpse of the huge pyramids of metal, gleaming silently like the refuse grounds of some forgotten El Dorado.

That evening Hathaway was waiting for him as he came down the hospital steps. Franklin waved him across the court, then led the way quickly to his car.

"What's the matter, Doctor?" Hathaway asked as Franklin wound up the windows and glanced around the lines of parked cars. "Is someone after you?"

Franklin laughed somberly. "I don't know. I hope not, but if what you say is right, I suppose there is."

Hathaway leaned back with a chuckle, propping one knee up on the dashboard. "So you've seen something, Doctor, after all."

"Well, I'm not sure yet, but there's just a chance you may be right. This morning at the Fairlawne supermarket . . ." He broke off, uneasily remembering the huge blank sign and the abrupt way in which he had turned back to the supermarket as he approached it, then described his encounter.

Hathaway nodded slowly. "I've seen the sign there. It's big, but not as big as some that are going up. They're building them everywhere now. All over the city. What are you going to do, Doctor?"

Franklin gripped the wheel tightly. Hathaway's thinly veiled amusement irritated him. "Nothing, of course. Damn it, it may be just autosuggestion; you've probably got me imagining—"

Hathaway sat up with a jerk, his face mottled and savage. "Don't be absurd, Doctor! If you can't believe your own senses what chance have you left? They're invading your brain, if you don't defend yourself they'll take it over completely! We've got to act now, before we're all paralyzed."

Wearily Franklin raised one hand to restrain him. "Just a minute. Assuming that these signs *are* going up everywhere, what would be their object? Apart from wasting the enormous amount of capital invested in all the other millions of signs and billboards, the amounts of discretionary spending power still available must be infinitesimal. Some of the present mortgage and discount schemes reach half a century ahead, so there can't be much slack left to take up. A big trade war would be disastrous."

"Quite right, Doctor," Hathaway rejoined evenly, "but you're forgetting one thing. What would supply that extra spending power? A big increase in production. Already they've started to raise the working day from twelve hours to fourteen. In some of the appliance plants around the city Sunday working is being introduced as a norm. Can you visualize it, Doctor—a seven-day week, everyone with at least three jobs?''

Franklin shook his head. ''People won't stand for it.''

''They will. Within the last twenty-five years the gross national product has risen by fifty percent, but so have the average hours worked. Ultimately we'll all be working and spending twenty-four hours a day, seven days a week. No one will dare refuse. Think what a slump would mean—millions of layoffs, people with time on their hands and nothing to spend it on. Real leisure, not just time spent buying things.'' He seized Franklin by the shoulder. ''Well, Doctor, are you going to join me?''

Franklin freed himself. Half a mile away, partly hidden by the four-story bulk of the Pathology Department, was the upper half of one of the giant signs, workmen still crawling across its girders. The airlines over the city had deliberately been routed away from the hospital, and the sign obviously had no connection with approaching aircraft.

''Isn't there a prohibition on subliminal living? How can the unions accept it?''

''The fear of a slump. You know the new economic dogmas. Unless output rises by a steady inflationary five percent the economy is stagnating. Ten years ago increased efficiency alone would raise output, but the advantages there are minimal now and only one thing is left. More work. Increased consumption and subliminal advertising will provide the spur.''

''What are you planning to do?''

''I can't tell you, Doctor, unless you accept equal responsibility for it.''

''Sounds rather quixotic,'' Franklin commented. ''Tilting at windmills. You won't be able to chop those things down with an ax.''

''I won't try.'' Hathaway suddenly gave up and opened the door. ''Don't wait too long to make up your mind, Doctor. By then it may not be yours to make up.'' With a wave he was gone.

On the way home Franklin's skepticism returned. The idea of the conspiracy was preposterous, and the economic arguments were too plausible. As usual, though, there had been a hook in the soft bait Hathaway dangled before him—Sunday working. His own consultancy had been extended into Sunday morning with his appointment as visiting factory doctor to one of the automobile plants that had started

Sunday shifts. But instead of resenting this incursion into his already meager hours of leisure he had been glad. For one frightening reason—he needed the extra income.

Looking out over the lines of scurrying cars, he noticed that at least a dozen of the great signs had been erected along the expressway. As Hathaway had said, more were going up everywhere, rearing over the supermarkets in the housing developments like rusty metal sails.

Judith was in the kitchen when he reached home, watching the TV program on the handset over the cooker. Franklin climbed past a big cardboard carton, its seals still unbroken, which blocked the doorway, kissed her on the cheek as she scribbled numbers down on her pad. The pleasant odor of pot-roast chicken—or, rather, a gelatine dummy of a chicken fully flavored and free of any toxic or nutritional properties—mollified his irritation at finding her still playing the Spot Bargains.

He tapped the carton with his foot. "What's this?"

"No idea, darling, something's always coming these days, I can't keep up with it all." She peered through the glass door at the chicken—an economy 12-pounder, the size of a turkey, with stylized legs and wings and an enormous breast, most of which would be discarded at the end of the meal (there were no dogs or cats these days; the crumbs from the rich man's table saw to that)—and then glanced at him pointedly.

"You look rather worried, Robert. Bad day?"

Franklin murmured noncommittally. The hours spent trying to detect false clues in the faces of the Spot Bargain announcers had sharpened Judith's perceptions, and he felt a pang of sympathy for the legion of husbands similarly outmatched.

"Have you been talking to that crazy beatnik again?"

"Hathaway? As a matter of fact, I have. He's not all that crazy." He stepped backward into the carton, almost spilling his drink. "Well, what is this thing? As I'll be working for the next fifty Sundays to pay for it I'd like to find out."

He searched the sides, finally located the label. *"A TV set?* Judith, do we need another one? We've already got three. Lounge, dining room, and the handset. What's the fourth for?"

"The guest room, dear; don't get so excited. We can't leave a handset in the guest room, it's rude. I'm trying to economize, but four TV sets is the bare minimum. All the magazines say so."

"*And* three radios?" Franklin stared irritably at the carton. "If we do invite a guest here how much time is he going to spend alone in his room watching television? Judith, we've got to call a halt. It's not as if these things were free, or even cheap. Anyway, television is a total waste of time. There's only one program. It's ridiculous to have four sets."

"Robert, there are *four* channels."

"But only the commercials are different." Before Judith could reply the telephone rang. Franklin lifted the kitchen receiver, listened to the gabble of noise that poured from it. At first he wondered whether this was some offbeat prestige commercial, then realized it was Hathaway in a manic swing.

"Hathaway!" he shouted back. "Relax, man! What's the matter now?"

"—Doctor, you'll have to believe me this time. I tell you I got on to one of the islands with a stroboscope, they've got hundreds of high-speed shutters blasting away like machine guns straight into people's faces and they can't see a thing, it's fantastic! The next big campaign's going to be cars and TV sets; they're trying to swing a two-month model change—can you imagine it, Doctor, a new car every two months? God Almighty, it's just—"

Franklin waited impatiently as the five-second commercial break cut in (all telephone calls were free, the length of the commercial extending with range—for long-distance calls the ratio of commercial to conversation was as high as 10:1, the participants desperately trying to get a word in edgeways to the interminable interruptions), but just before it ended he abruptly put the telephone down, then removed the receiver from the cradle.

Judith came over and took his arm. "Robert, what's the matter? You look terribly strained."

Franklin picked up his drink and walked through into the lounge. "It's just Hathaway. As you say, I'm getting a little too involved with him. He's starting to prey on my mind."

He looked at the dark outline of the sign over the supermarket, its red warning lights glowing in the night sky. Blank and nameless, like an area forever closed off in an insane mind, what frightened him was its total anonymity.

"Yet I'm not sure," he muttered. "So much of what Hathaway says makes sense. These subliminal techniques are the sort of last-ditch attempt you'd expect from an overcapitalized industrial system."

He waited for Judith to reply, then looked up at her. She stood in the center of the carpet, hands folded limply, her sharp, intelligent face curiously dull and blunted. He followed her gaze out over the rooftops, then with an effort turned his head and quickly switched on the TV set.

"Come on," he said grimly. "Let's watch television. God, we're going to need that fourth set."

A week later Franklin began to compile his inventory. He saw nothing more of Hathaway; as he left the hospital in the evening the familiar scruffy figure was absent. When the first of the explosions sounded dimly around the city and he read of the attempts to sabotage the giant signs, he automatically assumed that Hathaway was responsible, but later he heard on a newscast that the detonations had been set off by construction workers excavating foundations.

More of the signs appeared over the rooftops, isolated on the palisaded islands near the suburban shopping centers. Already there were over thirty on the ten-mile route from the hospital, standing shoulder to shoulder over the speeding cars like giant dominoes. Franklin had given up his attempt to avoid looking at them, but the slim possibility that the explosions might be Hathaway's counterattack kept his suspicions alive.

He began his inventory after hearing the newscast, discovered that in the previous fortnight he and Judith had traded in their

Car (previous model 2 months old)
2 TV sets (4 months)
Power mower (7 months)
Electric cooker (5 months)
Hair dryer (4 months)
Refrigerator (3 months)
2 radios (7 months)
Record player (5 months)
Cocktail bar (8 months)

Half these purchases had been made by himself, but exactly when he could never recall realizing at the time. The car, for example, he had left in the garage near the hospital to be greased, that evening had signed for the new model as he sat at its wheel, accepting the salesman's assurance that the depreciation on the two-month trade-in was virtually less than the cost of the grease job. Ten minutes later, as he sped along the expressway, he suddenly realized that he had bought a new car. Similarly, the TV sets had been replaced by identical models after developing the same irritating interference pattern (curiously, the new sets also displayed the pattern, but as the salesman assured them, this promptly vanished two days later).

Not once had he actually decided of his own volition that he wanted something and then gone out to a store and bought it!

He carried the inventory around with him, adding to it as necessary, quietly and without protest analyzing these new sales techniques, wondering whether total capitulation might be the only way of defeating them. As long as he kept up even a token resistance, the inflationary growth curve would show a controlled annual 10 percent climb. With that resistance removed, however, it would begin to rocket upward out of control. . . .

Then, driving home from the hospital two months later, he saw one of the signs for the first time.

He was in the 40 mph lane, unable to keep up with the flood of new cars, had just passed the second of the three cloverleafs when the traffic half a mile away began to slow down. Hundreds of cars had driven up onto the grass verge, and a large crowd was gathering around one of the signs. Two small black figures were climbing up the metal face, and a series of huge gridlike patterns of light flashed on and off, illuminating the evening air. The patterns were random and broken, as if the sign was being tested for the first time.

Relieved that Hathaway's suspicions had been completely groundless, Franklin turned off onto the soft shoulder, then walked forward through the spectators as the lights blinked and stuttered in their faces. Below, behind the steel palisades around the island, was a large group of police and engineers, craning up at the men scaling the sign a hundred feet over their heads.

Suddenly Franklin stopped, the sense of relief fading instantly. With a jolt he saw that several of the police on the ground were armed with shotguns, and that the two policemen climbing the sign carried submachine guns slung over their shoulders. They were converging on a third figure, crouched by a switchbox on the penultimate tier, a ragged bearded man in a grimy shirt, a bare knee poking through his jeans.

Hathaway!

Franklin hurried toward the island, the sign hissing and spluttering, fuses blowing by the dozen.

Then the flicker of lights cleared and steadied, blazing out continuously, and together the crowd looked up at the decks of brilliant letters. The phrases, and every combination of them possible, were entirely familiar, and Franklin knew that he had been reading them unconsciously in his mind for weeks as he passed up and down the expressway.

BUY NOW BUY NOW BUY NOW BUY NOW BUY NOW
NEW CAR NOW NEW CAR NOW NEW CAR NOW
YES YES YES YES YES YES YES YES YES YES YES

Sirens blaring, two patrol cars swung up onto the verge through the crowd and plunged across the damp grass. Police spilled from its doors, batons in their hands, quickly began to force back the crowd. Franklin held his ground as they approached, started to say: "Officer, I know the man—" but the policeman punched him in the chest with the flat of his hand. Winded, he stumbled back among the cars, leaned helplessly against a fender as the police began to break the windshields, the hapless drivers protesting angrily, those farther back rushing for their vehicles.

The noise fell away abruptly when one of the submachine guns fired a brief roaring burst, then rose in a massive gasp of horror as Hathaway, arms outstretched, let out a cry of triumph and pain, and jumped.

"But, Robert, what does it really matter?" Judith asked as Franklin sat inertly in the lounge the next morning. "I know it's tragic for his wife and daughter, but Hathaway was in the grip of an obsession. If he hated advertising signs so much why didn't he dynamite those we *can* see, instead of worrying so much about those we can't?"

Franklin stared at the TV screen, hoping the program would distract him.

"Hathaway was *right*," he said simply.

"Was he? Advertising is here to stay. We've no real freedom of choice, anyway. We can't spend more than we can afford; the finance companies soon clamp down."

"You accept that?" Franklin went over to the window. A quarter of a mile away, in the center of the estate, another of the signs was being erected. It was due east from them, and in the early-morning light the shadows of its rectangular superstructure fell across the garden, reaching almost to the steps of the French windows at his feet. As a concession to the neighborhood, and perhaps to allay any suspicions while it was being erected by an appeal to petty snobbery, the lower sections had been encased in mock-Tudor paneling.

Franklin stared at it numbly, counting the half-dozen police lounging by their patrol cars as the construction gang unloaded prefabricated grilles from a couple of trucks. Then he looked at the sign by the supermarket, trying to repress his memories of Hathaway and the pathetic attempts the man had made to convince Franklin and gain his help.

He was still standing there an hour later when Judith came in, putting on her hat and coat, ready to visit the supermarket.

Franklin followed her to the door. "I'll drive you down there, Judith," he said in a flat dead voice. "I have to see about booking a new car. The next models are coming out at the end of the month. With luck we'll get one of the early deliveries."

They walked out into the trim drive, the shadows of the great signs swinging across the quiet neighborhood as the day progressed, sweeping over the heads of the people on their way to the supermarket like the dark blades of enormous scythes.

ISAAC ASIMOV

Dreaming Is a Private Thing

Goods obviously can have a price assigned to them. But what of abilities—can we really determine the worth of something like *creativity?* This fine story by Isaac Asimov considers the merchandising of creativity, but it raises other important issues as well. It anticipates (as Frederik Pohl has pointed out) how science fiction often alerts us to what we could be worrying about in future years. A current controversy exists over the impact of sex and violence on television on the behavior of individuals and groups. As Dr. Asimov shows in this story, the advent of new technologies may make current concerns seem mild. But he also recognizes an important economic truth—there will always be a market for quality.

Isaac Asimov has not written very much science fiction in recent years, and that's a shame, because even if dreaming is a private thing, SF writers share their dreams (at least some of them) with us, and for that we are the richer.

Jesse Weill looked up from his desk. His old spare body, his sharp high-bridge nose, deep-set shadowy eyes, and amazing shock of white hair had trademarked his appearance during the years that Dreams, Inc. had become world-famous.

He said, "Is the boy here already, Joe?"

Joe Dooley was short and heavyset. A cigar caressed his moist lower lip. He took it away for a moment and nodded. "His folks are with him. They're all scared."

"You're sure this is not a false alarm, Joe? I haven't got much time." He looked at his watch. "Government business at two."

"This is a sure thing, Mr. Weill." Dooley's face was a study in earnestness. His jowls quivered with persuasive intensity. "Like I told you, I picked him up playing some kind of basketball game in the schoolyard. You should've seen the kid. He stunk. When he had his hands on the ball, his own team had to take it away, and fast, but just the same he had all the stance of a star player. Know what I mean? To me it was a giveaway."

"Did you talk to him?"

"Well, sure. I stopped him at lunch. You know me." Dooley gestured expansively with his cigar and caught the severed ash with his other hand. " 'Kid,' I said—"

"And he's dream material?"

"I said, 'Kid, I just came from Africa and—' "

"All right." Weill held up the palm of his hand. "Your word I'll always take. How you do it I don't know, but when you say a boy is a potential dreamer, I'll gamble. Bring him in."

The youngster came in between his parents. Dooley pushed chairs forward, and Weill rose to shake hands. He smiled at the youngster in a way that turned the wrinkles of his face into benevolent creases.

"You're Tommy Slutsky?"

Tommy nodded wordlessly. He was about ten and a little small for that. His dark hair was plastered down unconvincingly, and his face was unrealistically clean.

Weill said, "You're a good boy?"

The boy's mother smiled at once and patted Tommy's head maternally (a gesture which did not soften the anxious expression on the youngster's face). She said, "He's always a very good boy."

Weill let this dubious statement pass. "Tell me, Tommy," he said, and held out a lollipop which was first hesitantly considered, then accepted. "Do you ever listen to dreamies?"

"Sometimes," said Tommy in an uncertain treble.

Mr. Slutsky cleared his throat. He was broad-shouldered and thick-fingered, the type of laboring man that, every once in a while, to the confusion of eugenics, sired a dreamer. "We rented one or two for the boy. Real old ones."

Weill nodded. He said, "Did you like them, Tommy?"

"They were sort of silly."

"You think up better ones for yourself, do you?"

The grin that spread over the ten-year-old features had the effect of taking away some of the unreality of the slicked hair and washed face.

Weill went on, gently: "Would you like to make up a dream for me?"

Tommy was instantly embarrassed. "I guess not."

"It won't be hard. It's very easy. . . . Joe."

Dooley moved a screen out of the way and rolled forward a dream recorder.

The youngster looked owlishly at it.

Weill lifted the helmet and brought it close to the boy. ''Do you know what this is?''

Tommy shrank away. ''No.''

''It's a thinker. That's what we call it because people think into it. You put it on your head and think anything you want.''

''Then what happens?''

''Nothing at all. It feels nice.''

''No,'' said Tommy, ''I guess I'd rather not.''

His mother bent hurriedly toward him. ''It won't hurt, Tommy. You do what the man says.'' There was an unmistakable edge to her voice.

Tommy stiffened and looked as though he might cry, but he didn't. Weill put the thinker on him.

He did it gently and slowly and let it remain there for some thirty seconds before speaking again, to let the boy assure himself it would do no harm, to let him get used to the insinuating touch of the fibrils against the sutures of his skull (penetrating the skin so finely as to be almost insensible), and finally to let him get used to the faint hum of the alternating field vortices.

Then he said, ''Now would you think for us?''

''About what?'' Only the boy's nose and mouth showed.

''About anything you want. What's the best thing you would like to do when school is out?''

The boy thought a moment and said, with rising inflection, ''Go on a stratojet?''

''Why not? Sure thing. You go on a jet. It's taking off right now.'' He gestured lightly to Dooley, who threw the freezer into circuit.

Weill kept the boy only five minutes and then let him and his mother be escorted from the office by Dooley. Tommy looked bewildered but undamaged by the ordeal.

Weill said to the father, ''Now, Mr. Slutsky, if your boy does well on this test, we'll be glad to pay you five hundred dollars each year until he finishes high school. In that time all we'll ask is that he spend an hour a week some afternoon at our special school.''

''Do I have to sign a paper?'' Slutsky's voice was a bit hoarse.

''Certainly. This is business, Mr. Slutsky.''

"Well, I don't know. Dreamers are hard to come by, I hear."

"They are. They are. But your son, Mr. Slutsky, is not a dreamer yet. He might never be. Five hundred dollars a year is a gamble for us. It's not a gamble for you. When he's finished high school, it may turn out he's not a dreamer, yet you've lost nothing. You've gained maybe four thousand dollars altogether. If he *is* a dreamer, he'll make a nice living and you certainly haven't lost then."

"He'll need special training, won't he?"

"Oh, yes, most intensive. But we don't have to worry about that till after he's finished high school. Then, after two years with us, he'll be developed. Rely on me, Mr. Slutsky."

"Will you guarantee that special training?"

Weill, who had been shoving a paper across the desk at Slutsky and punching a pen wrong side to at him, put the pen down and chuckled. "Guarantee? No. How can we when we don't know for sure yet if he's a real talent? Still, the five hundred a year will stay yours."

Slutsky pondered and shook his head. "I tell you straight out, Mr. Weill—after your man arranged to have us come here, I called Luster-Think. They said they'll guarantee training."

Weill sighed. "Mr. Slutsky, I don't like to talk against a competitor. If they say they'll guarantee training, they'll do as they say, but they can't make a boy a dreamer if he hasn't got it in him, training or not. If they take a plain boy without the proper talent and put him through a development course, they'll ruin him. A dreamer he won't be, that I guarantee you. And a normal human being he won't be, either. Don't take the chance of doing it to your son.

"Now Dreams, Inc. will be perfectly honest with you. If he can be a dreamer, we'll make him one. If not, we'll give him back to you without having tampered with him and say, 'Let him learn a trade.' He'll be better and healthier that way. I tell you, Mr. Slutsky—I have sons and daughters and grandchildren so I know what I say—I would not allow a child of mine to be pushed into dreaming if he's not ready for it. Not for a million dollars."

Slutsky wiped his mouth with the back of his hand and reached for the pen. "What does this say?"

"This is just an option. We pay you a hundred dollars in cash right now. No strings attached. We'll study the boy's reverie. If we feel it's worth following up, we'll call you in again and make the five-hundred-dollars-a-year deal. Leave yourself in my hands, Mr. Slutsky, and don't worry. You won't be sorry.''

Slutsky signed.

Weill passed the document through the file slot and handed an envelope to Slutsky.

Five minutes later, alone in the office, he placed the unfreezer over his own head and absorbed the boy's reverie intently. It was a typically childish daydream. First Person was at the controls of the plane, which looked like a compound of illustrations out of the filmed thrillers that still circulated among those who lacked the time, desire, or money for dream cylinders.

When he removed the unfreezer, he found Dooley looking at him.

''Well, Mr. Weill, what do you think?'' said Dooley with an eager and proprietary air.

''Could be, Joe. Could be. He has the overtones, and for a ten-year-old boy without a scrap of training it's hopeful. When the plane went through a cloud, there was a distinct sensation of pillows. Also the smell of clean sheets, which was an amusing touch. We can go with him a ways, Joe.''

''Good.'' Joe beamed happily at Weill's approval.

''But I tell you, Joe, what we really need is to catch them still sooner. And why not? Someday, Joe, every child will be tested at birth. A difference in the brain there positively must be, and it should be found. Then we could separate the dreamers at the very beginning.''

''Hell, Mr. Weill,'' said Dooley, looking hurt. ''What would happen to my job then?''

Weill laughed. ''No cause to worry yet, Joe. It won't happen in our lifetimes. In mine, certainly not. We'll be depending on good talent scouts like you for many years. You just watch the playgrounds and the streets''—Weill's gnarled hand dropped to Dooley's shoulder with a gentle approving pressure—''and find us a few more Hillarys and Janows, and Luster-Think won't ever catch us. . . . Now get out. I want lunch, and then I'll be ready for my two o'clock appointment. The government, Joe, the government.'' And he winked portentously.

Jesse Weill's two o'clock appointment was with a young man, apple-cheeked, spectacled, sandy-haired, and glowing with the intensity of a man with a mission. He presented his credentials across

Weill's desk and revealed himself to be John J. Byrne, an agent of the Department of Arts and Sciences.

"Good afternoon, Mr. Byrne," said Weill. "In what way can I be of service?"

"Are we private here?" asked the agent. He had an unexpected baritone.

"Quite private."

"Then, if you don't mind, I'll ask you to absorb this." Byrne produced a small and battered cylinder and held it out between thumb and forefinger.

Weill took it, hefted it, turned it this way and that, and said with a denture-revealing smile, "Not the produce of Dreams, Inc., Mr. Byrne."

"I didn't think it was," said the agent. "I'd still like you to absorb it. I'd set the automatic cutoff for about a minute, though."

"That's all that can be endured?" Weill pulled the receiver to his desk and placed the cylinder in the unfreeze compartment. He removed it, polished either end of the cylinder with his handkerchief, and tried again. "It doesn't make good contact," he said. "An amateurish job."

He placed the cushioned unfreeze helmet over his skull and adjusted the temple contacts, then set the automatic cutoff. He leaned back and clasped his hands over his chest and began absorbing.

His fingers grew rigid and clutched at his jacket. After the cutoff had brought absorption to an end, he removed the unfreezer and looked faintly angry. "A raw piece," he said. "It's lucky I'm an old man so that such things no longer bother me."

Byrne said stiffly, "It's not the worst we've found. And the fad is increasing."

Weill shrugged. "Pornographic dreamies. It's a logical development, I suppose."

The government man said, "Logical or not, it represents a deadly danger for the moral fiber of the nation."

"The moral fiber," said Weill, "can take a lot of beating. Erotica of one form or another has been circulated all through history."

"Not like this, sir. A direct mind-to-mind stimulation is much more effective than smoking-room stories or filthy pictures. Those must be filtered through the senses and lose some of their effect in that way."

Weill could scarcely argue that point. He said, "What would you have me do?"

"Can you suggest a possible source for this cylinder?"

"Mr. Byrne, I'm not a policeman."

"No, no, I'm not asking you to do our work for us. The Department is quite capable of conducting its own investigations. Can you help us, I mean, from your own specialized knowledge? You say your company did not put out that filth. Who did?"

"No reputable dream-distributor. I'm sure of that. It's too cheaply made."

"That could have been done on purpose."

"And no professional dreamer originated it."

"Are you sure, Mr. Weill? Couldn't dreamers do this sort of thing for some small, illegitimate concern for money—or for fun?"

"They could, but not this particular one. No overtones. It's two-dimensional. Of course, a thing like this doesn't need overtones."

"What do you mean—overtones?"

Weill laughed gently. "You are not a dreamie fan?"

Byrne tried not to look virtuous and did not entirely succeed. "I prefer music."

"Well, that's all right, too," said Weill tolerantly, "but it makes it a little harder to explain overtones. Even people who absorb dreamies might not be able to explain if you asked them. Still, they'd know a dreamie was no good if the overtones were missing, even if they couldn't tell you why. Look, when an experienced dreamer goes into reverie, he doesn't think a story like in the old-fashioned television or book-films. It's a series of little visions. Each one has several meanings. If you studied them carefully, you'd find maybe five or six. While absorbing them in the ordinary way, you would never notice, but careful study shows it. Believe me, my psychological staff puts in long hours on just that point. All the overtones, the different meanings, blend together into a mass of guided emotion. Without them, everything would be flat, tasteless.

"Now, this morning I tested a young boy. A ten-year-old with possibilities. A cloud to him isn't just a cloud; it's a pillow, too. Having the sensations of both, it was more than either. Of course, the boy's very primitive. But when he's through with his schooling, he'll be trained and disciplined. He'll be subjected to all sorts of sensations.

He'll store up experience. He'll study and analyze classic dreamies of the past. He'll learn how to control and direct his thoughts, though, mind you. I have always said that when a good dreamer improvises—''

Weill halted abruptly, then proceeded in less impassioned tones, ''I shouldn't get excited. All I'm trying to bring out now is that every professional dreamer has his own type of overtones which he can't mask. To an expert it's like signing his name on the dreamie. And I, Mr. Byrne, know all the signatures. Now that piece of dirt you brought me has no overtones at all. It was done by an ordinary person. A little talent, maybe, but like you and me, he can't think.''

Byrne reddened a trifle. ''Not everyone can't think, Mr. Weill, even if they don't make dreamies.''

''Oh, tush,'' and Weill wagged his hand in the air. ''Don't be angry with what an old man says. I don't mean *think* as in *reason,* I mean *think* as in *dream.* We all can dream after a fashion, just like we all can run. But can you and I run a mile in under four minutes? You and I can talk, but are we Daniel Websters? Now when I think of a steak, I think of the word. Maybe I have a quick picture of a brown steak on a platter. Maybe you have a better pictorialization of it, and you can see the crisp fat and the onions and the baked potato. I don't know. But a *dreamer* . . . he sees it and smells it and tastes it and everything about it, with the charcoal and the satisfied feeling in the stomach and the way the knife cuts through it, and a hundred other things all at once. Very sensual. Very sensual. You and I can't do it.''

''Well, then,'' said Byrne, ''no professional dreamer has done this. That's something, anyway.'' He put the cylinder in his inner jacket pocket. ''I hope we'll have your full cooperation in squelching this sort of thing.''

''Positively, Mr. Byrne. With a whole heart.''

''I hope so.'' Byrne spoke with a consciousness of power. ''It's not up to me, Mr. Weill, to say what will be done and what won't be done, but this sort of thing''—he tapped the cylinder he had brought—''will make it awfully tempting to impose a really strict censorship on dreamies.''

He rose. ''Good day, Mr. Weill.''

''Good day, Mr. Byrne. I'll hope always for the best.''

Francis Belanger burst into Jesse Weill's office in his usual steaming tizzy, his reddish hair disordered and his face aglow with worry and a mild perspiration. He was brought up sharply by the sight of Weill's head cradled in the crook of his elbow and bent on the desk until only the glimmer of white hair was visible.

Belanger swallowed. "Boss?"

Weill's head lifted. "It's you, Frank?"

"What's the matter, boss? Are you sick?"

"I'm old enough to be sick, but I'm on my feet. Staggering, but on my feet. A government man was here."

"What did he want?"

"He threatens censorship. He brought a sample of what's going around. Cheap dreamies for bottle parties."

"God damn!" said Belanger feelingly.

"The only trouble is that morality makes for good campaign fodder. They'll be hitting out everywhere. And to tell the truth, we're vulnerable, Frank."

"*We* are? Our stuff is clean. We play up adventure and romance."

Weill thrust out his lower lip and wrinkled his forehead.

"Between us, Frank, we don't have to make believe. Clean? It depends on how you look at it. It's not for publication, maybe, but you know and I know that every dreamie has its Freudian connotations. You can't deny it."

"Sure, if you *look* for it. If you're a psychiatrist—"

"If you're an ordinary person, too. The ordinary observer doesn't know it's there, and maybe he couldn't tell a phallic symbol from a mother image even if you pointed them out. Still, his subconscious knows. And it's the connotations that make many a dreamie click."

"All right, what's the government going to do? Clean up the subconscious?"

"It's a problem. I don't know what they're going to do. What we have on our side, and what I'm mainly depending on, is the fact that the public loves its dreamies, and won't give them up. . . . Meanwhile, what did you come in for? You want to see me about something, I suppose?"

Belanger tossed an object onto Weill's desk and shoved his shirttail deeper into his trousers.

Weill broke open the glistening plastic cover and took out the enclosed cylinder. At one end was engraved in a too-fancy script in pastel blue: *Along the Himalayan Trail*. It bore the mark of Luster-Think.

"The Competitor's Product." Weill said it with capitals, and his lips twitched. "It hasn't been published yet. Where did you get it, Frank?"

"Never mind. I just want you to absorb it."

Weill sighed. "Today everyone wants me to absorb dreams. Frank, it's not dirty?"

Belanger said testily, "It has your Freudian symbols. Narrow crevasses between the mountain peaks. I hope that won't bother you."

"I'm an old man. It stopped bothering me years ago, but that other thing was so poorly done it hurt. . . . All right, let's see what you've got here."

Again the recorder. Again the unfreezer over his skull and at the temples. This time Weill rested back in his chair for fifteen minutes or more, while Francis Belanger went hurriedly through two cigarettes.

When Weill removed the headpiece and blinked dream out of his eyes, Belanger said, "Well, what's your reaction, boss?"

Weill corrugated his forehead. "It's not for me. It was repetitious. With competition like this, Dreams, Inc. doesn't have to worry yet."

"That's your mistake, boss. Luster-Think's going to win with stuff like this. We've got to do something."

"Now, Frank—"

"No, you listen. This is the coming thing."

"This?" Weill stared with half-humorous dubiety at the cylinder. "It's amateurish. It's repetitious. Its overtones are very unsubtle. The snow had a distinct lemon sherbet taste. Who tastes lemon sherbet in snow these days, Frank? In the old days, yes. Twenty years ago, maybe. When Lyman Harrison first made his Snow Symphonies for sale down South, it was a big thing. Sherbet and candy-striped mountaintops and sliding down chocolate-covered cliffs. It's slapstick, Frank. These days it doesn't go."

"Because," said Belanger, "you're not up with the times, boss. I've got to talk to you straight. When you started the dreamie business, when you bought up the basic patents and began putting them out, dreamies were luxury stuff. The market was small and individual. You could afford to turn out specialized dreamies and sell them to people at high prices."

"I know," said Weill, "and we've kept that up. But also we've opened a rental business for the masses."

"Yes, we have, and it's not enough. Our dreamies have subtlety, yes. They can be used over and over again. The tenth time you're still finding new things, still getting new enjoyment. But how many people are connoisseurs? And another thing. Our stuff is strongly individualized. They're First Person."

"Well?"

"Well, Luster-Think is opening dream palaces. They've opened one with three hundred booths in Nashville. You walk in, take your seat, put on your unfreezer, and get your dream. Everyone in the audience gets the same one."

"I've heard of it, Frank, and it's been done before. It didn't work the first time, and it won't work now. You want to know why it won't work? Because in the first place, dreaming is a private thing. Do you like your neighbor to know what you're dreaming? In the second place, in a dream palace the dreams have to start on schedule, don't they? So the dreamer has to dream not when he wants to but when some palace manager says he should. Finally, a dream one person likes, another person doesn't like. In those three hundred booths, I guarantee you, a hundred and fifty people are dissatisfied. And if they're dissatisfied, they won't come back."

Slowly Belanger rolled up his sleeves and opened his collar. "Boss," he said, "you're talking through your hat. What's the use of proving they won't work? They *are* working. The word came through today that Luster-Think is breaking ground for a thousand-booth palace in St. Louis. People can get used to public dreaming if everyone else in the same room is having the same dream. And they can adjust themselves to having it at a given time, as long as it's cheap and convenient.

"Damn it, boss, it's a social affair. A boy and a girl go to a dream palace and absorb some cheap romantic thing with stereotyped overtones and commonplace situations, but still they come out with stars sprinkling their hair. They've had the same dream together. They've gone through identical sloppy emotions. They're *in tune,* boss. You bet they go back to the dream palace, and all their friends go, too."

"And if they don't like the dream?"

"That's the point. That's the nub of the whole thing. They're bound to like it. If you prepare Hillary specials with wheels within wheels within wheels, with surprise twists on the third-level undertones, with clever shifts of significance, and all the other things we're so proud of, why, naturally, it won't appeal to everyone. Specialized dreamies are for specialized tastes. But Luster-Think is turning out simple jobs in

Third Person so both sexes can be hit at once. Like what you've just absorbed. Simple, repetitious, commonplace. They're aiming at the lowest common denominator. No one will love it, maybe, but no one will hate it."

Weill sat silent for a long time, and Belanger watched him. Then Weill said, "Frank, I started on quality, and I'm staying there. Maybe you're right. Maybe dream palaces are the coming thing. If so, we'll open them, but we'll use good stuff. Maybe Luster-Think underestimates ordinary people. Let's go slowly and not panic. I have based all my policies on the theory that there's always a market for quality. Sometimes, my boy, it would surprise you how big a market."

"Boss—"

The sounding of the intercom interrupted Belanger.

"What is it, Ruth?" said Weill.

The voice of his secretary said, "It's Mr. Hillary, sir. He wants to see you right away. He says it's important."

"Hillary?" Weill's voice registered shock. Then, "Wait five minutes, Ruth, then send him in."

Weill turned to Belanger. "Today, Frank, is definitely not one of my good days. A dreamer should be at home with his thinker. And Hillary's our best dreamer, so he especially should be at home. What do you suppose is wrong with him?"

Belanger, still brooding over Luster-Think and dream palaces, said shortly, "Call him in and find out."

"In one minute. Tell me, how was his last dream? I haven't absorbed the one that came in last week."

Belanger came down to earth. He wrinkled his nose. "Not so good."

"Why not?"

"It was ragged. Too jumpy. I don't mind sharp transitions for the liveliness, you know, but there's got to be some connection, even if only on a deep level."

"Is it a total loss?"

"No Hillary dream is a *total* loss. It took a lot of editing, though. We cut it down quite a bit and spliced in some odd pieces he'd sent us now and then. You know, detached scenes. It's still not Grade A, but it will pass."

"You told him about this, Frank?"

"Think I'm crazy, boss? Think I'm going to say a harsh word to a dreamer?"

And at that point the door opened and Weill's comely young secretary smiled Sherman Hillary into the office.

Sherman Hillary, at the age of thirty-one, could have been recognized as a dreamer by anyone. His eyes, though unspectacled, had nevertheless the misty look of one who either needs glasses or who rarely focuses on anything mundane. He was of average height but underweight, with black hair that needed cutting, a narrow chin, a pale skin, and a troubled look.

He muttered, "Hello, Mr. Weill," and half-nodded in hangdog fashion in the direction of Belanger.

Weill said heartily, "Sherman, my boy, you look fine. What's the matter? A dream is cooking only so-so at home? You're worried about it? Sit down, sit down."

The dreamer did, sitting at the edge of the chair and holding his thighs stiffly together as though to be ready for instant obedience to a possible order to stand up once more.

He said, "I've come to tell you, Mr. Weill, I'm quitting."

"Quitting?"

"I don't want to dream anymore, Mr. Weill."

Weill's old face looked older now than at any other time during the day. "Why, Sherman?"

The dreamer's lips twisted. He blurted out, "Because I'm not *living,* Mr. Weill. Everything passes me by. It wasn't so bad at first. It was even relaxing. I'd dream evenings, weekends when I felt like it, or any other time. And when I didn't feel like it, I wouldn't. But now, Mr. Weill, I'm an old pro. You tell me I'm one of the best in the business and the industry looks to me to think up new subleties and new changes on the old reliables like the flying reveries and the worm-turning skits."

Weill said, "And is anyone better than you, Sherman? Your little sequence on leading an orchestra is selling steadily after ten years."

"All right, Mr. Weill, I've done my part. It's gotten so I don't go out anymore. I neglect my wife. My little girl doesn't know me. Last week we went to a dinner party—Sarah made me—and I don't remember a bit of it. Sarah says I was sitting on the couch all evening just staring at nothing and humming. She said everyone kept looking at me. She cried all night. I'm tired of things like that, Mr. Weill. I want to be a normal person and live in this world. I promised her I'd quit, and I will, so it's good-bye, Mr. Weill.'' Hillary stood up and held out his hand awkwardly.

Weill waved it gently away. ''If you want to quit, Sherman, it's all right. But do an old man a favor and let me explain something to you.''

''I'm not going to change my mind,'' said Hillary.

''I'm not going to try to make you. I just want to explain something. I'm an old man, and even before you were born I was in this business, so I like to talk about it. Humor me, Sherman? Please?''

Hillary sat down. His teeth clamped down on his lower lip, and he stared sullenly at his fingernails.

Weill said, ''Do you know what a dreamer is, Sherman? Do you know what he means to ordinary people? Do you know what it is to be like me, like Frank Belanger, like your wife Sarah? To have crippled minds that can't imagine, that can't build up thoughts? People like myself, ordinary people, would like to escape just once in a while this life of ours. We can't. We need help.

''In olden times it was books, plays, movies, radio, television. They gave us make-believe, but that wasn't important. What *was* important was that for a little while our own imaginations were stimulated. We could think of handsome lovers and beautiful princesses. We could be attractive, witty, strong, capable—everything we weren't.

''But always the passing of the dream from dreamer to absorber was not perfect. It had to be translated into words in one way or another. The best dreamer in the world might not be able to get any of it into words. And the best writer in the world could put only the smallest part of his dream into words. You understand?

''But now, with dream-recording, any man can dream. You, Sherman, and a handful of men like you supply those dreams directly and exactly. It's straight from your head into ours, full strength. You dream for a hundred million people every time you dream. You dream a hundred million dreams at once. This is a great thing, my boy. You give all those people a glimpse of something they could not have by themselves.''

Hillary mumbled, ''I've done my share.'' He rose desperately to his feet. "I'm through. I don't care what you say. And if you want to sue me for breaking our contract, go ahead and sue. I don't care."

Weill stood up, too. "Would I sue you? . . . Ruth"—he spoke into the intercom—"bring in our copy of Mr. Hillary's contract."

He waited. So did Hillary and Belanger. Weill smiled faintly, and his yellowed fingers drummed softly on his desk.

His secretary brought in the contract. Weill took it, showed its face to Hillary, and said, "Sherman, my boy, unless you *want* to be with me, it's not right you should stay."

Then before Belanger could make more than the beginning of a horrified gesture to stop him, he tore the contract into four pieces and tossed them down the waste chute. "That's all."

Hillary's hand shot out to seize Weill's. "Thanks, Mr. Weill," he said earnestly, his voice husky. "You've always treated me very well, and I'm grateful. I'm sorry it had to be like this."

"It's all right, my boy. It's all right."

Half in tears, still muttering thanks, Sherman Hillary left.

"For the love of Pete, boss, why did you let him go?" demanded Belanger. "Don't you see the game? He'll be going straight to Luster-Think. They've bought him off."

Weill raised his hand. "You're wrong. You're quite wrong. I know the boy, and this would not be his style. Besides," he added dryly, "Ruth is a good secretary, and she knows what to bring me when I ask for a dreamer's contract. The real contract is still in the safe, believe me.

"Meanwhile, a fine day I've had. I had to argue with a father to give me a chance at new talent, with a government man to avoid censorship, with you to keep from adopting fatal policies, and now with my best dreamer to keep him from leaving. The father I probably won out over. The government man and you, I don't know. Maybe yes, maybe no. But about Sherman Hillary, at least, there is no question. The dreamer will be back."

"How do you know?"

Weill smiled at Belanger and crinkled his cheeks into a network of fine lines. "Frank, my boy, you know how to edit dreamies so you think you know all the tools and machines of the trade. But let me tell you something. The most important tool in the dreamie business is the dreamer himself. He is the one you have to understand most of all, and I understand them.

"Listen. When I was a youngster—there were no dreamies then—I knew a fellow who wrote television scripts. He would complain to me bitterly that when someone met him for the first time and found out who he was, they would say: 'Where do you get those crazy ideas?'

"They honestly didn't know. To them it was an impossibility to even think of one of them. So what could my friend say? He used to talk to me about it and tell me: 'Could I say, "I don't know"? When I go to bed, I can't sleep for ideas dancing in my head. When I shave, I cut myself; when I talk, I lose track of what I'm saying; when I drive, I take my life in my hands. And always because ideas, situations, dialogues are spinning and twisting in my mind. I can't tell you where I get my ideas. Can you tell me, maybe, your trick of *not* getting ideas, so I, too, can have a little peace?

"You see, Frank, how it is. *You* can stop work here anytime. So can I. This is our job, not our life. But not Sherman Hillary. Wherever he goes, whatever he does, he'll dream. While he lives, he must think; while he thinks, he must dream. We don't hold him prisoner; our contract isn't an iron wall for him. His own skull is his prisoner. He'll be back. What can he do?"

Belanger shrugged. "If what you say is right, I'm sort of sorry for the guy."

Weill nodded sadly. "I'm sorry for all of them. Through the years I've found out one thing. It's their business: making people happy. Other people."

ROBERT SILVERBERG

Company Store

The entrepreneurial spirit does find expression in contemporary science fiction. This interesting story conveys an important message: to be in debt is to be a slave. In an earlier era of America's history entire towns were controlled by business enterprises which rented the houses the workers lived in, owned the retail outlets that sold them the staples of life and buried them (for a price) when they died. These company towns—and the workers' dilemma—have been immortalized in song by Tennessee Ernie Ford in "Sixteen Tons."

The salesman in Silverberg's tale has a compulsive drive to sell. In fact, the salesman must sell or face destruction, a fate that does not occur in the real world, unless one considers unemployment to be a form of destruction. The law in the story is on the side of the seller—it is strictly "buyer beware." Although written before the consumer movement, "Company Store" vividly portrays the feeling of entrapment present in the buyer-seller relationship.

Robert Silverberg is one of the finest contemporary science fiction writers. The excellence and the poetry of his recent work has overshadowed his creative social criticism, exemplified by stories like "Going Down Smooth," "Black Is Beautiful," and the present story.

Colonist Roy Wingert gripped his blaster with shaky hands. He took dead aim at the slimy wormlike creatures wriggling behind his newly deposited pile of crates.

They told me this planet was uninhabited, he thought. *Hah!*

He yanked back the firing stud. A spurt of violet light leaped out.

His nostrils caught the smell of roasting alien flesh. Shuddering, Wingert turned away from the mess before him, in time to see four more of the wormlike beings writhing toward him from the rear.

He ashed those. Two more dangled invitingly from a thick-boled tree at his left.

Getting into the spirit of the thing now, Wingert turned the beam on them, too. The clearing was beginning to look like the vestibule of an abattoir. Sweat ran down Wingert's face. His stomach was starting to get queasy, and his skin was cold at the prospect of spending his three-year tour on Quellac doing nothing but fighting off these overgrown night crawlers.

Two more of them were wriggling out of a decaying log near his feet. They were nearly six feet long, with saw-edged teeth glistening in Quellac's bright sunlight. *Nothing very dangerous,* Wingert thought grimly. *Ho!* He recharged the blaster and roasted the two newcomers.

Loud noises back of him persuaded him to turn. Something very much like a large gray toad, seven or eight feet high and mostly mouth, was hopping toward him through the forest. It was about thirty yards away now. It looked very hungry.

Squaring his shoulders, Wingert prepared to defend himself against this new assault. But just as he started to depress the firing stud, a motion to his far right registered in the corner of his eye. *Another* of the things—approaching rapidly from the opposite direction.

"Pardon me, sir," a sharp crackling voice said suddenly. "You seem to be in serious straits. May I offer you the use of this Duarm Pocket Force-Field Generator in this emergency? The cost is only—"

Wingert gasped. "*Damn* the cost! Turn the thing on! Those toads are only twenty feet away!"

"Of course, sir."

Wingert heard a click, and abruptly a shimmering blue bubble of force sprang up around them. The two onrushing pseudotoads cracked soundly into it and were thrown back.

Wingert staggered over to one of the packing cases and sat down limply. He was soaked with sweat from head to foot.

"Thanks," he said. "You saved my life. But who the hell are you, and where'd you come from?"

"Permit me to introduce myself. I am XL-ad41, a new-model Vending and Distributing Robot manufactured on Densobol II. I arrived here not long ago, and, perceiving your plight—"

Wingert saw now that the creature was indeed a robot, roughly humanoid except for a heavy pair of locomotory treads. "Hold on! Let's go back to the beginning." The toad things were eyeing him hungrily from outside the force-field. "You say you're a new-model *what?*"

"Vending and Distributing Robot. It is my function to diffuse through the civilized galaxy the goods and supplies manufactured by my creators, Associated Artisans of Densobol II.'' The robot's rubberized lips split in an oily smile. ''I am, you might say, a mechanized Traveling Salesman. Are you from Terra, perhaps?''

''Yes, but—''

''I thought as much. By comparing your physical appearance with the phenotype data in my memory banks I reached the conclusion that you were of Terra origin. The confirmation you have just given is most gratifying.''

''Glad to hear it. Densobol II is in the Magellanic Cluster, isn't it? Lesser or Greater Cloud?''

''Lesser. One matter puzzles me, though. In view of your Terran origin, it seems odd that you didn't respond when I mentioned that I am a traveling salesman.''

Wingert frowned. ''How was I supposed to respond? Clap my hands and wriggle my ears?''

''You were supposed to show humor response. According to my files on Terra, mention of traveling salesmen customarily strikes upon a common well of folklore implanted in the subconscious, thereby inducing a conscious humor reaction.''

''Sorry,'' Wingert apologized. ''I'm afraid I never was too interested in Earth. That's why I signed on with Planetary Colonization.''

''Ah, yes. I had just concluded that your failure to show response to standard folklore indicated some fundamental dislocation of your position relative to your cultural *Gestalt.* Again, confirmation is gratifying. As an experimental model, I'm subject to careful monitoring by my makers. I'm anxious to demonstrate my capability as a salesman.''

Wingert had almost completely recovered from his earlier exertions. He eyed the two toad beings uneasily and said, ''That force-field generator—that's one of the things you sell?''

''The Duarm Generator is one of our finest products. It's strictly one-way, you know. *They* can't get in, but you can still fire at them.''

''What? Why didn't you tell me that long ago?'' Wingert drew his blaster and disposed of the toad creatures with two well-placed shots.

''That's that,'' he said. ''I guess I sit inside this force-field and wait for the next ones, now.''

''Oh, they won't be along for a while,'' the robot said lightly. ''The creatures that attacked you are native to the next continent. They're not found here at all.''

"Then how'd they get here?"

"I brought them," the robot said sunnily. "I collected the most hostile creatures I could find on this world, and left them in your vicinity in order to demonstrate the necessity for the Duarm Force-Field Generat—"

"*You* brought them?" Wingert rose and advanced on the robot menacingly. "Deliberately, as a sales stunt? They could have killed and eaten me!"

"On the contrary. I was controlling the situation, as you saw. When matters became serious I intervened."

"Get out of here!" Wingert raged. "Go on, you crazy robot! I have to set up my bubble. Go!"

"But you owe me—"

"We'll settle up later. Get going, *fast!*"

The robot got. Wingert watched it scuttle off into the underbrush.

He tried to control his rage. Angry as he was, he felt a certain amusement at the robot's crude sales tactics. It was clever, in a coarse way, to assemble a collection of menacing aliens and arrive at the last minute to supply the force-field. But when you poison a man in order to sell him the antidote, you *don't* boast about it afterward to the victim!

He glanced speculatively at the forest, hoping the robot had told the truth. He didn't care to spend his entire tour on Quellac fighting off dangerous beasts.

The generator was still operating; Wingert studied it and found a cam that widened the field. He expanded it to a thirty-yard radius and left it that way. The clearing was littered with alien corpses.

Wingert shuddered.

Well, now that amusement was over, it was time to get down to business. He had been on Quellac just an hour, and had spent most of that time fighting for his life.

The Colonists' Manual said, *"The first step for a newly arrived colonist is to install his Matter-Transmitter."* Wingert closed the book and peered at the scattered pile of crates that were his possessions until he spied the large yellow box labeled *Matter-Transmitter, Handle With Care*.

From the box marked *Tools* he took a crowbar and delicately pried a couple of planks out of the packing crate. A silvery metallic object was visible within. Wingert hoped the Matter-Transmitter was in working order; it was his most important possession, his sole link to far-off Terra.

The Manual said, *"All necessities of life will be sent via matter-transmitter without cost."* Wingert smiled. Necessities of life? He could have magneboots, cigars, senso tapes, low-power, short-range matter-transmitters, dream pellets, bottled Martinis and nuclear fizzes, simply by requisitioning them. All the comforts of home. They had told him working for Planetary Colonization was rugged, but it was hardly that. Not with the Matter-Transmitter to take the sting out of pioneering.

Unless, Winger thought gloomily, *that lunatic robot brings some more giant toads over from the next continent.*

Wingert opened the packing crate and bared the Matter-Transmitter. It looked, he thought, like an office desk with elephantiasis of the side drawers; they bulged grotesquely, aproning out into shovel-shaped platforms, one labeled *"Send"* and the other *"Receive."*

An imposing-looking array of dials and meters completed the machine's face. Wingert located the red Activator Stud along the north perimeter and jammed it down.

The Matter-Transmitter came quiveringly to life.

Dials clicked; meters registered. The squarish device seemed to have taken on existence of its own. The viewscreen flickered polychromatically, then cleared.

A mild pudgy face stared out at Wingert.

"Hello. I'm Smathers, from the Earth Office. I'm the company contact man for Transmitters AZ-1061 right through BF-80. Can I have your name, registry number, and coordinates?"

"Roy Wingert, Number 76-032-10f3. The name of this planet is Quellac, and I don't know the coordinates offhand. If you'll give me a minute to check my contract—"

"No need of that," Smathers said. "Just let me have the serial number of your Matter-Transmitter. It's inscribed on the plate along the west perimeter."

Wingert found it after a moment's search. "AZ-1142."

"That checks. Well, welcome to the Company, Colonist Wingert. How's your planet?"

"Not so good," Wingert said.

"How so?"

"It's inhabited. By hostile aliens. And my contract said I was being sent to an uninhabited world."

"Read it again, Colonist Wingert. As I recall, it simply said you would meet no hostile creatures where *you* were. Our survey team reported some difficulties on the wild continent to your west but—"

"You see these dead things here?"

"Yes."

"I killed them. To save my own neck. They attacked me about a minute after the Company ship dropped me off here."

"They're obviously strays from that other continent," Smathers said. "Most unusual. Be sure to report any further difficulties of this sort."

"Sure," Wingert said. "Big comfort *that* is."

"To change the subject," Smathers said frigidly, "I wish to remind you that the Company stands ready to serve you. In the words of the contract, *'All necessities of life will be sent via Matter-Transmitter.'* That's in the Manual too. Would you care to make your first order now? The Company is extremely anxious that its employees are well taken care of."

Wingert frowned. "Well, I haven't even unpacked, you know. I don't think I need anything yet—except—yes! Send me some old-fashioned razor blades, will you? And a tube of shaving cream. I forgot to pack mine, and I can't stand these new vibroshaves."

Smathers emitted a suppressed chuckle. "You're not going to grow a beard?"

"No," Wingert said stiffly. "They itch."

"Very well, then. I'll have the routing desk ship a supply of blades and cream to Machine AZ-1142. So long for now, Colonist Wingert, and good luck. The Company sends its best wishes."

"Thanks," Wingert said sourly. "Same to you."

He turned away from the blank screen and glanced beyond the confines of his force-field. All seemed quiet, so he snapped off the generator.

Quellac, he thought, had the makings of a darned fine world, except for the beasts on the western continent. The planet was Earth-type, sixth in orbit around a small yellow main-sequence star. The soil was red with iron salts, but looked fertile enough, judging from the thick vegetation pushing up all around. Not far away a sluggish little stream wound through a sloping valley and vanished in a hazy cloud of purple mist near the horizon.

It would be a soft enough life, he thought, *if no more toads showed up. Or worms with teeth.*

The contract specified that his job was to "prepare and otherwise survey the world assigned, for the purpose of admitting future colonists under the auspices of Planetary Colonization, Inc." He was an advance agent, sent out by the Company to smooth the bugs out of the planet before the regular colonists arrived.

For this they gave him $1000 a month, plus "necessities of life" via Matter-Transmitter.

There were worse ways of making a living, Wingert told himself.

A lazy green-edged cloud was drifting over the forest. He pushed aside a blackened alien husk and sprawled out on the warm red soil, leaning against the Matter-Transmitter's comforting bulk. Before him were the eight or nine crates containing his equipment and possessions.

He had made the three-week journey from Earth to Quellac aboard the first-class liner *Mogred.* Matter-transmission would have been faster, but a Transmitter could handle a bulk of 150 pounds, which was Wingert's weight, only in three 50-pound installments. That idea didn't appeal to him. Besides, there had been no Matter-Transmitter set on Quellac to receive him, which made the whole problem fairly academic.

A bird sang softly. Wingert yawned. It was early afternoon, and he didn't feel impatient to set up his shelter. The Manual said it took but an hour to unpack. Later, then, when the sun was sinking behind those cerise mountains, he would blow his bubble home and unpack his goods. Right now he just wanted to relax, to let the tension of that first fierce encounter drain away.

"Pardon me, sir," said a familiar sharp voice. "I happened to overhear that order for razor blades, and I think it's only fair to inform you that I carry a product of much greater face appeal."

Wingert was on his feet in an instant, glaring at the robot. "I told you to go away. A-W-A-Y."

Undisturbed, the robot produced a small translucent tube filled with a glossy green paste. "This," XL-ad41 said, "is Gloglam's Depilating Fluid, twelve units—ah, one dollar, that is—per tube."

Wingert shook his head. "I get my goods free, from Terra. Besides, I like to shave with a razor. *Please* go away."

The robot looked about as crestfallen as a robot could possibly look. "You don't seem to understand that your refusal to purchase from me reflects adversely on my abilities, and may result in my being dismantled at the end of this test. Therefore I insist you approach my merchandise with an open mind."

A sudden grin of salesman-like inspiration illuminated XL-ad41's face. "I'll take the liberty of offering you this free sample. Try Gloglam's Depilating Fluid and I can guarantee you'll never use a blade-razor again."

The robot poured a small quantity of the green fluid into a smaller vial and handed it to Wingert. "Here. I'll return shortly to hear your decision."

The robot departed, trampling down the shrubbery with its massive treads. Wingert scratched his stubbly chin and regarded the vial quizzically.

Gloglam's Depilating Fluid, eh? And XL-ad41, the robot traveling salesman. He smiled wryly. On Earth they bombarded you with singing commericals, and here in the wilds of deep space robots from Densobol came descending on you trying to sell shaving cream.

Well, if the robot salesman were anything like its Terran counterparts, the only way he'd be able to get rid of it would be by buying something from it. And particularly since the poor robot seemed to be on a trial run, and might be destroyed if it didn't make sales. As a onetime salesman himself, Wingert felt sympathy.

Cautiously he squeezed a couple of drops of Gloglam's Depilating Fluid into his palm and rubbed it against one cheek. The stuff was cool and slightly sharp, with a pleasant twang. He rubbed it in for a moment, wondering if it might be going to dissolve his jawbone, then pulled out his pocket mirror.

His face was neat and pink where he'd applied the depilator. He hadn't had such a good shave in years. Enthusiastically he rubbed the remainder of the tube on his face, thereby discovering that the robot had given him just enough to shave one cheek and most of his chin.

Wingert chuckled. Bumbling and pedantic it might be, but the creature knew a little basic salesmanship, at least.

"Well?" XL-ad41 asked, reappearing as if beckoned. "Are you satisfied?"

Grinning, Wingert said, "That was pretty sly—giving me enough to shave half my face, I mean. But the stuff is good; there's no denying that."

"How many tubes will you take?"

Wingert pulled out his billfold. He had brought only $16 with him; he hadn't expected to have any use for Terran currency on Quellac, but there had been a ten, a five, and a one in his wallet at blast-off time.

"One tube," he said. He handed the robot the tattered single. XL-ad41 bowed courteously, reached into a pectoral compartment, and drew out the remainder of the tube he had shown Wingert before.

"Uh-uh," the Earthman said quickly. "That's the tube you took the sample from—and the sample was supposed to be free. I want a full tube.

"The proverbial innate shrewdness of the Terran," XL-ad41 observed mournfully. "I defer to it."

It gave a second tube to Wingert, who examined it and slid it into his tunic. "And now, if you'll excuse me, I have some unpacking to do," Wingert said.

He strode around the smiling robot, grabbed the crowbar, and began opening the crate that housed his bubble home. Suddenly the Matter-Transmitter emitted a series of loud buzzes followed by a dull *clonk*.

"Your machine has delivered something," XL-ad41 ventured.

Wingert lifted the lid of the "*Receive*" platform and drew out a small package wrapped neatly in plastofil. He peeled away the wrapping.

Within was a box containing twenty-four double-edged blades, a tube of shaving cream and a bill folded lengthwise. Wingert read it:

Razor blades, as ordered		$00.23
Shaving cream, as ordered		00.77
Charge for transportation		50.00
	Total	$51.00

"You look pale," the robot said. "Perhaps you have some disease. You might be interested in purchasing the Derblong Self-Calibrating Medical Autodiagnostical Servomechanism, which I happen to—"

"No," Wingert said grimly. "I don't need anything like that. Get out of my way."

He stalked back to the Transmitter and jabbed down savagely on the Activator Stud. A moment later Smathers' bland voice said, "Hello, Colonist Wingert. Something wrong?"

"There sure is," Wingert said in a strangled voice. "My razor blades just showed up—with a $50 bill for transportation! What kind of racket is this, anyway? I was told that you'd ship my supplies out free of charge. It says in the contract—"

"The contract says," Smathers interrupted smoothly, "that all necessities of life will be transmitted without cost, Colonist Wingert. It makes no mention of free supply of luxuries. The Company would be unable to bear the crushing financial burden of transporting any and all luxury items a colonist might desire."

"Razor blades are luxury items?" Wingert choked back an impulse to kick the Transmitter's control panel in. "How can you have the audacity to call razor blades *luxury items?"*

"Most colonists let their beards grow," Smathers said. "Your reluctance to do so, Colonist Wingert, is your own affair. The Company—"

"I know. The Company cannot be expected to bear the crushing financial burden. Okay," Wingert said. "In the future I'll be more careful about what I order. And as for now, take these damned razor blades back and cancel the requisition." He dumped the package in the *"Send"* bin and depressed the control stud.

"I'm sorry you did that," Smathers said. "It will now be necessary for us to assess you an additional $50 to cover the return shipping."

"What?"

"However," Smathers went on, "we'll see to it after this that you're notified in advance anytime there may be a shipping charge on goods sent to you."

"Thanks," Wingert said hoarsely.

"Since you don't want razor blades, I presume you're going to grow a beard. I rather thought you would. Most colonists do, you know."

"I'm not growing any beards. Some vending robot from the Densobol system wandered through here about ten minutes ago and sold me a tube of depilating paste."

Smathers' eyes nearly popped. "You'll have to cancel that purchase," he said, his voice suddenly stern.

Wingert stared incredulously at the pudgy face in the screen. "Now you're going to interfere with that, *too?*"

"Purchasing supplies from anyone but the Company is a gross violation of your contract, Colonist Wingert! It makes you subject to heavy penalty! After all, we agreed to supply you with your needs. For you to call in an outside supplier is to rob the Company of its privilege of serving you, Colonist Wingert. You see?"

Wingert was silent for almost a minute, too dizzy with rage to frame words. Finally he said, "So I get charged $50 shipping costs every time I requisition razor blades from you people, but if I try to buy depilating paste on my own it violates my contract? Why, that's—that's usury! Slavery! It's illegal!"

The voice from the Matter-Transmitter coughed warningly. "Powerful accusations, Colonist Wingert. I suggest that before you hurl any more abuse at the Company you read your contract more carefully."

"I don't give a damn about the contract! I'll buy anywhere I please!"

Smathers grinned triumphantly. "I was afraid you'd say that. You realize that you've now given us legal provocation to slap a spybeam on you in order to make sure you don't cheat us by violating your contract?"

Wingert sputtered. "Spybeam? But—I'll smash your accursed Transmitter! *Then* try to spy on me!"

"We won't be able to," Smathers conceded. "But destroying a Transmitter is a serious felony, punishable by heavy fine. Good afternoon, Colonist Wingert."

"Hey! Come back here! You can't—"

Wingert punched the Activator Stud three times, but Smathers had broken the contact and would not reopen it.

Scowling, Wingert turned away and sat down on the edge of a crate.

"Can I offer you a box of Sugrath Anti-Choler Tranquilizing Pills?" XL-ad41 said helpfully. "Large economy size."

"Shut up and leave me alone!"

Wingert stared moodily at the shiny tips of his boots. The Company, he thought, had him sewed up neatly. He had no money and no way of returning to Earth short of dividing himself into three equal chunks and teleporting. And though Quellac was an attractive planet, it lacked certain aspects of Earth. Tobacco, for one. Wingert enjoyed smoking.

A box of cigars would be $2.40 plus $75 shipping costs. And Smathers would smirk and tell him cigars were luxuries.

Sensotapes? Luxuries. Short-range transmitters? Maybe those came under the contract, since they were tools. But the pattern was clear. By the time his three-year tour was up, there would be $36,000 in salary waiting in his account—minus the various accumulated charges. He'd be lucky if he came out owing less than $20,000.

Naturally, he wouldn't have that sort of money, and so the benevolent Company would offer a choice: either go to jail or take another three-year term to pay off your debt. So they'd ship him someplace else, and at the end of that time he'd be in twice as deep.

Year after year he would sink further into debt, thanks to that damnable contract. He'd spend the rest of his life opening up new planets for Planetary Colonizations, Inc., and never have anything to show for it but a staggering debt.

It was worse than slavery.

There had to be some way out.

But after ransacking the contract for nearly an hour, Wingert concluded that it was airtight.

Angrily he glared up at the beaming robot.

"What are you hanging around here for? You've made your sale. Shove off!"

XL-ad41 shook its head. "You still owe me $500 for the generator. And surely you can't expect me to return to my manufacturers after having made only two sales. Why, they'd turn me off in an instant and begin developing an XL-ad42!"

"Did you hear what Smathers said? I'll be violating my contract if they see me buying anything more from you. Go on, now. Take your generator back. The sale is cancelled. Visit some other planet; I'm in enough hot water as it is without—"

"Sorry," the robot said, and it seemed to Wingert that there was an ominous note in its mellow voice. "This is the seventeenth planet I've called at since being sent forth by my manufacturers, and I have no sale to show for it but one tube of Gloglam Depilating Fluid. It's a poor record. I don't dare return yet."

"Try somewhere else, then. Find a planet full of suckers and give 'em the hard sell. I can't buy from you."

"I'm afraid you'll have to," the robot said mildly. "My specifications call for me to return to Densobol for inspection after my seventeenth visit." A panel in the robot's abdomen opened whirringly and Wingert saw the snout of a Molecular Disruptor emerge.

"The ultimate sales tactic, eh? If the customer won't buy, pull a gun and *make* him buy. Except it won't work here. I haven't any money."

"Your friends on Terra will send some. I *must* return to Densobol with a successful sales record. Otherwise—"

"I know. They'll dismantle you."

"Correct. Therefore, I must approach you this way. And I fully intend to carry out my threat if you refuse."

"Hold on here!" a new voice cut in. "What's going on, Wingert?"

Wingert glanced at the Transmitter. The screen was lit, and Smathers' plump face glared outward at him.

"It's this robot," Wingert said. "It's under some sort of sales compulsion, and it just pulled a gun on me."

"I know. I saw the whole thing on the spybeam."

"I'm in a nice spot now," Wingert said dismally. He glanced from the waiting robot to the unsmiling Smathers. "If I don't buy from this robot, it'll murder me—and if I *do* buy anything, you'll spy it and fine me." Wingert wondered vaguely which would be worse.

"I stock many fine devices unknown on Earth," the robot said proudly. "A Pioneer-Model Dreeg-Skinner, in case there are dreegs on Quellac—though frankly I doubt that. Or else you might want our Rotary Diatom-Strainer, or perhaps a new-model Hegley Neuronic Extractor—"

"Quiet," Wingert snapped. He turned back to Smathers. "Well, what do I do? You're the Company; protect your colonist from this marauding alien."

"We'll send you a weapon, Colonist Wingert."

"And have me try to outdraw a robot? You're a lot of help," Wingert said broodingly. Even if he escaped somehow from this dilemma, he knew the Company still had him by the throat over the "Necessities of Life" clause. His accumulated shipping charges in three years would—

He sucked his breath in sharply. "Smathers?"

"Yes?"

"Listen to me: if I don't buy from the robot, it'll blast me with a Molecular Disruptor. But I *can't* buy from the robot, even if the Company would let me, because I don't have any money. Money's necessary if I want to stay alive. Get it? *Necessary?*"

"No," Smathers said. "I don't get it."

"What I'm saying is that the item I most need to preserve my life is money. It's a *necessity of life.* And therefore you have to supply me gratis with all the money I need, until this robot decides it's sold me enough. If you don't come through, I'll sue the Company for breach of contract."

Smathers grinned. "Try it. You'll be dead before you can contact a lawyer. The robot will kill you."

Sweat poured down Wingert's back, but he felt the moment of triumph approaching. Reaching inside his khaki shirt, he drew out the thick pseudoparchment sheet that was his contract.

"You refuse! You refuse to supply a necessity of life! The contract," Wingert declared, "is therefore void." Before Smathers' horrified gaze he ripped the document up and tossed the pieces over his shoulder carelessly.

"Having broken your end of the contract," Wingert said, "you relieve me of all further obligations to the Company. Therefore I'll thank you to remove your damned spybeam from my planet."

"*Your* planet?"

"Precisely. Squatter's rights—and since there's no longer a contract between us, you're forbidden by galactic law to spy on me!"

Smathers looked dazed. "You're a fast talker, Wingert. But we'll fight this. Wait till I refer this upstairs. You won't get out of this so easily!"

Wingert flashed a cocky grin. "Refer it upstairs, if you want. I've got the law on my side."

Smathers snarled and broke the contact.

"Nicely argued," said XL-ad41 approvingly. "I hope you win your case."

"I have to," Wingert said. "They can't touch me, not if their contract is really binding on both parties. If they try to use their spybeam record as evidence against me, it'll show you threatening me. They don't have a leg to stand on."

"But how about me? I—"

"I haven't forgotten. There is a Molecular Disruptor in your belly waiting to disrupt me." Wingert grinned at the robot. "Look here, XL-ad41, face facts: you're a lousy salesman. You have a certain degree of misused guile, but you lack tact, subtlety. You can't go selling people things at gunpoint very long without involving your manufacturers in an interstellar war. As soon as you get back to Densobol and they find out what you've done, they'll dismantle you quicker than you can sell a Dreeg-Skinner."

"I was thinking that myself," the robot admitted.

"Good. But I'll make a suggestion: I'll *teach* you how to be a salesman. I used to be one, myself; besides, I'm an Earthman, and innately shrewd. When I'm through with you, you move on to the next planet—I think your makers will forgive you if you make an extra stop—and sell out all your stock."

"It sounds wonderful," XL-ad41 said.

"One string is attached. In return for the education I'll give you, you're to supply me with such things as I need to live comfortably here on a permanent basis. Cigars, magneboots, short-range transmitters, depilator, etc. I'm sure your manufacturers will think it's a fair exchange, my profit-making shrewdness for your magneboots. Oh, and I'll need one of those force-field generators too—just in case the Company shows up and tries to make trouble."

The robot glowed happily. "I'm sure such an exchange can be arranged. I believe this now makes us partners."

"It does indeed," Wingert said. "As your first lesson, let me show you an ancient Terran custom that a good salesman ought to know." He gripped the robot's cold metal hand firmly in his own. "Shake, partner!"

RALPH WILLIAMS

Business as Usual, During Alterations

Throughout most of recorded history mankind has lived within an economy of scarcity. Only in the last half-century have technological developments made an economy of abundance possible, at least in the West and Japan. The costs involved in this process were high, not only in terms of human exploitation but also in more subtle ways. For example, the explosion of available consumer goods has produced considerable confusion, part of the "future shock" phenomenon of being surrounded by so much diversity that it is difficult to enjoy any of it.

Because technological change has been so rapid, entire industries have been created and wiped out almost overnight. The resourcefulness often shown by the businessman to these developments has been little short of amazing—the transition from a literally "horse-powered" transportation system to the automobile and from the blacksmith to the mechanic are but examples.

"Business as Usual, During Alterations" presents members of the business community facing the greatest crisis in the history of economic relationships. Competition is supposed to be the essence of the Free Enterprise System (at least on paper)—but it was never supposed to be like this.

The Sector Coordinator frowned, studying the report on his desk. In the concise symbology of sociodynamic calculus, it still covered several pages. "Preposterous!" he said. "Utterly preposterous!"

The Chief of the Observation Team nodded. "Quite," he agreed. "Valid, though."

"But it's ridiculous. Your prognosis indicates complete self-extermination by the natives of this planet . . . uh . . . 'Earth,' in less than one Galactic quarter. It's . . . well, *preposterous!*"

"Exactly," the observer said.

"But we can't have it. We *need* this planet. The only inhabited system in fifty light-years, a civilization just on the verge of technological expansion, young, vigorous—and now, *this*. We'll have to assume direct control, move in a full administrative staff . . . why, it will cost billions, we could set up a colony of our own almost as cheaply. There must be a mistake.'' The Coordinator flipped back through the pages.

''Ah,'' he exclaimed. ''Thought so. Here, this intergroup belligerence function, a purely inductive generalization which you apply in an unprecedented situation. Not valid. In effect, you are saying these people cannot adjust. Why, their whole history is one of adaptation—they take anything, absolutely anything, according to your observational data, and adapt it to their ends.''

The Chief Observer nodded. ''Individual ends, though, not social ends. That's the crux. Me first, to hell with the other guy. Works well enough when one man can't reach much farther than he can throw a rock, or shout orders more than a few hundred yards. Not so well, though, when you can say 'jump, frog,' to a whole continent at once, and back it up with hydrogen bombs. To control that level of power, you need cultural adaptability, instinctive or reasoned. These people don't have either.'' He paused and scratched thoughtfully at his chin, or what would have been his chin, if he had been human.

''I will admit, though, the math is a little shaky. So, we've prepared a check. With your approval, we intend to introduce a gadget to these people. Nonlethal, individually desirable, but culturally deadly—so presented that they can accept or reject it, with the choice spelled out for them. The beauty of it is, we kill two birds with one stone. If they accept—blooey goes their civilization; all we have to do is move in and fill the vacuum. If they reject, we don't have to move in, I'm wrong.''

''What kind of gadget?''

''Well, what kind of gadget would do it? Remember, a highly competitive culture, based on economy of scarcity; things—property, or its use—exchanged for services on an individual basis . . .''

''The matter duplicator!''

''Exactly.''

It was about midmorning, I suppose, when we began to hear the first rumors of the duplicator at Brown's.

One of the account clerks came running over to tell me about it during the morning coffee break. The story was that someone had invented a machine which could reproduce instantly, out of thin air, any physical object. She had it from one of the other girls, who got it from an elevator operator, who got it from a customer.

In a big store like Brown's, with so many women working, you hear all kinds of rumor. "Well, that's certainly very interesting," I told her. "What won't they think of next! I'll have to be sure to catch the eleven o'clock news."

A few minutes later, however, Pete Martens in Appliances called up to tell me it was on TV. "You'd better take a look, Mr. Thomas," he said. "If this isn't a gag, it's something pretty big."

"Thank you, Pete," I said. "I'll be right down." I don't keep a TV in my office; it's a bad example to set for executive personnel, I feel.

There were several knots of customers and salespeople clustered around the demonstrators in Appliances. Pete saw me step out of the elevator and opened up a place. "Right here, Mr. Thomas," he said.

I nodded thanks and looked at the screen. A man sat behind a desk, talking. On the desk was a black box, a cube about ten inches on a side, with two pans, side by side, on top—something like a kitchen scales. A red button was set in the face of the cube. Below it was a plate with some printing.

". . . Anything small enough to place on the pan," the man was saying, "absolutely anything." He picked up a pair of desk shears, tossed them on one pan, pushed the button. An identical pair instantly appeared on the other pan. He rummaged in his pocket, brought out a key ring, duplicated that. He took off his glasses, duplicated them.

"Or," he said, "you can do this. Hand me that other duplicator, please." A hand came into the picture, holding a contraption similar to the one the demonstrator had been using. He placed it on one pan, pushed the button, removed it and the duplicate. With a careless gesture, he swept the original machine off the desk. It crashed when it hit the floor. He smiled and looked into the camera.

"Don't worry, folks," he said. "There's plenty more where that came from." With the machine he had just made he duplicated another, another, another, until the desk was covered with them.

"How do they work?" I asked Martens.

He strugged. "Nobody knows. There were a couple of them sitting on the city hall steps this morning. No name plates, no identification, just a tag telling how to work them and something about chipping foundations. They had the back off one just before you came down; it looks like some sort of electronic gadget, but the studio engineers couldn't figure it out, so they sent a couple over to the university. Stumped them, too.'' He laughed nervously. ''Maybe the brownies left them.''

''. . . Just one thing to remember, folks,'' the TV was saying. I looked back at the screen. The duplicators had been removed, except for one, and the man was holding a hamster in the palm of one hand. ''*Don't* try to duplicate little Johnny because he's so cute you'd like a dozen of him.''

He placed the hamster on one pan, pushed the button. The duplicated hamster jumped high in the air at the moment of materialization and fell to the desk, jerking violently for a moment before it was still. The original crept to the edge of the pan and stared at it, nose twitching.

''Do you think it could be a hoax?'' I asked Martens. ''You know, trick photography, something like that?''

He shook his head. ''I don't think so. It's on the other channels too, this fellow's putting on the best show, but they're all full of it. Radio, too.''

''He's putting on a good show, all right.'' I looked at the customers around me, all hanging pop-eyed on the demonstrator's slightest move. ''If we just had a few thousand of those things here in the store right now, with all this buildup—''

''Well, yes,'' Martens said. ''It kind of scares me, though. You know, all those things, just make anything you want, as many as you want, zip, zip, zip, like that. What I mean, my brother *works* in a place where they make things like scissors. What about him?''

I nodded thoughtfully. ''I see what you mean. That duplicator, it could be a whole factory in itself, no materials costs, no labor costs—why, it'll wreck the whole price structure. No buying; we can set up a few duplicators and make our own merchandise. No inventory; we stock just one of everything. Receiving? We wipe out the whole department. Warehousing? Ditto.'' I began really to see possibilities. ''Pete,'' I said, ''you're right, this is big, really big.'' I looked around for a phone. ''I'd better call Mr. Brown right now.''

Mr. Brown must have been watching the same program at home. I could hear it in the background, something about bigger duplicators now.

''Yes, I know, John.'' His voice sounded dead. ''I've been watching it. Probably means the end of our whole economy, I suppose. Did you read what that tag on the machine said?''

''Martens said something about chipping foundations.''

''I copied it down—just a minute—here it is. There was something about how to operate the machine, then this: *'Warning! A push of the button grants your heart's desire. It is also a chip at the foundations of human society. A few billion such chips will bring it crashing down. The choice is yours.'* Well, I guess the chips are flying already. My General Motors stock—'' He groaned.

Over in the appliance department I caught a glimpse of the screen. A toy automobile was on one pan of the duplicator. The announcer was using a toy crane to lift duplicates off the other pan, ranging them in neat rows on the desk top.

''But what about the store, Mr. Brown?'' I asked.

''I don't know, John, I just don't know. You're there, you do the best you can, just hang tough till we see how things are going to work out.''

Hang tough! In this business, people who hang tough and wait to see how things work out get plowed under. If you want to stay in business, you get on top of trends and move with them. Well, Mr. Brown used to be a real merchant, he built Brown's up from a corner variety store; but that was forty years ago and we all get old.

''O.K., Mr. Brown,'' I said. ''I'll do what I can.''

''Fine, John, I know you will.''

He hung up. Before I could do the same, the operator broke in. ''Oh, Mr. Thomas,'' she said. ''Mrs. Jones wants you in Ladies' Wear; she says it's emergency.''

Mrs. Jones is one of those people to whom everything is an emergency, but Ladies' Wear is on the first floor, only a few aisles from the phone I had been using. ''Thank you, Connie,'' I said. ''I'll take care of it.''

When I got over there, Mrs. Jones was flustering around a stocky, middle-aged man who was fooling with something on the wrapping counter. It was a duplicator. He was trying to balance another on one of the pans. It kept tipping until he got a pencil fixed under the pan as a prop. He stepped back a little. ''Presto chango, abracadabra,'' he said, and pushed the button. The duplicator settled back on its base with a thump. There were now three of them—the original and one on each pan. The pencil fell away and rolled slowly off the counter. In the flesh, so to speak, it was a much more impressive operation than on TV.

He took one off, readjusted the pencil, and made another.

"You're the manager?" he asked me.

I nodded.

"How much?" He jerked his head at the two duplicators on the counter.

"I'm not sure I understand," I said cautiously. "You mean, you want to sell them to the store?"

"I do, indeed." He put the two original duplicators back in a cardboard carton and tucked in the flaps. "Come, come, I'm a busy man this morning. What have you got in the till there?"

It could be a con game, of course. Some sort of electronic flimflammery on the TV, and a confederate going down the street working sleight of hand in the business places— But, no, Mr. Brown had been getting it at home, too. Besides, it didn't *smell* like a con game. I rang "No Sale," took out the bills, and counted them—ninety-three dollars. I had guessed wrong bigger than that a lot of times before. I laid the money on the counter.

"O.K., bud, you're in business," the man said. He picked up the money and carton, turned and shoved through the crowd of employees and customers. No one paid him any attention. They were too busy staring at the duplicators.

I picked one up and looked at it. It weighed about fifteen pounds, just a black metal box with some plumbing at the top supporting the two pans, and a button to push. Under the button was the tag with simple instructions: *"When you push the button, any object placed on one pan will be duplicated on the other,"* and then the warning Mr. Brown had read to me. A nice piece of merchandise, no doubt about it.

"I'll give you two hundred for them," one of the customers said impulsively.

"Just a moment, please," I told him. I adjusted one duplicator on the pan of the other as I had seen the demonstrator do, pushed the button and held my breath. It worked.

"Here you are, sir," I said. "The price will be $19.98. Mrs. Jones, take the sale, please."

I made several more, checking the action. There was nothing to it.

Push the button, take one off, push the button again. By steadying the machine with your hand, you could get away from the pencil business.

The clerk from the next counter had been standing at my elbow, watching breathlessly. "Do you see how it's done?" I asked her. "You do? Good. Would you operate the machine, now? Just keep taking them off and pushing the button."

I looked around and saw the floor supervisor in the crowd. "Sam, get a couple of your people and clear off those blouses by the door. Handle the sales from there, no wrapping, cash and carry, $19.98 each, one to the customer. We'll use this counter to make them."

"Ah," a sardonic voice said at my side. "Business as usual, eh, while Rome burns." I knew the voice, as well as the style. Both belonged to George Beedle, our personnel manager. In the old days, before Dr. Elton Mayo invented Human Relations, personnel men were people who made out hire and fire slips, worked up wage rates and job qualifications, so forth. Now they are doctors of philosophy, fully prepared to instruct operating officers in the fine points of practical psychology, sociology, economics, epistemology, and the Sermon on the Mount. I enjoy arguing with George, it's amazing how erudite a person can be without having the slightest grasp of merchandising, but not when I have work to do.

"Go away, George," I said firmly. "I'm busy now."

He looked at me curiously. "Busy at what? Making money for Brown's? Here, let me show you how to do it the easy way."

He found a ten-dollar bill in his wallet, laid it on the pan of a duplicator. With his left forefinger, he pressed the button. As another ten-dollar bill appeared, he flipped it off the pan with his right forefinger, pressed again, flipped again. "I often wonder," he said dreamily, "what the vintners buy—" press, flip, press, flip, press, flip. The air was full of ten-dollar bills.

Two or three people started scrambling for them. The rest just stared.

I must confess I was flabbergasted, myself. This potentiality of the duplicator just had not occurred to me. Goods, yes, everybody makes goods, but only the government makes money—or perhaps I should say, used to make money.

"The marketplace, John," George said—press, flip, press, flip—"that's your little Republican tin god, and the lifeblood of the marketplace is money. What price money now?'' He picked up one of the bills, creased it, touched his lighter to it, and lit a cigarette. ''Good kindling, I suppose, if you have a fireplace.''

''Uh, yes,'' I said. I pulled myself together. He was wrong, of course, in a general sense. About ten-dollar bills, though, he was obviously right as rain. It was a dirty shame, just when we had an item as hot as these duplicators to move; but there it was. In the retail trade, you learn not to argue with facts or waste time in vain regrets. I caught Sam's eye and motioned him over. ''No cash sales,'' I told him. ''None whatever, personal checks only.''

''Checks can be duplicated, too,'' George reminded me, but he looked a little uncertain.

''What for?'' I said. ''A check isn't legal tender, it's a specific order from a specific person to transfer credit in a specific way. I don't need a duplicator, I can write all the bad checks I want without one.''

''Oh,'' George said.

I had been thinking while I was talking. A lot of those people look like the kind who might not have checking accounts.

''Wait a minute, Sam,'' I said. ''If they can't write a check, open a credit account for them. The main thing is, keep the merchandise moving. These duplicators are hot now, but they'll be dead as Moses tomorrow.''

''Right, Mr. Thomas, gotcha,'' Sam said. He hurried back to his counter. I called up the Credit Department and made arrangements to handle the accounts. ''If they've got a home address and a job,'' I said, ''that's good enough. Get their signature and give them the merchandise.''

George was still standing there, he had got back his normal self-assurance, a superior smirk on his face—the intellectual sophisticate, no Babbitt he, even if crass mercantile ventures did pay his salary. Sometimes George irritates me just a little.

''Well?'' I said.

''Nothing,'' he murmured, ''nothing at all. Just marveling at the business mind in operation. It's so beautifully oblivious. Here's a gadget that spells the absolute destruction of our economy. Are you worried? Only about how to make a fast buck spreading the plague.''

There must have been two hundred customers milling around in Ladies' Wear now, the word had spread fast. The duplicators were coming in a steady stream from the wrapping counter. Two girls from the Credit Department had just stepped out of the elevator and were hurrying over with big stacks of contracts under their arms. "That's what I get paid for," I told George, "moving merchandise. Other people get paid for worrying about the social implications."

"Exactly. And someone *has* been worrying about them. You read that tag, didn't you?"

"I read it," I admitted. "So what? With all the button pushing going on today, the few thousand I push won't make a bit of difference."

"It *will* make a difference. You just haven't stopped to think why that warning is there. Take a minute and stop thinking about these things as just a gadget people will pay twenty bucks for, think about what they can *do*. What happens to United States Steel when railroads can turn out all the rails they need, right on the ties ready to be spiked down, with a duplicator on a handcar? For that matter, what happens to the railroads when people can make their heavy freight on the spot, out of nothing, and don't have to move it from one end of the country to the other? What happens to General Motors when anybody who wants a new Chevy can borrow the neighbor's and make himself one? What happens to Westinghouse when Mrs. Jones can wander into Brown's with her duplicator under her arm, pick a new toaster off the counter and set it on the pan, walk out thirty seconds later with one of her own? If Westinghouse's troubles don't touch you, what happens to Brown's when she can do that? What happens—"

I didn't wait to hear anymore. There's no getting around it, George does have a vivid way of putting things. I could see now he was right, I hadn't been thinking about this thing, just reacting. There was a phone at the next counter. "Connie," I said, "get me a conference hookup immediately, all department heads." My tone must have hinted that when I said immediately, I meant right now. The call chimes were already beginning to sound as I hung up.

The first customers had begun to get their duplicators. Most were hurrying out of the store, but a few lingered, eyeing merchandise speculatively. One woman with an avaricious glint in her eye and a purposeful swing to her heavy body elbowed through them and came toward a rack of expensive cocktail gowns. "George!" I said. "Watch the phone!" By the time I got there, she had picked a rather gaudy sample from the rack and was folding it to lay on the pan of her duplicator. I reached over her shoulder and picked it off before she could push the button.

''I'm sorry, madam,'' I said firmly. ''We cannot allow customers to duplicate merchandise.''

She glared at me belligerently. ''Who says so?''

''The law says so.'' Possibly this was not exactly true, but I did not give her time to think about it. ''You are interested in this gown, madam?'' I said. ''Allow me.'' I put the dress back on the pan and pushed the button. ''There you are,'' I said. I glanced at the price tag—$98.75. ''The price is one dollar and ninety-eight cents. You have your credit card?'' She nodded uncertainly, looking shaken but not entirely convinced. ''Possibly,'' I said, ''you'd like a few more at this very low price.'' I went down the rack, picking half a dozen at random and duplicating them. ''If you find any that don't suit you, just mail them back, we'll give you full credit. Now, perhaps, a nice synthetic pseudomarten jacket, a beautiful syntho-silk bag, all at the same phenomenal discount, absolutely no down payment, you do not owe us one red cent until the first of next month.''

The saleswoman was standing there helplessly, her mouth open. ''I'll bill it,'' I told her shortly. ''You start wrapping the merchandise.'' It made several nice bulky packages, very hard to manage while holding the duplicator too. ''There you are, madam,'' I said, assisting her toward the door, ''and remember, this sale isn't just for today, every item Brown's sells can be duplicated for similar amazingly low prices, you need not even bring your own duplicator, we will have one on every counter for your convenience.''

I brushed past Sam on the way. ''Get those people with duplicators moving out of here,'' I said, ''drag counters around, block off the aisles, get a guard at the other doors. No one allowed in the store with duplicators. Then get duplicators around to each department as fast as you can, grab anybody you need to help you.''

I got back to George and found him holding the phone. ''They're all on,'' he said.

''Thank you, George.'' I picked up the phone.

''I suppose you've all had the word on these duplicators,'' I said. ''Is there anyone who hasn't?'' No one spoke. ''O.K., now here's what we've been doing down here on the first floor—'' I outlined what had happened. ''Up to now,'' I said, ''it's all been emergency action, off the cuff. Let's see if we can't get things a little better organized, get ahead of it. Any suggestions?''

''On this credit deal,'' Markov said, ''the way we're writing them up, most of these people are white card, a few pink. If there's much trade, we're going to be swamped up here trying to check accounts. How about that?''

''Give them all blue-card treatment for today,'' I said. ''We can get back into the routine when things settle down.'' At Brown's, a blue card is just like cash, only quicker, no restrictions on credit. All the customer has to do is show the card, the salesperson gets the account number on the slip, and that's that.

''O.K., but is anyone's credit any good, really, if we don't have money?''

''We haven't had money since 1933,'' I told him. ''Those green paper slips you carry around in your billfold are just credit tokens, to simplify the bookkeeping. Am I right, Joslyn?''

''More or less,'' Joslyn in Accounting said. ''Close enough for our purposes, anyway. Now, about that ninety-eight percent markdown you put on Ladies' Wear, it may work there; but how about other lines, especially under-a-dollar items. Can we sell a ten-cent article for two mills? And what about nonduplicable merchandise? You can't set a five-hundred-pound refrigerator on that pan.'' With the duplicator, of course, we didn't have to worry about original cost of duplicable items, that was nil. We still had overhead, though, and in modern retailing you don't operate on a fixed markup. Brown's had about a hundred thousand dollars worth of electronic calculating machinery to figure exact markup on each item, based on running inventory, actual departmental overhead, warehouse handling costs, amortization of fixtures, a dozen other factors.

''What about this,'' I said, ''a sliding markoff from ninety percent on cheaper articles to ninety-nine percent on big stuff, where duplicable. On the nonduplicable items, our price is straight ten percent of the price tag. What we want to remember is, these items may not be duplicable today, but they will be tomorrow, just as soon as somebody builds a bigger duplicator, and we have to clear out stock. If we can end up today with just one sample of everything we sell on the floor, and the warehouses bone-empty, that will be just right. With the duplicator, that's all we need to stay in business.''

I could almost hear the wheels whirring in Joslyn's head, they make exactly the same sound as an IBM comptometer. "I'll buy it," he said finally, "as a temporary measure to move the stuff, pending calculation. I suppose you do want me to throw out the old cards, start calculating new prices from scratch?"

"That's exactly what I want. Now, who's next?"

Toivo in Personnel, the man who does George's work while George is busy philosophizing, was. He wanted to know what the policy would be on employee discount on duplicators.

"No duplicator sales to employees," I told him. "Each employee will get one free, compliments of Brown's. 'Thou shalt not muzzle the ox—' On the other hand, you don't have to keep the feed box unlocked for him, either. They'll get the duplicators as they go home tonight, and they won't be allowed to bring them back into the store."

After that, Sam had a question about the instruction tags on the duplicators—he was not a department head, of course, but I had got him in on the roundup because he was in charge on the firing line. "Hadn't we ought to paint over that warning, or something?" he asked. "It's not a very good selling point."

"Have you lost any sales on it yet?" I asked.

"Well, no," he said.

"I think you'd better let it stand, then. There could be a point of liability involved if we removed it. This way, it's up to the buyer, he's been warned."

I won't say we settled all the problems the duplicator posed in half an hour, but we made a good running start.

"All very fine," George said as I hung up and mopped my face with a cashmere cardigan from the counter, "but what are you going to do about the mobs?"

"Mobs? What mobs?"

"Mobs," George said firmly. "You may not think that warning is important, but a lot of people do. They're worried about what's going to happen when the foundations are chipped away. So—let's get ours now, devil take the hindmost. I'm not just guessing about this, incidentally, I've been watching the TV while you were talking. Most of the trouble is still downtown, but it's coming this way. What do you intend to do about it?"

There was not a lot I *could* do. It's not a subject you hear discussed at retail conventions, but mob action is one of those things anyone with large areas of plate glass fronting on a busy thoroughfare thinks about now and then—usually on those gloomy occasions when you wake up at three-thirty in the morning and can't get back to sleep. In my own case, I had long ago decided on a basic principle: You can't fight it, so treat it like any other act of God, button up and ride with it. Luckily, we had stripped all the other departments to the bone to give a flying reserve on the first floor to handle contingencies. They were beginning to show up now, and I put them right to work.

"Clear out the windows," I said, "get it all out, don't leave even a necktie. How are those signs coming?" I had already put a crew to work on a collection of big signs and banners—"YOUR CREDIT IS GOOD AT BROWN'S"; "99% OFF—ALL ITEMS—UP TO 99% OFF"; "DUPLICATORS, $19.98, NO DOWN PAYMENT, YOUR CREDIT IS GOOD AT BROWN'S"; "GIGANTIC STOCK CLEARANCE, UP TO 99% OFF"—not very subtle, but the way I had it sized up, this was not a time for subtlety. We could whet down the rough edges later, the thing now was to keep moving.

"Get those signs in the windows," I said. "Fast. We don't want anything in there to catch a looter's eye, just the bargain hunters."

Markov was down on the first floor now. I called him over. "What's the absolute minimum for one of your girls to make up a contract and fill out a credit card?" I asked him.

"Those girls on the duplicators have got it down to about two minutes, now," he said.

"Not good enough. From now on, I don't want a person coming in this store without a credit card. There'll be a lot coming, and they won't be in a mood to stand in line. If you have to, just get their names and addresses and a signature. What we want to do is slow them up just a little as they come in the entrance, without building up too much pressure. That way, the wilder ones can zip by up the street while we bleed off the slower moving element, where our customers will be. Can you do it?"

Markov looked thoughtful. "I think so. We'll block off the entrances back about ten feet. That will leave a nice little wad of about fifty or so to slow things down. We'll move them on in through four aisles with two girls writing contracts at each aisle. Just getting minimum credit information like you say, I think we can move about eight hundred per hour per entrance."

"Sounds good," I said. "Get moving on it."

I got the floor supervisors together next and told them what we expected. "When the rush comes," I told them, "just get their credit card number and get the merchandise on a slip. Move everything you can, but don't waste time and don't get in any arguments. If anyone gets balky, load him down with merchandise and shove him out. If we let these people get out of hand once, we've had it."

"If it's going to be that bad, Mr. Thomas," Sansom from the Bootery said, "why don't we just lock up for today?"

"For two reasons: First, if we just lock up and go home, they can still break the locks, and we've got no one here to control things. The second reason is, we're not here just for fun, we're here to sell goods.

"Now, are there any other questions?"

There were several about technical aspects of handling the crowds, and we settled them in a hurry, because things were getting ready to pop. There was a commotion outside, and a dozen or so men jammed in the south entrance all at once. They stood there for a moment and looked uncertainly around. Before they had a chance to get their bearings, Markov was hustling them over to his account clerks. A good man, Markov, he was really out of place in Credit, he should have been on the floor.

Two of the customers had duplicators, and they were not about to check them. I saw my "no duplicator" rule was not going to work today. "Forget it," I told the clerks. "Just try to keep track of the merchandise and get on a slip."

By the time Markov had the first group checked through and turned loose with their bright new credit cards in their hands, every entrance was plugged. Luckily for us, the jewelry store two doors down hadn't got the word in time, or perhaps they just did not think fast enough. The more aggressive went past our windows full of sale signs, their eyes on the jewelry and knickknacks, and the meeker were crowded off into Brown's. In any group like this, there is always a small percentage of actively antisocial individuals and a large number who are just there, with no very sharp understanding of why. After the first few minutes of excitement, most of these latter were wishing they were home. While Brown's was not exactly home, it was comparatively homey. We got a few hoodlums, but they were watered down to where we could handle them. The rest were just people, a little more worked up than usual, but still customers.

I won't say we didn't have excitement, because we did. Anytime you get three or four thousand people milling around in a store, you are going to have excitement.

Brown's has a liquor department, on the fourth floor, where it is not conspicuous. What we want is the case-lot trade, not the after-closing half-pint customer. In spite of this, a few of the rowdier element did find their way to it. I got a trouble call a little after one.

A redheaded fellow was back of the counter, tossing bottles to the crowd. ''Here y'are, Mac,'' he said as I pushed up to the counter. ''Have one on Brown's, good old Brown's.'' He shoved a bottle of Black Label at me.

''Right,'' I said. I smashed the neck off on the counter edge. ''Cheers,'' I said, and tipped it up.

The redhead stared at me. ''Careful, bud,'' he said. ''You'll cut your tongue, I did once, trying that.''

''The way to do it,'' I explained. ''You hold your hand tight around the neck and let the whiskey run over your thumb.'' I showed him. ''Here, you have one.'' I grabbed another bottle, smashed the neck off, and handed it to him. He tried it, gingerly.

''No, not like that,'' I said impatiently, ''just shove your lip against your thumb, tip 'er up, let 'er go down. Like this.'' The nice thing about this is, by careful manipulation of your thumb you can seem to be taking a hefty swig, though actually drinking very little. I learned how in my younger days, while temporarily employed by the government in the retail blood-and-guts trade, through carefully observing my platoon sergeant. He had a reputation as a rough fast drinker, but always ended the evening on his own feet.

''This stuff is no good, anyway,'' I said. ''These square bottles don't give you a grip. Hand me a couple of those Lemon Hart.'' I broke the necks and gave him one. ''Mud in your eye.'' A hand reached past me for the bottle I had set down. I chopped at it and the man behind me yelped. ''Buy your own whiskey,'' I said coldly. ''Here, you,'' I told one of the clerks, ''this man wants a bottle of Scotch. Get on the ball, start serving the customers.''

Redhead already had a pretty good glow on when I got there, and Lemon Hart is 151 proof. By the time he had mastered the trick of drinking out of a broken bottle, I judged he was not in shape to bother us anymore. ''Get his credit card and bill him for two Black Label Scotch, two Lemon Hart rum, plus whatever else he handed out,'' I said. ''Then have the store police tuck him away.''

These things are not hard to handle, if you move in fast and keep jabbing. The basic principle is: Never react as the other fellow expects you to, let him worry about what you are going to do, rather than vice versa. And, of course, keep your eye on the objective, which in our case is to sell merchandise. It's surprising how few salespeople nowadays can seem to get that through their heads. They let the customer take the initiative. Once you do that, you are licked. You are not selling then, you are *buying,* regardless of which way the money goes.

I had occasion to think about this several times that afternoon. The young people we had on the floor could go through the motions, but they weren't really *selling*. I got another SOS, for example, from Sporting Goods.

"This gentleman wants to buy a pistol, but he doesn't have a permit," the salesman said nervously. A tall cadaverous individual was standing by the counter.

"Here's my permit," the man grated. He turned toward me. I found myself looking into the muzzle of a .30 Luger. "Now I want bullets, and quick."

"I see," I said. I noticed the safety was on. I glanced at the counter. There was no open box of ammunition. We do not, of course, keep loaded pistols in stock. "Just what do you wish to use the pistol for, sir," I asked him. "Target, sport, or . . . uh . . . defense?"

"To shoot people with," the man said grimly. "From now on, there is no law, it's survival of the fittest. I intend to survive."

"In that case," I said, "might I suggest a somewhat more advanced weapon? Son, reach me one of those Stens from up over the rack, please."

"No false moves!" the man warned harshly. "I have you both covered!"

"Right," I agreed. "No false moves. There you are, sir, a genuine Sten, the submachine gun favored by British commandoes in World War II. One of the most reliable and fastest firing hand weapons ever designed." I worked the action a few times and showed him how to release and insert the magazine. As I did so, I smeared the price tag with my thumb. "Only $179.50, sir," I said, "complete with two fully loaded magazines, guaranteed to comply with pertinent provisions of the Federal Firearms Act." He picked it up eagerly, his eyes shining like a four-year-old who has just seen Wyatt Earp's Ned Buntline Special hanging on the Christmas tree.

"Now," I said, "if I could have your credit card, please, while the clerk gets your ammunition—get out a dozen boxes of that .38 Short back on the lower right-hand shelf, please, the stuff in the green boxes with the white trademark." I got the account number and began writing up the sale. "You'll need something to carry the ammunition and other gear, of course. How about one of our new Everest Assault Paks, crafted after those used by Tensing Norkay and Sir Edmund Hillary in the conquest of Everest? And a holster for the pistol, we have a beautiful item here by Lawrence, specially designed for quick draw from any position—"

"Wasn't that just a little, uh, unethical?" the clerk asked as we watched the man swagger out, his Everest Assault Pak dragging heavily at his narrow shoulders, the hand-tooled Lawrence holster bulking on his hip, the Sten under his arm.

"Under ordinary circumstances," I admitted, "yes. Today, no. We're required by law to disable those Stens, but we're not required to tell the customer just what we did to them, he's supposed to know the law himself. If we had given that fellow a gun that would shoot, or ammo to fit that pistol, he'd be dead in half an hour, and he might hurt someone else, too. This way, he'll be picked up in ten minutes, no damage done, no one hurt, I don't think we'll even be gigged on selling that pistol without a permit. If we are, we've got a hundred and sixty extra on the Sten to help pay the fine, that's our fee for taking the chance.

"Now, one more thing. When things settle down again, remind me to give you a few pointers on tie-in sales and knowing your merchandise, not to mention showing initiative in dealing with customers. Jobs may be hard to get, son, when this duplicator really starts working."

Well, the boy could take a hint, you have to give him that. For the rest of the day there was a pretty steady stream of people leaving Sporting Goods with Stens under their arms and Everest Assault Paks on their backs. I had to send three more people over to help him, and when I checked a little later he had moved all the old ammunition, some of it dating back to the time I had been in Sporting Goods myself—not at any ninety-nine percent discount, either. On guns and ammunition we were sticking to straight list, except for the one thousand percent markup on the Stens, which he had kept.

It didn't make any difference to the customers. They were people who took seriously that business about foundation chipping, and they were all convinced Times Square would be a jungle tomorrow—professorial types mostly, like the fellow with the Luger. I have noticed before that people who have the most faith in the efficacy of shooting other people often seem to be those who have not tried it often.

Finally, about ten in the evening, the National Guard moved in, and we were able to close up.

By that time, the first shock was over, people were getting used to the duplicator. Their eyes no longer popped when the duplicate appeared out of thin air, easy terms and low prices were not such a novelty anymore, they were beginning to pick and choose.

No one had been able to figure out how the duplicating effect was generated, but the engineers had found it was transmitted to the pans over a simple metallic circuit. With that much known, larger duplicators were obviously feasible. As soon as we were sure of this, we had got out wires to our suppliers canceling all current orders—tough on them, no doubt, but we weren't in business for our health.

Back in the receiving warehouse, our building maintenance crew had already got a big duplicator working, just the works from a small one coupled to two big aluminum sheets. They were making TV sets when I went back to check after closing the store—for some reason there had been a big run on TVs, you would think everyone already had one, but apparently not. One man was pushing the button and two more were picking them off with forklifts and running them over to a stack against the wall.

It seemed to me they were getting a little too enthusiastic about it. I wanted some inventory on heavy stuff, just enough so we didn't have to run our model back and make one every time we sold a store or daveno, the small articles we could make right at the counter as we sold them; but until things settled down I didn't want a big stock.

"O.K., boys," I told them. "You can close up now and go home. There's a pile of duplicators by the door, take one as you go out. Take a couple for the kids, too, if you'd like." I had decided to drop the one-to-a-customer rule. We had sold over two thousand that day at twenty dollars, another twelve or fifteen hundred at prices down to five dollars, but toward the end of the day we couldn't keep them moving even at a dollar fifty. Tomorrow, they'd be breakfast food prizes.

I went back up front. The store was a mess, but the counters and shelves all had a lovely bare look and the stock runners were still hauling bale after bale of contracts over to the elevators. I felt pretty good about it.

We had turned the coffee shop over to the military for a command post, I was still not entirely easy about vandalism. George was there, sitting at the coffee-smeared counter with a second lieutenant. Walkie-talkies, field rations, and miscellaneous gear were piled on the tables. A sergeant was reading comic books from the rack by the door and a couple of Guardsmen were sleeping in booths. It looked very homey and quiet.

"Ah," George said, "the man with the ball-point pen, bowed by the weight of three and a quarter percent he stands, say what immortal hand or eye, framed thy fearful symmetry. Sit down, John, have a cup of coffee. Lieutenant Simond, Mr. Thomas. You and the lieutenant should get along, John, he's another merchant prince, from the supermarket in the next block."

Simond blushed, a nice-looking crew-cut young fellow. George is a little disconcerting, when you don't know him well, and he seemed rather above himself tonight. In fact, for a man who had put in a big day—even George had been working toward the last—he seemed somewhat *too* jovial. I looked at him closely.

"That's right, John," he said cheerfully. "At the end of the day's occupation, when the world looks rancid and sour, comes that pause for a soothing libation, which is known as the 'cocktail hour.' " He pulled a bottle from his pocket. "Here, put some of this in your coffee, you'll feel better."

"Thank you, George," I said. The bottle in the bottom file drawer is not a custom at Brown's, I don't believe in drinking in the store and George knows it; but there is a time and place for making an issue of rules, and there is a time and place for not doing so.

George lifted his cup. "To Western Civilization," he said, "drowned by the mill that ground out salt. *Skoal!*"

"Oh, now—" I said.

"Oh, now, yourself, John. Let's not kid ourselves, just because it takes a day or two for the machinery to fall apart. You've kept on top so far by moving fast and taking advantage of the mob's stupidity. The fact still remains, this machine makes every man self-sufficient, it takes the stickum right out of society. Pretty soon, people are going to get wise to that. Who's going to buy your gadgets then, who's going to buy beans from Lieutenant Simond here when they can drop a jar of caviar on the pan and, presto—'' He made a motion of jabbing a button.

''Well, let's wait and see,'' I said. ''It may not be quite so bad as you think.''

''It's *worse* than I think,'' George said stubbornly.

I shrugged and sipped at my coffee. I didn't believe it, there have always been merchants, ever since the Stone Age, come war, revolution, or cataclysm, people have bought and sold. Still, it's hard to argue with logic.

Simond cleared his throat. ''Not to change the subject,'' he said, ''but about that bean business Mr. Beedle mentioned—'' He paused diffidently.

''Yes?'' I said. As far as I was concerned, a new subject was welcome. The comfortable satisfaction I had felt when I sat down was all gone. George often does that to me. ''What about beans?''

''Well, I've been thinking about it, he's right, you know, not very many people *will* buy beans and chuck roast, when they can eat wild rice and smoked pheasant breast. So, you know what I've been thinking? I think what we'll have to have, instead of a supermarket, is a sort of superdelicatessen. Just one item each of every fancy food from all over the world, thousands and thousands, all different ''

''It won't work,'' George said with weary kindness. ''That's what I've just been explaining to John here. Why should I buy my pickled hummingbird tongues from you, when I can keep a can on my own shelf and duplicate it *ad nauseam?*''

''*Ad nauseam,* that's why,'' Simond said earnestly. ''Beans you can eat every day. Pickled hummingbird tongues, you can't. You know when we first started selling these frozen TV dinners, we ran into something funny. The first couple of weeks, they'd go like crazy. Then they'd die. We'd change suppliers, same story. Hot, then cold. Finally, somebody got an idea. You take the Mexican dinner, that's a good seller, I like it myself. You taste the first one, it's delicious. The next, not quite so good. The third or fourth one, eating's a chore, and by the tenth you can't stand the sight of even the wrapper—"

"C rations," I put in.

"That's it, same thing. The trouble is, each one is as exactly like the other as they can be made. You eat one, you've had them all. So, we passed the word to our supplier. Now, he changes the formula every week, a little more pepper, a few less beans, a different cut of meat, so forth. People think they are getting the same thing, but it's just enough different to keep them coming back for more."

"I see what you mean," I said thoughtfully. "In the past, we've sold standardization because it was a scarce commodity. Now, the shoe is on the other foot, we'll sell diversity. Instead of offering the customer a choice of GE or Westinghouse refrigerator, we'll offer a choice of any refrigerator built, anywhere—" A sudden thought struck me. "Damn it," I said unhappily. "We *still* can't get away from our suppliers."

"Not only that," George offered helpfully. "Those samples you're going to offer a choice of are practically all going to be handmade models, remember that. Also, you're not going to get away with duplicating them for nothing. I think you already broke the law when you duplicated the trademarks on those cartons. Even if you didn't, it's not going to take much extension of present legislation to make it illegal to copy any manufactured article without paying royalty."

How right he was. I was way ahead of him. The whole picture was beginning to firm up in my mind now, and I was not very happy at what I thought I saw.

I looked at my watch. "Turn on that TV, please, George," I said. "It's time for the late news."

". . . And that's the situation with regard to the duplicator, the biggest news in the world today," the announcer said. "Now, for a quick rundown of expert opinion, how the duplicator will affect you and me in the days ahead. First to Detroit, Mr. William Peterkin . . ."

". . . Mr. Peterkin, what, in your opinion, will be the single most noticeable effect of the duplicator on the auto industry?"

Mr. Peterkin looked bloodshot and haggard, it was obvious that he had put in a busy day, too.

"Well, I should say elimination of our dependence on expensive tooling and assembly lines. We have a lot of things on the drawing boards—fuel injection, interesting ideas in body design, electronic shifting, even a sort of, you might say, 'electronic chauffeur,' to remember previously traveled routes and drive them for you—all sorts of things that haven't been put on the market because of production difficulties. Now, well, all I can say is, watch the news for the next few months. Suddenly it's going to be, not 1960, but about 2160.

"How about employment, Mr. Peterkin? A lot of people have been worrying about their jobs. How does that look in your industry?"

"That's kind of a funny thing. You know, when we first got the word about this thing, this duplicator, we immediately started thinking in terms of pretty drastic retrenchment. Then, when we got down to cases and started figuring what to cut, where, it turned out we didn't have much fat to spare. Engineers, draftsmen, designers; we need about six times as many as we have. Nut-twirlers and button-pushers on assembly lines will go; but mechanics, craftsmen who can take a blueprint and turn out a piece to specified tolerance . . . well, we can't get them from other industries, they're in the same boat, so it looks like we'll go into a big training program immediately, coupled with a heavy recruiting drive—"

"Great," I said. "There goes our help, just like wartime. We can't compete when they're offering Rosie the Salesgirl four bucks an hour to be Rosie the Riveter."

". . . And now," the announcer said, "Washington, the Department of Commerce—"

". . . The outlook for all forms of surface transport, and certain categories of air transport, is fluid. It has not yet been determined if the duplication effect can be extended over metallic or wireless circuits for any distance. Should remote duplication prove feasible, rolling stock and roadbeds, trucks and barges, will become obsolete. Increases forecast in total tonnages moved, however, may require marked expansion of terminal facilities—"

". . . Wall Street—"

". . . After a heavy selling wave, industrials and utilities recovered surprisingly by closing time—"

". . . Treasury's abrupt withdrawal of all legal tender. While the duplicator can help ease tremendous task of expanding and modernizing banking's physical plant, there simply are not enough people—"

''You get the picture?'' I said. ''The same old rat race, only twice as furious. We've been running like mad all day, just to get back to where we were.''

George shook his head slowly. ''You're wrong, John. Not back to where we were. This morning, we had an economy of scarcity. Tonight, we have an economy of abundance. This morning, we had a money economy—it *was* a money economy, even if credit was important. Tonight, it's a credit economy, one hundred percent. This morning, you and the lieutenant were selling standardization. Tonight, it's diversity.

''The whole framework of our society is flipped upside down.'' He frowned uncertainly. ''And yet, you're right too, it doesn't seem to make much difference, it *is* still the same old rat race. I don't understand it.''

''Well, maybe the framework is just not so important as you thought, George,'' I said. ''Anyway, *you* puzzle about it. I haven't got time, right now. Tomorrow's going to be a busy day, and probably the next several after it.'' I finished my coffee and stood up. ''If you fellows will excuse me, I'm going home to bed.''

And that was the first day of the duplicator, the day that set the pattern.

MACK REYNOLDS

Criminal in Utopia

Mack Reynolds is a unique writer in modern science fiction—student of political economy, world traveler, the son of radical parents, and himself a onetime lecturer for the Socialist Labor Party. He is one of the few to treat such issues as Third World development problems, multinational corporations, and the connections between economic relationships and modernization. Over the years he has built an enormous body of work on socioeconomic themes.

"Criminal in Utopia" finds him at the top of his form as he portrays a society operating entirely on the principle of credit. The story is really a careful extrapolation of present trends and conditions—certainly the Western world has already reached the point where serious alterations in the supply of credit would result in severe social and economic dislocations.

On a personal level, most of us are aware of the revolutionary effect on purchasing patterns and mercantile life caused by the proliferation of credit cards, which are now accepted for such diverse goods and services as gas, food, clothing, entertainment, and college tuition. While it is true that credit (at least in small amounts) is now relatively easy to obtain, the system has a number of disconcerting side effects, not the least of which is the amount of information on the personal lives of millions accumulating in the memory banks of computers. There are legal means developing to stop this practice. On the other hand, the development of credit has led to a variety of rackets involving theft and fraud. Mack Reynolds turns his attention to the latter problem with a story that proves that even in the future, skillful individuals will find a way to beat the system.

I

Rex Moran dialed his wrist teevee phone for the time and looked at the clock face that appeared on the screen. A robot voice said, "When the bell rings it will be exactly two minutes until eight hours." A tiny bell rang.

Rex Moran grunted and looked about the small apartment. He had better get going.

First, though, he took his Universal Credit Card from an inner pocket of his jerkin and inserted it in the slot of his standard teevee phone which sat on his living *cum* bedroom's sole table. He said into the screen, "Credit balance check, please."

Within moments, a robot voice said, "Ten shares of Inalienable Basic. No shares of Variable Basic. Current cash credit, one dollar and twenty-three cents."

"One dollar and twenty-three cents," he muttered. "Holy living Zoroaster. I didn't think I'd have to start with that little on hand."

He dialed Credit and waited until a face faded in on the screen. It was a businesslike, brisk, possibly impatient face.

"Jason May, here. Assistant Credit Manager, Inalienable Basic Dividends," he said.

Rex Moran put his Uni-Credit Card on the screen and said, "I'd like an advance on my dividends."

The other was seated at a desk. "Just a moment, please," he said and touched a button. He listened to a report on a desk phone screen then looked back at Moran. "You're already two months ahead."

"I know that," Rex Moran said doggedly, "but it's an emergency."

"It is always an emergency, Mr. Moran," the other said flatly. "What is the emergency? Your records show that you are almost invariably as far ahead as you can get on your monthly dividends. As you must know, the government charges interest on such advances. In the long run, Mr. Moran, you lose."

"I know, I know," Rex Moran said, an element of complaint in his voice. "I've had a long set of bad luck. One thing after another."

"What is the current emergency, please?"

Rex Moran wished he had thought this out in more detail before launching into his fling. He said, "I've got a sick brother, I have to go help."

"Where is this brother, Mr. Moran?"

"In Panama City."

"One moment, please." The other went back to one of his desk screens. In only moments he looked up again with a sigh.

"Mr. Moran, the computer banks have no records of you having a brother at all, in Panama City or anywhere else. Request denied. And Mr. Moran . . ."

"Yeah?" Rex Moran said in disgust.

"It is a minor offense to lie to a credit manager in attempt to secure an advance on dividends. I shall take no action on this occasion, but the fact will be entered on your record in the computer banks."

"Oh, great," Rex Moran growled. He flicked off his screen. "I didn't expect that to work anyway," he muttered.

He thought over his plans for a few minutes, then squared his shoulders and dialed the local branch of the ultra-market, on his auto-delivery box. He was a man in his early thirties, mildly burly in build and with a not really unpleasant but a broken face of one who has either seen military combat, or perhaps been a pugilist. In actuality, neither was the case.

The ultra-market in the screen, he dialed the children's toy section, boys' toys, and then military-type toys. He finally narrowed it down to guns and dialed one that came to only seventy-cents. It would have to do. He put his Uni-Credit Card in the slot, his thumbprint on the screen and ordered the toy.

Within minutes, it was in the auto-delivery box, and he put it in the side pocket of his jerkin. It was on the smallish side, but black and at any distance at all realistic enough for his purpose.

He moved over to his library booster teevee screen and dialed a newspaper, then the paper of two weeks previous and the obituaries. He went through several papers before he found the one that seemed most likely, by the address and the information in the item, and made some notes with his stylo.

Finally, he dialed the address and waited until a face faded in on his phone screen.

The other frowned at him, in lack of recognition.

Rex Moran said, "Mr. Vassilis? My name is Roy McCord."

The other was a tired-looking obvious aristocrat, perhaps a few years the other side of sixty.

Still frowning, he said, "What can I do for you, Mr. McCord?"

"I just got back into town and heard the bad news. I'm a friend—forgive me, Mr. Vassilis—*was* a friend of Jerry Jerome."

The other's face lightened slightly and then went sad. "Ah, I see. I am afraid he hadn't mentioned your name, but then Jerome had many friends of whom I knew little."

"Yes, sir. I'd like the opportunity to offer my condolences in person," Rex Moran began.

The older man was frowning slightly and began to respond.

But Moran hurried on. "But I also have something of Jerry's that I suppose should go to you."

Rex Moran managed to look slightly embarrassed. "Well, sir, I . . . well, I think it would be better if I just brought it over."

The other was mystified. However, he shrugged. "Very well, young man. Let me see, I shall be free at, say nine hours this morning, and should be able to give you a few minutes."

"Fine, sir. I'll be there." Rex Moran switched off the screen before the other could say anything further.

For a moment he stared down at the blank screen, then shifted muscles in his shoulders. "First step," he said. "So far, so good. Maybe I shouldn't have used this phone, but in the long run it won't make any difference."

He didn't take the vacuum tube transport from his own building, knowing that a record was kept of all trips in the computer banks, and the john-fuzz might trace back later on his Uni-Credit Card number. Instead, he walked several blocks and entered a public terminal.

He looked up at the map and selected another terminal a couple of blocks from his destination, then entered the next twenty-seater going through that point. After putting his credit card in the payment slot, he realized that with the buying of the toy gun, he probably had only a few cents left to his balance. He didn't even have enough credit to get back to his apartment if this little romp pickled. What a laugh that would give the boys if he had to walk home.

He left the vacuum-tube transport terminal and walked to the building where Vassilis lived. This was the crucial point now. If there were others present, his plan had come a cropper. However, if he had read between the lines correctly, the senior Mr. Vassilis lived alone in his apartment in this swank neighborhood.

There was an identity screen in the front entry. Keeping his fingers crossed that his Universal Credit Card wouldn't be required for entrance, he said into the screen, "Roy McCord, on appointment to see Mr. Frank Vassilis."

The door opened, and he entered.

There were two elevators. He entered one and said, "The apartment of Frank Vassilis."

The Vassilis apartment was on the top floor but one. Rex Moran got out of the elevator, found a door with the Vassilis name on it and activated the door screen. When it lit up, he said into it, "Roy McCord, calling on Mr. Vassilis, by appointment."

The door opened, and he stepped through.

And came to a halt. The man standing there in a dark suit was not the Mr. Vassilis he had spoken to earlier on the teevee phone. This worthy was a stiffish type, of possibly fifty. His eyes went up and down Rex Moran superciliously, taking in the less than elegant suit, taking in the rugged features.

He said, "Yes, sir. Mr. McCord? The master is awaiting you in his escape room."

The *master?* Holy jumping Zoroaster, Vassilis had a man servant. Whoever heard of personal servants in this day and age? The obituary had hinted that the old boy was upper class, but Moran hadn't been thinking in terms of something so rich as an establishment with a servant.

However, he followed along. It was the largest apartment he could offhand ever remember being in. They went down one hall, turned right and down another one.

There wasn't even an identity screen on the door before which they stopped. The servant knocked gently and opened the door before there was any reply. Evidently, old Vassilis was expecting him, all right.

The servant stood stiffly and said, "Mr. McCord."

The elderly man Rex Moran had talked to on the teevee phone earlier looked up from where he sat in a comfort chair, a small magnifying glass in one hand, a dozen or so stamps on a small table before him. He was evidently a philatelist.

He said, "Ah, yes, Mr. Roy McCord, Jerome's friend. Please come in." As the servant had before him, he took in Moran's clothing and general appearance, and his eyebrows went up slightly. "Now, what is it I can do for you, Mr. McCord?"

Rex Moran looked at the servant.

Vassilis said, "That will be all, Franklin."

Franklin turned and left, closing the door quietly behind him.

No need to mince around. Rex Moran brought the toy gun from his pocket briefly, let the other see it and returned it to his side pocket, but still holding it in his hand.

He said, "This is a romp, Mr. Vassilis."

The other goggled at him. "You . . . you mean you are a thief? That you got into my home on false pretenses?"

Moran let his face go empty. "I wouldn't put it that way. Let's just say that I'm tired of not getting my share of the cake. And since the powers that be won't give it to me, I'm taking it."

The old man stared at him. "You are a fool, young man."

''Maybe, maybe not.'' Rex Moran jiggled the gun in his side pocket suggestively.

''Being a thief doesn't make sense in this day. Society has made arrangements to defend itself against the thief. There's not enough profit in petty crime to pay off.''

Rex Moran grinned at him sourly. ''I didn't exactly have petty crime in mind, Mr. Vassilis. Now, hand me your credit card.''

''What other kind of crime is possible? Nobody but I can spend my dollar credits. I can't give them away, gamble them away, throw them away, be cheated out of them. Only *I* can spend my dividends.''

''We'll see about that.'' Rex Moran nodded. ''Now, let's have your Universal Credit Card.'' He jiggled the gun in his pocket again.

The older man contemptuously took a beautiful leather wallet from an inner pocket and brought forth a standard Uni-Credit Card. He handed it over.

Moran said, ''You have a vacuum delivery box in this room? Oh, yeah, here we are. Zoroaster, look at the size of it! Now that's the advantage of being an upper class like you, Mr. Vassilis. You should see the teeny auto-delivery box in my mini-apartment. If I want anything of any size at all, I've got to use the box down in the lobby of the crummy building I'm in. Now, with a nice big auto-delivery box like this anything you wanted would have to be really supersize before you couldn't get it delivered right here into your escape room.''

Vassilis said, ''You are a fool, young man. The officials will be after you in no time flat.''

Moran grinned at him and sat down before the box, keeping one eye on the other. He put the card in the teevee screen's slot and said, ''Credit balance, please.''

A robot voice said, ''Ten shares of Inalienable Basic. Two thousand and forty-six shares of Variable Basic. Current cash credit, forty-two thousand and twenty-nine dollars and eighteen cents.''

Rex Moran whistled. ''Two-thousand-and-forty-six-shares-of-Variable!''

Vassilis grunted contempt of him.

Moran dialed the ultra-market, then sports, then firearms, then handguns. He finally selected a .38 Recoilless and dialed it and a box of cartridges.

He thought for a moment, then dialed photography and selected a Polaroid-Pentax and some film for it.

''Might as well do this up brown,'' he said conversationally to the older man. ''Might as well put a *generous* hole in that credit balance.''

''There'll be no hole—as you call it—at all,'' Vassilis said bitterly. ''When I report this thievery, the authorities will return to my account the sum involved in any deprecations you have performed.''

Rex Moran dialed men's clothing and took his time selecting a full outfit, including shoes.

''Now, this is the crucial point,'' he said thoughtfully, to no one in particular. He dialed jewelry and finally selected a two-thousand-dollar diamond ring.

''I guess that's it,'' he said. Then, ''Oh, one other thing.'' He dialed sports again, and camping, and eventually a length of rope.

He turned back to Frank Vassilis. ''And now, old man, come on over here and stick your thumbprint on this order screen.''

''Suppose I refuse?''

Rex Moran grinned at him. ''Why should you? Like you said, when you report this, the authorities will return your credit dollars to you and come looking for me. You're not losing anything.''

The older man, grumbling, came erect in his chair. He came over to the auto-delivery box and, with a sneer of contempt for his intruder, stuck his right thumbprint on the screen.

Moments later, the articles had arrived.

Vassilis returned to his comfort chair.

Rex Moran began fishing the articles he had ordered from the box. He loaded the gun, put it next to him, within handy reach and then dressed in his new clothes. He took up the camera and slung it over his shoulder. He looked at the ring admiringly and tucked it away in an inner pocket, and then the gun.

He muttered, ''I have half a mind to order a few more of these but that big a drain on your account all at the same time might throw some relays and have the computer people check back.''

''Thief,'' Vassilis said bitterly.

Moran grinned at him. ''What's your beef? It won't be you who loses.''

He took up the rope. ''First we'll tie you up a bit, old chum-pal, and then we'll call in Franklin, or whatever you called him, and do a job on him.''

''You'll never get away with this, you young cloddy,'' the old man bit out.

''Famous last words,'' Moran grinned back at him.

II

Back on the street, he realized it was going to be necessary to walk to his next destination. His credit standing simply did not allow even such a small sum as riding in the vacuum tubes. However, happily, it wasn't as far as all that. As he walked, he took the toy gun from his pocket and threw it into a waste receptacle. He had the real thing now. He found the neighborhood and had a choice of three alternatives. He took the smallest of the shops and entered.

There were even a few display cases. How anachronistic could you get? He grunted sour amusement to himself; here was the last of the kulaks, the last of the small businessmen.

A quiet man of about fifty entered from a back room and took Rex in before saying in a soft voice, "Yes, sir, what can I do for you?"

Rex Moran went into his act. Hesitantly, he said, "I understand that you sometimes buy personal property."

"That is correct. Buy and sell. But what type of property, Mr. . . . ?"

"Adams," Rex Moran said. "Timothy Adams. I have a ring that used to belong to my mother. It is of no value to me, now, and I thought . . . well, I might as well realize what dollar credit value it has."

"I see. Please sit down, Mr. Adams. Heirloom jewelry is a bit of a drug on the market, but we can take a look." He sat himself behind a desk and motioned to a straight chair.

Rex Moran sat down and brought the diamond ring from his pocket and proffered it. The other took it and set it on the table. He looked at Rex Moran thoughtfully. "This is a very modern setting, Mr. Adams. I had gained the impression that it was an older piece your mother had left you."

"Oh, no," Rex Moran said. "She bought it not too very long before she died. If I had a wife, or someone, I might give it to her, but I haven't."

The other looked at him evenly. "Mr. Adams, I am not a fence, you know. This is a legitimate business."

"Fence?" Rex Moran said blankly.

"I buy and sell such items as art objects and jewelry, but I do not receive stolen goods. Where did you say your mother bought this?"

"On a vacation in Common Eur-Asia. In Budapest, I think, or possibly Belgrade."

"So it would be untraceable here in the United States of the Americas."

"Why, it never occurred to me."

The shop owner took up the ring and looked at it thoughtfully. He brought a jeweler's glass from a drawer and peered through it.

He put it down finally and looked at Rex Moran. "I'll give you two hundred dollars for it."

"Two hundred dollars! My mother said she paid more than two thousand."

"Then she paid too much. The markup on jewelry is very high, Mr. Adams, and such items as this can take a very long time to move."

Rex Moran thought about it. "Make it three hundred."

The other considered that. "Very well," he said finally. "But I am making a mistake."

"Yeah," Rex Moran said sourly. He brought his Uni-Credit Card from his pocket and stuck it into one of the slots on the other's Exchange Screen.

The shop owner put the ring in a drawer, brought forth his own Universal Credit Card and put it into the other exchange slot. He said into the screen, "Please transfer the amount of three hundred dollars from my account to this other card."

A robot voice said, "Transfer completed."

Rex Moran retrieved his Uni-Credit Card and came to his feet. "I still think I was robbed," he muttered.

The other said nothing, simply sat there and watched after him as Rex Moran left the shop.

Well, he now had three hundred dollars to his account. That was a damn sight less than he had expected to get. However, he hadn't dared buy a more expensive piece of jewelry than the two-thousand-dollar piece, on Vassilis's credit card. There would have been more of a chance of the shop owner checking on such an item. More chance of it being able to be traced. Besides, if he had drained Vassilis's account too badly, there might have been a computer check at that point.

He strode rather rapidly to the nearest vacuum-tube transport terminal and into it, wanting to get out of the neighborhood as quickly as possible. He took a two-seater vehicle to the downtown area of the pseudo-city, if a pseudo-city can be said to have a downtown area.

When he left the vacuum tube, it was to emerge in the vicinity of several restaurants. It was just about noon, but since he hadn't been able to afford breakfast, he was feeling hunger. Well, three hundred dollars was three hundred dollars, and he might as well blow himsself to a fairly good repast in an auto-cafeteria.

He selected one and sat himself down at a table and stared down at the menu listed on the tabletop. To hell with anything based on Antarctic krill, plankton protein, or soy beans; he was up to some real animal protein and Zoroaster could take the cost.

He put his credit card in the table slot, his thumbprint on the screen and dialed chicken and a mug of sea-booze. He would have liked a shot of pseudo-whiskey to begin, but his funds weren't that unlimited.

His wrist teevee phone buzzed.

He looked down at it in some surprise. He had it set on Number One Priority, and only two people in the world were eligible to break in on him on that priority, and he certainly was not expecting a call from either.

But there was a strange face in the tiny screen. Strange and severe.

The voice said, "This is Distribution Service, Subdivision Police. Rex Moran, you are under arrest for attempt to violate regulations pertaining to usage of the Universal Credit Card. Report immediately to the nearest Police Administrative Station. Failure to do so will compound the felony."

"Get lost, fuzz-john," Rex Moran snarled. He snapped the instrument off, then stared down at the blank screen in dismay. What had gone wrong? Especially, what had gone wrong so quickly? It had to be something to do with his selling that damned ring. But what? He had expected the ring to stay in that tiny shop, waiting for a customer for months, perhaps even years. And even then, when it was resold, the transaction should never have appeared on the computer records, except as an exchange of dollar credit from the purchaser's account to the shopkeeper's.

What foul luck! Vassilis must have put in an immediate alarm, and the police must have contacted every place in town where Rex Moran could possibly dispose of the purloined ring.

He had to think fast. They'd be after him now. Damn and double damn. He wouldn't even be able to return to his mini-apartment. He was on the run, and for a meaningless amount such as three hundred dollars, and even that now was of no use. He wouldn't dare use his credit card; the computers were surely watching for him.

They could also zero in on his wrist teevee phone. He reached down, in disgust, and began to rip it off. However, the screen lit up again, and a new face was there.

A voice rasped, ''Now hear this, all citizens. Crimes against the government of the United States of the Americas have been committed by Rex Moran, including assault, robbery, sale of stolen property, and attempted misuse of the Universal Credit Card. All citizens are requested to cooperate in his apprehension. The criminal is dangerous and armed. Here is his face.''

Rex groaned when his face appeared on the tiny screen. Happily, it was a fairly old photo, and taken before some of his present scarred features had become what they were.

He ripped the instrument from his wrist and flung it into a corner. At this early hour there were no others present in the auto-cafeteria, thank the living Zoroaster for that.

He came to his feet and hurried for the door. In the far distance, he could hear a siren. Undoubtedly, it was for him. You didn't hear police sirens that often in the pseudo-cities of the Ultra-Welfare State.

He hurried down the street and turned a corner as quickly as possible. He dared not use the vacuum tube. He dared not summon a floater, for that matter.

But that brought something to mind.

He found a fairly isolated spot and waited until a pedestrian came along. He brought his gun from his pocket and said, ''Hold it, chum-pal.''

The other looked at him, down at the gun, up into Rex Moran's face again and blanched. ''Why, why you're the criminal just flashed on the teevee.''

''That's right, chum-pal, and you look just like the sort of chum-pal who'd cooperate with a man with a shooter trained on his tummy.''

The other was wide-eyed and ashen. ''Why . . . why, of course.''

''Okay. Quick now, dial a floater on your wrist teevee phone.''

''Of course, of course. Don't be nervous.''

''I'm not nervous.'' Rex Moran grinned at him and jiggled the gun up and down. ''Hurry it up.''

The other dialed, and within moments an auto-floater cab turned the corner and pulled up next to them at the curb. The door opened.

Rex said, ''Quick, put your Uni-Credit Card in the slot.''

Even as the other was doing so, Moran was climbing into the back seat of the floater. He rasped, ''Put your thumbprint on the screen.''

While the other did that, Rex Moran was dialing his destination, not letting the other see.

He reached out suddenly and grasped the other's wrist teevee phone and ripped it off and stuck it in his pocket. He pulled the credit card from the floater's slot and handed it back to his victim.

"There," he said, "don't say I didn't do you a favor. Think of all the trouble you'd have if you didn't have a credit card."

He slammed the door shut and the floater took off.

Rex Moran said into the vehicle's screen, "Maximum speed, please."

A robot voice said, "Yes, sir."

He couldn't afford to stay in the floater for very long. Just enough to get out of this neighborhood. As soon as that cloddy he had just stuck up back there reported to the police, they'd check through the computers for the floater's destination. There'd be a record, based on the number of the victim's Uni-Credit Card. A record of *everything* seemingly went into the computer banks. Why not? He growled sourly; evidently their capacity was almost infinite.

Yes, they'd check the destination of his trip. However, he was not quite so silly as to go all the way to the destination he had dialed. About halfway there, at a traffic control stop, he opened the door and left the floater to go on its own.

He ducked down a side street and took of at right angles to the avenue along which the floater was progressing.

Rex Moran now had a double problem. He grimaced wryly. An *immediate* double problem, that was. For one thing, he was still hungry. For another, he had to get off the streets. Citizens weren't likely to pay overmuch attention to the Distribution Service police calls over the teevee phone screens, but there was always the exception. Given time, someone would spot and report him, in spite of the poor photograph which just had been broadcast.

He could hear the stolen wrist teevee phone buzz in his pocket and brought it forth, flicking the tiny stud which prevented it from transmitting his face.

It was the same official as before, and he was making the same broadcast, but now reporting Rex Moran as last seen in that part of town where he had dialed the floater. Evidently his victim had reported.

That also meant they would know that Moran had the stolen wrist teevee phone and would shortly be zeroing in on it. He threw the instrument into the gutter and ground a heel down on it.

He had to get off the streets.

And suddenly he knew where to go.

In this vicinity there was a posh restaurant of which he had heard but had never been able to afford, nor had he really ever expected to be able to afford it. Well, things were different now.

He entered the building and took the elevator to the penthouse restaurant known as the Gourmet Room. The day was more advanced now, and upperclass office workers were beginning to stream in for the midday meal.

He avoided looking impressed at the ostentatious swank of this rendezvous of the ultra wealthy and thanked his stars that he had thought of acquiring his present clothing. A headwaiter approached diffidently. In all his life, Rex Moran had never eaten in a restaurant which boasted live waiters. Now he tried to look unimpressed.

''A single, sir?'' the maître d'hôtel said.

''Please,'' Rex Moran told him, keeping his voice softly modulated and as though such surroundings were an everyday affair for him. ''If possible, a table set back somewhere. I have a bit of figuring to do.''

''Certainly, sir. This way.''

He was seated in an out-of-the-way alcove which suited his needs perfectly.

The maître d' snapped his fingers, and a waiter scurried up.

There was no menu. It was that kind of a restaurant.

The maître d' said unctuously, ''Sir, today the Gratin de langoustines Georgette is superb.''

Rex Moran hadn't the vaguest idea what langoustines Georgette might be, but he made a face as though considering.

''What else might you recommend?'' he said.

''The chef has surpassed himself with the poulet docteur.''

''That sounds good.''

The waiter made a note.

''And a half bottle of Sylvaner of the Haut-Rhin, perhaps?''

''Fine.''

Salad and dessert were settled upon, and then the maître d' and the waiter were gone.

Rex Morgan sighed inwardly and looked around. The only other diner within his immediate vicinity had his back to Moran.

He unslung the Polaroid-Pentax from his shoulder and brought from his pocket the cassette of film. He inserted it in the camera. Then he took from his inner pocket the Universal Credit Card he had appropriated from Frank Vassilis and examined it with care, spending particular time on the thumbprint.

Finally, he propped the card against the small vase in the table center, which held a single black rose, and focused the camera on it. He clicked the shutter then drew the photo from the camera back and stared at it. It didn't quite do. He tried again, getting the camera closer to the subject. He took half a dozen shots before he came up with as near a duplicate of the Universal Credit Card's thumbprint as he could hope for.

He put the credit card away, the camera back in its case and brought forth his penknife. He was busily trimming the photo to be the exact size of a thumbprint when the waiter turned up with his first course.

Poulet docteur turned out to be the best chicken dish he had ever tasted. And the wine was excellent.

In the middle of his salad course, and before dessert, he came suddenly to his feet and hurried toward the reception desk *cum* cashier's booth. It was there that the payment screen for the ultraswank restaurant was to be found.

And it was there that the maître d'hôtel stood, his eyebrows politely raised now.

Rex Moran said to him hurriedly, "I have just thought of something I must attend to. Please hold my dessert for me. And, please, keep an eye on my camera over there, will you?"

The maître d' looked over at Moran's table. The camera sat upon it. He said, "Why, of course, sir."

Rex Moran left, still projecting an air of a suddenly remembered matter that must urgently be taken care of.

Down on the street he grimaced. One camera sacrificed to the game. However, he had no need of it now.

He was still in one of the best sections of town. He made his way toward a nearby hotel, holding a handkerchief over his face, as though trying to extract something from his left eye. There were quite a few pedestrians at this time of the day.

In the hotel, he approached the lone clerk at the reception desk. Now, he had to take his chances. If the man recognized him from the police broadcast—Rex Moran was on a spot.

He said, "I would like a small suite. Nothing ambitious. Living room, bedroom, bath. I doubt if I'll be entertaining."

"Why, yes, sir, of course." The other looked beyond Moran. "Ah, your luggage, sir?"

"I have no luggage," Rex Moran said, offhandedly. "I just came in from the coast. Plan to do some shopping here for my wardrobe. Always buy my things here in the East. California styles are ludicrous."

"Yes, sir, of course." The clerk motioned in the direction of the teevee screen slot on the desk. "Would you wish to register?"

"I'd rather see the suite, before deciding," Rex Moran said. "I'll register up there, if it's satisfactory."

"Oh, I'm sure it will be, sir. Let me suggest Suite Double A."

"Double A," Rex Moran said and made his way to the bank of elevators.

Inside the first elevator, he said, "Suite Double A."

"Yes, sir," a robot voice said.

Suite Double A was several stories up. Rex Moran emerged from the elevator, looked up at the direction signs on the wall and made his way to the suite in question.

It was quite the most elaborate quarters in which Rex Moran had ever been. Not that that was the issue, he would have taken the accommodations whatever they had resembled.

He approached the room's teevee phone screen and said into it, "This suite seems adequate, I'll take it."

A robot voice said, "Very good, sir. If you'll just put your Uni-Credit Card in the slot."

Rex Moran took a deep breath. He brought the card of Frank Vassilis from his pocket, inserted it in the slot. Then he brought forth the photo he had taken of the Vassilis right thumbprint and laid it in the screen. He picked it up again, immediately.

A robot voice said, "Thank you, sir."

Rex Moran took another deep breath and let it hiss out again between his teeth.

"*Zo-ro-as-ter*. I think it worked."

He dialed the time. It was midafternoon.

He grinned exuberantly. He had it licked. Unless there was something he didn't know about, he absolutely had it licked.

He dialed Service and said to the screen, ''I'd like to lay in a stock of potables. Let me see. Let's say a bottle of Scotch, one of cognac, one of Metaxa, one of Benedictine, one of Cherry Heering, one of Chartreuse—yellow, of course, not the green—one of Pernod, absinthe if available but otherwise the ordinary will do.''

A robot voice said, ''Sir, in the New Carlton all these can be dialed on the auto-bar.''

''I know, I know, but I like to mix my own.''

''Very good, sir. They will be delivered through the auto-bar, sir.''

''Mind,'' Rex Moran said, ''the best quality.''

''Always, sir.''

Still grinning widely, he went over to the suite's auto-bar and took up the bottle of Glengrant Scotch and held it up to the light approvingly. In his whole life he had been lushed up exactly once on Scotch. The stuff was worth its weight in rubies since Central Production had discontinued the use of cereals for beverages.

He dialed for soda and sipped away at it approvingly, even as he strode up and down the room, considering his immediate future.

He wondered briefly how you went about getting a mopsy up to your quarters in a hostelry as posh as the New Carlton. But he had better draw the line there, anyway. It was no use pushing your luck. Some wheel might come off. She might have seen the police teevee alarm on him.

What the hell else was there in the way of unrealized lifelong ambitions?

Caviar. He had never eaten his fill of caviar. In fact, the amount of caviar he had eaten in his whole life could have come out of a two-ounce jar of the precious stuff.

Fine. He dialed Service again and had a pound jar of caviar sent up, along with sweet butter, toast, chopped eggs, and chopped onion. While he was at it, he ordered a large amount of smoked sturgeon and smoked salmon.

While he waited for this order, he built himself another Scotch and soda. Glengrant. He'd have to remember that name, on the off chance that he'd ever have another opportunity such as this.

He spent the rest of the day indulging himself in every food and drink ambition he could ever remember having had. And in getting well smashed and surfeited with rich edibles to the point that, when dinner time arrived, he had no appetite, to his disgust. He wanted to order a real gargantuan meal.

His last vague memory was of staggering into the bedroom and dialing the bed to ultimate softness before throwing himself into it.

In the morning, he should have awakened with some sort of hangover, but the gods were still with him; either that or there was another good mark to chalk up for Glengrant whiskey. He awoke grinning up at the ceiling. He had slept like a log.

He dialed the time at the bedside teevee phone and didn't bother to look into the screen at the clock. A robot voice said, "When the bell rings it will be exactly nine minutes to eight hours."

Ha! Nine minutes to go.

He dialed breakfast, a monstrous breakfast, and had it delivered to the auto-table next to the bed. Fresh mango juice, papaya, eggs in black butter, caviar again, toast, fried tomatoes, coffee; double orders of all.

Groaning satisfaction, he ate.

By the time breakfast was over, it was past eight o'clock.

All right, he grinned jubiliantly, time to get busy.

He went to the teevee phone screen and dialed the local branch of the ultra-market and men's furnishings. He took his time selecting a new change of clothing. That accomplished he dialed the order, put Vassilis' card in the slot and laid the photo of the thumbprint on the screen and took it off again immediately.

The clothing arrived in minutes, and he dressed after showering and shaving in the bathroom.

He returned to the teevee phone screen and dialed the ultra-market once again. He began ordering items, in fine discrimination, and had the time of his life unwrapping and examining them as they arrived. His loot piled up.

At about ten o'clock, he decided really to do it up brown and dialed a floater sales outlet. He ordered a sports model private floater and instructed them to send it over to the hotel's parking area on automatic.

At ten minutes after ten, the identity screen on the door lit up. There were two men there, one in uniform.

The one in plain clothes said disgustedly, "All right, come along."

The one in uniform looked at all the purchases strewn around the room, wrapping paper and string everywhere. "Zoroaster," he snorted.

They took him down the elevator, through the lobby, out to the street where a police floater awaited. The uniformed one drove manually. Rex Moran sat in the back with the other.

The plainclothesman said sourly, "You must have had the time of your life."

Rex Moran laughed.

"Big joke," the other said. "We almost nabbed you there in the auto-cafeteria. We should have zeroed in on you, instead of trying to arrest you by teevee phone."

"I wondered why you didn't," Rex Moran said. "Police inefficiency."

They took him to the local offices of the Bureau of Distribution Services, to an elevator and then to the third floor where he was ushered into the presence of Marvin Ruhling himself.

Ruhling looked at him and said, "Very funny, ordering even a sports floater."

Rex laughed and took a chair. The uniformed policeman left but the plainclothesman also sat down. His face was as disgusted as that of the Supervisor.

Marvin Ruhling said, "Holy jumping Zoroaster, what kind of heat do you think Vassilis is going to stir up?"

Rex Moran said reasonably, "Never let him know what really happened. He wasn't doing any harm. He had a little excitement."

"A little excitement, you damn cloddy. Suppose he had dropped dead of a heart attack or something? Not to mention that pedestrian you forced at gunpoint to get a floater for you."

Rex said, "Well, you asked for it. You wanted authenticity. You got it."

"Authenticity," the plainclothesman grunted digustedly. "Which reminds me, we better get that teevee police broadcast killed, or the next time Rex goes out on the street somebody'll shoot him."

Ruhling said to Rex Moran, "Well, your conclusions?"

"That we've got to do something to the cards. Something to guarantee the thumbprint is legitimate. Otherwise, a real bad-o could locate some upperclass cloddy without any immediate friends or relatives, take him out somewhere and finish him off and hide the body, then take the Uni-Credit Card and head off into some other part of the country and, using the same system I did, duplicate photographically the thumbprint. And for the rest of his life he could milk the dividends that would accrue on the upperclass cloddy's credit account from his Variable Basic."

Marvin Ruhling looked at him sourly. "What could we do to the credit cards?"

"Search me. That's up to the engineers. Maybe something in the card, or on the screen, to detect body heat. I don't know. But I proved the cards vulnerable the way they are."

"What else?"

Rex Moran thought about it. He shook his head. "I just mentioned it to Fred, here, on the way over. That system of making a citizen arrest himself and turn himself over to the nearest police station doesn't wash. Oh, I admit it saves manpower, ordinarily, but when you get a cloddy vicious enough to be carrying a shooter, then you should zero in on his wrist teevee phone, assuming he's silly enough to be carrying one, without warning."

"Rex is obviously right on that one," the plainclothesman said.

Marvin Ruhling sighed deeply. "All right," he said. "You won your bet. You were able to beat the rap, exist in comfort for a full twenty-four hours, without any dollar credits."

He glared at his underling. "But I'd sure as the holy living Zoroaster like to see you do it six months from now, when I've cleared up some of those loopholes you used."

Rex Moran grinned at him. "It's a bet," he said.

JOHN T. PHILLIFENT

Owe Me

Large corporate structures, like all large bureaucratic structures, mold the lives of the men and women who work in them. Novels like *The Man in the Gray Flannel Suit* and nonfiction works such as *The Organization Man* discuss the problems of routine, conformity, and drabness that pervade the modern business organization. The seemingly heartless removal of employees after decades of service and the lack of security for white-collar workers of all types is one aspect of this problem, as is the "gold watch and a thank you" treatment of those who make it to retirement, men and women who (in many cases) look back on a career devoid of meaning.

"Owe Me" is a story of one of the important stock characters in science fiction—the deviant—the individual who refuses to accept the system as it is and who struggles to change it. Mr. Smith is a man with enormous creative talents who simply will not play the game. There is a strong tendency for large bureaucratic structures to "reward" the people who work in them by promoting them from positions where their creative abilities are being utilized to administrative positions for which they are not suited or qualified (the Peter Principle) or in which they are unhappy. The term "desk jockey" is understood in many different cultures—and for many the Desk is a prison. This story also explores a question addressed in this book by Isaac Asimov: how can you put a price on creativity? Smith's answer is that salaries, royalties, and status are *never* enough.

Conway Morriss sagged back in his managerial chair and contemplated the forthcoming interview with considerable distaste. A glance at the digital wall clock showed him 10.14.50. He promised himself a clear fifteen minutes out of a very full morning to finding out why, at least. A discreet chime interrupted his train of thought, heralded his secretary's voice.

"Mr. Smith is here, Mr. Morriss."

Morriss scowled. "Very well, Hilda, send him in, and no more incalls until I say."

The door murmured open, clicked shut again. Smith came across the tread-deadening carpet to halt and stand, casually erect in front of the desk, meeting the manager's irritated stare with a calmness that hinted of underlying amusement and curiosity. For a long moment there was nothing said, Morriss taking the opportunity to study Smith all over again. A tall man, lean and loose-jointed, almost gangling, yet with an aura of self-confidence that went well with his rakehell hair-style, eagle-beak nose, and cool gray eyes retreating into shadow under a clifflike brow. It was a face full of character, yet the man was little better than a janitor, a night watchman, even if the post was overdignified with the title of security guard. An important post all the same. Morriss Micro-Modules had plenty of stuff to tempt a certain type of intruder.

"You wanted to see me, Mr. Morriss?" Smith sounded idly curious.

"I wouldn't say I *want* to see you, Smith." Morriss shook his head. "I have little choice, seeing that I, personally, hired you in the first place. I'm not in the habit of passing the buck, but I tell you frankly I am not looking forward to this, nor to what I shall have to do immediately afterward." He saw Smith's inquiring look, and jabbed at the folder on his desk. "I have your personnel file here, naturally, and heading it is a letter, a personal letter to me from Harvey Bander, recommending you. Harvey's a good friend of mine, as well as being in a similar line of business. So again I have little choice. Either that letter is an arrant forgery, or you somehow managed to fool Harvey into trusting you. Now that you've been caught I have to ring and tell him. Warn him. But before I do that I have to deal with you. The truth. Sit down."

Smith looked for a chair, adjusted it, sat, and the submerged curiosity was plainer on his face now. "I reckon you will ring Harvey Bander when we're through here, Mr. Morriss, just to set your mind at rest, but you won't surprise him at all. He knows me pretty well."

"Does he know you're a common thief? At least? Or possibly something a lot worse, an industrial snoop?" Morriss meant to keep his voice controlled but the mere thought of an outsider prowling through his files and records made his blood pressure and voice rise. In the gadgetry business fortunes can be made and lost on exclusive know-how. Smith smiled now, not unkindly.

"We can wash out 'thief,' at least," he suggested mildly. "The records don't show anything missing that I took. As for the other thing, that could be harder to disprove, but maybe we'll get to it. Just what did Stoltz report to you, anyway?"

"How did you know it was Stoltz?" Morriss felt belated caution. Smith didn't even begin to look like a guilty man caught out. "Not that it matters," he resumed, "since you've as good as admitted . . . What the devil are you doing?"

Smith had risen to his feet smoothly and was holding a small something he had taken from a hip pocket, aiming it slowly around the office. "Just making sure we're not bugged," he said, and Morriss snorted.

"*This* interview is not being recorded, believe me."

"I do. There's one mike in your left-hand drawer, one in the intercom, one in the terminal console, and one over there in that wall unit, but they're all inert right now. That's all right. It's the nonofficial ones, that you might not know about, that I'm looking for." Smith completed a careful full revolution, shrugged, and nodded. "It's all right. Nothing here."

Morriss snorted again. "What are you trying to pull? A gadget that small that could sweep a room this size that easily . . . is strictly from TV fantasy. You have your nerve, trying that kind of bluff on me, of all people."

"No bluff. This works. I made it myself." Smith sat again. "We can get to that later. Tell me about Stoltz's report."

Morriss, fighting the feeling that he was the interviewee rather than the other way around, shuffled a sheet of paper where he could glance at it for reference.

"No need to quote the exact words. In essence, it was Stoltz's shift after yours. He made his rounds conscientiously. He found doors open, drawers open, files open, terminal readouts left switched on . . . where they had no business to be. In places where he isn't allowed to be himself. Nor any security guard. Except in an emergency. And none was registered. So he made report to that effect. It had to be you, or some confederate you let in. Snooping into things and places where only myself and three other people have any rightful access!"

"That's fair," Smith admitted. "Of course, he wouldn't know if anything had been taken."

"Right. *I* won't know until Ratcliffe has finished checking. But don't get any notion that will let *you* off the hook!"

"Did Lem Stoltz offer any reason why I would be so dim as to leave things that way for him . . . or anyone else . . . to find?"

"Not his place. But he did suggest that perhaps you were smart enough to be able to open all those off-limit restrictions, only you didn't know how to shut them up again."

"It's a thought. He's a good man, Stoltz. One of the few who checks everything he's supposed to, not like some who do a once-around quick and forget it. You'd do well to keep him on."

"Now see here!" Morriss felt it was time he got back on top again. "Are you suggesting this was all a deliberate plan of yours?"

"Just that. It's been reported, and here I am, in disgrace. Weren't you just a little bit surprised that I checked in this morning all normal? To fit your picture I should have been a hundred miles away by now. Incidentally I can open, and shut, any door, drawer, lock, cabinet, or storeroom in this establishment, Mr. Morriss. In fact I have been doing just that every night shift in the three months I've been here."

"My God!" Morriss felt sweat start on his face. "And you think you can con me into believing that you're *not* into industrial espionage! You must take me for a full-marks fool!"

"Maybe I do, in a way. I take you for an honest man anyway, and that can come close to the same thing, sometimes."

"Why don't I pick up this phone," Morriss growled, "and call the law right now, and have you put away?"

"Couple of reasons. One, you don't want that kind of publicity. Two, you'd have a job thinking up a charge that would stick. Let me give you a third, a better one." Smith rose again, approached the desk. Morriss peered up at him in sudden apprehension. The man had a wild, corsair look about him, almost piratical. He had produced yet another something from a pocket.

"This"—he held it between finger and thumb of his left hand—"is quite a toy. Starting here"—he indicated the plain end—"is a nine-volt cell, the kind you supply for those wrist radios you market. Next to it is a chip, the sixty-four-circuit assembly . . . it's the Mark IX module that turned out to have undesirable characteristics and was scrapped, remember? And then a YIG crystal cluster, another one that came out wrong in the melt, the Y4C multiplier . . ."

"They were all consigned to scrap. Weren't they?"

"Not yet. You have two thousand of those in a store bin. And be glad of that. There's a few more bits and pieces, all odds or rejects, and then we get to this." He indicated the other end now. "Remember that experimental laser-kit you got the contract for? Schools and hobbyists and instructional classes? Remember, too, that somebody set up the wrong figures and pulled off a thousand quartz rods that were too damned fine to be any good for anything? Well now . . . there's a bit more to it than that, naturally, but the point is, everything here is from your own stock bins and more than half of it is reject or scrap.''

''Our reject rate is no higher than . . .'' Morriss tried, but Smith wasn't listening to him. He changed hands, felt in another pocket.

''Recognize that?'' he asked. Morriss took the slim slab of metal, some three inches by two, mirror-finish one side, rough cast the other, scratched his memory, found the reference.

''That's a base plate, one we use for our microportable TV.''

''Right. It's vanadium steel, one-eighth of an inch thick, and a swine to cut, but you have to have it, as the only substantial bit in the whole assembly. Holds everything else together. Now . . .'' Smith reached for a couple of financial reports, gray-backed volumes that were identical save for the monthly imprint. He arranged them parallel with an inch gap separating them, laid the metal plate to bridge the gap. A third volume on top reduced the gap still more. He made a careful adjustment to a knurled collar around the waist of the thing in his hand, then brought the thin quartz rod close to one edge of the metal, using the third volume as a guideline for his hand.

''The circuitry,'' he murmured, as if talking to himself, ''does things to concentrate the final output into a beam with a cross section considerably finer than a hair. So the temperature in that beam section is something ferocious.''

Morriss saw the quartz tip move steadily along, saw a needle point of intense glare and a spit of microscopic sparks.

''Of course,'' Smith mused, ''that beam range is only a shade more than an inch, but what more do you need?'' He reached the far edge, lifted the gadget away. The mirror surface looked as if it had been scored with a needle, until Smith picked up the uncovered half and handed it across. ''It's cold,'' he said, ''and a clean cut. Mind your fingers, that edge is like a razor.''

Morriss stared at the clean edge and had no words. He gazed up at Smith, and still the words wouldn't come. Smith grinned easily, took the cut plate back. ''Just to show off,'' he said, almost apologetically, and took up a rubber band from the desk tray. Diving into his pocket again he brought out a stub of chalk-white stuff. ''Borax stick,'' he explained. ''It helps.'' He rubbed it delicately and sparingly on both cut surfaces, maneuvered them back together, slipped the band around to hold them, made another adjustment to the thing in his hand. This time Morriss saw a faint fan of blue from that quartz tip. Less than a minute later the plate was whole again, only now it was a staring impossibility, one half of it mirror-smooth, the other half rough-cast finish. It was the same on the other side. Morriss turned it over, foolishly, just to check. His eyes could barely detect the join ridge.

"Try that on Dommy Richards, and watch his face," Smith suggested, and for a moment, Morriss grinned in anticipation, anxious to see what his chief engineer would make of it. But the mirth evaporated quickly.

"All right, Smith . . . if that *is* your name . . . what's it all about? You have obviously laid on this whole charade deliberately. But why?"

Smith's grin was guarded now. He held out the gadget for Morriss to take. It was respectably heavy, looked like a fat black pencil with a chrome waistline. Morriss put it down, watched Smith settle back in his chair.

"I don't have to tell you," the inventor said, "that it's a surefire hobby item. That's your field. Battery life is around eight hours continuous. And all the components are your own stock run or standard products. Here"—he fished out a folded paper from an inside pocket, leaned to toss it onto the desk—"is the detailed guts of it, circuitry and parts named. You know the prices, the costing, the potential market. Go ahead and analyze it market-wise. Say, for three months."

Morriss almost asked, "Why three months?" But his own wit caught up in time to stop that gaffe. There would be a flush of competition just as soon as other hobby houses could lay hands on a sample and strip it. "Three months would be optimistic," he substituted. "Things catch on fast in this business."

"Yes, but . . . at least half the items in there are wild. Nonstandard. And you're the only one with the production details on file, the know-how. So you have the edge all the way. Still, three months would do for starters. And"—as Morriss reached for his terminal console—"it might be better on your desk comp, not *that* thing. Just as well not to have anything on permanent record just yet."

"You don't miss a trick, do you?" Morriss muttered, his fingers dancing over his desk computer. This *was* his field, and his fingers were sure, the LEDs flickering their swift responses. He had already intuited a final figure, but it was still something of a shock to see the results come up in hard green. It was big. The hobby market could pay very well if the item was right. And this was. It had a thousand potential uses. Morriss schooled his face. He was first and foremost a businessman. When he had said he wasn't in the habit of passing the buck he had spoken truly. He grasped the nettle firmly now.

"All right," he said, meeting Smith's stare. "How much?"

Smith leaned back in his chair and chuckled. "Comes the hard part. I'm as big a fool as the next man in some ways, Mr. Morriss. One of my follies is that I like to kid myself I'm a fair judge of character. So when you say 'How much?' like that, we both know what you mean. Only, I'm not selling anything. What you have there is all your own property. Even the paper and ink of the diagram is company stock. It's all yours anyway. Free!"

Morriss took two full minutes and several deep breaths and still his voice came out shrill. "You can't *do* that! Man, do you know what this thing is worth?"

"Don't tell me, I don't want to know. I'm no good at that kind of figuring, never was. No, it's a gift. If handing you back your own property can be classified as a gift. No sale, anyway."

Morriss shook his head helplessly. He wanted to get up and stride about, and shout, and *do* something. But Smith just sat there, serene and unmoved.

"There has got to be more to it than that," he insisted. "Three months you've worked here. In your own time, out of establishment components, you have produced something that will sell by the million. Yes, million! And now you're giving it away, to me. Smith, there has to be a string somewhere!"

"Well now," Smith nodded slowly, "there is a place where you could tie a string or two, if you want to. There are things you could do for me, again if you feel you want to. This is where it comes in, am I a judge of character?"

"Ah!" Morriss began to feel more comfortable. "What . . . a job?"

"Hah!" Smith laughed openly now. "You run true to pattern. Mr. Morriss. No, no job. Hell, what do I want with a job?"

"But, man, at a salary at least ten times what we've been paying you. And worth every cent of it, for a man who can do this kind of trick . . ." He saw that Smith was still grinning, still shaking his head. "No?"

"No. I don't have a lot of use for money."

That statement was so outrageous that Morriss could only gape.

''What you can do,'' Smith murmured, ''if you want to, three little things. First, clear my wage check to the end of the month.''

''No problem.'' Morriss stretched out his hand. ''A word to the cashier.''

''And while you're doing that, the second thing. Have him fix up an unlimited credit account on you, in the name of Magruder Smith.''

Morriss drew his hand back sharply, all his instincts screaming against such a deal. He hoped it didn't show on his face, but Smith had sharp eyes.

''You don't like that? You're thinking I might walk out of here and run up a few bills to take you for maybe half a million or some such figure? Now why would I do a thing like that? How good a character judge are *you,* Morriss?'' Smith wrinkled his brow in curiosity. ''Can I eat more than one meal at a time, wear more than one outfit, sleep in more than one bed at a time? Who can? As I said, I have little use for money. So long as I have enough fare to the next place, I'll get by.''

''But . . .'' Morriss hesitated, ''a checking account! What for?''

''Just a thought. I might be back this way sometime, who knows? Still, forget that. Do it this way. Your word that if ever I have need of money, or a favor of some kind, I can call on you. Call it an obligation. How's that?''

Morriss looked down at the gadget, then at his figure estimates, then back to Smith, and felt foolish. ''You'd accept just my word?''

''I'll take that chance, sure.''

''You said that I run true to form. Like Harvey Bander? You made this kind of deal with him?''

''And a few more, yes. I move around a lot. And that's the third thing you can do for me. You have other friends, Mr. Morriss. Write me a letter or two, like the one Harvey Bander wrote. That's all. That's it. I'd like to be moving on again.''

This time Morriss took three minutes of baffled thought, then stretched his hand again to the intercom. ''You'll have your wages, and your credit account. And three letters. I'm willing to take a chance on you, Smith. But there's a thing you can do for me, in a moment. Ah, Willmot, Morriss here. I'd like you to raise a new credit account. Yes, the name is Magruder Smith . . .'' It took only a few minutes. As Morriss released the switch and sat back the unusual forename rang a long-forgotten bell in his mind. ''Magruder Smith?'' he murmured. ''I have heard that name before, haven't I?''

"Maybe. You want to know why I choose to live this way, right? Well, that's part of it. A long time ago now, full of bright and shiny ambition, I started up my own business. This line, but nothing this size . . ."

"*This* was a shoestring outfit once," Morriss interrupted. "and it took a lot of damned hard work to build it up to what you see now."

"I appreciate that. I know. I had ideas, and they worked. I made a lot of money fast. And then, it seemed like all at once, there I was at a desk, dealing, trading, arguing, trying to tell other people what to do, and how to do it, watching them do it, and worrying . . . a load on my back all the time, ulcers getting a grip on my guts. All that, while I paid men on the shop floor to do what *I* wanted to do. It was no good. I sold out. I quit. Money wouldn't buy me what I wanted, and I can't be idle. I need problems, but I like to be free to pick my own. This way . . . I can. That's it."

"You'd be worth a lot to me," Morriss murmured, scribbling hurriedly. "Your own office, work your own hours, all the facilities, references . . ."

"On an income I'd have to pay taxes, file returns. And it can get lost or stolen. You realize if I got mugged in a dark alley tonight I wouldn't lose a thing? I have nothing to lose. I'm rich enough, in the only way inflation can't touch. I know eight or ten people like you who owe me, should I ever be in need. Who can steal that?" He rose and stood by the desk as Morriss finished the last letter and folded all three into an envelope. "You better have this, too." He produced a card with a circuit diagram on it. "That's my bug-finder. My own. It works. You can get yourself one made up. But, take my advice, don't sell it. Let a professional bugman get a good look at that and he'll figure out a bug to beat it. I could. And one last thing." This was another paper with a long screed on it. "You have pretty good security arrangements here, but there are a few weak spots. That's a list of them, and how to tighten them up a bit. All right? Thanks for everything. See you around sometime, maybe."

For a long while after Smith had gone Morriss sat still at his desk, deep in thought. The man was smart obviously. But crazy, too. No home, no roots, no money in the bank, no security, not even an automobile! Just a bum, wandering from job to job. It was no way for a man to live. So why, Morriss demanded of himself savagely, why was he so achingly envious?

ARTHUR C. CLARKE

Patent Pending

The author of *Childhood's End, Rendezvous with Rama,* and *Imperial Earth* certainly needs no introduction. However, Clarke's excellence as a novelist has tended to obscure his skill as a master of the short story. Future critics and historians of science fiction may indeed discuss Clarke for his contributions to the short story rather than the quality of his longer work. In "Patent Pending" he addresses himself to one of the truisms of economic life—if you outlaw the product, you increase the demand (or certainly the price). In the United States, the experience of Prohibition and, more recently, legalities over marijuana have supplied us with considerable evidence in this regard, as have the books banned in Boston or any other number of examples. In the film *2001: A Space Odyssey,* Clarke projected a future that included Pan American and Howard Johnsons. Here Clarke portrays a business opportunity of the future that promises great rewards, but which carries with it certain risks.

There are no subjects that have not been discussed, at some time or other, in the saloon bar of the White Hart—and whether or not there are ladies present makes no difference whatsoever. After all, they came in at their own risk. Three of them, now I come to think of it, have eventually gone out again with husbands. So perhaps the risk isn't on their side at all. . . .

I mention this because I would not like you to think that all our conversations are highly erudite and scientific, and our activities purely cerebral. Though chess is rampant, darts and shove-ha'penny also flourish. The *Times Literary Supplement,* the *Saturday Review,* the *New Statesman* and the *Atlantic Monthly* may be brought in by some of the customers, but the same people are quite likely to leave with the latest issue of *Staggering Stories of Pseudoscience.*

A great deal of business also goes on in the obscurer corners of the pub. Copies of antique books and magazines frequently change hands at astronomical prices, and on almost any Wednesday at least three well-known dealers may be seen smoking large cigars as they lean over the bar, swapping stories with Drew. From time to time a vast guffaw announces the denouement of some anecdote and provokes a flood of anxious inquiries from patrons who are afraid they may have missed something. But, alas, delicacy forbids that I should repeat any of these interesting tales here. Unlike most things in this island, they are not for export. . . .

Luckily, no such restrictions apply to the tales of Mr. Harry Purvis, B.Sc. (at least), Ph.D. (probably), F.R.S. (personally I don't think so, though it *has* been rumored). None of them would bring a blush to the cheeks of the most delicately nurtured maiden aunts, should any still survive in these days.

I must apologize. This is too sweeping a statement. There was one story which might, in some circles, be regarded as a little daring. Yet I do not hesitate to repeat it, for I know that you, dear reader, will be sufficiently broad-minded to take no offense.

It started in this fashion. A celebrated Fleet Street reviewer had been pinned into a corner by a persuasive publisher, who was about to bring out a book of which he had high hopes. It was one of the riper productions the ''and-then-the-house-gave-another-lurch-as-the-termites-finished-the-east-wing'' school of fiction. Eire had already banned it, but that is an honor which few books escape nowadays, and certainly could not be considered a distinction. However, if a leading British newspaper could be induced to make a stern call for its suppression, it would become a best-seller overnight. . . .

Such was the logic of its publisher, and he was using all his wiles to induce cooperation. I heard him remark, apparently to ally any scruples his reviewer friend might have, ''Of course not! If they can understand it, they *can't* be corrupted any further!'' And then Harry Purvis, who has an uncanny knack of following half a dozen conversations simultaneously, so that he can insert himself in the right one at the right time, said in his peculiarly penetrating and noninterruptable voice: ''Censorship does raise some very difficult problems, doesn't it? I've always argued that there's an inverse correlation between a country's degree of civilization and the restraints it puts on its press.''

A New England voice from the back of the room cut in: ''On *that* argument, Paris is a more civilized place than Boston.''

"Precisely," answered Purvis. For once, he waited for a reply.

"O.K." said the New England voice mildly. "I'm not arguing. I just wanted to check."

"To continue," said Purvis, wasting no more time in doing so, "I'm reminded of a matter which has not yet concerned the censor, but which will certainly do so before long. It began in France, and so far has remained there. When it *does* come out into the open, it may have a greater impact on our civilization than the atom bomb.

"Like the atom bomb, it arose out of equally academic research. *Never,* gentlemen, underestimate science. I doubt if there is a single field of study so theoretical, so remote from what is laughingly called everyday life, that it may not one day produce something that will shake the world.

"You will appreciate that the story I am telling you is, for once in a while, secondhand. I got it from a colleague at the Sorbonne last year while I was over there at a scientific conference. So the names are all fictitious: I was told them at the time, but I can't remember them now.

"Professor—ah—Julian was an experimental physiologist at one of the smaller, but less impecunious, French universities. Some of you may remember that rather unlikely tale we heard here the other week from that fellow Hinckelberg, about his colleague who'd learned how to control the behavior of animals through feeding the correct currents into their nervous systems. Well, if there *was* any truth in that story—and frankly I doubt it—the whole project was probably inspired by Julian's papers in *Comptes Rendus*.

"Professor Julian, however, never published his most remarkable results. When you stumble on something which is really terrific, you don't rush into print. You wait until you have overwhelming evidence—unless you're afraid that someone else is hot on the track. Then you may issue an ambiguous report that will establish your priority at a later date, without giving too much away at the moment—like the famous cryptogram that Huygens put out when he detected the rings of Saturn.

"You may well wonder what Julian's discovery was, so I won't keep you in suspense. It was simply the natural extension of what man has been doing for the last hundred years. First the camera gave us the power to capture scenes. Then Edison invented the phonograph, and sound was mastered. Today, in the talking film, we have a kind of mechanical memory which would be inconceivable to our forefathers.

But surely the matter cannot rest there. Eventually science must be able to catch and store thoughts and sensations themselves, and feed them back into the mind so that, whenever it wishes, it can repeat any experience in life, down to its minutest detail.''

''That's an old idea!'' snorted someone. ''See the 'feelies' in *Brave New World.*''

''All good ideas have been thought of by somebody before they are realized,'' said Purvis severely. ''The point is that what Huxley and others had talked about, Julian actually did. My goodness, there's a pun there! Aldous—Julian—oh, let it pass!

''It was done electronically, of course. You all know how the encephalograph can record the minute electrical impulses in the living brain—the so-called 'brain waves,' as the popular press calls them. Julian's device was a much subtler elaboration of this well-known instrument. And, having recorded cerebral impulses, he could play them back again. It sounds simple, doesn't it? So was the phonograph, but it took the genius of Edison to think of it.

''And now, enter the villain. Well, perhaps that's too strong a word, for Professor Julian's assistant Georges—Georges Dupin—is really quite a sympathetic character. It was just that, being a Frenchman of a more practical turn of mind than the Professor, he saw at once that there were some milliards of francs involved in this laboratory toy.

''The first thing was to get it out of the laboratory. The French have an undoubted flair for elegant engineering, and after some weeks of work—with the full cooperation of the Professor—Georges had managed to pack the 'playback' side of the apparatus into a cabinet no larger than a television set, and containing not very many more parts.

''Then Georges was ready to make his first experiment. It would involve considerable expense, but as someone so rightly remarked you cannot make omelets without breaking eggs. And the analogy is, if I may say so, an exceedingly apt one.

''For Georges went to see the most famous gourmet in France, and made an interesting proposition. It was one that the great man could not refuse, because it was so unique a tribute to his eminence. Georges explained patiently that he had invented a device for registering (he said nothing about storing) sensations. In the cause of science, and for the honor of the French cuisine, could he be privileged to analyze the emotions, the subtle nuances of gustatory discrimination, that took place in Monsieur le Baron's mind when he employed his unsurpassed talents? Monsieur could name the restaurant, the chef and the menu—everything would bc arrangcd for his convenience. Of course, if he was too busy, no doubt that well-known epicure, Le Compte de—

"The Baron, who was in some respects a surprisingly coarse man, uttered a word not to be found in most French dictionaries. '*That* cretin!' he exploded. 'He would be happy on English cooking! No, *I* shall do it.' And forthwith he sat down to compose the menu, while Georges anxiously estimated the cost of the items and wondered if his bank balance would stand the strain. . . .

"It would be interesting to know what the chef and the waiters thought about the whole business. There was the Baron, seated at his favorite table and doing full justice to his favorite dishes, not in the least inconvenienced by the tangle of wires that trailed from his head to that diabolical-looking machine in the corner. The restaurant was empty of all other occupants, for the last thing Georges wanted was premature publicity. This had added very considerably to the already distressing cost of the experiment. He could only hope that the results would be worth it.

"They were. The only way of *proving* that, of course, would be to play back Georges's recording. We have to take his word for it, since the utter inadequacy of words in such matters is all too well known. The Baron *was* a genuine connoisseur, not one of those who merely pretend to powers of discrimination they do not possess. You know Thurber's 'Only a naïve domestic Burgundy, but I think you'll admire its presumption.' The Baron would have known at the first sniff whether it was domestic or not—and if it had been presumptuous he'd have smacked it down.

"I gather that Georges had his money's worth out of that recording, even though he had not intended it merely for personal use. It opened up new worlds to him, and clarified the ideas that had been forming in his ingenious brain. There was no doubt about it: all the exquisite sensations that had passed through the Baron's mind during the consumption of that Lucullan repast had been captured, so that anyone else, however untrained he might be in such matters, could savor them to the full. For, you see, the recording dealt purely with emotions: intelligence did not come into the picture at all. The Baron needed a lifetime of knowledge and training before he could *experience* these sensations. But once they were down on tape, anyone, even if in real life he had no sense of taste at all, could take over from there.

"Think of the glowing vistas that opened up before Georges's eyes! There were other meals, other gourmets. There were the collected impressions of all the vintages of Europe—what would connoisseurs not pay for them? When the last bottle of a rare wine had been broached, its incorporeal essence could be preserved, as the voice of Melba can travel down the centuries. For, after all, it was not the wine itself that mattered, but the sensations it evoked . . .

"So mused Georges. But this, he knew, was only a beginning. The French claim to logic I have often disputed, but in Georges's case it cannot be denied. He thought the matter over for a few days: then he went to see his *petite dame*.

" 'Yvonne, *ma chéri,*' he said, 'I have a somewhat unusual request to make of you . . .' "

Harry Purvis knew when to break off in a story. He turned to the bar and called, "Another Scotch, Drew." No one said a word while it was provided.

"To continue," said Purvis at length, "the experiment, unusual though it was, even in France, was successfully carried out. As both discretion and custom demanded, all was arranged in the lonely hours of the night. You will have gathered already that Georges was a persuasive person, though I doubt if Mam'selle needed much persuading.

"Stifling her curiosity with a sincere but hasty kiss, Georges saw Yvonne out of the lab and rushed back to his apparatus. Breathlessly, he ran through the playback. It worked—not that he had ever had any real doubts. Moreover—do please remember I have only my informant's word for this—it was indistinguishable from the real thing. At that moment something approaching religious awe overcame Georges. This was, without a doubt, the greatest invention in history. He would be immortal as well as wealthy, for he had achieved something of which all men had dreamed, and had robbed old age of one of its terrors. . . .

"He also realized that he could now dispense with Yvonne, if he so wished. This raised implications that would require further thought. *Much* further thought.

"You will, of course, appreciate that I am giving you a highly condensed account of events. While all this was going on, Georges was still working as a loyal employee of the Professor, who suspected nothing. As yet, indeed, Georges had done little more than any research worker might have in similar circumstances. His performances had been somewhat beyond the call of duty, but could all be explained away if need be.

"The next step would involve some very delicate negotiations and the expenditure of further hard-won francs. Georges now had all the material he needed to prove, beyond a shadow of doubt, that he was handling a very valuable commerical property. There were shrewd businessmen in Paris who would jump at the opportunity. Yet a certain delicacy, for which we must give him full credit, restrained Georges from using his second—er—recording as a sample of the wares his machine could purvey. There was no way of disguising the personalities involved, and Georges was a modest man. 'Besides,' he argued, again with great good sense, 'when the gramophone company wishes to make a *disque,* it does not enregister the performance of some amateur musician. *That* is a matter for professionals. And so, *ma foi,* is *this.*' Whereupon, after a further call at his bank, he set forth again for Paris.

"He did not go anywhere near the Place Pigalle, because that was full of Americans and prices were accordingly exorbitant. Instead, a few discreet inquiries and some understanding cabdrivers took him to an almost oppressively respectable suburb, where he presently found himself in a pleasant waiting room, by no means as exotic as might have been supposed.

"And there, somewhat embarrassed, Georges explained his mission to a formidable lady whose age one could have no more guessed than her profession. Used though she was to unorthodox requests, *this* was something she had never encountered in all her considerable experience. But the customer was always right, as long as he had the cash, and so in due course everything was arranged. One of the young ladies and her boy friend, an *apache* of somewhat overwhelming masculinity, traveled back with Georges to the provinces. At first they were, naturally, somewhat suspicious, but as Georges had already found, no expert can ever resist flattery. Soon they were all on excellent terms. Hercule and Susette promised Georges that they would give him every cause for satisfaction.

"No doubt some of you would be glad to have further details, but you can scarcely expect me to supply them. All I can say is that Georges—or rather his instrument—was kept very busy, and that by the morning little of the recording material was left unused. For it seems that Hercule was indeed appropriately named. . . .

"When this piquant episode was finished, Georges had very little money left, but he did possess two recordings that were quite beyond price. Once more he set off to Paris, where, with practically no trouble, he came to terms with some businessmen who were so astonished that they gave him a very generous contract before coming to their senses. I am pleased to report this, because so often the scientist emerges second best in his dealings with the world of finance. I'm equally pleased to record that Georges had made provision for Professor Julian in the contract. You may say cynically that it was, after all, the Professor's invention, and that sooner or later Georges would have had to square him. But I like to think there was more to it than that.

"The full details of the scheme for exploiting the device are, of course, unknown to me. I gather that Georges had been expansively eloquent—not that much eloqence was needed to convince anyone who had once experienced one or both of his playbacks. The market would be enormous, unlimited. The export trade alone could put France on her feet again and would wipe out her dollar deficit overnight—once certain snags had been overcome. Everything would have to be managed through somewhat clandestine channels, for think of the hubbub from the hypocritical Anglo-Saxons when they discovered just what was being imported into their countries. The Mother's Union, The Daughters of the American Revolution, The Housewives League, and *all* the religious organizations would rise as one. The lawyers were looking into the matter very carefully, and as far as could be seen the regulations that still excluded *Tropic of Capricorn* from the mails of the English-speaking countries could not be applied to this case—for the simple reason that no one had thought of it. But there would be such a shout for new laws that Parliament and Congress would have to do something, so it was best to keep under cover as long as possible.

"In fact, as one of the directors pointed out, if the recordings were banned, so much the better. They could make more money on a smaller output, because the price would promptly soar and all the vigilance of the Customs Officials couldn't block every leak. It would be Prohibition all over again.

"You will scarcely be surprised to hear that by this time Georges had somewhat lost interest in the gastronomical angle. It was an interesting but definitely minor possibility of the invention. Indeed, this had been tacitly admitted by the directors as they drew up the articles of association, for they had included the pleasures of the cuisine among 'subsidiary rights.'

"Georges returned home with his head in the clouds, and a substantial check in his pocket. A charming fancy had struck his imagination. He thought of all the trouble to which the gramophone companies had gone so that the world might have the complete recordings of the Forty-eight Preludes and Fugues or the Nine Symphonies. Well, *his* new company would put out a complete and definite set of recordings, performed by experts versed in the most esoteric knowledge of East and West. How many opus numbers would be required? That, of course, had been a subject of profound debate for some thousands of years. The Hindu textbooks, Georges had heard, got well into three figures. It would be a most interesting research, combining profit with pleasure in an unexampled manner. . . . He had already begun some preliminary studies, using treatises which even in Paris were none too easy to obtain.

"If you think that while all this was going on, Georges had neglected his usual interests, you are all too right. He was working literally night and day, for he had not yet revealed his plans to the Professor and almost everything had to be done when the lab was closed. And one of the interests he had had to neglect was Yvonne.

"Her curiosity had already been aroused, as any girl's would have been. But now she was more than intrigued—she was distracted. For Georges had become so remote and cold. He was no longer in love with her.

"It was a result that might have been anticipated. Publicans have to guard against the danger of sampling their own wares too often—I'm sure *you* don't, Drew—and Georges had fallen into this seductive trap. He had been through that recording too many times, with somewhat debilitating results. Moreover, poor Yvonne was not to be compared with the experienced and talented Susette. It was the old story of the professional versus the amateur.

"All that Yvonne knew was that Georges was in love with someone else. That was true enough. She suspected that he had been unfaithful to her. And *that* raises profound philosophical questions we can hardly go into here.

"This being France, in case you had forgotten, the outcome was inevitable. Poor Georges! He was working late one night at the lab, as usual, when Yvonne finished him off with one of those ridiculous ornamental pistols which are *de rigueur* for such occasions. Let us drink to his memory.''

''That's the trouble with all your stories,'' said John Beynon. ''You tell us about wonderful inventions, and then at the end it turns out that the discoverer was killed, so no one can do anything about it. For I suppose, as usual, the apparatus was destroyed?''

''But no,'' replied Purvis. ''Apart from Georges, this is one of the stories that has a happy ending. There was no trouble at all about Yvonne, of course. Georges' grieving sponsors arrived on the scene with great speed and prevented any adverse publicity. Being men of sentiment as well as men of business, they realized that they would have to secure Yvonne's freedom. They promptly did this by playing the recording to *le Maire* and *le Préfet,* thus convincing them that the poor girl had experienced irresistible provocation. A few shares in the new company clinched the deal, with expressions of the utmost cordiality on both sides. Yvonne even got her gun back.''

''Then when—'' began someone else.

''Ah, these things take time. There's the question of mass production, you know. It's quite possible that distribution has already commenced through private—*very* private—channels. Some of those dubious little shops and notice boards around Leicester Square may soon start giving hints.''

''Of course,'' said the New England voice disrespectfully, ''you wouldn't know the *name* of the company.''

You can't help admiring Purvis at times like this. He scarcely hesitated.

''Le Société Anonyme d'Aphrodite,'' he replied. ''And I've just remembered something that will cheer *you* up. They hope to get round your sticky mails regulations and establish themselves before the inevitable congressional inquiry starts. They're opening up a branch in Nevada: apparently you can still get away with anything there.'' He raised his glass.

''To Georges Dupin,'' he said solemnly. ''Martyr to science. Remember him when the fireworks start. And one other thing—''

''Yes?'' we all asked.

''Better start saving now. And sell your TV sets before the bottom drops out of the market.''

PHILIP K. DICK

Captive Market

Philip K. Dick is another outstanding writer of short fiction whose work at this length has been ignored because of his more famous novels, such as the Hugo Award–winning *The Man in the High Castle.* He enjoys a high reputation among academic and other "serious" critics of science fiction and is particularly well known in Eastern and Western Europe. Dick has always stressed the ambiguous nature of "reality" in his work, and this trend has intensified in recent years.

Webster's Seventh defines monopoly as "exclusive ownership through legal privilege, command of supply, or concerted action." To a considerable extent, modern corporate capitalism was built on monopoly and monopolistic practices. But monopoly, especially in terms of "command of supply," can also be *situational.* If the conditions are right, an individual with the proper skills and resources can find him/herself in control of a well-defined market whose members have no alternative *but* to do business.

Saturday morning, about eleven o'clock, Mrs. Edna Berthelson was ready to make her little trip. Although it was a weekly affair, consuming four hours of her valuable business time, she made the profitable trip alone, preserving for herself the integrity of her find.

Because that was what it was. A find, a stroke of incredible luck. There was nothing else like it, and she had been in business fifty-three years. More, if the years in her father's store were counted—but they didn't really count. That had been for the experience (her father made that clear); no pay was involved. But it gave her the understanding of business, the feel of operating a small country store, dusting pencils and unwrapping flypaper and serving up dried beans and chasing the cat out of the cracker barrel where he liked to sleep.

Now the store was old, and so was she. The big, heavyset, black-browed man who was her father had died long ago; her own children and grandchildren had been spawned, had crept out over the world, were everywhere. One by one they had appeared, lived in Walnut Creek, sweated through the dry, sun-baked summers, and then gone on, leaving one by one as they had come. She and the store sagged and settled a little more each year, became a little more frail and stern and grim. A little more themselves.

That morning very early Jackie said: ''Grandmaw, where are you going?'' Although he knew, of course, where she was going. She was going out in her truck as she always did; this was the Saturday trip. But he liked to ask; he was pleased by the stability of the answer. He liked having it always the same.

To another question there was another unvarying answer, but this one didn't please him so much. It came in answer to the question: ''Can I come along?''

The answer to that was always *no*.

Edna Berthelson laboriously carried packages and boxes from the back of the store to the rusty, upright pickup truck. Dust lay over the truck; its red-metal sides were bent and corroded. The motor was already on; it was wheezing and heating up in the midday sun. A few drab chickens pecked in the dust around its wheels. Under the porch of the store a plump white shaggy sheep squatted, its face vapid, indolent, indifferently watching the activity of the day. Cars and trucks rolled along Mount Diablo Boulevard. Along Lafayette Avenue a few shoppers strolled, farmers and their wives, petty businessmen, farmhands, some city women in their gaudy slacks and print shirts, sandals, bandannas. In the front of the store the radio tinnily played popular songs.

''I asked you a question,'' Jackie said righteously. ''I asked you where you're going.''

Mrs. Berthelson bent stiffly over to lift the last armload of boxes. Most of the loading had been done the night before by Arnie the Swede, the hulking, white-haired hired man who did the heavy work around the store. ''What?'' she murmured vaguely, her gray, wrinkled face twisting with concentration. ''You know perfectly well where I'm going.''

Jackie trailed plaintively after her, as she reentered the store to look for her order book. ''Can I come? Please, can I come along? You never let me come—you never let *anybody* come.''

''Of course not,'' Mrs. Berthelson said sharply. ''It's nobody's business.''

"But I *want* to come along," Jackie explained.

Slyly, the little old woman turned her gray head and peered back at him, a worn, colorless bird taking in a world perfectly understood. "So does everybody else." Thin lips twitching in a secret smile, Mrs. Berthelson said softly: "But nobody can."

Jackie didn't like the sound of that. Sullenly, he retired to a corner, hands stuck deep in the pockets of his jeans, not taking part in something that was denied him, not approving of something in which he could not share. Mrs. Berthelson ignored him. She pulled her frayed blue sweater around her thin shoulders, located her sunglasses, pulled the screen door shut after her, and strode briskly to the truck.

Getting the truck into gear was an intricate process. For a time she sat tugging crossly at the shift, pumping the clutch up and down, waiting impatiently for the teeth to fall into place. At last, screeching and chattering, the gears meshed; the truck leaped a little, and Mrs. Berthelson gunned the motor and released the hand brake.

As the truck roared jerkily down the driveway, Jackie detached himself from the shade by the house and followed along after it. His mother was nowhere in sight. Only the dozing sheep and the two scratching chickens were visible. Even Arnie the Swede was gone, probably getting a cold Coke. Now was a fine time. Now was the best time he had ever had. And it was going to be sooner or later anyhow, because he was determined to come along.

Grabbing hold of the tailboard of the truck, Jackie hoisted himself up and landed facedown on the tightly packed heaps of packages and boxes. Under him the truck bounced and bumped. Jackie hung on for dear life; clutching at the boxes he pulled his legs under him, crouched down, and desperately sought to keep from being flung off. Gradually the truck righted itself, and the torque diminished. He breathed a sigh of relief and settled gratefully down.

He was on his way. He was along, finally. Accompanying Mrs. Berthelson on her secret weekly trip, her strange covert enterprise from which—he had heard—she made a fabulous profit. A trip which nobody understood, and which he knew, in the deep recesses of his child's mind, was something awesome and wonderful, something that would be well worth the trouble.

He had hoped fervently that she wouldn't stop to check her load along the way.

With infinite care, Tellman prepared himself a cup of "coffee." First, he carried a tin cup of roasted grain over to the gasoline drum the colony used as a mixing bowl. Dumping it in, he hurried to add a handful of chicory and a few fragments of dried bran. Dirt-stained hands trembling, he managed to get a fire started among the ashes and coals under the pitted metal grate. He set a pan of tepid water on the flames and searched for a spoon.

"What are you up to?" his wife demanded from behind him.

"Uh," Tellman muttered. Nervously, he edged between Gladys and the meal. "Just fooling around." In spite of himself, his voice took on a nagging whine. "I have a right to fix myself something, don't I? As much right as anybody else."

"You ought to be over helping."

"I was. I wrenched something in my back." The wiry, middle-aged man ducked uneasily away from his wife; tugging at the remains of his soiled white shirt, he retreated toward the door of the shack. "Damn it, a person has to rest, sometimes."

"Rest when we get there." Gladys wearily brushed back her thick, dark-blonde hair. "Suppose everybody was like you."

Tellman flushed resentfully. "Who plotted our trajectory? Who's done all the navigation work?"

A faint ironic smile touched his wife's chapped lips. "We'll see how your charts work out," she said. "Then we'll talk about it."

Enraged, Tellman plunged out of the shack, into the blinding late-afternoon sunlight.

He hated the sun, the sterile white glare that began at five in the morning and lasted until nine in the evening. The Big Blast had sizzled the water vapor from the air; the sun beat down pitilessly, sparing nobody. But there were few left to care.

To his right was the cluster of shacks that made up the camp. An eclectic hodgepodge of boards, sheets of tin, wire and tar paper, upright concrete blocks, anything and everything dragged from the San Francisco ruins, forty miles west. Cloth blankets flapped dismally in doorways, protection against the vast hosts of insects that swept across the campsite from time to time. Birds, the natural enemy of insects, were gone. Tellman hadn't seen a bird in two years—and he didn't expect to see one again. Beyond the camp began the eternal dead black ash, the charred face of the world, without features, without life.

The camp had been set up in a natural hollow. One side was sheltered by the tumbled ruins of what had once been a minor mountain range. The concussion of the blast had burst the towering cliffs; rock had cascaded into the valley for days. After San Francisco had been fired out of existence, survivors had crept into the heaps of boulders, looking for a place to hide from the sun. That was the hardest part: the unshielded sun. Not the insects, not the radioactive clouds of ash, not the flashing white fury of the blasts, but the sun. More people had died of thirst and dehydration and blind insanity than from toxic poisons.

From his breast pocket, Tellman got a precious package of cigarettes. Shakily, he lit up. His thin, clawlike hands were trembling, partly from fatigue, partly from rage and tension. How he hated the camp. He loathed everybody in it, his wife included. Were they worth saving? He doubted it. Most of them were barbarians, already; what did it matter if they got the ship off or not? He was sweating away his mind and life, trying to save them. The hell with them.

But then, his own safety was involved with theirs.

He stalked stiff-legged over to where Barnes and Masterson stood talking. "How's it coming?" he demanded gruffly.

"Fine," Barnes answered. "It won't be long, now."

"One more load," Masterson said. His heavy features twitched uneasily. "I hope nothing gets fouled up. She ought to be here any minute."

Tellman loathed the sweaty, animal-like scent that rolled from Masterson's beefy body. Their situation wasn't an excuse to creep around filthy as a pig . . . on Venus, things would be different. Masterson was useful, now; he was an experienced mechanic, invaluable in servicing the turbine and jets of the ship. But when the ship had landed and been pillaged . . .

Satisfied, Tellman brooded over the reestablishment of the rightful order. The hierarchy had collapsed in the ruins of the cities, but it would be back strong as ever. Take Flannery, for example. Flannery was nothing but a foul-mouthed, shanty-Irish stevedore . . . but he was in charge of loading the ship, the greatest job at the moment. Flannery was top dog, for the time being . . . but that would change.

It had to change. Consoled, Tellman strolled away from Barnes and Masterson, over to the ship itself.

The ship was huge. Across its muzzle the stenciled identification still remained, not yet totally obliterated by drifting ash and the searing heat of the sun.

U.S. ARMY ORDNANCE
SERIES A-3 (b)

Originally, it had been a high-velocity "massive retaliation" weapon, loaded with an H-warhead, ready to carry indiscriminate death to the enemy. The projectile had never been launched. Soviet toxic crystals had blown quietly into the windows and doors of the local command barracks. When launching day arrived, there was no crew to send it off. But it didn't matter—there was no enemy, either. The rocket had stood on its buttocks for months . . . it was still there when the first refugees straggled into the shelter of the demolished mountains.

"Nice, isn't it?" Patricia Shelby said. She glanced up from her work and smiled blearily at Tellman. Her small, pretty face was streaked with fatigue and eyestrain. "Sort of like the trylon at the New York World's Fair."

"My God," Tellman said, "you remember that?"

"I was only eight," Patricia answered. In the shadow of the ship she was carefully checking the automatic relays that would maintain the air, temperature, and humidty of the ship. "But I'll never forget it. Maybe I was a precog—when I saw it sticking up I knew someday it would mean a lot to everybody."

"A lot to the twenty of us," Tellman corrected. Suddenly he offered her the remains of his cigarette. "Here—you look like you could use it."

"Thanks." Patricia continued with her work, the cigarette between her lips. "I'm almost done— Boy, some of these relays are tiny. Just think." She held up a microscopic wafer of transparent plastic. "While we're all out cold, this makes the difference between life and death." A strange, awed look crept into her dark-blue eyes. "To the human race."

Tellman guffawed. "You and Flannery. He's always spouting idealistic twaddle."

Professor John Crowley, once head of the history department at Stanford, now the nominal leader of the colony, sat with Flannery and Jean Dobbs, examining the suppurating arm of a ten-year-old boy. "Radiation," Crowley was saying emphatically. "The overall level is rising daily. It's settling ash that does it. If we don't get out soon, we're done.''

''It's not radiation,'' Flannery corrected in his ultimately certain voice. ''It's toxic crystalline poisoning; that stuff's knee-deep up in the hills. He's been playing around up there.''

''Is that so?'' Jean Dobbs demanded. The boy nodded his head not daring to look at her. ''You're right,'' she said to Flannery.

''Put some salve on it,'' Flannery said. ''And hope he'll live. Outside of sulfathiazole there's not much we have.'' He glanced at his watch, suddenly tense. ''Unless she brings the penicillin, today.''

''If she doesn't bring it today,'' Crowley said, ''she'll never bring it. This is the last load; as soon as it's stored, we're taking off.''

Rubbing his hands, Flannery suddenly bellowed: ''Then get out the money!''

Crowley grinned. ''Right.'' He fumbled in one of the steel storage lockers and yanked out a handful of paper bills. Holding a sheaf of bills up to Tellman he fanned them out invitingly. ''Take your pick. Take them all.''

Nervously, Tellman said, ''Be careful with that. She's probably raised the price on everything, again.''

''We've got plenty.'' Flannery took some and stuffed it into a partly filled load being wheeled by, on its way to the ship. ''There's money blowing all over the world, along with the ash and particles of bone. On Venus we won't need it—she might as well have it all.''

On Venus, Tellman thought, savagely, things would revert to their legitimate order—with Flannery digging sewers where he belonged. ''What's she bringing mostly?'' he asked Crowley and Jean Dobbs, ignoring Flannery. ''What's the last load made up of?''

''Comic books,'' Flannery said dreamily, wiping perspiration from his balding forehead; he was a lean, tall, dark-haired young man. ''And harmonicas.''

Crowley winked at him. ''Uke picks, so we can lie in our hammocks all day, strumming 'Someone's in the Kitchen with Dinah.' ''

''And swizzle sticks,'' Flannery reminded him. ''In order that we may all the more properly flatten the bubbles of our vintage '38 champagne.''

Tellman boiled. ''You—degenerate!''

Crowley and Flannery roared with laughter, and Tellman stalked off, smoldering under this new humiliation. What kind of morons and lunatics were they? Joking at a time like this . . . He peered miserably, almost accusingly, at the ship. Was this the kind of world they were going to found?

In the pitiless white-hot sun, the huge ship shimmered and glowed. A vast upright tube of alloy and protective fiber mesh rising up above the tumble of wretched shacks. One more load, and they were off. One more truckful of supplies from their only source, the meager trickle of uncontaminated goods that meant the difference between life and death.

Praying that nothing would go wrong, Tellman turned to await the arrival of Mrs. Edna Berthelson and her battered red pickup truck. Their fragile umbilical cord, connecting them with the opulent, undamaged past.

On both sides of the road lay groves of lush apricot trees. Bees and flies buzzed sleepily among the rotting fruit scattered over the soil; every now and then a roadside stand appeared, operated by somnambulistic children. In driveways stood parked Buicks and Oldsmobiles. Rural dogs wandered here and there. At one intersection stood a swank tavern, its neon sign blinking on and off, ghostly pale in the midmorning sun.

Mrs. Edna Berthelson glared hostilely at the tavern, and at the cars parked around it. City people were moving out into the valley, cutting down the old oak trees, the ancient fruit orchards, setting up suburban homes, stopping in the middle of the day for a whiskey sour and then driving cheerfully on. Driving at seventy-five miles an hour in their swept-back Chryslers. A column of cars that had piled up behind her truck suddenly burst forth and swung past her. She let them go, stony-faced, indifferent. Served them right for being in such a hurry. If she always hurried like that, she would never have had time to pay attention to that odd ability she had found in her introspective, lonely drives; never have discovered that she could look "ahead," never have discovered that hole in the warp of time which enabled her to trade so easily at her own exorbitant prices. Let them hurry if they wanted. The heavy load in the back of the truck jogged rhythmically. The motor wheezed. Against the back window a half-dead fly buzzed.

Jackie lay stretched out among the cartons and boxes, enjoying the ride, gazing complacently at the apricot trees and cars. Against the hot sky the peak of Mount Diablo rose, blue and white, an expanse of cold rock. Trails of mist clung to the peak; Mount Diablo went a long way up. He made a face at a dog standing indolently at the side of the road, waiting to cross. He waved gaily at a Pacific Telephone Co. repairman, stringing wire from a huge reel.

Abruptly the truck turned off the state highway and onto a black-surfaced side road. Now there were fewer cars. The truck began to climb . . . the rich orchards fell behind and gave way to flat brown fields. A dilapidated farmhouse lay to the right; he watched it with interest, wondering how old it was. When it was out of sight, no other man-made structures followed. The fields became unkempt. Broken, sagging fences were visible occasionally. Torn signs, no longer legible. The truck was approaching the base of Mount Diablo . . . almost nobody came this way.

Idly, the boy wondered why Mrs. Berthelson's little trip took her in this direction. Nobody lived here; suddenly there were no fields, only scrub grass and bushes, wild countryside, the tumbled slope of the mountain. A rabbit hopped skillfully across the half-decayed road. Rolling hills, a broad expanse of trees and strewn boulders . . . there was nothing here but a state fire tower, and maybe a watershed. And an abandoned picnic area, once maintained by the state, now forgotten.

An edge of fear touched the boy. No customers lived out this way . . . he had been positive the battered red pickup truck would head directly into town, take him and the load to San Francisco or Oakland or Berkeley, a city where he could get out and run around, see interesting sights. There was nothing here, only abandoned emptiness, silent and foreboding. In the shadow of the mountain, the air was chill. He shivered. All at once he wished he hadn't come.

Mrs. Berthelson slowed the truck and shifted noisily into low. With a roar and an explosive belch of exhaust gases, the truck crept up a steep ascent, among jagged boulders, ominous and sharp. Somewhere far off a bird cried shrilly; Jackie listened to its thin sounds echoing dismally away and wondered how he could attract his grandmother's attention. It would be nice to be in front, in the cabin. It would be nice—

And then he noticed it. At first he didn't believe it . . . but he *had* to believe it.

Under him, the truck was beginning to fade away.

It faded slowly, almost imperceptibly. Dimmer and dimmer the truck grew; its rusty red sides became gray, then colorless. The black road was visible underneath. In wild panic, the boy clutched at the piles of boxes. His hands passed through them; he was riding precariously on an uneven sea of dim shapes, among almost invisible phantoms.

He lurched and slid down. Now—hideously—he was suspended momentarily halfway *through* the truck, just above the tail pipe. Groping desperately, he struggled to catch hold of the boxes directly above him. "Help!" he shouted. His voice echoed around him; it was the only sound . . . the roar of the truck was fading. For a moment he clutched at the retreating shape of the truck; then, gently, gradually, the last image of the truck faded, and with a sickening crunch, the boy dropped to the road.

The impact sent him rolling into the dry weeds beyond the drainage ditch. Stunned, dazed with disbelief and pain, he lay gasping, trying feebly to pull himself up. There was only silence; the truck, Mrs. Berthelson, had vanished. He was totally alone. He closed his eyes and lay back, stupefied with fright.

Sometime later, probably not much later, he was aroused by the squeal of brakes. A dirty, orange state maintenance truck had lurched to a stop; two men in khaki work clothes were climbing down and hurrying over.

"What's the matter?" one yelled at him. They grabbed him up, faces serious and alarmed. "What are you doing here?"

"Fell," he muttered. "Off the truck."

"What truck?" they demanded. "How?"

He couldn't tell them. All he knew was that Mrs. Berthelson had gone. He hadn't made it, after all. Once again, she was making her trip alone. He would never know where she went; he would never find out who her customers were.

Gripping the steering wheel of the truck, Mrs. Berthelson was conscious that the transition had taken place. Vaguely, she was aware that the rolling brown fields, rocks and green scrub bushes had faded out. The first time she had gone "ahead" she had found the old truck floundering in a sea of black ash. She had been so excited by her discovery that day that she had neglected to "scan" conditions on the other side of the hole. She had known there were customers . . . and dashed headlong through the warp to get there first. She smiled complacently . . . she needn't have hurried, there was no competition here. In fact, the customers were so eager to deal with her, they had done virtually everything in their power to make things easier for her.

The men had built a crude strip of road out into the ash, a sort of wooden platform onto which the truck now rolled. She had learned the exact moment to "go ahead"; it was the instant that the truck passed the drainage culvert a quarter mile inside the state park. Here, "ahead," the culvert also existed . . . but there was little left of it, only a vague jumble of shattered stone. And the road was utterly buried. Under the wheels of the truck the rough boards thumped and banged. It would be bad if she had a flat tire . . . but some of them could fix it. They were always working; one little additional task wouldn't make much difference. She could see them, now; they stood at the end of the wooden platform, waiting impatiently for her. Beyond them was their jumble of crude, smelly shacks, and beyond that, their ship.

A lot she cared about their ship. She knew what it was: stolen army property. Setting her bony hand rigidly around the gearshift knob, she threw the truck into neutral and coasted to a stop. As the men approached, she began pulling on the hand brake.

"Afternoon," Professor Crowley muttered, his eyes sharp and keen as he peered eagerly into the back of the truck.

Mrs. Berthelson grunted a noncommittal answer. She didn't like any of them . . . dirty men, smelling of sweat and fear, their bodies and clothes streaked with grime, and the ancient coating of desperation that never seemed to leave them. Like awed, pitiful children they clustered around the truck, poking hopefully at the packages, already beginning to pluck them out onto the black ground.

"Here now," she said sharply. "You leave those alone."

Their hands darted back as if seared. Mrs. Berthelson sternly climbed from the truck, grabbed up her inventory sheet and plodded up to Crowley.

"You just wait," she told him. "Those have to be checked off."

He nodded, glanced at Masterson, licked his dry lips, and waited. They all waited. It had always been that way; they knew, and she knew, that there was no other way they could get their supplies. And if they didn't get their supplies, their food and medicine and clothing and instruments and tools and raw materials, they wouldn't be able to leave in their ship.

In this world, in the "ahead," such things didn't exist. At least, not so anybody could use them. A cursory glance had told her that; she could see the ruin with her own eyes. They hadn't taken very good care of their world. They had wasted it all, turned it into black ash and ruin. Well, it was their business, not hers.

She had never been much interested in the relationship between their world and hers. She was content to know that both existed, and that she could go from one to the other and back. And she was the *only* one who knew how. Several times, people from this world, members of this group, had tried to go "back there" with her. It had always failed. As she made the transition, they were left behind. It was her power, her faculty. Not a shared faculty—she was glad of that. And for a person in business, quite a valuable faculty.

"All right," she said crisply. Standing where she could keep her eye on them, she began checking off each box as it was carried from the truck. Her routine was exact and certain; it was part of her life. As long as she could remember she had transacted business in a distinct way. Her father had taught her how to live in a business world; she had learned his stern principles and rules. She was following them now.

Flannery and Patricia Shelby stood together at one side; Flannery held the money, payment for the delivery. "Well," he said, under his breath, "now we can tell her to go leap in the river."

"Are you sure?" Pat asked nervously.

"The last load's here." Flannery grinned starkly and ran a trembling hand through his thinning black hair. "Now we can get rolling. With this stuff, the ship's crammed to the gills. We may even have to sit down and eat some of that *now.*" He indicated a bulging pasteboard carton of groceries. "Bacon, eggs, milk, real coffee. Maybe we won't shove it in deep-freeze. Maybe we ought to have a last-meal-before-the-flight orgy."

Wistfully, Pat said, "It would be nice. It's been a long time since we've had food like that."

Masterson strode over. "Let's kill her and boil her in a big kettle. Skinny old witch—she might make good soup."

"In the oven," Flannery corrected. "Some gingerbread, to take along with us."

"I wish you wouldn't talk like that," Pat said apprehensively. "She's so—well, maybe she *is* a witch. I mean, maybe that's what witches were . . . old women with strange talents. Like her—being able to pass through time.''

''Damn lucky for us,'' Masterson said briefly.

''But she doesn't understand it. Does she? Does she know what she's doing? That she could save us all this by sharing her ability. Does she know what's happened to our world?''

Flannery considered. ''Probably she doesn't know—or care. A mind like hers, business and profit—getting exorbitant rates from us, selling this stuff to us at an incredible premium. And the joke is that money's worth nothing to us. If she could see, she'd know that. It's just paper, in this world. But she's caught in a narrow little routine. Business, profit.'' He shook his head. ''A mind like that, a warped, miserable flea-sized mind . . . and *she* has that unique talent.''

''But she can *see,*'' Pat persisted. ''She can see the ash, the ruin. How can she not know?''

Flannery shrugged. ''She probably doesn't connect it with her own life. After all, she'll be dead in a couple of years . . . she won't see the war in her real time. She'll only see it this way, as a region into which she can travel. A sort of travelogue of strange lands. She can enter and leave—but we're stuck. It must give you a damn fine sense of security to be able to walk out of one world into another. God, what I'd give to be able to go back with her.''

''It's been tried,'' Masterson pointed out. ''That lizardhead Tellman tried it. And he came walking *back,* covered with ash. He said the truck faded out.''

''Of course it did,'' Flannery said mildly. ''She drove it back to Walnut Creek. Back to 1965.''

The unloading had been completed. The members of the colony were toiling up the slope, lugging the cartons to the check area beneath the ship. Mrs. Berthelson strode over to Flannery, accompanied by Professor Crowley.

''Here's the inventory,'' she said briskly. ''A few items couldn't be found. You know, I don't stock all that in my store. I have to send out for most of it.''

''We know,'' Flannery said, coldly amused. It would be interesting to see a country store that stocked binocular microscopes, turret lathes, frozen packs of antibiotics, high-frequency radio transmitters, advanced textbooks in all fields.

''So that's why I have to charge you a little dearer,'' the old woman continued, the inflexible routine of squeeze. "On items I bring in—" She examined her inventory, then returned the ten-page typewritten list that Crowley had given her on the previous visit. "Some of these weren't available. I marked them back order. That bunch of metals from those laboratories back East—they said maybe later." A cunning look slid over the ancient gray eyes. "And they'll be very expensive."

"It doesn't matter," Flannery said, handing her the money. "You can cancel all the back orders."

At first her face showed nothing. Only a vague inability to understand.

"No more shipments," Crowley explained. A certain tension faded from them; for the first time, they weren't afraid of her. The old relationship had ended. They weren't dependent on the rusty red truck. They had their shipment; they were ready to leave.

"We're taking off," Flannery said, grinning starkly. "We're full up."

Comprehension came. "But I placed orders for those things." Her voice was thin, bleak. Without emotion, "They'll be shipped to me. I'll have to pay for them."

"Well," Flannery said softly, "isn't that too damn bad."

Crowley shot him a warning glance. "Sorry," he said to the old woman. "We can't stick around—this place is getting hot. We've got to take off."

On the withered face, dismay turned to growing wrath. "You ordered those things! You *have* to take them!" Her shrill voice rose to a screech of fury. "What am I supposed to do with them?"

As Flannery framed his bitter answer, Pat Shelby intervened. "Mrs. Berthelson," she said quietly, "you've done a lot for us, even if you wouldn't help us through the hole in your time. And we're very grateful. If it wasn't for you, we couldn't have got together enough supplies. But we really have to go." She reached out her hand to touch the frail shoulder, but the old woman jerked furiously away. "I mean," Pat finished awkwardly, "we can't stay any longer, whether we want to or not. Do you see all that black ash? It's radioactive, and more of it sifts down all the time. The toxic level is rising—if we stay any longer it'll start destroying us."

Mrs. Edna Berthelson stood clutching her inventory list. There was an expression on her face that none of the group had ever seen before. The violent spasm of wrath had vanished; now a cold, chill glaze lay over the aged features. Her eyes were like gray rocks, utterly without feeling.

Flannery wasn't impressed. "Here's your loot," he said, thrusting out the handful of bills. "What the hell." He turned to Crowley. "Let's toss in the rest. Let's stuff it down her goddamn throat."

"Shut up," Crowley snapped.

Flannery sank resentfully back. "Who are you talking to?"

"Enough's enough." Crowley, worried and tense, tried to speak to the old woman. "My God, you can't expect us to stay around here forever, can you?"

There was no response. Abruptly, the old woman turned and strode silently back to her truck.

Masterson and Crowley looked uneasily at each other. "She sure is mad," Masterson said apprehensively.

Tellman hurried up, glanced at the old woman getting into her truck, and then bent down to root around in one of the cartons of groceries. Childish greed flushed across his thin face. "Look," he gasped. "Coffee—fifteen pounds of it. Can we open some? Can we get one tin open, to celebrate?"

"Sure," Crowley said tonelessly, his eyes on the truck. With a muffled roar, the truck turned in a wide arc and rumbled off down the crude platform, toward the ash. It rolled off into the ash, slithered for a short distance, and then faded out. Only the bleak, sun-swept plain of darkness remained.

"Coffee!" Tellman shouted gleefully. He tossed the bright metal can high in the air and clumsily caught it again. "A celebration! Our last night—last meal on Earth!"

It was true.

As the red pickup truck jogged metallically along the road, Mrs. Berthelson scanned "ahead" and saw that the men were telling the truth. Her thin lips writhed; in her mouth an acid taste of bile rose. She had taken it for granted that they would continue to buy—there was no competition, no other source of supply. But they were leaving. And when they left, there would be no more market.

She would never find a market that satisfactory. It was a perfect market; the group was a perfect customer. In the locked box at the back of the store, hidden down under the reserve sacks of grain, was almost two hundred and fifty thousand dollars. A fortune, taken in over the months, received from the imprisoned colony as it toiled to construct its ship.

And *she* had made it possible. She was responsible for letting them get away after all. Because of her shortsightedness, they were able to escape. She hadn't used her head.

As she drove back to town she meditated calmly, rationally. It was totally because of her: she was the only one who had possessed the power to bring them their supplies. Without her, they were helpless.

Hopefully, she cast about, looking this way and that, peering with her deep inner sense, into the various "aheads." There was more than one, of course. The "aheads" lay like a pattern of squares, an intricate web of worlds into which she could step, if she cared. But all were empty of what she wanted.

All showed bleak plains of black ash, devoid of human habitation. What she wanted was lacking: they were each without customers.

The patterns of "aheads" was complex. Sequences were connected like beads on a string; there were chains of "aheads" which formed interwoven links. One step led to the next . . . but not to alternate chains.

Carefully, with great precision, she began the job of searching through each of the chains. There were many of them . . . a virtual infinity of possible "aheads." And it was her power to select; she had stepped into that one, the particular chain in which the huddled colony had labored to construct its ship. She had, by entering it, made it manifest. Frozen it into reality. Dredged it up from among the many, from among the multitude of possibilities.

Now she needed to dredge another. That particular "ahead" had proven unsatisfactory. The market had petered out.

The truck was entering the pleasant town of Walnut Creek, passing bright stores and houses and supermarkets, before she located it. There were so many, and her mind was old . . . but now she had picked it out. And as soon as she found it, she knew it was the one. Her innate business instinct certified it; the particular "ahead" clicked.

Of the possibilities, this one was unique. The ship was well-built, and thoroughly tested. In "ahead" after "ahead" the ship rose, hesitated as automatic machinery locked, and then burst from the jacket of atmosphere, toward the morning star. In a few "aheads," the wasted sequences of failure, the ship exploded into white-hot fragments. Those, she ignored; she saw no advantage in that.

In a few "aheads" the ship failed to take off at all. The turbines lashed; exhaust poured out . . . and the ship remained as it was. But then the men scampered out, and began going over the turbines, searching for the faulty parts. So nothing was gained. In later segments along the chain, in subsequent links, the damage was repaired, and the takeoff was satisfactorily completed.

But one chain was correct. Each element, each link, developed perfectly. The pressure locks closed, and the ship was sealed. The turbines fired, and the ship, with a shudder, rose from the plain of black ash. Three miles up, the rear jets tore loose. The ship floundered, dropped in a screaming dive, and plunged back toward the Earth. Emergency landing jets, designed for Venus, were frantically thrown on. The ship slowed, hovered for an agonizing instant, and then crashed into the heap of rubble that had been Mount Diablo. There the remains of the ship lay, twisted metal sheets, smoking in the dismal silence.

From the ship the men emerged, shaken and mute, to inspect the damage. To begin the miserable, futile task all over again. Collecting supplies, patching the rocket up . . . The old woman smiled to herself.

That was what she wanted. That would do perfectly. And all she had to do—such a little thing—was select that sequence when she made her next trip. When she took her little business trip, the following Saturday.

Crowley lay half buried in the black ash, pawing feebly at a deep gash in his cheek. A broken tooth throbbed. A thick ooze of blood dripped into his mouth, the hot salty taste of his own body fluids leaking helplessly out. He tried to move his leg, but there was no sensation. Broken. His mind was too dazed, too bewildered with despair, to comprehend.

Somewhere in the half-darkness, Flannery stirred. A woman groaned; scattered among the rocks and buckled sections of the ship lay the injured and dying. An upright shape rose, stumbled, and pitched over. An artificial light flickered. It was Tellman, making his way clumsily over the tattered remains of their world. He gaped foolishly at Crowley; his glasses hung from one ear and part of his lower jaw was missing. Abruptly he collapsed face-forward into a smoking mound of supplies. His skinny body twitched aimlessly.

Crowley managed to pull himself to his knees. Masterson was bending over him, saying something again and again.

"I'm all right," Crowley rasped.

"We're down. Wrecked."

"I know."

On Masterson's shattered face glittered the first stirrings of hysteria. "Do you think—"

"No, Crowley muttered. "It isn't possible."

Masterson began to giggle. Tears streaked the grime of his cheeks; drops of thick moisture dripped down his neck into his charred collar. "She did it. She fixed us. She wants us to stay here."

"No," Crowley repeated. He shut out the thought. It couldn't be. It just couldn't. "We'll get away," he said. "We'll assemble the remains—start over."

"She'll be back," Masterson quavered. "She knows we'll be here waiting for her. Customers!"

"No," Crowley said. He didn't believe it; he made himself not believe it. "We'll get away. We've *got* to get away!"

ROBERT SHECKLEY

Something for Nothing

At the height of his writing activity, Robert Sheckley was one of the most prolific and consistently good authors in science fiction. Most of his early fiction reads as well today as it did when it was written in the fifties and sixties, especially his stories with social themes, and he is still going strong. Sheckley is in many ways a bitter writer with an acid pen, very much anti-establishment and in favor of the nonconformist. He has little use for large institutions that push people around and control their lives (see his "The Academy"). At the same time, his view of human nature is basically pessimistic.

"Something for Nothing" recalls one of Robert A. Heinlein's favorite expressions: TANSTAAFL, or "there ain't no such thing as a free lunch." Modern marketing practices and techniques usually offer less than they promise. Here Sheckley gives us a tale about greed and the acquisitive process, featuring a protagonist who gets somewhat more than he bargained for.

But had he heard a voice? He couldn't be sure. Reconstructing it a moment later, Joe Collins knew he had been lying on his bed, too tired even to take his waterlogged shoes off the blanket. He had been staring at the network of cracks in the muddy yellow ceiling, watching water drip slowly and mournfully through.

It must have happened then. Collins caught a glimpse of metal beside his bed. He sat up. There was a machine on the floor, where no machine had been.

In that first moment of surprise, Collins thought he heard a very distant voice say, "There! *That* does it."

He couldn't be sure of the voice. But the machine was undeniably there.

Collins knelt to examine it. The machine was about three feet square and it was humming softly. The crackle-gray surface was featureless, except for a red button in one corner and a brass plate in the center. The plate said, CLASS-A UTILIZER, SERIES AA-1256432.

And underneath, WARNING! THIS MACHINE SHOULD BE USED ONLY BY CLASS-A RATINGS!

That was all.

There were no knobs, dials, switches or any of the other attachments Collins associated with machines. Just the brass plate, the red button and the hum.

"Where did you come from?" Collins asked. The Class-A Utilizer continued to hum. He hadn't really expected an answer. Sitting on the edge of his bed, he stared thoughtfully at the Utilizer. The question now was—what to do with it?

He touched the red button warily, aware of his lack of experience with machines that fell from nowhere. When he turned it on, would the floor open up? Would little green men drop from the ceiling?

But he had slightly less than nothing to lose. He pressed the button lightly.

Nothing happened.

"All right—*do* something," Collins said, feeling definitely let down. The Utilizer continued to hum softly.

Well, he could always pawn it. Honest Charlie would give him at least a dollar for the metal. He tried to lift the Utilizer. It wouldn't lift. He tried again, exerting all his strength, and succeeded in raising one corner an inch from the floor. He released it and sat down on the bed, breathing heavily.

"You should have sent a couple of men to help me," Collins told the Utilizer. Immediately, the hum grew louder and the machine started to vibrate.

Collins watched, but still nothing happened. On a hunch, he reached out and stabbed the red button.

Immediately, two bulky men appeared, dressed in rough work-clothes. They looked at the Utilizer appraisingly. One of them said, "Thank God, it's the small model. The big ones is brutes to get a grip on."

The other man said, "It beats the marble quarry, don't it?"

They looked at Collins, who stared back. Finally the first man said, "Okay, Mac, we ain't got all day. Where you want it?"

"But where do you come from?" Collins asked. "And *why?*"

"We come from the Powha Minnile Movers, Incorporated," the man said. "And we come because you wanted movers, that's why. Now, where you want it?"

"Go away," Collins said. "I'll call for you later."

The moving men shrugged their shoulders and vanished. For several minutes, Collins stared at the spot where they had been. Then he stared at the Class-A Utilizer, which was humming softly again.

Utilizer? He could give it a better name.

A Wishing Machine.

Collins was not particularly shocked. When the miraculous occurs, only dull, workaday mentalities are unable to accept it. Collins was certainly not one of those. He had an excellent background for acceptance.

Most of his life had been spent wishing, hoping, praying that something marvelous would happen to him. In high school, he had dreamed of waking up some morning with an ability to know his homework without the tedious necessity of studying it. In the army, he had wished for some witch or jinn to change his orders, putting him in charge of the day room, instead of forcing him to do close-order drill like everyone else.

Out of the army, Collins had avoided work, for which he was psychologically unsuited. He had drifted around, hopeing that some fabulously wealthy person would be induced to change his will, leaving him Everything.

He had never really expected anything to happen. But he was prepared when it did.

"I'd like a thousand dollars in small unmarked bills," Collins said cautiously. When the hum grew louder, he pressed the button. In front of him appeared a large mound of soiled singles, five- and ten-dollar bills. They were not crisp, but they certainly were money.

Collins threw a handful in the air and watched it settle beautifully to the floor. He lay on his bed and began making plans.

First, he would get the machine out of New York—upstate, perhaps—someplace where he wouldn't be bothered by nosy neighbors. The income tax would be tricky on this sort of thing. Perhaps, after he got organized, he should go to Central America, or . . .

There was a suspicious noise in the room.

Collins leaped to his feet. A hole was opening in the wall, and someone was forcing his way through.

"*Hey,* I didn't ask you anything!" Collins told the machine.

The hole grew larger, and a large, red-faced man was halfway through, pushing angrily at the hole.

At that moment, Collins remembered that machines usually have owners. Anyone who owned a wishing machine wouldn't take kindly to having it gone. He would go to any lengths to recover it. Probably, he would stop short of—

"Protect me!" Collins shouted at the Utilizer, and stabbed the red button.

A small bald man in loud pajamas appeared, yawning sleepily. "Sanisa Leek, Temporal Wall Protection Service," he said, rubbing his eyes. "I'm Leek. What can I do for you?"

"Get him out of here!" Collins screamed. The red-faced man, waving his arms wildly, was almost through the hole.

Leek found a bit of bright metal in his pajamas pocket. The red-faced man shouted, "Wait! You don't understand! That man—"

Leek pointed his piece of metal. The red-faced man screamed and vanished. In another moment the hole had vanished too.

"Did you kill him?" Collins asked.

"Of course not," Leek said, putting away the bit of metal. "I just veered him back through his glommatch. He won't try *that* way again."

"You mean he'll try some other way?" Collins asked.

"It's possible," Leek said. "He could attempt a microtransfer, or even an animation." He looked sharply at Collins. "This is your Utilizer, isn't it?"

"Of course," Collins said, starting to perspire.

"And you're an A-rating?"

"Naturally," Collins told him. "If I wasn't, what would I be doing with a Utilizer?"

"No offense," Leek said drowsily; "just being friendly." He shook his head slowly. "How you A's get around! I suppose you've come back here to do a history book?"

Collins just smiled enigmatically.

"I'll be on my way," Leek said, yawning copiously. "On the go, night and day. I'd be better off in a quarry."

And he vanished in the middle of a yawn.

Rain was still beating against the ceiling. Across the air-shaft, the snoring continued, undisturbed. Collins was alone again, with the machine.

And with a thousand dollars in small bills scattered around the floor.

He patted the Utilizer affectionately. Those A-ratings had it pretty good. Want something? Just ask for it and press a button. Undoubtedly, the real owner missed it.

Leek had said that the man might try to get in some other way. What way?

What did it matter? Collins gathered up the bills, whistling softly. As long as he had the wishing machine, he could take care of himself.

The next few days marked a great change in Collins's fortunes. With the aid of the Powha Minnile Movers he took the Utilizer to Upstate New York. There, he bought a medium-sized mountain in a neglected corner of the Adirondacks. Once the papers were in his hands, he walked to the center of his property, several miles from the highway. The two movers, sweating profusely, lugged the Utilizer behind him, cursing monotonously as they broke through the dense underbrush.

"Set it down here and scram," Collins said. The last few days had done a lot for his confidence.

The moving men sighed wearily and vanished. Collins looked around. On all sides, as far as he could see, was closely spaced forest of birch and pine. The air was sweet and damp. Birds were chirping merrily in the treetops, and an occasional squirrel darted by.

Nature! He had always loved nature. This would be the perfect spot to build a large, impressive house with swimming pool, tennis courts and, possibly, a small airport.

"I want a house," Collins stated firmly, and pushed the red button.

A man in a neat gray business suit and pince-nez appeared. "Yes, sir," he said, squinting at the trees, "but you really must be more specific. Do you want something classic, like a bungalow, ranch, split-level, mansion, castle or palace? Or primitive, like an igloo or hut? Since you are an A, you could have something up-to-the-minute, like a semiface, an extended new or a sunken miniature."

"Huh?" Collins said. "I don't know. What would you suggest?"

"Small mansion," the man said promptly. "They usually start with that."

"They do?"

"Oh, yes. Later, they move to a warm climate and build a palace."

Collins wanted to ask more questions, but he decided against it. Everything was going smoothly. These people thought he was an A, and the true owner of the Utilizer. There was no sense in disenchanting them.

"You take care of it all," he told the man.

"Yes, sir," the man said. "I usually do."

The rest of the day, Collins reclined on a couch and drank iced beverages while the Maxima Olph Construction Company materialized equipment and put up his house.

It was a long-slung affair of some twenty rooms, which Collins considered quite modest under the circumstances. It was built only of the best materials, from a design of Mig of Degma, interior by Towige, a Mula swimming pool and formal gardens by Vierien.

By evening, it was completed, and the small army of workmen packed up their equipment and vanished.

Collins allowed his chef to prepare a light supper for him. Afterward, he sat in his large, cool living room to think the whole thing over. In front of him, humming gently, sat the Utilizer.

Collins lighted a cheroot and sniffed the aroma. First of all, he rejected any supernatural explanations. There were no demons or devils involved in this. His house had been built by ordinary human beings, who swore and laughed and cursed like human beings. The Utilizer was simply a scientific gadget, which worked on principles he didn't understand or care to understand.

Could it have come from another planet? Not likely. They wouldn't have learned English just for him.

The Utilizer must have come from the Earth's future. But how?

Collins leaned back and puffed his cheroot. Accidents will happen, he reminded himself. Why couldn't the Utilizer have just *slipped* into the past? After all, it could create something from nothing, and that was much more complicated.

What a wonderful future it must be, he thought. Wishing machines! How marvelously civilized! All a person had to do was think of something. Presto! There it was. In time, perhaps, they'd eliminate the red button. Then there'd be no manual labor involved.

Of course, he'd have to watch his step. There was still the owner—and the rest of the A's. They would try to take the machine from him. Probably, they were a hereditary clique . . .

A movement caught the edge of his eye and he looked up. The Utilizer was quivering like a leaf in a gale.

Collins walked up to it, frowning blackly. A faint mist of steam surrounded the trembling Utilizer. It seemed to be overheating.

Could he have overworked it? Perhaps a bucket of water . . .

Then he noticed that the Utilizer was perceptibly smaller. It was no more than two feet square and shrinking before his eyes.

The owner! Or perhaps the A's! This must be the microtransfer that Leek had talked about. If he didn't do something quickly, Collins knew, his wishing machine would dwindle to nothingness and disappear.

"Leek Protection Service," Collins snapped. He punched the button and withdrew his hand quickly. The machine was very hot.

Leek appeared in a corner of the room, wearing slacks and a sports shirt, and carrying a golf club. "Must I be disturbed every time I—"

"Do something!" Collins shouted, pointing to the Utilizer, which was now only a foot square and glowing a dull red.

"Nothing I can do," Leek said. "Temporal wall is all I'm licensed for. You want the microcontrol people." He hefted his golf club and was gone.

"Microcontrol," Collins said, and reached for the button. He withdrew his hand hastily. The Utilizer was only about four inches on a side now and glowing a hot cherry red. He could barely see the button, which was the size of a pin.

Collins whirled around, grabbed a cushion and punched down.

A girl with horn-rimmed glasses appeared, notebook in hand, pencil poised. "With whom did you wish to make an appointment?" she asked sedately.

"Get me help fast!" Collins roared, watching his precious Utilizer grow smaller and smaller.

"Mr. Vergon is out to lunch," the girl said, biting her pencil thoughtfully. "He's dezoned himself. I can't reach him."

"Who *can* you reach?"

She consulted her notebook. "Mr. Vis is in the Dieg Continuum and Mr. Elgis is doing field work in Paleolithic Europe. If you're really in a rush, maybe you'd better call Transferpoint Control. They're a smaller outfit, but—"

"Transferpoint Control. Okay—scram." He turned his full attention to the Utilizer and stabbed down on it with the scorched pillow. Nothing happened. The Utilizer was barely half an inch square, and Collins realized that the cushion hadn't been able to depress the almost invisible button.

For a moment Collins considered letting the Utilizer go. Maybe this was the time. He could sell the house, the furnishings, and still be pretty well off . . .

No! He hadn't wished for anything important yet! No one was going to take it from him without a struggle.

He forced himself to keep his eyes open as he stabbed the white-hot button with a rigid forefinger.

A thin, shabbily dressed old man appeared, holding something that looked like a gaily colored Easter egg. He threw it down. The egg burst and an orange smoke billowed out and was sucked directly into the infinitesimal Utilizer. A great billow of smoke went up, almost choking Collins. Then the Utilizer's shape started to form again. The old man nodded curtly.

"We're not fancy," he said, "but we're reliable." He nodded again and disappeared.

Collins thought he could hear a distant shout of anger.

Shakily, he sat down on the floor in front of the machine. His hand was throbbing painfully.

"Fix me up," he muttered through dry lips, and punched the button with his good hand.

The Utilizer hummed louder for a moment, then was silent. The pain left his scorched finger and, looking down, Collins saw that there was no sign of a burn—not even scar tissue to mark where it had been.

Collins poured himself a long shot of brandy and went directly to bed. That night, he dreamed he was being chased by a gigantic letter A, but he didn't remember it in the morning.

Within a week, Collins found that building his mansion in the woods had been precisely the wrong thing to do. He had to hire a platoon of guards to keep away sightseers, and hunters insisted on camping in his formal gardens.

Also, the Bureau of Internal Revenue began to take a lively interest in his affairs.

But, above all, Collins discovered he wasn't so fond of nature after all. Birds and squirrels were all very well, but they hardly ranked as conversationalists. Trees, though quite ornamental, made poor drinking companions.

Collins decided he was a city boy at heart.

Therefore, with the aid of the Powha Minnile Movers, the Maxima Olph Construction Corporation, the Jagton Instantaneous Travel Bureau and a great deal of money placed in the proper hands, Collins moved to a small Central American republic. There, since the climate was warmer and income tax nonexistent, he built a large, airy, ostentatious palace.

It came equipped with the usual accessories—horses, dogs, peacocks, servants, maintenance men, guards, musicians, bevies of dancing girls and everything else a palace should have. Collins spent two weeks just exploring the place.

Everything went along nicely for a while.

One morning Collins approached the Utilizer, with the vague intention of asking for a sports car, or possibly a small herd of pedigreed cattle. He bent over the gray machine, reached for the red button . . .

And the Utilizer backed away from him.

For a moment, Collins thought he was seeing things, and he almost decided to stop drinking champagne before breakfast. He took a step forward and reached for the red button.

The Utilizer sidestepped him neatly and trotted out of the room.

Collins sprinted after it, cursing the owner and the A's. This was probably the animation that Leek had spoken about—somehow, the owner had managed to imbue the machine with mobility. It didn't matter. All he had to do was catch up, punch the button and ask for the Animation Control people.

The Utilizer raced down a hall, Collins close behind. An under-butler, polishing a solid gold doorknob, stared openmouthed.

"Stop it!" Collins shouted.

The under-butler moved clumsily into the Utilizer's path. The machine dodged him gracefully and sprinted toward the main door.

Collins pushed a switch and the door slammed shut.

The Utilizer gathered momentum and went right through it. Once in the open, it tripped over a garden hose, regained its balance and headed toward the open countryside.

Collins raced after it. If he could get just a little closer . . .

The Utilizer suddenly leaped into the air. It hung there for a long moment, then fell to the ground. Collins sprang at the button.

The Utilizer rolled out of the way, took a short run and leaped again. For a moment, it hung twenty feet above his head—drifted a few feet straight up, stopped, twisted wildly and fell.

Collins was afraid that, on a third jump, it would keep going up. When it drifted unwillingly back to the ground, he was ready. He feinted, then stabbed the button. The Utilizer couldn't duck fast enough.

"Animation Control!" Collins roared triumphantly.

There was a small explosion, and the Utilizer settled down docilely. There was no hint of animation left in it.

Collins wiped his forehead and sat on the machine. Closer and closer. He'd better do some big wishing now, while he still had the chance.

In rapid succession, he asked for five million dollars, three functioning oil wells, a motion-picture studio, perfect health, twenty-five more dancing girls, immortality, a sports car and a herd of pedigreed cattle.

He thought he heard someone snicker. He looked around. No one was there.

When he turned back, the Utilizer had vanished.

He just stared. And, in another moment, *he* vanished.

When he opened his eyes, Collins found himself standing in front of a desk. On the other side was the large, red-faced man who had originally tried to break into his room. The man didn't appear angry. Rather, he appeared resigned, even melancholy.

Collins stood for a moment in silence, sorry that the whole thing was over. The owner and the A's had finally caught him. But it had been glorious while it lasted.

"Well," Collins said directly, "you've got your machine back. Now, what else do you want?"

"*My* machine?" the red-faced man said, looking up incredulously. "It's not my machine, sir. Not at all."

Collins stared at him. "Don't try to kid me, mister. You A-ratings want to protect your monopoly, don't you?"

The red-faced man put down his paper. "Mr. Collins," he said stiffly, "my name is Flign. I am an agent for the Citizens Protective Union, a nonprofit organization, whose aim is to protect individuals such as yourself from errors of judgment."

"You mean you're not one of the A's?"

"You are laboring under a misapprehension, sir," Flign said with quiet dignity. "The A-rating does not represent a social group, as you seem to believe. It is merely a credit rating."

"A what?" Collins asked slowly.

"A credit rating." Flign glanced at his watch. "We haven't much time, so I'll make this as brief as possible. Ours is a decentralized age, Mr. Collins. Our businesses, industries and services are scattered through an appreciable portion of space and time. The utilization corporation is an essential link. It provides for the transfer of goods and services from point to point. Do you understand?"

Collins nodded.

"Credit is, of course, an automatic privilege. But, eventually, everything must be paid for."

Collins didn't like the sound of that. *Pay?* This place wasn't as civilized as he had thought. No one had mentioned paying. Why did they bring it up now?

"Why didn't someone stop me?" he asked desperately. "They must have known I didn't have a proper rating."

Flign shook his head. "The credit ratings are suggestions, not laws. In a civilized world, an individual has the right to his own decisions. I'm very sorry, sir." He glanced at his watch again and handed Collins the paper he had been reading. "Would you just glance at this bill and tell me whether it's in order?"

Collins took the paper and read:

One Palace, with Accessories	Cr. 450,000,000
Services of Maxima Olph Movers	111,000
122 Dancing Girls	122,000,000
Perfect Health	888,234,031

He scanned the rest of the list quickly. The total came to slightly better than eighteen billion Credits.

"Wait a minute!" Collins shouted. "I can't be held to this! The Utilizer just dropped into my room by accident!"

"That's the very fact I'm going to bring to their attention," Flign said. "Who knows? Perhaps they will be reasonable. It does no harm to try."

Collins felt the room sway. Flign's face began to melt before him.

"Time's up," Flign said. "Good luck."

Collins closed his eyes.

When he opened them again, he was standing on a bleak plain, facing a range of stubby mountains. A cold wind lashed his face and the sky was the color of steel.

A raggedly dressed man was standing beside him. ''Here,'' the man said and handed Collins a pick.

''What's this?''

''This is a pick,'' the man said patiently. ''And over there is a quarry, where you and I and a number of others will cut marble.''

''Marble?''

''Sure. There's always some idiot who wants a palace,'' the man said with a wry grin. ''You can call me Jang. We'll be together for some time.''

Collins blinked stupidly. ''How long?''

''You work it out,'' Jang said. ''The rate is fifty credits a month until your debt is paid off.''

The pick dropped from Collins's hand. They couldn't do this to him! The Utilization Corporation must realize its mistake by now! *They* had been at fault, letting the machine slip into the past. Didn't they realize that?

''It's all a mistake!'' Collins said.

''No mistake,'' Jang said. ''They're very short of labor. Have to go recruiting all over for it. After the first thousand years you won't mind it.''

Collins started to follow Jang toward the quarry. He stopped.

''The first *thousand* years? I won't live that long!''

''Sure you will,'' Jang assured him. ''You got immortality, didn't you?''

Yes, he had. He had wished for it, just before they took back the machine. Or had they taken back the machine *after* he wished for it?

Collins remembered something. Strange, but he didn't remember seeing immortality on the bill Flign had showed him.

''How much did they charge me for immortality?'' he asked.

Jang looked at him and laughed. ''Don't be naive, pal. You should have it figured out by now.''

He led Collins toward the quarry. ''Naturally, they give *that* away for nothing.''